To Ben

ANOTHER LIFE

K.L. SHANDWICK

Copyright © 2019 K.L. Shandwick

All rights reserved.

The author has asserted their moral right under the Copyright, Designs and Patents Act, 1988, to be identified as the author of this work.

All Rights reserved. No part of this publication may be reproduced, copied, stored in a retrieval system, or transmitted, in any form or by any means, without the prior written consent of the copyright holder, nor be otherwise circulated in any form of binding or cover other than that in which it is published and without a similar condition being imposed on the subsequent purchaser.

This book is a work of fiction. Names, places, characters, band names and incidents are the product of the author's imagination or names are used within the fictitious setting. Any resemblance to actual persons living or dead, band names or locales are entirely coincidental unless quoted as artists.

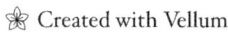 Created with Vellum

DEDICATION

Another Life is a story which may affect individuals who have faced the loss of a loved one. We all face this as it is part of life, and most of us go on to live life without the person we lost. Although the story is not the same, this book is dedicated to a family I have never met, but whose story touched me. This book is for Joey Rott and his family, who have first-hand experience with the help and love of Dana to live another life.

Cassia Rott (known and loved as Casi)
Sept 25, 1979 - Feb 8, 2016

CHAPTER ONE

Tears blurred my vision as I stared motionless at the single black scuff mark on the otherwise pristine white wall in front of me. I was on my knees, my mind numb to the worrying news I had heard and what it meant for us. Distracting myself, I reflected on earlier that night and images immediately began to float through my mind.

Earlier that evening

My aching limbs felt like lead weights, but my mental strength persisted, fueled by the vibrant energy of our chanting fans. Jogging back on stage, I stood beneath the relentless searing heat of the fifty plus spotlights. I was all but spent, my tired body running on pure adrenaline from the frenzied reaction of the crowd.

A single bead of perspiration coursed its way down my face and my heart pumped rapidly as I spotted Fletch grabbing his shiny black bass guitar.

Further wet droplets flew more freely from my dark, sweat-drenched hair as I nodded quickly at our drummer Scuds, then leaned forward, taking my old trusty Fender from its stand.

Lifting the frayed woven guitar strap over my head, I swiped up a towel from in front of the drum platform and rubbed vigorously at my face and hair.

Throwing it behind me, I plugged the jack from my rig into my guitar and spun around, flashing my practiced rock star smile as I addressed the eager faces of our most avid followers.

"What?" I goaded, addressing them by cupping the shell of my ear and pretending not to hear them. They roared in response. "You want some more?" I screamed into the mic, in no doubt they did. Their reaction was wild. I smirked knowingly and bobbed my head acknowledging their unified positive replies.

It had been almost two hours since our music lovers had risen to their feet at the sound of the first note we'd played, yet they had waited patiently after we'd left the stage, confident of their reward of one last number for their dedication to our band.

Casting my bleary eyes over the sea of jostling heads packed into the sweltering conditions of a sixteen-thousand capacity venue, I was reminded of how lucky I was. My racing heart clenched as I soaked in the enthralled mob's admiration, then I struggled for a second when my throat tightened as an unexpected wave of emotion threatened to overwhelm me. Hearing the deafening roar of appreciation at the end of a tour always caught me unaware.

The venue management were pissed because we'd already overrun on the set time, plus we had another commitment to move on to. Yet who were we to deny the mass of adoring rock fans their one last treat? I raised my hand and my heart rate spiked as the rowdy cheers and whistles instantly died and the auditorium fell quiet.

Commanding the instant silence of a mass of people always made my heart falter. The quiet magnified my awareness of the electric anticipation of the excited horde as they held their breaths and waited for the intro to that one last song.

Stepping out to perform the swansong of any tour was always special. Especially when we knew the demand was for the number that started it all and the song that had kick started SinaMen on the road to success.

Encores were a common event for a famous band like us, but this time the last performance had more significance because it was the end of an era for me.

Thinking about the significance of the number as I prepared to perform, I turned and stole another glance at my beautiful wife, Grace, waiting patiently in the wings. My brow creased briefly with concern when my eyes connected with hers.

Grace rarely complained about anything, so I'd been watching her closely during the previous couple of weeks. The tour had taken its toll on my heavily pregnant wife; a stubborn woman, who had refused to quit traveling with me to rest.

Completing SinaMen's tour in front of a lively audience made me thankful for life as a musician. The incredible opportunities it had afforded me sometimes took my breath away. Tonight was no exception, and with one last commitment before we went home, I felt relieved Grace had made it to the end of our road tour without any complications to add to her condition.

We were also thankful for the added bonus of finishing the tour in our home state because there was no long trip back at the end of a punishing three-week schedule. Playing eleven sold out venues and four jam-packed stadiums, with TV and radio station interviews in between, had left us with virtually no downtime to recover.

Cranking up my charisma, I connected with the rowdy concertgoers by pouring feeling into the song, whipping up their enthusiasm, and having them join in and belt out the chorus by pointing the microphone at them.

Their response produced an earsplitting rendition covering every single word on point like they were the rock stars themselves. When the song came to an end we didn't drag out the curtain call. Instead the band gathered in a huddle at the front of the stage and bowed in unison. I looked again to my gorgeous attentive wife with a mixture of relief and excitement that we'd made it through to the last gig.

Wiping my face again, I threw my damp towel out into the crowd and a cacophany of sound swelled from the back of the auditorium, the deafening noise reaching me all the way at the front. I glanced down toward a young bottle blonde who had caught the discarded towel and she held it up to her face.

Women and men hit on me all the time and I never understood why someone would go nuts for my sweaty T-shirts and discarded towels. The last thing on Earth I'd want to own was a sweat-stained piece of material from anyone who wasn't my wife.

Being groped by groupies and fans of all flavors annoyed me to no end. I was a married man, and where I used to suck it up and laugh it off when I was single, now all I wanted was Grace. She was my soulmate, my perfect match, and as everyone who knew us said, she was the better half of me.

In fact, when I'd met her, Grace had knocked me off my feet and taken my breath away, and before I knew it she'd quickly become my world. It hardly felt possible that two years had gone by since we'd married, because every day felt like a vacation with her around.

This is what made tonight's concert even more special. Grace and I were stoked at the prospect of becoming doting parents, and in preparation of the baby's arrival I'd taken a year's paternity leave from the band.

Smiling widely, Grace looked radiant and happy as I walked across the stage. Sometimes when I looked at her, I almost busted a nut in my jeans she was so hot. Even after all this time she was still the most beautiful woman I'd ever encountered.

She looked striking with her long wild dark hair, cute as fuck button nose and massive almond-shaped eyes, and since she was pregnant, her huge round belly.

My heart flipped as she walked over toward me with those ruby-red lips framing her gorgeous mouth and I saw how the light caught the twinkle in her huge shining gray eyes. In that precise moment I had never felt more in love with Grace.

"You okay, Baby? Should we go home to bed?"

"Don't be silly, Cole; I'm fine, honey. Besides, the launch is on the way. Finish this one last obligation," she said shaking her head. "The venue isn't far, ten blocks over I think, and we only need to stay an hour or so, right?" she asked glancing at her watch. "Two half-hour sets you said?"

Grace continued to use her persuasive ways and eventually convinced me to attend the launch party for a new band recently signed to our label. I knew if I had pressed any further my wife would only have dug her heels in harder. Figuring it was better to get my appearance over with than cause her more stress by arguing, I decided to make good on the promise I'd made to attend.

∼

Scanning the dimly lit, grungy looking space, relief washed over me when I caught sight of my wife still sitting in the booth where I'd left her. She was rocking a fabulous figure-hugging dress she'd squeezed herself into despite her bump. Its brilliant white color immediately set her apart from everyone else in the room. With or without the dress, Grace would have stood out anyway.

Men never looked twice at my wife; it only took them one glance, and they became transfixed by the way she was put together. Usually she would have been on my arm, but in her condition, I was concerned about how the events of the day had affected her. Also, with the heavy vibrations from the drum and bass players in the band, I had parked her ass as far away from the stage as I could.

I had seated Grace in the large sectional booth on the far side of the dance floor where I knew she'd be safe from the crowd, and when I glanced over and saw her still there, I excused myself from my three bandmates and cut straight across the dance floor toward her.

The break in the music set was welcome, and I felt all tension leave my body when the heavy metal band took a fifteen-minute interlude.

The new signing, Stone Gorge, weren't the best musicians I'd heard, but decent enough for us to wait it out for the first half of their gig. As this was an exclusive launch party the press was in attendance and the label had wanted our band to show some support for them.

In general terms, I didn't mind obliging because giving back was important, but on this occasion my wife's wellbeing took priority. After the long day we'd had I wanted to take her home.

As I neared Grace, she glanced up, and a smile tugged at her lips when her gorgeous eyes connected with mine. A smile also spread on my lips and widened affectionately as I approached.

My eyes narrowed suspiciously when I saw she was talking to a known skinny blonde groupie called Bekki. I'd seen her around with Scuds from time to time and fortunately, she wasn't someone I'd dipped my wick in before.

Bekki was so busy running off at the mouth she hadn't noticed I was behind her. My jaw ticked in frustration when I caught some of the comments she made and heard what the conversation was about.

"Oh my god, if I had a guy with a fine ass like his in my bed, I'd never leave it," she confessed.

Having no idea who she was talking about, I decided to cut in on the gossip. "Oh, yeah? Who's the lucky guy?" My voice was laced with sarcasm as I eyed Grace and bit back a grin.

Glancing over her shoulder, Bekki caught sight of me and gasped for breath, swallowed roughly and cringed.

Moving my position to see both her and Grace better, my eyes darted to Bekki. When she averted her gaze, I noted how uneasy she was. Turning my attention back to my wife I saw her wince. It was at this point the penny dropped. This wasn't idle female chitchat between two women. Bekki was stating an opinion and from her reaction when I confronted her, I knew instinctively she had been talking about me.

Unperturbed by Bekki's comment, Grace chuckled and shook her head, "Your timing is awful," she admonished, glancing up at me, but the twinkle in her eyes told me she was flattered by the groupie's envious remark. Bekki's crimson face and zero eye contact on the other hand, was a rare reaction from someone normally so brazen.

"Ah, I wasn't supposed to hear that, was I?" I asked, letting the lecherous groupie know I knew her comment was directed toward Grace about me. "But now that I have, I couldn't agree with you more," I replied sliding my hand around my wife's shoulder.

Crouching down beside her, I pressed my lips gently to hers, in no hurry to pull them away, but I did. "Great advice. Grace you should listen to Bekki," I affirmed, playfully, making a joke from Bekki's comment.

Relief washed through the groupie's worried eyes and she rolled them like she was more pissed with herself than me. It served her right, she shouldn't have been drooling like that about another woman's husband.

"You're incorrigible," Grace scolded me again, but I heard the hint of humor in her tone and knew she was enjoying both Bekki's discomfort and my unwillingness to let the subject slide.

Standing straight, I glared down as Bekki continued to look away. It struck me then that Bekki was losing her looks, but that didn't surprise me with the rock and roll lifestyle she led. The girl had been burning the candle at both ends and it showed.

"If you'll excuse us, I came to ask my beautiful wife to dance," I explained, and held my hand out theatrically for Grace. Slipping hers into mine, I helped her to her feet and led her onto the dance floor.

"That was so naughty, Cole." Grace chuckled. "And why are we on the dance floor when there's no music?" she asked.

"Who needs music when I have an angel in my arms? Are those harps I hear?" Grace looked at the ceiling dismissing my corny line. Pulling her snug little body close to mine with our hands held close to my heart, I pressed my cheek to hers.

"I can't dance without music," she insisted through a giggle.

Unperturbed, I thought for a moment. "You like Halestorm, right? Here's to Us?" She nodded but looked confused, then she shook her head in silent protest. "There you go. We'll dance to that. Forget these deadbeats, we'll have our own silent disco. How does that sound?"

"You are way too corny and romantic to be a rock star," she stated, with a look that told me she adored me.

"Yep, but don't tell them that," I whispered conspiratorially and winked. "Actually, it's because I'm a rock star that I can choose to dance with my girl in a room full of people without music, and none of them will bat an eyelid."

The smile Grace gave me was almost contemptuous, as if she didn't believe me. Narrowing her eyes, she glanced around the room scrutinizing everyone in turn and when she was done I felt her body relax when she realized my assumption was probably right.

Giving them the once-over myself, I saw most of them were stoned, and I knew unless someone was taking off their clothes, making an ass of themselves buck naked, or competing in a wet T-shirt competition, no one cared.

We danced slowly to the song in our heads, mentally singing it, and a couple of times I'd forget and sing out a line. "Want to get a room?" I whispered in Grace's ear after a couple of minutes. It was only a little after midnight, and even though I had asked, we continued to shuffle around to the song in our heads.

At first Grace didn't reply and was determined to see the gig through, but I knew with only five weeks to go until her due date, she was having trouble sleeping. She needed her rest because she'd been struggling with growing pains and indigestion. When she wasn't disturbed with those, her sleep was disrupted by her frequent trips during the night to pee.

"Does this mean I'm on a promise?" she asked, lowering her eyes and pretending to act coy.

"Always, Baby," I replied, stroking her back, then I cupped my hand at the base of her skull and pulled her head closer. I pressed an affectionate kiss to her forehead and pulled back to look at her.

We both chuckled as I slipped my hand into Grace's and led her over to the guys in my band to say our goodnights.

"Damn, Cole," Scuds protested when I leaned in for a hug, "next you'll be telling us you can only come on tour if Grace can come too. Oh, wait, you did that already," he teased, shaking his head.

"Yeah, don't forget I've seen how many attempts you've had over the years trying to find a girl like Grace. Wait until it's your turn and we'll see how great you are at controlling these feelings if you find her."

"Pussy whipped," Moz declared, through a cough and Fletch grinned widely. I sighed and gave him an is-that-the-best-you've-got look.

"Ah, come on, look at her. This little dude's ready to drop, give the guy a break," Fletch offered, as he came to my rescue by nodding at Grace's belly.

"See, he's the only one among you with any sense of occasion," I agreed.

I was happy to own how my behavior had changed. When I met Grace, she was the one girl I never saw coming, and the only one I never wanted to get away from. Our relationship was built on trust and Grace made me want to be 'the real me' and not the front man from a band living up to the expectations of the public. People could think as they liked and judge me how they wanted to, but I was damned if I'd let them dictate when I could put her first.

Hugging the guys one by one, each of them wished Grace well, and we headed for the door just as Stone Gorge took their places behind their instruments on the small stage again.

As we were driven home in the back of the black Sedan Grace snuggled in beside me, her head on my shoulder and she sighed, contentedly. "How did I live without you?"

"I've got no idea, Baby, it must have been miserable for you," I replied, trying to keep a serious tone to my voice.

Turning her face up to look at me she laughed, "You're an ass, you know that?"

"Ah, you mean I'm a fine ass," I corrected, reiterating Bekki's description of me, and Grace burst out laughing.

"That poor girl's face," she muttered reflecting on the incident and it was my turn to laugh.

"She's lucky you're secure. If a guy made a remark like that to me about you, I'd knock him the fuck out. Any man fantasizing about being in bed with you that isn't me doesn't deserve to live," I stated.

"Oh, I adore the caveman that threatens to break free in you at times."

"Yeah?" I asked, pretending I took her seriously.

"Hell, yeah, it's hot," she agreed.

"How hot?"

"Hmm," she hummed, chuckling as she processed my question and I took a moment just to look at her. Pregnancy made Grace radiantly beautiful and the way the moonlight caught her features enthralled me. My eyes settled on her soft plump lips and I fought the urge to kiss her as I waited for her reply. "On a scale of one to five, maybe a four."

Inhaling deeply, I sighed, pretending I felt let down. "Only a four, huh? And what would it take to get a five?" I wondered aloud.

"Sing to me. You have no idea what your voice does to me, Cole

Harkin. Goose bumps doesn't even begin to explain what that rich tone of yours does to me. All I know is I want to rip off your clothes."

Immediately I began singing the old Joe Cocker hit, "You Can Leave Your Hat On," causing her to crack up laughing, before she lurched forward, holding her belly.

Laughter gave way to concern as I furrowed my brow and looked her over.

"Jesus, are you okay?"

"Yeah," she replied, rubbing her lower belly as she straightened her spine in the seat. "The sooner this little cherub is on the outside now the better," she muttered.

We sat quietly in the car after this, me holding her close and rubbing her arm. Fortunately, by the time we made it through the gates to our home, the pain she'd felt had subsided.

"Good God, please don't look at me. I'm a mess," she muttered, dumping her designer purse on the floor when she caught sight of herself in our entrance hall mirror.

"Nonsense Baby, I'm still very attracted to you, never been more so than right now. Check you out? Hair like this," I commented, grabbing a handful of her wild, dark silky mane and sifting my fingers through it. Kissing her cheek, I added, "and when I see this gorgeous face with your sexy as fuck full lips, and this amazing belly..." I stopped talking when my emotions overwhelmed me and I had to kiss her instead.

Passion tore through me as soon as her tongue slid over mine, and my heart rate kicked up its pace. As fire began to flow through my veins, my grip tightened further as my dick strained hard in my jeans.

A soft erotic moan travelled between Grace's mouth and mine and with my arms at full stretch given her bump, I grabbed two handfuls of her ass.

"Dear God in Heaven, will you two get a room?" Matty, our housekeeper had wandered into the hallway and beat a hasty retreat to the kitchen.

"Jesus, Matty, will you get yourself a pair of noisy clogs and stop creeping the fuck up on us? Besides, it's the middle of the night; you should be in bed." I called back. Grace burst out laughing and swatted my arm.

"Stop it, you'll make her uncomfortable and she'll leave."

"You think? The woman lives to give me shit. Where else would she get away with talking to her boss the way she talks to me?"

"Well, she's right. We should go up to our bedroom," Grace suggested, but suddenly doubled over in pain again.

"Are you okay?" I asked as I bent over with her and held her tight.

"Fu— jeez," she replied, unable to answer as she rubbed her belly and breathed her way through the pain. When her discomfort subsided, she took another deep breath and straightened up. "Wow, that was intense."

"Should we go to the hospital?" I asked, my arms tightening protectively in support.

"Pfft, because I've had a twinge? You want them to laugh at us?" she replied in a matter-of-fact tone. From my perspective she'd had more than a few twinges in the previous few days.

"I don't want you to be in pain."

"Then you shouldn't have gotten me pregnant." She smirked and stepped away from me, but barely made it up the sixth step before she doubled over again. Turning to look at me she shrugged. "Maybe a trip to the hospital isn't such a bad idea."

CHAPTER TWO

*G*rabbing the keys from the bowl in the hallway where Stuart, one of my house staff had left them, I turned Grace back in the direction of the front door. She had already packed bags in preparation for the hospital and stuffed them in the trunk of all three cars we made use of. After helping her into the car passenger seat I slid behind the wheel and my chest felt tight.

As I drove out through the heavy privacy gates of our home it dawned on me that Stuart should have driven, but I wasn't thinking straight, and it hadn't occurred to me to call him out of his room. It was fortunate I had only been drinking water all night out of concern for my wife.

Grace messaged her Obstetrician, dropped her cell into her oversized purse and placed it on the floor as another contraction ripped through her. When her discomfort finally subsided, it gave me a short window of calm to talk to her.

"Thirty-five weeks is still good, right?" Slamming my foot on the gas, I turned my nervous gaze from the rain lashed windshield to eye her with concern. The windshield wipers beat in a rhythm which sounded faster and louder than usual as I waited for her to respond. I was naturally concerned because she'd missed her previous two doctor's appointments due to us being on the road, but when I challenged her about this Grace had insisted, she and the baby would be fine.

Until week thirty three Grace's pregnancy had been a textbook one—apart from the discomfort of needing to pee all the time and some niggling pains she assured me was to be expected as the birth date grew nearer.

Pain clouded my gorgeous wife's normally vibrant gray eyes when she looked back at me, her appearance did nothing to reassure me. Clutching her swollen belly, the agony was clear in her face as she nursed her bump with her hands.

"Yeah, another three weeks and they'd class her as full-term, so I guess our baby should be—" Another painful contraction caught her already labored breathing and interrupted the reassurance I had desperately sought. My chest tightened further, my anxiety increasing because apart from the actual birth, seeing Grace doubled up in pain was the part I'd been dreading the most from her condition.

Gripping the steering wheel, I noted my sweaty palms clung desperately to it as anxiety threatened to take over when I heard how deeply she inhaled in her effort to manage her pain. I was impressed by my wife's conscious effort to remain in control of her labor.

As time passed, she began to moan louder in discomfort and my heart jolted with anxiety each time I heard it. Nausea came in a wave and I swallowed it down because it wasn't time and no matter how much we'd talked about the birth, I wasn't prepared. Watching the love of my life in pain was hell. Even if it was necessary to bring the new life we had created together into this world.

When another contraction wore off an additional concern sprang to mind. "Your obstetrician's office replied to your message, right?"

Grace reached down, dragged her huge purse full of shit onto her lap and rummaged around inside. Finally, she pulled out her cell phone and let the heavy bag slide back to the floor.

The bright blue screen instantly glowed, lighting up the surrounding blanket of darkness inside the car. Swiping the small screen, she lifted her cell to her ear, and I knew she had received a voicemail.

"Yeah," she barely managed to breathe before another pain took her attention. Relief washed over me, glad that someone with the expertise to help Grace would be waiting for her on arrival.

I glanced at the digital clock on the dashboard panel: 3:21 a.m. Beside it was the date: January 7th, and I noted that until now it wasn't one which held any significance for me. A swell of excitement from inside reminded me it would be the day to surpass all the days of my life. The day my first child would be born and the beginning of a new life for Grace and me.

It took seven more contractions, three minutes apart, before we arrived at the Memorial Hospital entrance. Abandoning our imposing black SUV in the no-parking zone, I ran around the hood and yanked open the door so forcefully the vehicle rocked on its axel. Gripping Grace by the arms, I spoke in a gentle, encouraging tone.

"That's it, Baby, you're doing great, we're here. It won't be long before the doc can assess you and give you some drugs for the pain. No giving away our bedroom secrets when he does, by the way," I joked, trying to ease the tension that had returned to the situation as we made our way into the hospital.

Grace scoffed at my comment as we entered the foyer and another painful wave stopped her dead in her tracks. She clung to the long metal door handle to steady herself while a kind, middle-aged hospital orderly appeared from nowhere with a wheelchair. I helped him ease my wife into it as her pain subsided again.

"Looks like we got ourselves an expensive new addition to the family on the way," he teased, and I grinned in relief at his attempt to take the sting out of Grace's discomfort.

"Hey, you're that Cole erm…"

"Yeah, but I'm not the major attraction here, right?" I warned, and he glanced down at my wife and nodded.

As the contraction waned, Grace glanced up at the orderly and cussed under her breath. "This kid can have anything she wants, no questions asked. She just needs to be here already." Another groan tore from her throat and she doubled over again, cradling her belly and I prayed for a quick end to this experience for her.

We rode the elevator to the fifth floor, where an obstetric nurse was waiting, clipboard in hand. Her beady eyes widened in surprise when she recognized who I was. I scowled and shot her a warning look not to acknowledge me. The last thing my wife needed was a fangirl fawning over me while she was in pain.

"Dr. Ken is waiting for you, Grace. If you'll follow me, I'll get you settled and let him know you've arrived. There are a few papers to sign, Cole, but we can figure those out once we get Grace settled." Insurance, I figured, dismissing it. Nothing was as important as Grace's comfort.

Minutes passed after we entered the room and the Obstetric nurse squirted monitoring gel and attached monitoring pads to Grace's bump. A wave of emotion swelled in my throat at the sound of our daughter's steady heartbeat as it echoed loudly through the room. It was no secret we were having a girl; Grace had told everyone.

I noted the equipment had begun to record a series of squiggly lines onto the folded paper attached to a tray underneath. The nurse then focused on checking Grace's vitals before she turned to us and smiled.

"Grace, your blood pressure is perfect right now. This..." she stated, pointing at the two traces being recorded, "top trace is your baby's heart rate and you can see it fluctuate here. This means she's awake and active right now. The graph at the bottom is showing us your contractions are every three minutes, which is regular and exactly what we like to see."

"That's the baby's heartbeat?" I asked, pointing out the inked recording of it.

"Yes." She smiled. "Your baby's heart rate is increasing with each contraction at present, which is perfectly normal." I smiled in awe of this.

Discussing the birthing plan with Grace, the nurse informed us Grace would have a shot of steroids to help mature the baby's lungs for the birth.

As she was finishing talking, Dr. Ken strode into the room, looking like he'd come straight from a movie set with his expensive stethoscope around his neck and a pristine white laboratory coat covering his designer clothing. He had glossy blond hair, unblemished skin, and perfect, even white teeth. Way too attractive for a guy touching my wife.

Although I respected his profession, I hated that he was such a good-looking dude, because he had Grace's permission to explore the most intimate parts of her body. Keeping my jealousy in check, I reminded myself he had clinical reasons for doing this.

Discussing the history of the previous few hours, it became clear Grace was unsure as to whether the sac of fluid around our baby had broken, admitting to small frequent trickles of liquid with each contraction.

After examining her abdomen, Dr. Ken confirmed the baby's head was low in Grace's pelvis and informed us he needed to take a swab from inside her entrance to make sure our baby hadn't been exposed to any infection. My jaw ticked with tension at the thought of this.

Preparing an examination pack on a small mobile cart, the nurse rolled it close to the bed as the doctor washed his hands. After drying them, he snapped on some gloves and sat down on a stool at the edge of the bed, positioning Grace lower in preparation for the procedure.

After ensuring her hygiene he explained, "I'm using a speculum and once I take a germ culture I'll also take a small swab test to check for the presence of amniotic fluid. This is important as your baby is a little premature and early rupture can predispose the increased risk of infection."

Watching intently from the side of the bed, my beady, concerned eyes flicked from what he was doing at the business end to Grace's face, and I noted her pain-filled eyes stare up into mine for reassurance.

"You're doing great, Baby."

Grace's body sagged and she sighed with my encouragement, and my gaze returned to focus on the young doctor's face. A frown creased his brow and his eyes narrowed, widened then shot in my direction. When he held my gaze a second too long I sensed something was wrong.

"Nurse, can you position the light closer please?" he instructed, focusing back on the point of interest between Grace's legs again.

Hovering in the background, the nurse jumped, startled with the sharpness in his tone. Stepping forward, she repositioned the spotlight, and as her eyes fell between Grace's legs a look of worry flitted through them. A short gasp hitched in her breath and Dr. Ken's eyes darted to hers.

"What is it?" I asked, sensing immediately something was wrong.

"I'm collecting some samples to send to the laboratory for culture. Once I've done this, I'll answer any questions you have," the doctor said shutting me down.

Hearing our baby's heart rate spike instantly in protest to his ministrations distracted me from him, but when I looked back at the doc he was handing the slides to the nurse. Standing quickly, he tidied everything back on the tray, flicked off the rubber gloves and discarded them into a stainless steel pedal bin.

With his back to us he washed his hands before he turned and addressed us. "Give me a few minutes to fill out the pathology and microbiology forms and I'll come back to talk to you."

Grace looked completely unfazed by the examination and continued breathing through the contractions once he'd left the room. When she hadn't asked questions, I convinced myself it was my ignorance that had made me think there was something wrong, but my fears rose again when the doctor was still absent some fifteen minutes later.

Between contractions as we waited there were pockets of normality where Grace and I discussed some practical plans for after our daughter was born, but as time went on I became increasingly frustrated and a nagging doubt grew at the back of my mind the longer he took to return.

Watching Grace continue to suffer made my chest tight, heightening my awareness of every breath I took. I'd never suffered from anxiety, but I recognized this was probably what was going on, given how useless I felt. I was used to controlling situations not being controlled.

Reflecting on everything I'd witnessed since arriving at the hospital, the only positives were the baby's steady heartbeat and with each contraction, although agony for Grace, it meant we were one step closer to the birth of our precious baby.

When the door to our room slowly cracked open, the doctor stepped inside. The reluctant way he dragged his feet toward the bed almost freaked me out. I sensed hesitancy and dread in his presence. Gone was the chirpy, suave, and extremely self-assured authoritarian, and in his place was a young, dejected looking character who was almost unrecognizable as the same man.

I felt an aura of humility instead of how the doctor usually commanded respect, and there something else about his mood I couldn't define in that moment.

As he lowered himself gently onto the bed, the door opened again, and the nurse who'd been attending to Grace reentered the room. I felt her reluctance to be present and her gaze fell to the floor.

Sitting silently we waited for Grace's contraction to ebb away. My heartbeat pounded in fear while I watched Dr Ken draw several deep breaths.

A couple of times he swallowed roughly and closed his eyes as if what he needed to say was somehow painful for him and highly significant for us.

Frustration and anguish clashed in my gut, knotting it tight and I dug deep to find patience I never knew I possessed until that moment; either that or it was the unparalleled level of fear for our future which, until then, had prevented me from speaking out.

"What is it?" I eventually asked when the wait finally overwhelmed me.

Staring worriedly at me, it felt like an age before the young doctor found his courage, blinked, and took a deep breath. From the anticipation in those seconds, I knew he had no comforting words in what he needed to tell us.

Scanning the room for everything tangible to our situation, all I could see were the monitors that showed how Grace and the baby were coping; from what the nurse had explained before nothing had changed. When yet another contraction tailed off, Grace smiled reassuringly to me then again toward the doctor and the nurse.

Suddenly I noticed how young the nurse appeared and how upset she looked. My heart almost tore from my chest with a wave of fear and anticipation, and I instinctively knew whatever they had to say was going to change us.

While I silently prayed for everything to be okay, the door unexpectedly opened again and a small balding man stepped inside.

Initially I thought he may have been the pediatrician; dressed in his green scrubs. I have no idea why, perhaps because my mind wasn't willing to acknowledge the unspoken truth, that there was something wrong.

Standing next to the nurse, the new member of the medical team also avoided my gaze. I was about to ask who he was when Dr. Ken cleared his throat and caught my attention again.

"Grace," he said to gain her focus.

Looking nervously to me, he said her name again. "Grace, Cole..." He paused and swallowed audibly, his hesitancy made my heart beat erratically.

Inside my head I screamed for him to spit out whatever was wrong, as my heart tried to ignore the signs of concern I had seen in his eyes. Blood whooshed rapidly through my ears, and I wished it could have been loud enough to drown out any potentially bad news. I was already in shock and I had yet to learn why.

Grace's pain-filled eyes went wide with alarm at his assertive tone, her gaze switching from me to the doctor then back to me. My hand automatically sought hers and I gripped it tight.

"When I examined you, Grace, I saw something of concern. There are some changes in your cervix, and I've sent some slides to the laboratory and now we wait for the expert's opinion."

"What is it? What's wrong? Does she need antibiotics? Surgery? God, is the baby infected or something?" My rapid questions came without filter or any thought for how Grace was feeling. The look of concern on the doctor's face ramped up my distress.

"At this point, I wouldn't be willing to hazard a guess." He stopped talking and stared blankly at Grace who was interrupted by another contraction.

At first, I thought she hadn't heard him because she continued to breathe through her pain as she had with all the others, then I realized the doctor was waiting for her to finish. *What the hell could be wrong? She's been fine apart from these twinges.*

Fighting my impulse to question him further, I waited for Grace to focus because we both needed to be informed. When the contraction subsided, my wife stared fearfully at her doctor.

"Grace, because you're in established labor our priority is to help you to deliver your baby. This means we need to take you to the operating room straightaway. Your progress appears okay at present, but a vaginal birth is not an option. Your baby will become distressed if we leave it much longer."

"What?" My sharp, loud response startled the doctor as I tried to absorb the worrying situation we suddenly faced. Anguish dragged me to my feet.

"What do you think it is? Why can't she have a vaginal delivery?" Ignoring me, the doctor focused his attention on Grace. "What's wrong with her cervix? Grace had an examination at the start of her pregnancy, right, Baby?" I persisted, turning to look to her for reassurance.

Grace's eyes grew wide, but she frowned and went into the throes of another contraction before she could say anything. The contractions had changed and appeared to be almost continuous.

"Her test came back normal," I added, looking back to the doctor but he didn't reply. Panic set in and my heart began throwing out crazy arrhythmic beats in distress as my breathing became shallow and faster. *This can't be happening.* "Did you hear me?" I probed again.

The helpless look the doctor gave me crushed me. "You're right. Grace was screened, and the results *were* normal at that time," he confirmed quietly. "But I'm asking you to trust me, Grace can't deliver normally."

No. No. NO! A tight band of pressure squeezed my brain until I thought I'd have a stroke. All my reasoning fought for me not to accept what he'd stated. As a result, the pressing tension made me feel as if my skull was going to explode.

"Is this why she's been in so much pain lately?" I enquired, eyeing him carefully.

"It's entirely possible the cell changes were still at undetectable levels when Grace was screened, but yes, undoubtedly it would have caused her pain."

"Cell changes?" The anguish in my voice was apparent.

"I'm so sorry we don't have time for further explanations until after we operate. Our priority is to make Grace comfortable right now and to ensure your baby is born safely. The only way to do this is with emergency surgery."

I could have continued to force the issue because Grace and I needed an explanation; but in terms of prioritizing the immediate situation, the doctor was right. Grace had to be helped to bring our baby into the world and everything else had to wait. I figured once the baby was born we'd be in a better position to investigate where to get help to make Grace well again.

"Stay strong, Baby, we'll get through this. Trust me, we're going to find out what's going on with you and get the best guys in the business to fix it."

As I rambled on, spouting meaningless words in my efforts to make Grace feel safe, she focused her energy on her labor pains and the safe delivery of our daughter. Not once from when Dr. Ken gave us this news until she was ready for the operating room, did Grace break down, show distress, or ask any questions.

"Let's get on with what needs to be done," Grace stated to Dr. Ken in an expressionless tone. She sounded as if she had detached herself from everyone else in the room.

The moment Grace gave her consent to the surgical procedure, the nurse and the other guy in scrubs, whom I learned was the anesthesiologist, moved in and prepared my courageously calm girl for the operating room.

As the birth was an emergency procedure and the baby still premature, Grace was given the steroid shot for our daughter's lungs, and with no time for anything other than a full general anesthetic, I wasn't allowed to stay with her for the birth of our baby.

As they wheeled her through the operating room doors, I held Grace's hand, bent down and kissed her. Smoothing her hair, I forced a soft smile as my worried eyes met hers and my heartbeat battered erratically in denial.

"Stay strong, beautiful. I'll be right here waiting for you when you wake up. I love you so much. Forget everything else and concentrate on you and our baby. Don't worry, we'll work out the rest."

Too choked to say anything else, I stood up straight and watched them wheel her inside the room and I tried not to cry. Bawling was the last thing I wanted to do when Grace was being so brave.

Pain seared through my body as I watched my world lying helpless on the gurney. Holding my breath, I waited until the sound of the heavy operating room door clicked shut and I fell to my knees on the floor.

I was still in the same position when my tears had dried and I continued to stare at the single dark mark on the wall. With my mind back in the present, I still struggled to make sense of the grim expression on the doctor's face and how he avoided expanding on what was wrong with my wife.

We came to the hospital to have a baby, to be a family. Being left alone in a corridor with more questions than answers wasn't how this was supposed to go. Why would the doctor refuse to comment on what he suspected, yet act with such certainty regarding the surgery for Grace? How could emergency surgery pose less of a risk to her and our baby?

Every minute I waited for news felt excruciatingly long. As I sat there undisturbed, I willed someone to come out and find me; to tell me Grace and our baby were perfectly fine, and to say that the doctor was wrong.

CHAPTER THREE

"Cole?" Hearing the obstetrician's questioning tone drew me out of my daydream.

I glanced up from the floor and his worried expression sent fear coursing through my body. As I scrambled to my feet, my throat tightened and the crushing pain in my chest felt suffocating at the thought there may be something wrong with Grace or our child.

"Breathe," the doctor coaxed in a gentler tone than he'd used before, and I suddenly snapped out of the panic attack I was having. My anxious eyes frantically searched his face as I waited for him to update me.

"Yes?"

Anguish darkened his expression as he drew in a deep breath and held it, and my heart stalled. Averting his eyes from my gaze he shook his head, and I grew more impatient, my eyes riveted to him.

"Shall we have a seat?" he asked, gesturing with an outstretched hand at the row of blue plastic chairs lining the corridor.

Meekly, I sat down without taking my eyes off him and he did the same. Turning his body to face me, he placed his hands in his lap and gave me a sympathetic stare. I almost screamed because of how unhurried he appeared.

"First, you have a baby daughter. She's fine, vitals are all good, but as you know she's a few weeks early, so she's going up to the neonatal unit for observation for a short time. We're always cautious for the first day or two with our premature babies because those last few weeks can make a difference to their adaptation from the womb."

"And Grace?" I asked concerned.

The doctor rubbed his brow before he looked me square in the eye. Taking a deep breath, he shook his head. "There's no easy way to say this, Cole. Grace has cancer."

Initially I thought I'd misheard him. Then a wall of shock blindsided me and my heart sank to my stomach and my heart stalled again. "Wh... No... Bullshit, you're wrong," I argued, "you're a liar. How can you say something like this?" My tone was sharp—aggressive—and I sprang to my feet, my heart thudding faster than I'd ever felt it before. I ran my fingers through my hair then grabbed two clumps of it in my fists.

My stomach lurched and the taste of bile in my throat made my stomach roll again. I began to walk away as anger, aggression, and instant denial built up inside, then I turned and strode back to challenge him.

"Dude, we've just had a baby, she can't be sick," I scoffed. "This is bullshit. I won't hear it. You saw Grace; she's the picture of health. We came here to have a fucking baby."

"Cole, I need you to sit down because there is much more I need to tell you and it's important you hear what I have to say," he ordered in a much sterner but quiet voice.

"When I examined Grace, I knew immediately her cervix was unhealthy. I couldn't confirm a diagnosis until I had pathology results to support my clinical findings. However, when we operated, I'm afraid it was much worse than I had imagined, because there was no mistaking what we found when I opened Grace's abdomen."

For a moment the doctor fell silent, then he sighed heavily, like it was killing him to tell me this news, almost as much as it was killing me to hear what he had to say. I immediately sensed disappointment in the way he exhaled.

Gripping my upper arm, he shook his head again. "Cole, what I'm saying is Grace's cancer is so extensive and far advanced its inoperable. I'm at a loss as to how she didn't collapse before now. Grace may only have weeks, if not days, left to live."

My breath hitched in fright even before his devastating words sank in. Shock then made my deflated lungs heave for air, and in that horrible moment, it felt as if my ruptured heart had stopped beating... yet still I breathed.

"The spread has ravished her body, affecting her rectum, bladder, the anterior wall of her uterus, small bowel and liver. Probably why she's been having so much pain during the past couple of weeks."

"But they implied at her prenatal checks the pains were normal toward the end... never mind, how soon can she have treatment?" I asked, still clinging to hope.

"No, Cole, you aren't taking in what I've told you. There *is* no treatment. In fact, I am telling you here instead of with Grace because I'm not sure how, or if she'll recover from the surgery."

Turning my head, I glanced down the clinical setting of the hospital corridor and watched people at the far end wandering around, attending to their normal business, while I stood trying to imagine the nightmare of my future with a dying wife and a new baby girl to take care of.

There had been plenty of times in my life when I had thought life was cruel, but the full horror of the countless situations I'd heard of in life had never truly hit home.

Tragedies mostly happened to other people, although there had been a few times in my personal life where heartbreak had struck, like when my father had died. Back then there had been a period of adjustment for us beforehand.

My father's death had been a gradual process, allowing my mother, my brother, and me time to accustom ourselves to living without him. By the time he'd died we'd been resigned to his fate as we watched him decline and fade away. It was nothing like what I faced alone in the sterile corridor as fate hung in the balance with our future at its mercy.

"At the moment, Grace has been moved to our Intensive Care Unit and is very heavily sedated. Your daughter, like I assured you, is doing fine. You can see them both as soon as they have been made comfortable upstairs." I noted there were no congratulations like there would usually have been when a child was born.

"Is there someone we can call to be with you?" When I didn't respond, my mind numb from the news, he spoke again. "Let's walk down here to the relatives' room and I'll explain what's going to happen."

Following behind him, I walked half the length of the hallway and entered a small box room. It looked comfortable in pastel shades of green and I immediately associated it with bad news. It was a carbon copy of the décor at the hospice my father had gone into.

Holding his palm out, Dr. Ken gestured for me to take a seat, but I chose to remain standing. "Tell me," I urged. Again, he persuaded me to take a seat and at his insistence I sat.

"As I explained before, there are metastases or secondary cancers in many of her other organs. We had a few complications with the delivery because of Grace's condition, but the baby is quite well, breathing on her own, and warming up nicely."

For a long moment I couldn't think, and then the enormity of what he'd said threatened to make me lose control, but I knew I couldn't do that. "Tell me what to do," I whispered, as tears rolled down my cheeks as the full impact of my helpless situation became overwhelming.

"Grace is dying, Cole. There is probably very little time; especially now she's been compromised further by the surgery. She is going to be extremely weak when we reduce the sedation and if she wakes up she'll be in a lot of pain."

If she wakes? Springing to my feet again, my lungs felt so tight, as if they'd burst right out of my chest at any second. A wave of fear and despair at losing Grace brought one lump after another into my throat, and I fought the sickening sensation of losing my grasp on reality.

"Please tell me this isn't true," I begged, anger swelling inside until I was suddenly furious at the injustice of life.

Placing his hand on my forearm, his sad gaze was filled with sorrow. "Cole, I wish to God I could tell you differently, but I can't. Grace will deteriorate rapidly from now on. We're doing everything we can to make her comfortable. Do you have anyone we can call to come and be with you?" he prompted again.

Digging in my back jeans pocket, I took out my cell as the doctor continued to try to inform me about their excellent palliative care program. His hard sell on how they could give Grace a good end wasn't something I wanted to hear, so I ignored him completely and called my mom.

"Mom, it's me. I need you to come to the hospital."

"Has Grace had the baby?" she asked with all the bubbly excitement of an expectant grandmother.

"Yes, she's here, but Grace is sick." Closing the call out before she could ask any questions, I stuck my cell in my jacket pocket and the dreadful reality about Grace hit me on a whole other level. The painful truth of all the information the doctor had told me ran over me like a dump truck.

To be frank, I don't recall the next few hours after that, but I do remember someone giving me a shot and I guess I blacked out for a while.

When I finally came to, I initially thought I'd had a horrendously bad trip but, unfortunately, I hadn't dabbled in drugs for over six years. Clocking an oxygen flow gauge on the wall I remembered where I was and realized I was lying in a hospital bed. The nightmare I thought I'd escaped about Grace had followed me into my devastating reality.

For the first twenty-four hours my dying wife lay unconscious; heavily sedated as she recovered from her surgery. I trudged back and forth; torn between needing to be at her bedside and learning my duties as a first-time father in the Neonatal Intensive Care Unit or NICU. Thankfully, the Adult Intensive Care Unit and this were on the same floor.

When my mom showed up, the sense of relief I had expected to feel when she walked through the door never happened. There *was* no escape from the impending misery and heartache I faced.

I believed no one else could possibly understand the depth of despair I felt. This was *my* walk to walk. Only I knew what I felt in my heart, and to say I was disappointed to learn this didn't even begin to cut it.

I barely remember some fragmented moments of going through the motions in the hospital. Flitting back and forth between Grace; who was lucid for small periods of time, and the baby care unit, to carry out the endless routines of feeding and diaper changes of the too tiny, helpless infant in my care.

The only thing that stood out in my memory was when the pediatric nurse placed Layla's semi-naked body under my T-shirt, against my skin. During those few brief minutes the hurt I felt in my heart temporarily dissipated. I sighed deeply when Layla squirmed contentedly as she soaked up my warmth when I cradled her protectively against me. Then, when I felt her little heart beating close to mine through her teeny bony chest, I choked up with the indescribable distress I felt, and my tears fell again.

From that moment on, I tried to block out any and all attempts to share my grief. Despite my family's many attempts to help me face a future without Grace, I couldn't bare my heart to them, preferring to shut down. For a while I refused to participate in life because I felt if I did, it meant I would have accepted it would be without Grace and I was neither prepared or ready to do this.

However, no amount of denial could take away Grace's silent killer. No matter how hard it was to accept, five short ugly days after Layla entered this world, my beautiful wife, Grace, left it. I was a mess, yet she was devastatingly brave and serenely calm at the end when her life was abruptly stilled at 7:48 a.m. in the morning.

Dr. Ken had been right; the open surgery had exposed the extent of the cancer and the proliferation of the disease after this completely overwhelmed her body. Words meant in comfort about Grace having seen Layla and holding her in her arms before she died infuriated me.

There were no words of condolence I found comfort in and they were crass remarks borne out of unempathetic ignorance because five fucking days was no time to give a lifetime of bonding to our baby before her mom was gone forever.

Staring numbly at Grace's lifeless body it was difficult to comprehend that she had been so full of sass, and vitality on our last night together. Less than a week later our happily ever after had been ripped from our grasp by some stealthy form of terminal illness. And I was left furious at the world.

The circumstance forced upon me was unfathomable, but this was my new reality. Neither of us could ever have imagined when Grace waved that simple piece of plastic with those two thin pink lines in my face, her body had already been preparing her goodbye.

The swiftness of Grace's death didn't grant us the privilege of time. No part of me was willing nor able to accept how quickly she was taken from me. There hadn't even been the time or the clarity of mind to think of all the things I had wanted to say. It left me with tender loving feelings I wished I had told her about when I'd still had the chance.

Pity those thoughts only came to mind after she'd passed, because they were very intimate and heartfelt sentiments, which now remained trapped inside my head and my heart and with nowhere to go now. We were robbed of what so many couples took for granted; to watch each other change with the passing years, to raise a family, and to grow old together.

However, what I was most incredibly bitter about was how Grace would never see the beautiful precious child she gave her life for, robbed of watching her daughter blossom from the tiny bud she had left behind.

∼

"The vultures are circling outside, Cole. Thank God, Mom and I have never been in the limelight with you so they're not looking for us. Although, I did see a couple of photographers lurking in the foyer by the elevators on the ground floor."

The press was incidental to what was happening, and I shrugged off my brother, Dorian's comment. Preparing to leave the hospital the day after Grace died, with our six-day-old baby, was soul crushing. Supported by my mom and my brother, I had no choice but to go home.

Seeing my normally youthful looking mom appear old and haggard —her face etched with the strain of grief almost as much as mine—

made me feel sick. She had arrived at the hospital from our hometown in Delaware the day Layla was born, and I vaguely remembered her prompting me to eat. Being so absorbed in my grief, I'd only fleetingly considered the impact on her and how she'd carried me through every step of the way as Grace lay dying.

There wasn't a single minute during the day when Grace or Layla didn't have either one of us in support. Mom had been right there, traveling the same path of tragedy beside me, and I'd hardly noticed her.

It had never occurred to me until that moment, as we were leaving the hospital, how she must have felt as she left me behind each night, wondering how to prepare the house for my baby daughter's homecoming.

Due to my fame, word had gotten out about Grace, like it always did when there was some juicy new information about Cole Harkin, lead singer from SinaMen. But I was so overawed; I couldn't begin to concern myself with their intrusive lack of decorum.

The hounding press was a breed of desensitized people with no morality for the life changing situations of others, and news of Grace's death was a huge deal to them. As such, my bandmates had been stalked incessantly as soon as the story had broken.

Sensationalizing my wife's tragic demise, they focused on her type of cancer and speculated as to whether I was to blame by way of my previous promiscuity, insinuating this could have been a possible contributor to the development of the disease.

Their presumption was the lowest blow because I was clean. Ironically, I'd never been with any girl without wrapping up first, apart from Grace, and I'd been regularly tested. Apart from this, after being faithful to Grace for the two years we'd been together, this media assumption had come as a major insult to me. Their negativity of the man I was sat heavily with me, and I found their damning judgmental assumptions of my character degrading.

Unlike me, Grace had a history of unprotected sex with several partners and was on the pill when I met her. She had also been in three long-term relationships.

Too grief stricken to fight this point on my own, my brother

Dorian took up the mantle, incensed they would target me on such a day and in this way.

From my perspective, I felt ashamed for the reporters who hadn't focused on the real story. There was the unspoken sadness of the child who'd lost her mother and the man who had lost his beautiful wife. Instead they had chosen to pitch their story on the seedy side of cervical cancer and apportioning blame on me.

Stepping out into the cold, gray day, I was instantly reminded of the intrusion and brutal lack of morals among the press as a hungry pack of reporters huddled around me. Anticipating this, I had covered Layla's car seat with a white knitted shawl, obscuring her identity from them.

Walking in time with me, camera bulbs flashed as insensitive questions were hurled in a cacophony of jumbled noise. No one appeared to care how devastated I was by the shock of my sudden loss or my concern for the tiny baby I carried. Someone even waved a grubby cheap notepad in my face and asked for my autograph.

Squaring up to them Dorian let loose calling them a tirade of names and a whole bunch of more degrading terms I thought were too good for them.

Personally, I didn't even acknowledge their presence; instead securing Layla's car seat in the back of the car, and focusing on getting the hell out of there to keep my baby safe. For most of my time in the public eye I had been relentlessly scrutinized. I knew if they drew a reaction from me it would give a new story legs for them to run with instead. This was why I chose to treat them with the attention they deserved—indifference.

Even after we had driven away my mom sighed in relief and expressed her disgust at how they'd behaved. I was so bereft at leaving Grace behind in the morgue I couldn't even muster the strength to respond.

Dorian had flown in from Maine and when he saw the mess I was, he immediately got together with my mom, Derek, my manager and Angus and Dinah, my wife's parents, to plan her funeral. Everyone tried their best to get me involved, but I was too heartbroken to deal with the practicalities of it all.

As Grace's husband, I knew I should have done better, but I felt utterly overwhelmed any time anyone brought up the subject. The thought of saying this final goodbye to my beautiful young wife slayed me.

My wife had passed on what her final wishes were to me, and I understood her need to have the last word on this. Her request for privacy was a given, due to the way the press had constantly invaded it whenever we stepped outside the house.

Being buried on our property meant we had some control. Derek had the funeral director sign a nondisclosure agreement and her casket was delivered in an unmarked van.

Paul and Stuart, two of our estate managers, rigged up a wooden trailer they used for transporting hay and harnessed two black stallions Stuart had hand-reared from our stables to take Grace from our house on her final journey to the meadow.

Diane and Peter, our landscape gardeners, had draped the old wagon trailer with ivory sheer material panels, then decorated it with ivory calla lilies, vine leaves, and lilac wisteria from Grace's favorite parts of our gardens.

The final effect looked stunningly elegant and fitting for someone as beautiful as Grace. As horrible as the day was, my wife would have been happy with what her family and friends did out of love as we lay her to rest.

Heavy rain pelted the manmade lake surrounding us. The droplets bouncing in a noisy musical roar in the otherwise quiet pasture. The island and lake had been designed by Grace and landscaped by Diane and Peter with a working crew from town in the months after we moved.

When I recalled how excited Grace was when our landscapers brought her design to life, what she'd called her 'reflective serenity concept' it made my heart clench. The south section of our property ran along the intersection between the Reed Creek and New River, so it hadn't been too difficult to redirect some water to flood a small amount of acreage on the lower part of the meadow.

Grace had romantic visions of it being a place for us to escape to away from our kids for the night when our teenagers became too much. I never thought for a moment, when I agreed to the plan, it would become her final resting place.

With her casket safely transported from our pontoon boat onto the island, I stood bewildered at the thought of how I'd cope with the enormity of bringing up a female child alone. A Roman Catholic priest delivered the final sermon over her open grave before her mahogany-colored coffin was lowered into the ground.

As we stood by her graveside under the large willow trees on the tiny island, I hated everything surrounding me and I struggled for breath. Flanked by my brother, mother, and Grace's parents, we each threw a single yellow rose down into the hole where she lay and said our silent goodbyes.

Layla was back at the house and my mind turned to my poor tiny child. At least she'd been spared the sight of laying her mother into the ground. Apart from this, the only comforting thought I took away with me that day was I'd achieved the request she had asked for, no prying eyes of the press.

Grace's last request was for me to sing a song for her after everyone had gone. I sang, "Stairway to Heaven" by Led Zeppelin and almost choked on every word. Then Stuart brought the pontoon boat back and picked me up. I was soaked to the skin by then, but he hugged me anyway, then he quietly led me home.

CHAPTER FOUR

Following Grace's burial, those first few weeks at home were an alcoholic blur; my mom, my brother, and the house staff having taken over because I had all but ceased to function. Three weeks in, my mom and Dorian had taken up residence at my place, banned alcohol deliveries to my home, and their sometimes worried but mostly stony faces watched every move I made.

Naturally they were sad and concerned, and frankly I'd given them due cause, because everything in life had taken a back seat as I wallowed in pity somewhere between grief and denial.

Hygiene, eating, even Layla, became someone else's responsibility as I got lost in an alcoholic haze as I tried to drown my thoughts by getting lost in an abyss. Mom overrode her grief and fears with practicality, and with Layla needing twenty-four-hour care; she had interviewed and hired a local, highly qualified nanny for her.

It had been almost four weeks after Grace died, by the time Grace's parents finally found the courage to leave. Sad eyes still swollen with tears gazed into mine when I made a rare appearance downstairs as Stuart prepared their ride.

"Promise us you'll get yourself straight and cherish Layla," Angus hugged me and pleaded, with a voice that broke when he mentioned Layla's name.

"Make Grace proud and bring her up in the way she would have wanted," Dinah stated, sniffing back her tears.

"Of course, I just need some time," I agreed, too wounded by the way they looked at me, and by then I'd have promised them anything to get them to leave.

Their way of dealing with the loss of their daughter was by highlighting constant reminders and sharing memories of her. It may have comforted them, but their comments had felt like jagged knives gutting me.

Those early days were a blur as Mom, Dorian, Matty and the others took responsibility for everything because I had ceased to function, and as January slid into February my life was still on hold.

When a month and a day had passed, my mom lost patience with me when I had declined an invite for the fourth day running to take a short walk around the grounds with my daughter in her stroller.

"The fresh air will do you good," she advised, as she walked closer to my bed. Sitting down, she laid a gentle hand on my shoulder. "There are no words to describe what your heart feels like right now. I can vouch for that. Your life ahead will be very different to the one you envisioned with Grace, but have faith. With the love of your daughter, in time you'll learn to live again."

Angrily I sat bolt upright, baring my teeth to my mother, fury at my situation oozing from every pore. "No words?" I scoffed. "Mom, I have plenty of words and this faith that you talk about... it... it's bullshit. How am I supposed to believe in anything when life threw a curve ball so hard in my face, it not only knocked me on my ass, but it's paralyzed my mind, heart, and my soul, huh?"

"I know it's—"

"No, Mom. You may know a lot, but you *don't* know *this*. You and Dad had a *whole* life together before he was taken. Ours was just beginning. God barely gave Grace the time to bond, to smile down at her tiny daughter with a lifetime of love that had to be crammed into five short days. And what about our baby? What about Layla? Helpless, motherless, defenseless from a lifetime of questions that begin with 'what if' and answers that disappoint as they begin with 'if only'? What of the tears our daughter will shed over the years in the future for the woman who gave her life and she'll never know?"

My mom sat passive and silent during my rant with her hands neatly folded in her lap, her sad eyes brimming with tears at my words, then she shrugged. She had no reply to the injustice of the circumstance I had found myself in because nothing she could say could change this.

"Layla was left motherless... before she could even focus to look back at her mother's face. God gave them *no* time, *us* no time, before he killed our ties that bound each of us together as a family."

For the first time, I saw the look on Mom's face change. Adopting a stern, you've-pushed-me-too-far look, she stood, straightened her back, and crossed her arms across her chest.

"Get out of that bed right now and get washed. You stink. This bedroom smells like a distillery. Now, I know you're grieving, but you still have a baby daughter to take care of. Grace would have gone peacefully in the knowledge you'd protect her child with your life."

When I didn't move she threw her hands up in the air.

"Fine, have it your way. I'm leaving. It's time, Cole. Time you got your grieving head out of your self-absorbed ass and started to care for that precious bundle lying two doors down being cared for by a stranger. Don't shame yourself by sullying Grace's memory."

Hearing my mom's comment about ruining Grace's memory halted my current thoughts and I stared pointedly up at her. I thought her words were the lowest of blows at a time when I was already guilt-ridden about how Grace had died.

A part of me even thought I had killed her, because I figured if I hadn't gotten her pregnant she'd still have been with us.

Personally, I'm ashamed to say I didn't connect with Layla at all because of the horrible circumstances surrounding her birth. I supposed blaming myself for knocking Grace up was partly the reason for that.

In the early days, there wasn't that instant 'fall in love' moment from me for Layla. I'd heard this mentioned so many times when I watched other new fathers on YouTube, and I wondered how different this would have been if I hadn't known Grace was dying.

Most of the time since I'd arrived at the hospital with her, until we left without her, was a blur; yet there were agonizing memories of our stay, which felt as if I were experiencing them in slow motion at the time.

I had vivid memories of staring helplessly down at Grace as she lay unconscious, and in another I was being ushered robotically into the NICU staring into a bassinet where a newborn baby lay.

Forcing a smile toward me, the nurse glanced down at my baby. I followed her gaze and saw a tiny naked baby girl lying peacefully on her back. I expected to feel something, *anything*, for her, but I didn't.

Denial swept through me and I begged God to tell me this was all a bad dream. *Any second I'll wake up and Grace will be in the shower singing like she does every morning when I open my eyes.*

Still focusing my gaze on our child, I was ashamed at how disconnected I felt. I silently asked for her forgiveness, because the shock and pain of what was happening to my wife overrode everything with such excruciating pain, I had no capacity for anything else.

The last emotion I could feel was love, and I swore no one would get under my skin again if this were the outcome. It was a decimating once-in-a-lifetime deal.

My unstable emotional state was a constant swirl of conflicting or free-falling feelings brought on by dark thoughts full of anger. Those periodically culminated in bitter words of vengeance against anyone who looked at me in a way I perceived to be wrong.

Mom wasn't kidding. She left within the hour and her dressing down of me had the desired effect. I dragged my ass out of bed because she was right; none of this was my baby daughter, Layla's fault. The poor little soul hadn't asked to be born, and as much as I wanted to, I knew I couldn't spend the next eighteen years of her life in bed wallowing in self-pity, denial, and grief.

Fighting against the dark thoughts within myself, I had no other option but to live the rest of my journey on earth missing the love of my life. There was nothing I could do about missing Grace, and I knew I had to somehow find a way to respect her memory and myself.

Dealing with grief taught me I wasn't a brave man, but I had to push back my selfish temptations and try to live up to the person Grace would have expected me to be. Like her name, I couldn't afford the luxury of falling from Grace.

Padding through to the bathroom, I stared at the gaunt figure in the mirror and considered how my hurt, tormented appearance may have made my mom and brother feel when they looked at me. It was the first time I considered anything other than dying in the previous month.

My normally short, dark-brown hair was overgrown on the top; my hazel eyes, which Grace always told me sparkled with mischief, looked lifeless, and my facial hair was no longer an attractive closely groomed beard, but a fully-fledged bush any mountain man would have been proud of. I sighed deeply and went through the motion of splashing water on my face to wake myself up before I stepped into the shower.

Ten minutes later, I dragged my weary ass into some clean jeans and shuffled barefooted along the hall past the first door—the one Grace had used as a dressing room for all her shit—and opened the second. The calming, pale pink decor with the dreamy cloud murals, hand-painted by Grace, was yet another reminder of what I'd lost.

For a second, I squeezed my eyes shut when a vision of my wife looking sexy in an old button-down shirt of mine with paint in her hair flashed through my mind. I hesitated as a pang of hurt crushed my chest and stood clutching tightly to the polished glass handle. The smooth cool glass in my palm soothed me as I fought against my anger.

"You're just in time, Cole. Layla is about ready for dinner. Are you going to feed her?" My eyes sprang open, and I glanced at the tall dark-haired girl with a golden tan and a sunny smile, looking intently back at me.

"Maybe I'll just sit here for a while." For a moment I saw the hesitation in her thought, but she quickly moved out of the nursing chair and moved over to the self-contained kitchen area specifically designed in the nursery and began mixing a bottle for my daughter. "Harper," she informed me by way of introduction. It was the first time I'd actually paid any attention to her.

Without responding, I sat quietly observing how Grace had thought of everything necessary for taking care of Layla's needs as Harper busied herself until Layla began fussing; then became more vigorous in her protest of having to wait for attention.

Turning to face me, she tipped her chin at the cradle. "Could you please pick your daughter up and hold her for a few moments while I finish preparing her formula?" Harper's voice was even, and the way she prompted me was matter-of-fact, but she didn't fool me for a second. I knew she was prompting me to have contact with my daughter.

Too tired to argue, and irritated by Layla's lusty yelling, I slid my large hand gently beneath her and lifted her carefully out of her crib. The smell of baby poop instantly filled my nostrils. "Jeez, she stinks," I muttered and carried her over to the changing table equipped with clean clothing, diapers, wipes—the works.

"Can you stop doing that and come over here to clean her up, please?" I asked in a tone that had a hint of frustration and horror at the prospect of having to do it. My baby was a month old, and apart from the black newborn tar stuff and the French mustard looking poops she'd had in the first few days, I hadn't cleaned her butt.

"I can't mix her food and clean poop at the same time. It isn't hygienic. You're going to have to do it because you don't know how to make her formula." Gesturing her head at Layla, she grabbed a bottle brush and some sterilizer before adding, "Look at her, poor little soul, she can't wait. The poop will burn her delicate skin."

Cussing under my breath, I sighed heavily and lifted my daughter over my shoulder while I dug into one of the small compartments for a clean diaper and some wipes. As I stood up straight, the hand resting over her butt suddenly felt warm.

Swapping my hands over, I checked it out and wrinkled my nose in disgust because Layla had shit all the way through her onsie. "Damn," I cussed again, laying her flat on her back on the changing mat. Grabbing a few wet wipes from the packet, I cleaned the offending gift off of my hand.

Harper turned to look at me and smirked. "Your child has a hidden talent for doing that," she commented deadpan and placed the newly made bottle into a bowl before running the water in it to cool the newly made formula.

"There's nothing hidden about it. It's splattered all over my fucking hand, and through her clothes I might add. Is it normal for shit to ooze from a diaper and spread out like this? I mean judging by the amount in that bottle it's multiplied tenfold in her gut," I commented dryly, as I began to pop the fasteners and peel Layla's clothing away. Harper kept her back to me and didn't comment, but I heard the soft chuckle she made.

It took me a good three minutes to wipe the shit from her back, between her legs, and halfway up her ass, and all the while she was stubborn and uncooperative, kicking her legs, clenching her fists, and baring the back of her throat at me with some belly busting yells.

By the time I was finished making her clean and decent again, she was a purple hot mess; her normally pale skin tinted by how pissed she was by my interruption of her glory at sitting in her own pile of manure. Gently, I picked her up and calmed her the fuck down before I even attempted to put a new diaper back on her.

Lifting Layla gingerly from the changing mat, I did what they taught me in the hospital and pulled her body close, chest to chest with mine. Splaying my huge rough hand across her tiny, silky back I took a deep, deep breath at how warm and perfect she felt skin to skin.

A lump of emotion swelled in my throat as the fragrant smell of her baby hair hit my nostrils. I cleared my clogged throat when the tiny little person I'd helped to create wriggled and nuzzled closer. When her hissy fit finally ebbed she became a quiet, contented, and innocent little bundle in my arms. When she started to coo I felt my hard, frozen heart melt.

Layla was half Grace, half me, and my mom was spot on. If I had anything to be thankful for in this whole fucked-up, devastating situation, it had to be the beautiful child Grace had left behind. A tear ran down my face, but I only knew I was crying when I felt Layla's wet little head nuzzle into my neck. Then she cooed louder.

"I... I think I will feed her, if you don't mind," I heard myself say. A camera click drew my attention to Harper, and she stood holding her phone high in the air. I immediately frowned.

"Don't worry, I'm not going to sell it. It's for you and Layla to keep as a memory of the first time you visited her here in the nursery." My heart squeezed tight and my small smile was immediate, if a little guilty. Layla was a month old, and this was the first time I'd braved the few steps from my bedroom to where she slept. *Shame on me.*

I was also embarrassed for thinking the worst of Harper's motive, but for the previous six years of my fame, the people who had taken candid pictures of me usually sold them to the highest bidder.

"Thanks, that's really thoughtful of you," I mumbled, a little concerned at how shitty my appearance had been when I looked in the mirror earlier. I placed Layla back on the changing mat and fought her fresh protests as I wrestled her into a badly positioned diaper.

When I had secured the tabs as best I could, I picked her up again and slowly lowered myself into the nursing chair. It rocked back and forth as I repositioned my baby into the crook of my arm. Harper's smile was encouraging as she walked toward me with my daughter's bottle. Crouching beside me, she gently placed a small bib under Layla's chin.

Immediately, my feisty little daughter protested at being disturbed again and her lungs delivered a twenty-decibel yell in my direction. Taking the bottle from Harper, I quickly shoved the nipple into Layla's mouth and silence reigned. Harper and I both shared a small smile, then she turned and went back to what she was doing at the sink.

Greedily, Layla slurped the formula like she'd been starved for weeks. Sometimes she'd suck until she had no more breath left in her lungs and then she'd release, causing bubbles of air to fill the bottle before she'd have at it again.

After Layla grunted like she was going to produce another mess, ungraciously farted, and burped her way through her lunch, Harper offered to dress her again.

"It's okay, I'll do it. My mom wanted to take her for a walk in the fresh air, but she read me the riot act and left," I shared with no hint of humor. "I'll take her. Go take a couple of hours for yourself and I'll let you know when we get back." A warm smile lit up Harper's face and she nodded.

"Sounds like a plan. Thanks, I have some laundry to take care of so that would be great," she replied. The smile she gave me was big and bright and not the kind anyone with laundry would give. It was a smile of approval for me finally waking up to my responsibilities as Layla's father.

CHAPTER FIVE

During the first year after Grace had died nothing inspired me. My total disinterest in life, apart from Layla, continued to worry Dorian—a single, quiet guy who had, by then, rerooted himself permanently in my house.

At the nine-month mark, he sat me down and did some straight talking about how he saw things, and at that point I was still too lost to disagree.

"I've called a local architect to come and discuss building a house next door to this one for me. Nothing fancy, just a space of my own. What we have here is a long-term situation, and I figured it was time I did something about these temporary living arrangements."

My house was massive, even emptier without Grace, and there were plenty of spare rooms to create a suite for him, but Dorian was determined to have a place to call home. I couldn't fault him for that.

Being a computer geek, he carried his business in a soft-top sports bag and a fine leather satchel. He'd been known to work from all around the world because as long as there was Internet and electricity, Dorian's office went with him. It wasn't a surprise he wanted to stay; we'd always been close, and he wanted to be near Layla and me.

By the time he'd been with me almost a year, he'd all but driven me crazy with his techno music while he worked and punk rock when he relaxed. If I'd ever asked myself the question, who the fuck relaxes to punk? I had the answer. Being a rocker, the tunes he played were disturbing to my ears and as irritating as marker pens squeaking painfully on a whiteboard.

It was the music that finally broke my patience at his intrusion, and with plenty of land around the property, I was thankful he'd taken the decision out of my hands. My only stipulation was soundproof walls and acoustic glass to deaden the drone from his taste in music.

Secretly, the concept of Dorian living right next door actually appealed to me. It was a win-win situation because as Layla grew she'd have her uncle next door, and when I went back to work; he'd be able to oversee her welfare while I was away on the road.

Going away was a subject that had been a constant blot on my mind once I'd had some space and time to absorb Grace's passing.

Eventually, my sense of perspective returned, and I was finally able to consider how my wife suddenly dying had impacted the lives of my bandmates. They had all been incredibly supportive but had ultimately been left hanging since my bereavement. It was another thought that depressed me, because with a tiny infant to care for, my mind just wouldn't go there.

Then as time ticked by, I struggled between depression and dread as Layla's first birthday approached. The day she was born was anything but happy. There was no excitement leading up to my daughter's milestone because it was the day my life as a father had begun and my ability to feel any real joy had come to an end.

It was a blessing that Harper was so in tune with Layla—instilling a sense of fun into an otherwise dull world for her, with me as her father —and Harper had proved her patience by putting up with me. The girl never complained about anything and took everything thrown at her in her stride, and because of this, we'd effortlessly grown to be close friends.

With each day that passed, Layla's features changed and the resemblance to Grace as a child became more remarkable. There were times when she stole the breath from my chest when she'd give me a look, scrunch up her nose, or make an expression that brought my late wife right back into the room.

The fleeting lighter moments we shared felt like a sliver of light, like the glow of something bright from the other side of a door. The door of grief was still heavy and firmly closed in my mind, but I figured if anyone could shift my dark depressive state, it would be Layla.

When my daughter's birthday arrived, it was a difficult day—a highly emotional day—and apart from the hour where we opened her gifts, sang "Happy Birthday," and shared a small tea party, my evening was spent in deep reflection. It was the night I tried to face some of the demons I had blocked from my mind.

In my bedroom closet, stacked high and out of sight, was a small six by nine inch box I'd been given by the staff at the hospital before we'd left. I'd stowed it away the minute we'd arrived home. Moving the small bedroom chair to the door, I climbed up and shoved the items away that I had originally used to hide it.

Taking the box from the shelf, I stepped down from the chair and slowly walked to my bed. As I sat down, my eyes came to rest on the poignant picture on the lid of the box. The image of a mother's curled hand with the fist of a newborn resting in it made my stomach clench. I sighed heavily and swallowed back a rising burn from deep in my throat as the warning of it threatened me with tears.

Smoothing my hand over the board, I covered the picture with mine as memories flashed in front of my closed eyes of the anguish-stricken faces of all those connected with our harrowing tragic event.

Drawing a deep breath, I placed my fingertips on the edge of the box and flipped off the lid. My breath hitched and my heart momentarily stopped when a long lock of Grace's smooth dark hair snaked around all the other items.

My eyes instantly shut out the tangible evidence of my once vibrant beauty lying curled in the box in front of me. It took courage for me to touch it, but I lifted it out, slid it slowly through my fingers and held it to my nose. Inhaling deeply, I expected to find a reminder of her in it, but all it smelled of was the cardboard box itself.

Gently, I smoothed it out on top of the white comforter and noted the dark color was still as vivid as the hair on her head had been when she'd died. I turned my attention back to the box. Scanning over the items, I noted Grace's hospital bracelet and I swallowed, remembering the way the nurse smiled as she tagged her when we had first arrived.

A pile of Polaroid pictures, pink baby name tags, and a little book full of all Layla's important birth details—weight, length, head circumference—lay inside. I picked up a small piece of the monitor tracing used to measure Grace's contractions and Layla's heartbeat, before I noticed a piece of card with two painted palm prints of Grace's, one of hers on its own and one with Grace's in purple with Layla's pale pink handprint carefully placed inside.

Pain, pleasure, and everything in between flowed through my veins as I stared again with a swell of sadness at the inside of the box. A lump in my throat swelled tight, temporarily suffocating me from drawing another breath and tightened my chest. The sensation overwhelmed me, pulling me to my feet in distress.

Gulping for air, I staggered into my bathroom and clung to the sink in the vanity unit until my knuckles blanched white. Quickly, the sight disappeared when a wave of tears blurred my vision.

"Fuck," I screamed loudly. I banged my fist on the wooden surround, then turned toward the shower stall and repeated the action. To my shock a large crack appeared in the toughened glass, bringing me instantly to my senses.

A soft knock sounded at the door, followed by Harper's alarmed voice as the door cracked open. "Cole, are you, okay..." Her voice trailed away as I came from the bathroom and noted her eyes had fallen on the box on my bed.

"Yeah, I..." Gesturing toward the box, I shrugged, not trusting myself to explain for fear of losing my composure again.

"Sorry, I heard you shout and thought for a second you'd hurt yourself," she offered by way of her intrusion.

"I did," I admitted, although not in the way she had thought. I nodded my head toward the contents spilled onto the bed. "Thought I was brave enough to go there. I guess it was a mistake."

Instead of leaving, Harper pushed the door farther open and wandered closer to the bed. Meeting her back at the bedside, I stared intently, watching her looking down to avoid looking toward the bed myself.

"Are these from the day Layla was born?" she probed. Normally I'd have told her to mind her own goddamned business, but for some reason I drew strength from having her there. Maybe because she had no memories of Grace, and therefore nothing of her own to share about her that my mind could use as a trigger to fuck me over with.

"Would you mind?" Glancing up at me with kind eyes, Harper's gaze was soft—sympathetic—but her voice was laced with sad curiosity. I nodded my head, thinking if she saw them first it would somehow soften the blow when I took another look.

"Layla definitely takes after her mother." Harper's innocent comment made my breath hitch. Hearing the audible sound I made, she glanced at me with concern. "Sorry, I shouldn't have—"

"Yeah, yeah you should have. She is, and she's getting more like her every single day."

"This may sound awkward, given what you guys were going through at the time, but Grace looks so happy with Layla in her arms. The look of love just flies right out of the picture. They look perfect together."

Giving her a look of suspicion, I couldn't stop myself from checking out the tiny Polaroid photograph she held in her hand. Taking it from her for closer inspection, I noted my grazed and bruised knuckles from my run-in with the shower stall.

Turning away from her, I sat down heavily on the bed and let out a deep sigh as I focused on one of the last pictures of Grace for the first time. I stared at the memory caught on camera for me and Layla of the day she was born.

Every observation Harper had made was true. If Grace had lived to be a hundred years, I figured I'd never have witnessed a happier, more contented smile on her lips, or the look of love that emanated from her bright blue eyes toward our baby daughter. It had been one of her two lucid days; the picture had been taken two days after Layla had been born. I had needed to feel detached in order to get through it as I watched her say hello and goodbye to our child.

Absentmindedly, I traced my fingertip delicately over the snap, my head already wondering if it could be expertly processed into a larger frame for Layla to keep.

"May I?" Harper interjected as she pointed to the rest of the pile of prints. I nodded and she scooped them together in one hand. Flipping through them she made no comment until she came to the final one and I heard her gasp.

Faltering, she slowly lowered the photographs back onto the bed and stood. "I'm sorry for the intrusion, I've overstepped... I just thought... I'll leave you to it. I'd better get back and check on Layla, she should be waking from her nap soon," she babbled hurriedly as she made for the door. Sensing her discomfort, my eyes narrowed as she opened it.

"Harper?" I probed in a questioning tone.

With her hand on the doorknob, she stopped opening the door but stayed facing away from me.

"Yeah?"

"Thanks. Your 'intrusion' as you call it was most welcome. It gave me the strength I need right now to help me move forward with this. I'd been dreading opening this box... you made it a damned sight easier for me to..." *To what? Put these memories to rest?* I didn't know how to finish what I'd started to say.

"Glad I could be here for you. Thank you for letting me in," she replied, before opening the door fully and closing it softly behind her.

Inhaling deeply, I exhaled and returned my focus to the mementos on the bed. Picking the pictures up, I flicked slowly through them until I came to the last one.

The second I saw it, my heart splintered and my mind traveled faster than the speed of light to the moment in the picture. In my hand, captured for posterity, was the last kiss in life I ever gave to my beautiful dying wife.

The memory of that day had sat heavily on my chest like some cruel medieval torture implement, unrelenting and designed to inflict the maximum pain, which it had.

If the picture was meant to comfort me, it didn't. If it was designed to commemorate the awful experience, it did that for the sake of others, because in my mind it was a daily vivid event and I had no use for such an image.

Going back to the palm print image, I placed my hand on top of the two already there and I groaned, heaved a heavy sigh, then returned the items to the box. After placing it neatly back in its place in the closet, I closed the door. I had an overwhelming emotional need to be close to my daughter.

Pushing open the door of the nursery, Harper's eyes caught mine and I saw she'd been crying. After seeing the picture of myself with Grace at the end of her life, I couldn't blame her.

"Want to take an hour out? It's been a heavy day. I'd like a little alone time with my daughter."

Harper gave me a knowing smile, one that hinted Layla was exactly what I needed to escape my feelings of despair.

"Absolutely. I could do with a change of sweater. Your gorgeous, but highly productive, daughter slobbered down my back when she ate too much cake."

A chuckle escaped my lips as I shook my head. "That's my little rocker girl, living life to excess," I replied, and my grin grew bigger.

If you need me, you know where I am," she offered and scooted out the door before I could argue with her.

"So…" I began as I sat down, placing Layla on my knee. She was facing me, her bright gray eyes in an innocent stare. Gazing up at me, she lay quietly, as if I held the answers to the universe in my grasp.

"What are we gonna do with you, Baby?" I asked sadly, while I thought of something else to say.

Layla lurched forward and grabbed my beard. "It isn't spiky, right? It's soft and loveable. Your mom loved my beard," I added, suddenly realizing I'd shared something about Grace with Layla without a second thought.

Grabbing a fistful, my daughter held it tight and pulled my face forward. The child's grip was a force I never knew such a little person could possess. "Ouch," I muttered, one hand leaving her body to circle her fist, thus preventing her from ripping a chunk of my beard clean off my face.

"Ow," I scowled again and Layla immediately let out a gummy, wide-mouthed laugh.

"Seriously, Baby? You almost disfigured me and it's funny?"

The sterner I spoke, the more infectious her laughter became until she had me laughing aloud too.

"I can see I'm going to have to up my game in the scolding department," I told her through another chuckle.

Once her laughing wound down, Layla yawned and I cradled her in my arms. When I stared down at my sleepy looking infant, I felt my heart clench and I admitted she had fast become my world. A sobering thought washed over me. At some point I was going to have to go back to work and leave her and this thought hurt me more than I ever knew it would.

I had no concerns over the day-to-day childcare for my daughter. My mom was a hard woman to please and she'd chosen well, because Harper was sweet-natured, coolheaded, and more than capable of taking care of Layla.

Matty, our housekeeper, was like a second mom and had been with me since the week after Grace and I had moved in. I knew she'd be an awesome backup for Harper if she ever needed anything.

In fact, all my employees were akin to family since Grace had passed; and the fact my brother, Dorian, was a permanent fixture was incredibly comforting to me as well. The acid test wouldn't be who could look after Layla once I was back out there, it would be who would look after me?

Derek, my manager knew how close we were as a band and had no doubt I'd be supported to the max by them on the road and so after consultations with my counselor, my mom, Dorian, my manager, and the band, I decided to go back to work.

In my line of work everyone thought it would be better for Layla to grow up not expecting me to be home all the time. As much as I hated this idea, I could see their reasoning behind it. If Layla was too young to remember anything else she may regard this as normal.

Having been home for so long, I found the prospect of getting back out there daunting: both from the prospect of being sociable to people, and the soul-crushing dilemma of not having daily physical contact with my daughter.

Dorian, Stuart, and Matty pushed advancements in social media forward as an argument for keeping in touch with Layla every day. The last thing I had wanted was to miss key milestones in my baby's life by being gone.

Eventually, I resigned myself to the fact that Skype was better than nothing for keeping in touch with my daughter, but I also stipulated that none of the tours lasted for more than a month at a time.

So, fifteen months after my daughter was born, and I was widowed, I was reluctantly thrust back into the public eye, severed abruptly from the secluded limbo I had found myself in since Grace's death.

Scuds, Moz, and Fletch, my bandmates, had been amazingly patient and supportive of me. All three were single guys, but we'd played together since before we'd turned twenty years old, and after almost ten years together—six of those famous—there wasn't anything we wouldn't have done for each other.

The guys loved Grace almost as much as me, and fortunately, not one of them wavered in their loyalty to me. This lack of pressure helped me to get my head straight enough to return to the band.

At first our rehearsals were slow. Music had been the last thing on my mind and the last song I had played was the song for my wife. God alone knows how I got through that first emotional day back without breaking down in tears. Half the songs we sang had been inspired by Grace.

I underestimated the power of music—less than a week in—my fingers felt less stiff and my effortless fretwork had returned. I poured my feelings into the songs as they began to course through my veins; the melodies making my heart feel lighter. Playing our familiar songs came effortlessly, their words reminding me of happier times, of emotional times, and of Grace.

In time life found its new normalcy. Mine was boozing on the road to forget and drying out at home. Unlike Scuds and Moz, I did what I needed to do to avoid women when I was on tour. I'd married Grace, and I didn't want to be with anyone else.

On several occasions, during the first month on the road, the guys tried to hook me up with some groupie as a way of pushing past my grief. None of them really understood what it was like to lose someone who was irreplaceable.

Meet and greets, partying, and being sociable in a room full of fine-looking women with the smell of perfume in the air, didn't come easy for me. My head was still locked down with the memory of Grace, while my body's physical needs defied my honoring her by rebelling in my pants.

After I met Grace, I never wanted anyone else. She was an intricate mix of wildly sexy and soberingly cute and so incredibly intoxicating. The instant chemistry between us was electric. Witnessing Scuds balls deep in a blow job made me hard, despite my grief and I was riddled with guilt because even after her death my faith was still Grace's.

Life on the road was hard in the circumstance I'd found myself in. Being famous as well, I was wary and being extra careful because I knew women saw me as vulnerable prey. The same could have been perceived by the guys. In the past everyone wanted to know me... until they did.

CHAPTER SIX

Four years later
Plane hopping had become second nature and whenever possible on tour I'd make it back to see Layla, even if it was only for a day. However, during a rare two days back in the USA to accept an award, I hit the skids because I was so near, but just too far from home to go back there. My work schedule was so tight there wasn't the time to make a visit.

I always had trouble sleeping in hotel beds, and given my mood was full of frustration because of the near miss to visit my daughter, I decided to hit the hotel bar.

Six shots after I'd slopped into the empty cocktail lounge, I glanced over at the bored, tired looking barman. Draining the remains of my bitter drink, I gasped loudly and slid the stubby whiskey tumbler back across his varnished wooden counter. "Again," I instructed nodding at my empty glass.

When he eyed me with contempt, I could almost hear his thoughts, that I was some famous rock musician punk he had no respect for.

Watching his shoulders hunch in disappointment because I wanted another drink, he turned, his broad back facing me as he grabbed what

I'd asked for. Returning to the counter with the half empty bottle of bourbon, he poured a large measure of the amber liquid. I smiled at it because I knew it would help to dull my senses and maybe even let me get some sleep.

As my bleary eyes met his, I could see he was pissed as all hell that I was keeping him from his bed. Checking my watch, I noted it was 2:40 a.m. and I sighed. Cutting him some slack, I asked for another refill, told him to mark it to my tab and I headed in the direction of the elevator bank.

It was rare for me to visit a hotel bar, but my dark mood had led to deep, dark thoughts, triggering another wave of depression. This wasn't the first time I'd questioned the value of life, and if it hadn't been for Layla, I knew I'd have opted out. The barman probably saved me, but no one would ever know this.

Pulling my hotel suite keycard from my leather jacket pocket, I waved it in front of the electronic pad until I heard the click and saw the red light turn green. Shoving the door wide, I entered the plush surroundings my years of wealth and status had afforded me.

I had found nothing that could rewire my brain to forget, and nothing could bring back Grace: my sweet, vibrant, and beautiful woman. As was usual when I was drunk, my mind wandered to a scene ingrained there, always set on replay at the most inappropriate times.

It was of me blinking through tears as I held my wife's fragile, disease-ravaged body in my arms as she was dying. My heart and soul felt utterly wrecked by the totally debilitating helplessness at the imminent loss of the only girl I'd ever loved.

Like her name suggested, Grace dealt with death with the utmost dignity, smiling courageously and with affection toward me through her devastating pain; staying calm in the face of death. Deep down I knew she did this for me because I'd been scared, and I was afraid to lose her.

Leaning in close to her face, I barely felt her weak feathery breath on my cheek, and I pressed my tear-soaked lips softly against her pale dehydrated ones. With tears dropping from my eyes, I kissed her goodbye for the last time in life. As I pulled back to look at her, she inhaled for the last time and her breathing immediately ceased.

ANOTHER LIFE

Nothing could ever have prepared me for what happened to Grace. I'd gone from a time where elation and hope filled my heart and it had instantly turned into despair. Instead of a lifetime of happiness ahead, we were thrown into circumstances where life and death played out simultaneously.

When the prognosis was days rather than weeks, Grace's impending final moments I'd imagined a harrowing scene in my tortured imagination as one where I fell to the floor, my legs giving out as I screamed loudly and unashamedly in my grief, begging for God to give her back to me.

However, in the very moment when her death came, and I thought my delicate heart would combust or shatter beyond repair, it did neither.

Staring down at her lifeless body, still warm, but at peace, a tight band formed in my chest, the likes of which I had never experienced before. My heart, instead of becoming filled with excruciating pain, felt numb and frozen.

I looked at the girl I thought I would love forever, and for a moment, I felt detached as a multitude of emotions crammed into my head, and I couldn't think for the static noise and a crushing pain that dulled my senses.

Despite my grief at losing Grace, I thought I would love her for all of my life. Instead of allowing the threatening mountain of grief I'd suppressed to overwhelm me, it was anger that took over. Robbed of our future as a family, I felt far too incensed at the world to allow my heart to break. Then the dam of misery caught up to me and it broke me.

For that first month after my girl had died, I couldn't see the purpose of her life, nor mine for that matter. After all, I had felt she was meant to love me, and me only her, so what was the point of going on without her? *Layla.*

The sunny, if somewhat reserved, disposition I'd always been known for, changed the day I found out Grace was dying. Up until then her optimism had always fueled mine.

From the day the oncologist sat wearily by her bedside and discussed her palliative care until the day she passed five days later,

Grace never shed a tear. Not in front of me anyway. I'd like to say I was as brave as her, but I wasn't.

In truth, I was warring with the enormous emotional misery I felt because of something so profound and life changing; no amount of resourcefulness could ever combat it.

Severe bitterness took over, and although I hid it well from Grace, everyone else bore the wrath of my fury. Naturally, I was as angry as fuck… with my wife, with her OBGYN team, and I blamed them for their lack of diligence, for ruining what should have been a lasting love story between Grace and me. But most of all, I was angry at the world for leaving my beautiful little daughter without her mom.

Throwing down the bourbon, I winced as it burned my throat then my chest, before the pain slowly ebbed away as it settled in my stomach.

Placing the glass on the bedside table, I unbuckled my black leather belt and slid it through the loops until it was free of my jeans. Winding it around my hand, I walked over toward the dresser and set it down, taking my wallet out of my back pocket and leaving it beside it.

Placing my hands on the dresser, I bent to look at my reflection in the mirror and I hated the gaunt, haunted figure of the man who looked back. Time had changed me. Grief had stolen my smile and dulled my normally bright, hazel eyes.

There were dark purple circles under those dull, bloodshot eyes, the same eyes that even I knew once held a mixture of wickedness and amusement in their glint. I had a beard that made me look like some evil pirate from a B-rated movie, so overgrown and unappealing, but it covered a lot of my ashen complexion.

My loss had made a significant difference, ravaging my once appealing appearance, and it had left me looking like a disheveled shell of the man Grace knew.

Standing tall, I exhaled heavily and sounded defeated as my heavy heart tightened painfully in my chest. The burden of work reminded me of my public face, It was in conflict with my fears as the anxious, private man caring for a motherless child; the only real, tangible evidence of the love and life we had shared.

It was a much different life than the one I'd envisioned with Grace, but I knew no matter how deeply my personal loss had affected me; I had to go on for Layla.

Postponing the tour once again could kill the band, I knew that, and following the advice of everyone else had given me purpose—a mission—but it was making my daughter fret, and I knew before long it would eventually lead to her feeling unhappy.

I hated the thought of my daughter being unhappy because of what I did. When Mom had hired Harper, it was on a seven-year contract to ensure Layla's stability in her formative years. Her thinking at the time being that Layla would then be old enough to travel with me with a personal tutor and chaperone, or by then my music career would be on the slide.

At the back of my mind, the time-limited contract was never far from my mind, especially with Layla getting older. With a sense of panic and a little over a year to figure out what was next for Layla, time had begun to look short.

Without her nanny, I knew I'd feel hopeless about facing the future. Plus, Layla idolized her, and in turn, so did I. She kept my daughter happy, grounded, and secure, and those were the most important things I had to focus on. Having Harper by my side was far better than facing Layla's future upbringing alone.

The problem for me was Harper was young and very pretty. Being a nanny to a rock star should have been an exciting adventure for her. Instead, she'd been hired into a house full of grief and had pretty much had to figure things out for herself.

Before coming to us, Harper had been a bright college student learning all aspects of early childhood development and she had taught Pilates and yoga to fund further training as a nanny. Everyone in the household worried because of her age and thought her position wasn't a role Harper would have aspired to do for the rest of her life, given her looks and abilities.

This thought depressed me as I unzipped my fly, dropped my jeans to my ankles, and stumbled out of them. Picking them up off the floor, I slung them over a high-backed chair. Eyeing the wet bar, I strode toward it without thinking, opened it and took out two dinkies of Irish whiskey.

Making my way back to the nightstand by the bed, I cracked the seal on both bottles, refreshing the half-drunk bourbon from my time in the elevator, before I shrugged myself out of my jacket.

Drinking usually eased my pain and helped me get some rest, but even as I crawled onto the huge, empty bed; I could tell it was going to be one of those nights where my mind kept my memories active.

True to form, one question led to another inside my head. *What will happen to Layla when it's time for Harper to leave? How can I work and travel with a seven-year-old? Who'll help Layla with all the girl stuff growing up? Puberty, tits, bras, periods, boys. Fuck. How do I balance my little daughter's life with the kind of work I do?* Hundreds of questions: all about Layla, my precious, vulnerable little girl. With no answer to my questions forthcoming, another familiar emotion came over me— helplessness.

Helplessness turned to restlessness, which turned into anger once again. "Fuck!" I screamed in frustration to no one in particular, then at everyone... mostly at God.

Whoever said, 'The good Lord doesn't give you more than you can handle,' had a warped sense of justice, because I hadn't been handling anything very well at all since Grace had died. In fact, I was barely coping with my job, and that was all an act.

Even years after Grace's death, I was *still* a broken wreck, unable to be the parent my daughter needed because I had to work.

The only comfort I appeared to have found was at the bottom of an empty glass, even though I knew I couldn't rely on alcohol to solve my problems and it would eventually make me less capable of taking care of Layla.

CHAPTER SEVEN

*D*awn brought more than daylight with it the following morning. It brought clarity of mind despite my hangover. Somewhere between night and day, I'd had an image of my sad little girl looking lost and waiting for me to come home. It wasn't a lie... call it a sixth sense, but I knew my baby's needs were growing.

Being a latchkey kid myself when I was growing up, I'd had my share of those feelings. Where my parents worked hard, they never took the time to really get to know me. Maybe 'took the time' isn't the right way to describe it; perhaps 'had the time' was a better description.

However, the same didn't apply to me. There was enough money in the bank to last a lifetime and then some. There and then I decided the counselors were wrong. My place wasn't doing what I did before; it was doing what came after.

Where I should have been wasn't a thousand miles from home making other people happy, while my daughter and I sucked it up and suffered in silence to keep the record company and promoters happy.

If my followers truly cared about me and my music, they'd understand I needed the space to work through my grief—even years later—

and to support my daughter away from the public eye. So, as if I had walked out of my haze, I realized where I needed to be and I called Derek, my manager, to tell him to cancel the last three shows.

"You sure you want to do this? People will have gone to a heap of expense to come to Bueno Aires for the gig," he asked, his loaded question designed to guilt me into performing. "Some will have travelled the length of South America," he added as if this would change my mind.

Obviously, it wasn't a decision I had taken lightly, and I was sorry to those I'd inconvenienced and let down, but most them weren't living their lives for other people. It felt time I took charge of myself and did the same.

"Yeah, I'm sorry, but I'm out," I stated firmly. Derek knew I was no stranger to hard work before Grace died, and I loved my fans and followers. His problem wasn't my problem because I loved my little daughter, and it was about time I demonstrated this.

"At least get a doctor's certificate for stress or something; otherwise it'll cost all parties involved the same as the gross national product of a developing country." I nodded even though he couldn't see me. He was right, this way the fans would get their money back.

"Done. I'm flying back to Richmond, Virginia today. I'll ask the doc for a home visit for tomorrow."

"Well, if you're sure?" he said hesitantly, and I could practically hear him swear in his head. "I'll get onto the promoters and set the shitstorm in motion. Any idea how long you want to take out?"

"Indefinitely. Years, if I need to. For good, if that's what the record company decides." Once I had made my mind up, there was no going back. It felt strangely liberating.

Quitting the call, I breathed a sigh of relief and checked my chunky gold Rolex, a gift from Grace for our first anniversary. It was 7:30 a.m. *Layla will be eating breakfast.*

Selecting the Skype app, I called Harper's phone and seconds later she replied.

"Hey, Harper, how's my baby?" I asked, noting my voice sounded lighter than it had since the moment I found out about Grace.

"Oh, hi, Cole, she's becoming sassier and smarter every day, not to mention how cute she is," she replied. Harper my daughter's nanny's sweet face beamed a bright sunny smile before she turned her cell camera around to show me Layla.

"Layla, your daddy's on Skype."

Throwing her head up to look at the screen I noted Layla's jet-black hair in two thick bunches at the sides of her head.

"Daddy," Layla mumbled excitedly around a mouth full of Froot Loops that almost fell out of her mouth. She clamped her hand over it and quickly disappeared when she jumped down from the counter stool.

Next thing I knew, the screen was shaking.

"Hold on, Layla." I imagined Layla tugging on Harper's arm. "Give me a sec, Cole," Harper instructed me as she laid her cell on the counter and I watched the kitchen ceiling fan whirl fast above it.

Seconds later, Layla's little out of focus nose came into view, followed quickly by her mouth as it grinned widely in closeup. I heard Harper gently admonish her, "No, Baby, you have to hold it a little farther away or Daddy will only see part of your beautiful face."

"Oh, okay, but I want to kiss him," she replied, sounding a little confused at Harper's request.

"Of course you can kiss the screen when Daddy has finished talking to you, but for now you have to let me hold it so as you can talk with him and see him at the same time. If it's too close, you won't see his gorgeous face when he's talking."

"Ah," she decided like she suddenly understood. "I see you, Daddy, do you see me?" she asked, leaning forward again and not completely trusting Harper's word.

"I do, Baby, and you look even more beautiful than you did yesterday," I told her honestly.

The shy smile in response was to die for. "Look at me, Daddy, I've got brunches." Twirling her hair in both hands she gave me a toothy grin.

"Bunches," Harper corrected her softly with a chuckle in her voice.

"When can you not be on the cell phone and give me proper

huggles?" Her needy question caught me off guard, because she had never expressed anything like it so plainly before. I was immediately thankful that she'd saved it until now to do so, because suddenly not being with her made my heart bleed.

"What would you say if I offered to share your Froot Loops with you tomorrow?" I enquired, dying to tell her I was on my way.

For a second, she glanced behind her at her bowl then turned her attention back to me. A frown creased her tiny brow, as she covered her mouth for a second then sighed. "To be honest, Daddy, I don't think there will be any left by tomorrow. I'm pretty hungry after sleeping all night."

A soft chuckle passed my lips when I realized she didn't have the insight to know what I had meant by my statement.

"Ah, well how many are left in the box?" I asked.

"Harper? My daddy wants to know how many Loop Froots are in the box, can you look? Do you want her to count them, Daddy?"

I chuckled again at her reversing the name, "Harper, are there enough Froot Loops left for me to have breakfast tomorrow?"

"Sure, it's a new box," Harper informed me from somewhere behind the cell phone.

"Don't you want Loops today? We'll have to figure out how to put them into the cell phone. Maybe if you call on the house phone it would be better because that's bigger," Layla reasoned.

"No, Baby, you don't understand. What would you say if I said I'm coming home and I'll be there when you wake up tomorrow?" I clarified.

Layla's eyes flicked up past the screen and I knew she was looking at Harper. "Would it be okay if my daddy came to see me?" When she sought permission from her nanny, my heart sank to my stomach and almost broke, but it wasn't her fault she was confused at times and didn't understand how things were.

Not being able to be with her was so hard. I hadn't seen her for three long weeks, and although her words stung, they made my decision to quit the tour and go home valid.

"This is your daddy's house, Layla, you know he lives here. Has to go to work, but he just told you he's coming home. Isn't that the best news ever?"

Watching Layla's face as it broke into a huge wide grin made my heart clench. "Amazing news," she agreed. "Daddy, will you bring Mommy with you? She isn't inside Harper's cell phone like you are."

I choked. For a few indescribable seconds I couldn't speak, wouldn't speak, because for the first time since I'd buried Grace, Layla had thrown me a curve ball with her request.

As if Harper felt the weight of Layla's question, she quickly interjected and covered my silence. "Sweetheart, why don't you go back and finish your cereal before it gets soggy, like a good girl, then we'll get ready for our playdate with Jaden and Tom," she coaxed.

Without waiting for Layla to reply, she added, "Just a sec, Cole, I'm just helping her down from the counter." Once again she laid the cell phone down, face up on the counter and lifted Layla down, placing her back on the floor. Picking her cell up, I saw Layla scoot around the kitchen counter and she disappeared from sight.

Harper's interruption had given me the time I had needed to gather my composure before she turned it to face herself.

"Sorry, I'm back," she informed me, as if I couldn't see that she was.

"Thanks for that," I mumbled quietly, without needing to explain what I was thankful for.

"Anytime," she soothed with a sad smile.

"As you heard, I'm coming home."

She smiled and widened her eyes like she was excited. "How long will you be here? I'll let Matty know because she hadn't planned anything special for dinner this week. I've just been eating the kind of stuff Layla does," she added sheepishly.

"I'm coming home today. I'll grab something to eat on the plane. Tell Matty not to worry about tonight... we'll have takeout. I'll catch up with her then and she can draw up some menus for us all after that."

"So you're coming home for more than a day?" she asked sounding surprised.

"Yeah, I figured it was time I got to know my daughter," I replied, in an apologetic tone.

Harper pouted her lips and glanced over to where I knew Layla was eating her breakfast then looked more intensely back at me.

"You know her, Cole. Don't do this to yourself. You had all those firm commitments before…" She paused, unsure of how to phrase it. "And Layla… she knows you love her."

"Sometimes, just loving someone isn't enough; it's how you act that's important."

Harper's bright blue eyes softened, and she gave me a slow smile. "You're a good man, Cole Harkin, and when Layla realizes you're coming home to stay, she'll probably pee her pants with excitement," she mused and chuckled as she glanced affectionately past the phone again.

Chatting with Harper for another few minutes, I managed to glean where they were headed and what the family they were visiting was like. Not that I didn't trust Harper's judgment, but knowing who Layla's playmates were would be my starting point for the first conversation I had with her when I returned home.

Once my call with Harper had ended, I knew it was important for me to get out of the city before the news broke regarding my no-show. There was no doubt I'd lose fans, and some would be angry, but that was better than losing my daughter.

Another call to Derek informed me the news would be out by 9:00 a.m. Checking the time, I saw it was a little after 8:10 a.m. *Shit! I need to move. Derek arranged a car for 8:30 a.m and after a smooth transition I was on my way home. I called Fletch, my bandmate, from the car and he wasn't surprised.*

"Take as long as you need. It'll give us the opportunity to do a few collaborations with some other bands. We want you to concentrate on making yourself happy, Cole."

Deep inside I knew my mood swings and drinking had been getting worse. Although it had been a long time since I'd lost Grace, most days my grief still felt as raw as the day she died.

SinaMen as a band had worked relentlessly for almost ten years, until Grace died. But after she'd passed I found listening to my own music too emotive. This was partly the reason for my relapse; playing the songs our fans expected to hear sometimes cut me to the quick; especially the ones written about Grace.

    The gods were in my favor because, luckily, my emotional breakdown had happened on a Sunday and the street outside the hotel was still quiet.

CHAPTER EIGHT

*A*s predicted by Derek, the shit storm I'd created was less than kind toward me. Personally, I couldn't have given a fuck, because I felt compelled to be with my daughter. Circumstances had been difficult since Grace's death, and until I had woken up knowing for the first time what to do, I had been in denial.

That fact had come as a revelation to me, and I had ignored all but Layla's basic needs as her dad in the process. On the way back from the airport to home, I sat in the car Derek had sent to meet me and wondered if I'd used the band as an excuse not to get close to Layla.

Did I really do that? If I did, was it because she looked the spitting image of her mom or had I a deeper, more basic reason than that, such as me being scared to death of losing her too?

Admitting my fears about losing her sent a pang of shock to my chest. It took my breath away. I shook my head because the thought was incomprehensible. *Surely God wouldn't be so cruel as to rob me of both of my girls?* Problem was, I had no trust in God anymore.

Even though I felt I had lost my faith, I defied myself by continuing to pray: for Layla's safety, for strength, for guidance. The contradiction didn't sit well with me because I was so pissed at the way Grace had died. I struggled with the concept of having someone I was supposed to believe in inflicting such misery and pain on people who had placed their trust in him.

I was still chewing over the hole in my beliefs when the driver pulled up to the heavy metal gates and I took the electronic remote from my carry-on. Pointing it at the metal barriers they clunked noisily before the wired buzzing sound signaled their parting.

Coming home used to give me a sense of relief, but ever since Grace had gone, the initial moment I caught sight of the house always filled my heart with sorrow. It sank instantly and a nauseous feeling rose up in my throat. Everywhere I looked I saw Grace: in the landscape, in the tub, the shower, by the dresser brushing out her long raven hair.

Mixed memories stirred strong emotions, both happy and sad. Images of the once vibrant, bubbly little beauty who lit up the room just by being in it, compared with the drained, exhausted skeletal frame robbed of her life by the ravaging disease that destroyed her.

Stepping out of the car, I stood staring up at the huge U-shaped, three-story building. It was the round attic room window that had sold us on the house as the romanticism of storing our family heirlooms in the attic overtook the practicalities of owning such a large property with such extensive grounds.

There were thousands of square feet of the house we never used. Matty and Stuart had a suite of rooms in the west wing, while Fred and Ramona, our maintenance man and housemaid lived off the premises. Peter and Diane, our landscapers and ground team lived in the East Wing. Harper had a suite of rooms next to Layla's suite which included a playroom, bathroom, and bedroom. My bedroom was down the hall from Harper and Layla's.

Opening the door, I stepped inside and closed it quietly behind me. The click of the latch sounded hollow as I glanced over to the sweeping staircase. The same staircase I'd carried Grace up two at a time the first night we'd moved in. I smiled at the memory of her surprised little face when I lifted her up and threw her over my shoulder because I couldn't wait to get her into my bed.

Throwing her playfully in the center of the mattress, I had tickled her within an inch of her life, and if I thought about it hard enough, I swear I could still hear her laughing at times. I smiled sadly at the memory.

Since she'd gone, when I looked up in that direction, or I glanced around the wide imposing hallway, there was an ache in my heart that wouldn't go away. All our dreams about filling our home full of babies and pets were now dust.

Inhaling sharply, I pulled myself up straight, realizing how low I'd slumped, and I wandered into the kitchen. Matty was kneading dough on a large wooden board and the smell of freshly cooked banana bread wafted intoxicatingly around the kitchen.

"Oh, you're here!" she exclaimed, immediately abandoning the beige lump of uncooked whatever, wiping her hands on a cloth, and hurrying over in front of me.

"Where else would I be?" I countered.

"You'll have to hug me if you don't want that black button-down shirt covered in flour," she joked with a welcoming smile.

Dipping to take her small frame in my arms, I squeezed her affectionately and let her go. Stepping back, I mirrored her smile. "Layla and Harper not back yet?"

Matty looked over her shoulder, already on her way back to the dough. Grabbing it in her hand she sprinkled flour from the shaker onto the board and began manipulating it by folding it in different directions.

"They're with Jaden and Tom's family. Cressida is a lovely woman and the boys are five and six years old, so around Layla's age. Cressida is pregnant again, so I think inviting our guys over there is her way of keeping hers out of trouble. You know Harper, she's got that schoolmarm look nailed and everyone behaves when she's around."

I chuckled at her description. It wasn't something I'd personally seen from Harper, so I noted in my mind to look out for it.

"All right then, I guess if no one is here I'll jump in the shower and grab a change of clothing," I replied.

"Wait. I'm glad you're home. Want to tell me how long it's for this time?"

"Indefinitely. It's time I gave my daughter my full attention. I blew the last three gigs... oh, that reminds me, can you ask William Martin to make a house call this evening on his way home?"

"You sick?" she enquired, her eyebrows shooting into her hairline as her shoulders shot to her ears at the mention of our family doctor.

"No, no, nothing like that. Relax. I just need a note to be written to get out of our contract. It's for the promoters to give to the insurance company to bail everyone out." I watched Matty visibly relax and nod.

"Thank the Lord. Right, I'll be on it as soon as I get this bread in the oven. Go take your shower and take a nap. You look like shit... and have a shave," she ordered as an afterthought.

Turning to look over my shoulder I smirked. She was right; I did look like shit. "Yes, Mom," I replied sarcastically and was immediately hit on the back of the head with a small ball of dough.

"What the fuck was that for?" I asked, chuckling through the question.

"For being a smart-ass when I'm trying to pretend not to care too much," she replied.

"You can pretend all you want, you know you love me," I informed her, winking and dodging another dough ball. "And you can come and pick this shit off my polished floor in a hurry. If it marks it I'm deducting the cost of the polish out of your wages," I added, as I took the stairs two at a time before I could gauge a reaction.

Having banter with Matty lightened my mood for a few minutes, but as soon as I opened my bedroom door, I swear Grace's smell still lingered inside.

Immediately my heart felt heavy, the ache inside still raw with the constant reminders all around me. Harper and Matty had disposed of her clothing long ago, it was something I couldn't face. I'd taken most of Grace's personal effects: her driver's license, passport, jewelry, and placed them all in my personal safety deposit box at the bank until such time when Layla was old enough to have them. So even though there was only a perfume bottle remaining of hers, Grace was still very much present in our bedroom.

Everywhere I looked she was there, because every stick of designer furniture, every luxury patterned fabric and the white throws on our bed, as well as every piece of wall art I saw, had been chosen by her.

Taking another deep breath, I tried to keep a handle on my depressed emotions as I went into the bathroom and turned on the shower.

Whether it was being home or the previous night's lack of sleep I wasn't sure, but I was suddenly tired to the bone and didn't linger under the hot steaming water jets. Drying myself, I slid between my crisp cotton sheets and promptly fell asleep.

"Daddy. Daddy?" The small sweet voice broke into my slumber, but it was like music to my ears. Cracking an eye open I quickly rose to rest my head on my elbow when my tiny gorgeous girl stared me square in the eye, her size exactly the right height to place her head just above the deep spring mattress and level with my face.

"Ah, hey, my little beauty, how have you been?" I asked shifting position to sit up as I lifted her up onto my lap. I leaned back against the headboard, taking her with me, and her ear rested over my heart.

"Good," she replied not moving.

"Good?" I enquired and waited for more, my hand automatically splaying the length of her body and tucking her little arm behind her.

"Yeah, apart from Jaden peeing in his mom's huge flowery pot plant in the backyard and getting his tush smacked. His daddy told him he'd get jail time for getting his pee pee out in public."

Conscious she was lying on me, I tried not to laugh because of how serious her tone was. "Oh, Baby, I don't know if you should be hanging with boys that get their pee pees out," I agreed.

Sitting up to look at me, she stared me straight in the eye, her huge gray expressive ones looking into mine like what she had to tell me was highly important. "It's okay, Daddy. I don't think you'll have to worry about that because Cressida, that's his mom by the way, she told him if he did it again, she'd cut his wiener off. A wiener is a pee pee, right?" I nodded, too amused to speak in case I laughed.

"Well," she started in an all-knowing way, the expression on her face almost making me bust she was so serious, "If I know Jaden Callahan, he won't listen. His dad says he never listens. So I don't think Jaden will have his pee pee much longer, because he keeps doing the stuff he's told not to."

"Hmm, maybe I need to check out this Jaden for myself. What do you say we invite him and his family over for a cookout this Sunday?"

"Here? In this house?" she asked, her voice rising incredulously.

"Where else, Baby Girl? Of course it'll be here."

A frown creased her brow and she shook her head. "I'm not allowed kids over to play," she argued, as a matter-of-fact.

"Since when?"

"Since Matty told Harper no kids because their mommies all wanted to get into your pants." Right when Layla told me this; I heard Harper's voice on the landing.

"Layla, you're taking a very long time finding the hair clip jar," she mused.

"She's with me, Harper." Hearing her approach, I called out again, "It's okay, you can come in. I'm decent. Well as decent as a man can be naked in bed," I added as she pushed open the door. I hadn't meant anything by it, and I don't even know why I mentioned the last part, but once I said it I had to own it.

"This little miss freaked me out by staring into my face while I was asleep, but you know what? I can't think of a better sight to wake up to," I admitted, looking at Layla as I spoke to Harper.

"I know, she's a doll, isn't she? Sometimes I feel I lucked out being able to care for her. She's a treasure," she added.

"And a pleasure. You told Cressida I was a pleasure to care for and that Daddy was amazing."

Harper blushed crimson; the color not only reaching her cheeks, but also staining the skin on her neck a deep red.

"Thanks, Layla, but you should finish that sentence because I said he was an amazing dad."

"Ouch, that burst my bubble. For a moment I thought you had designs on me, Harper." As soon as my remark was out I wanted to punch myself in the head.

This was the twenty-six-year-old nanny to my motherless child and I had crossed the line with my inappropriate shit.

In all the time she had been with me, we'd enjoyed a relaxed relationship and I classed her as family. During all those years I never been remotely flirtatious or overstepped my position as her employer.

"Layla, let's go downstairs and let your daddy get dressed. Matty has made the banana bread you begged her for this morning." At the mention of Matty's baking, Layla scooted off the bed.

Layla ran out the door faster than I knew her legs could carry her, her heavy little footsteps retreating into the distance. Glancing back at Harper, I caught her discomfort with my comment as she began to close my bedroom door.

"Thanks, Harper," I mumbled, as the door closed softly behind her. "Fuck," I cussed, banging my head back against the headboard in frustration. For a moment I sat stunned at what I'd done. Since the day I met Grace I'd never really flirted. yet my stupid fucked up mind had inadvertently done it with the one person I need the most.

CHAPTER NINE

For several minutes after Layla and Harper had gone back downstairs I stared into space, my mind completely blank. Eventually I decided the only thing I could do was apologize and hope Harper didn't hold a grudge.

Reluctantly, I dragged my ass out of bed and prepared to eat a huge chunk of humble pie, in the attempt of building the bridge I should never have tried to cross in the first place.

Dressing in a clean pair of jeans and a soft blue T-shirt, I entered my bathroom to take another leak and wash my hands and face before heading downstairs.

Glancing in the mirror as I peed, I saw what Matty saw. The ratty beard I'd spent a long time hiding behind had to go. Shaking myself down, I wiped and tucked my flaccid dick away.

Turning toward the sink I grabbed the state-of-the-art electric razor Grace had bought me the Christmas before she died. I sighed heavily at the memory of her grinning when she'd opened the box and chuckled.

"One day... it's all coming off," she'd joked, "I figured I'd buy this for the time when you're ready." Grace had only ever seen me without my beard in pictures. Another pang of regret stabbed me in my chest.

"Guess I'm ready now, Grace," I muttered aloud, and shook off the wave of emotion that threatened to interrupt my flow when I switched it on. The low steady buzz of the blades vibrating together, with the high and low pitched crunching sounds as my beard disappeared, felt cathartic.

Slowly, inch by inch, my paler skin came into view. Too late, I saw the difference between the exposed and unexposed skin and how hollow my cheeks were through the weight loss I suffered over time when my appetite disappeared.

By the time the beard was gone, I looked almost as ill as Grace appeared in those few short days right at the end. My face resembled footage I'd seen of prisoners of war in old news reels.

Stunned by how haunted I looked, I could hardly ignore the effects of neglect due to my mental state, because the visual representation looking back at me in the mirror shocked me to my core. I wasn't pretty to look at, but my face was evidence of how ravaged my heart was by losing my wife.

For a moment I felt too weak to fight back, until the image of Layla broke into my selfish thoughts. It was enough of a wake-up call to ensure I fought myself back to health... if not for me, for her.

Grace was gone and, ultimately, I was all Layla had, so I owed it to her to change my errant ways and claw my body back to its peak of physical fitness.

For years I had been acting as if losing Grace was exclusive to me, but as I continued to stare at my wasted appearance, I knew I had to fight my way out of my grief and find the strength to take care of my daughter. Another thought gripped me, which was one day Layla would truly realize what it was she had lost, and I had to be ready to support her when that day happened.

Suddenly I had purpose and understood what I needed to do. No matter how difficult the previous years had been, it was what I did in the future that would support my little girl to balance and accept the circumstances Grace had left us in. Somehow, I had to find ways of bridging the gaps. How... I had no idea.

"Daddy, you're taking a very long time up here," Layla told me, breaking into my thoughts. "Where's your face hair?" she asked, coming up close and staring up my long body with her huge rounded eyes. Bending, I picked her up and she instantly palmed the smooth skin on my face and inspected it thoroughly. "I like this better than that fuzzy jaggy stuff all over your chin," she admitted.

A grin spread over my face. "You look handsome when you smile, Daddy. Look you have cute holes here," she pointed out, poking a finger in each of my dimples. "Much better than when you're like this," she added, pulling a stern scowling face and pinching her lips into a line.

"Hmm, I look like that, huh?"

"Mm-hm, lots, like when you stare out the window in the kitchen," she nodded as she hummed the sound.

My daughter was right. Looking out at our backyard always reminded me of Grace. I guess my thoughts were less private during those times than I thought; if my expression told my story. "Then I need to smile more, eh?" I asked.

"Yay, I'd like that," she raved excitedly, wrapping her tiny arms around my neck as she brought her little cheek next to mine. The feel of her soft skin on my face warmed the chill in my heart.

Leaning her head back enough to look at me, she held my gaze for a second before she planted a kiss square on my lips. "Come on, Daddy, before Harper eats all the banana bread. Matty always has to hide it from her."

I chuckled again at the thought of Matty doing this. "All right. Lead the way, Baby. I'd hate to miss a slice of the good stuff on my first day home."

Layla wriggled free, and I slid her down my body until her feet hit the floor. Grabbing my hand, she put her weight into tugging me along with her, grinning back at me repeatedly as we made our way downstairs.

As we reached the kitchen, Layla let go my hand and ran ahead. The loss of her skin against mine made my heart clench again, because I'd missed almost nineteen months of her little life touring.

Suddenly I was riddled with guilt because the little person I'd given life to—the same one her mother had given her life for—had taken so much in her stride, but the balance of her care wasn't distributed as equally as it should have been.

Entering the kitchen, I saw Harper and Matty chatting. Harper was leaning on the kitchen counter on one side, Matty facing her from the other. Both were hugging mugs of coffee, mirroring their stance. The normalcy of the scene sent a warm feeling through me. Turning to look at me, Matty rounded the counter.

"Here he is. May I have mine now?" Layla asked expectantly.

Matty smiled affectionately and bent to speak to my daughter. "Yep, you did a great job, and wow, look at how handsome your daddy is now he doesn't have that animal stuck to his chin."

Layla squinted in my direction as did Harper, and I watched Harper fight a smile that threatened to break free. "I said the zackt same thing," Layla agreed, looking pleased with herself as she climbed up on the stool.

Placing two slices of banana bread and a coffee on the countertop, then a glass of milk and one slice for Layla beside mine, Matty wandered over to the pantry and pulled out her purse. I'd never understood her need to bring it downstairs to the kitchen all the time.

"Right, Harper told me about the takeout food. I'm not gonna argue because you look like you could use the extra calories with all that junk they feed you on the road, but starting tomorrow, I'm gonna fatten up that skinny, lanky ass of yours and get some vitamins inside of you. You're going on a healthy eating plan. Lean fillet steak, slow baked jacket potatoes, and plenty of salad for dinner tomorrow night. You may want to take tomorrow's menu into consideration when you're ordering later."

Instead of being pissed at being told what to eat, it felt good to be mothered by Matty for a change. She was right; a long stretch of poor takeout food on the bus and the standard hotel food menus meant I ate the same old greasy shit everywhere.

If I'd had the slightest reservations about ditching the tour and being home, the warm welcome from my daughter, the familiar faces of Matty and Harper, and Matty's straight talking made me feel glad to be back.

During the hour after Matty's departure, Layla kept Harper and I entertained with her sweet chatty nature. Every time I had spoken to my daughter, while I was away, there had always been something new that had taken me by surprise. It was clear Harper was dedicated and had given my daughter plenty of attention, because of the level of conversation she had.

What I loved was how Harper had taught Layla to think for herself: to form opinions and not be afraid to express herself. Grace would have been proud of how far she had come in such a short time and how she appeared to cope with Grace's absence.

Despite my offer of takeout, Matty had made Layla's favorite dinner: macaroni and cheese with tiny cherry tomatoes laced through it and a crisp cheese topping. It was exactly how she liked it. I sat with my little girl as she ate dinner, humming and mming in delight as she ate her way through it. When my doctor arrived for the house call, Harper took Layla upstairs to prepare her bath before bed.

William had no hesitation in writing a certificate to say I was burned out. Letting people down wasn't in my nature, even though I knew I'd done the right thing for my daughter and myself.

The doc was frank and expressed his concern at how I looked. I'd tried to pass it off as losing the beard, but I hadn't missed the second glance and shock on his face when I opened the front door to him when he'd first arrived.

Once William had left and I'd updated Derek, Layla was already tucked up in bed. Part of me had wanted more time with her, but it wasn't about what I wanted. It had made sense not to involve her in the takeout because she now went to bed at 7:30 p.m., and the counselor had suggested, maintaining her usual schedule was important to help her feel secure.

By 8:00 p.m. my daughter was sound asleep, having conned me into not one, but two bedtime stories. Reading about fairies and witches, hobgoblins, and too many other characters to recollect had made me feel closer to her for a few minutes.

As I read, Harper had ordered the takeout, and by the time I went back downstairs to the kitchen, she was setting the table in preparation of the food arriving.

With my mind flitting back to Layla's comment about not having kids at the house, I told Harper to organize a cookout with Matty for the following Sunday, and to invite the family of the playdate over, returning the favor.

My body was still keyed up from the decisions I'd made and I opened a bottle of wine, opting to stay away from hard liquor. Sliding onto a seat at the dining table, I poured two glasses of Merlot for us. Harper was finished placing the silverware and I felt her awkwardness about my earlier comment.

"Come... sit down and relax," I told her at the exact second the gate buzzer sounded. Harper looked at me, a little unsure of what to do, then went to the intercom and buzzed the delivery guy through the outer gate.

"I'm on it," Stuart called from the hallway when the car drove up and delivered the Chinese food. Bringing it into the kitchen, Stuart and I exchanged pleasantries about me being back and with the promise to catch up soon, he left, leaving Harper and I alone.

Harper hung back while we spoke, then grabbed a jug, filled it with iced water, and came over to the table. Years of learning to read women told me she wasn't entirely comfortable. Then it dawned on me that this was the first time we'd spent the evening together without someone or other hanging around.

Gesturing toward the food I nodded. "Dig in."

At my instruction, Harper began opening the boxes, dishing out some rice and passing it to me, slipping duck dumplings onto her plate and passing the second box on. This continued until we both had a little of everything on our plates.

Lifting my fork, I began to eat, and Harper silently did the same. In my head I had figured I'd apologize after dinner, but the pause in the conversation between us was killing me so I decided to get it out of the way.

"Look, Harper," I began, and her eyes snapped to mine. She was nervous, and my heart ached because it was the last emotion I had wanted to her to feel. "I'm really sorry about earlier... upstairs? I totally forgot myself and it was a shitty thing to do. I really don't know where that came from. It won't happen again," I stated firmly,

"Well, what I mean is if it does it'll be from years of stupid banter on—"

"It's fine. No harm done," she interrupted before I could finish, "and you were being honest; you were naked." Her cheeks flushed, and she tucked her hair behind her ear. My eyes fell to her jawline and I stared a moment longer than I should have at her silky, soft-looking skin.

"Wow. Matty has always pointed out how observant you are, but she never told me about the X-ray vision."

The color in her cheeks deepened and I could see I'd embarrassed her again. "Fuck, sorry. I don't know what's the matter with me, saying all this inappropriate shit," I apologized.

"I'm twenty six, Cole. Men have flirted with me before."

"I wasn't flirting. I didn't mean it like that. It was—"

"Banter, I know," she finished again then stabbed her fork in her food a few times without any attempt to eat it.

"Look, the last thing I'd ever want to do is make you feel uncomfortable around me. Layla thinks you're all her Disney Princesses rolled into one, and if I'm honest, I think you're pretty incredible too... I mean you keep my daughter stable and happy, and that's worth the world to me right now."

Harper's eyes softened, and her hand automatically moved to my wrist.

"It's fine," she softly said, dismissing my explanation. "What you've been through is awful, Cole. We've all felt some of your pain. It's good to see you smile. You have a nice smile." Harper shook her head like she'd forgotten her place then moved swiftly on.

"I may not have known Grace, but I joined this family when the impact shook your household to the core. And Grace was Layla's mom. That fact isn't lost on me, Cole. Matty and the rest of the staff also lost Grace and you must know we're all with you in this." I nodded, my throat too closed with emotion to have held a reply for a moment.

"What I see is a man who's still grieving. A man who wants to do his best for everyone, but who is forgetting to take care of himself. I know it's not my place to say this because I'm only Layla's nanny, but I care."

"After the time you've spent here, you aren't only Layla's nanny, you're the key to my daughter's happiness right now. She's only dealing with Grace's death so well because you're like a second mother to her." A soft squeeze on my wrist told me my statement meant a lot to her.

Reaching for the stemmed glass of wine, I stared out of the kitchen doors and threw the whole contents of the smooth liquid down my throat. Placing the wine glass back on the table, I lifted the bottle and poured myself another.

"I've been a mess. I *am* a mess," I admitted, in a rare moment of candor. "Some days I feel nothing and others I feel as if I can't go on. Layla is my only reason to live," I added dryly.

"No. Layla is your *main* reason to live," Harper corrected.

Turning my head, I narrowed my eyes and saw a culmination of feelings from compassion to alarm on her face.

"What happened with Grace was so horribly unjust. Some nights when I heard you crying, the pain in my heart... crushed me, and I didn't even know her. When I first got here, the sorrow in this house was so dense I felt like I couldn't breathe. There were nights when I cried myself to sleep thinking about Layla and your beautiful family being destroyed by that horrible disease. Anyone would feel the way you do right now."

Hearing Harper validate all I was going through helped. I had never aired my feelings this way before. It hadn't been my intention to do so, but to know she understood—that they all understood—meant everything and helped me to understand I wasn't the only person in the household missing Grace.

"I feel so angry with the world," I admitted, shaking my head. "Since Grace died, I've never been so careless about my life." My confession brought a fresh lump to my throat, and too late I realized I had no more fight in me to swallow it down.

Tears came and I let them flow unashamed. Even though Harper was my employee, it felt safe to cry. "I can't get past her, you know? I loved her so much," I whispered. "She was my world," I added even less audibly.

Moving quickly, Harper enveloped me in her arms and her hug felt firm, safe, and comforting. Rubbing my back in a soothing rhythm, she encouraged me to cry, and I let the grief I'd fought to suppress on so many other occasions expel from my body.

It must have been a pathetic sight to see, me sitting at the table with our food barely touched while my child's nanny rocked me back and forth, but I didn't care, nor could I have helped, giving myself up to the sad feelings inside my shattered heart.

I wasn't sure how long we'd been there when I finally pulled myself together. With my face close to Harper's neck, I began to feel calm. Inhaling the scent of a woman who wasn't trying to entice me felt unnerving. Pulling my head back to look at her, my face was only inches from hers.

"Thank you," I mouthed, and without thinking, I pressed my lips to hers in gratitude for her empathy and support. Realizing I'd kissed her, I jumped to my feet. "Fuck. I'm sorry." Running my hand through my hair, I gestured my other hand helplessly toward her because it felt as if I'd been unconsciously hitting on her from the moment I'd arrived home.

"Shh, you're fine, Cole. You haven't done anything wrong. I feel privileged you felt safe enough to share your feelings with me." Her tone intimated what I'd done was no big of a deal, and I stole a glance at her, which immediately made me feel better.

"Can I say something?" Her tone was even and apparently unaffected by what I'd done.

"Sure."

"You need help and I know you won't accept more counseling. I heard you yelling all the way down here in the kitchen the last time," she informed me, giving me a wry smirk.

I nodded. She was right, I wouldn't. "What kind of help?"

"Me. Let me support you. Nothing heavy. Maybe the healthy body, healthy mindset kind of stuff. I'm qualified for that remember? Layla starts at the Montessori school in the fall, which is three weeks from now. I'll write you a yoga program to start you off, then we can get into a routine when Layla's in school."

"You'd give up your free time like that for me?"

"No. You'd be joining me in my regular morning sessions. It'll help me keep up my teaching skills. I was going to take on a couple of clients in my free time, but I can do you instead," she suggested. Harper's face blushed again, and for a second I had no idea why she was having this reaction, then the 'I can do you' comment registered with me.

"Done. But I insist on paying you as my trainer. The thought of working with anyone else right now is too much, but I guess I should warn you... I'm not the easiest person to get along with."

"I figured as much," she commented truthfully, "but I'd be happy to take you on." I stared intensely at the beautiful, kindhearted girl in front of me and considered her proposal. If anyone could help me get back on track, it was her.

"Jeez, but I'm a mess," I admitted, running my fingers through my hair.

"Yeah, at times you are, but you're getting better, Cole. Recognizing things need to change is the first step back to health; the rest we'll work out as we go."

"Anyone ever told you you're amazing?" I asked because I genuinely thought she was.

"No one of rock star status, but I'll take it," she replied, and we both laughed.

"Well, you are. Thank you for all you do for me and Layla. We appreciate your support."

"My pleasure. She makes my job easy."

"Implying I don't?" I chuckled.

"I'm not your nanny," she teased.

"Sometimes I forget that, huh?" I was thinking back on how I'd just poured my heart out.

"I'm here for you too, Cole. You're a lovely man. You just have to admit you need a little help to get back on your feet after everything you've been through. It needs to come from within though. No one can do it for you, no matter how much we'd all like to."

"Jesus, are you nagging already? I thought you said the training doesn't start for another three weeks?"

Harper laughed and stood lifting her plate. "You can start by getting some proper rest. You've had a long day. Get yourself to bed and I'll clear all this away."

Pushing out of my chair, I almost went to hug her again, then thought better of it and nodded.

"Thanks, Sweetheart, g'night."

CHAPTER TEN

When Harper mentioned the cookout to Layla, my daughter quickly used this to her advantage and invited two more girls and their families before Harper drew a line. By Saturday, Matty was almost as excited as my daughter because we hadn't entertained at the house since before Grace had passed.

Thinking I'd need a little moral support from a few friendly faces, I invited my nearest neighbor and fellow musician, Max Ingle, and his wife, Sarah-Jayne, along with their daughter, Lucinda, to keep me company.

When Grace was alive, Max's place had been a regular haunt for my girl, who was close to Sarah-Jayne, and Max was the only guy outside of the house and the band I'd conversed with about Grace since she'd died. I could be myself with him.

Come Sunday morning, everything was in place and I felt a little more relaxed for having taken Harper's advice and had caught up on a few good nights' sleep. Layla was beside herself with excitement and had been wandering around the house in her bright pink princess bathing suit, since a little after 5:00 a.m.

Waking me up had become a habit of Layla's since I'd been home, but seeing her excited, smiling face lifted my heart. If I'm honest, although her resemblance to her mom was uncanny, she made me forget the bad times and kept me firmly in the present.

~

It was little after 1:00 p.m. when Layla came bursting excitedly into my office to tell me the guests had arrived. Grabbing me by my hand in her now familiar eager way to place me where she wanted, she dragged me along behind her until we reached the kitchen door.

"Now, Daddy, I've warned Jaden not to pee *anywhere*," she told me, crossing her arms in front of her then swiping them wide with her palms faced down to emphasize how serious she was. "And I'll be watching him so you don't need to worry," she added, nodding in her organized tone.

For a second, I wondered whether I wanted to know my innocent little daughter was waiting for the moment when her little friend got his wiener out and whether this really was Jaden's party piece.

I hadn't entertained anyone at the house since Grace had died, and facing a few people in my own backyard suddenly felt more daunting than stepping out on stage in front of thousands of people.

Performing was what I did for a living, and even in the darkest of times, I could still be relied on to put on a show, but the people I was meeting knew my daughter almost as well as I did.

Stepping out through the open patio doors, I stared down at the strangers milling around by the pool, and as if Harper had a sixth sense about my feelings, she turned to look at us. Smiling, her bright blue eyes met mine, and even from this distance I felt more reassured.

Excusing herself, she wandered down the side of the pool to meet me. Layla broke away from me and ran to talk to her friends.

"Hey, how are you feeling?" Harper asked, her tone soft and her eyes searching my face. Realizing it was the first time we'd really spoken since my breakdown a few days before, I felt a little embarrassed about displaying my vulnerabilities in front of her.

"Good... better. Thanks for—"

"Don't mention it. I'm glad I was there," she offered, knowing exactly what I had been about to say and not letting me finish.

"Take a deep breath because they are all, with the exception of Sarah-Jayne, fangirling," she told me, and I gave her a pissed-off look and a wry smirk.

"Cole, let me introduce you to Cressida, she's—"

About to pop, I thought staring down at her huge pregnant belly and an instant pang of hurt shot through me.

"Jaden and Tom's mom," I interjected. I rubbed my sternum and tried to ease the ache in my chest. I also needed everyone to know I knew something of my child's life.

"Yes! Oh. My. God. Cole Harkin knows who I am," she gushed, turning to look at the two other women who stood gawking at me. I wished I had a buck for every time someone bragged about this.

"How could I not when there are threats to cut off your son's wiener?" I replied with a flirty wink.

Cressida crumpled her body with laughter, her bones looking like they'd instantly melted during our little conversation. "Jesus, Layla told you that? I guess my husband and I had better think before we express any more thoughts in future."

"Cole," Sarah-Jayne's soft feminine tone smoothly interrupted, rescuing me from the awkwardness of the moment, as she stepped forward and hugged me tight. "You look like you needed some help," she whispered, and I squeezed the hand she had slipped into mine.

Pulling back to look at her I flashed her a genuine grin. "Sarah-Jayne," I mused, holding her away from me. My eyes raked down her outfit and I noted how lovely she was. "Glad you guys could make it on short notice. You look beautiful as always. Is Max in the pool house?" I asked, knowing full well he'd be propping up the bar away from the other women present.

"Where else would you find him on a Sunday afternoon?" she joked.

Sliding an arm over her shoulder, I began to lead us toward the pool house door when Harper stepped forward, blocking my way. She shrugged her shoulders and glanced at the other two women who had been watching my interaction with Cressida.

"Tammy and Francessca this is—"

"Oh. My. God. Cole Harkin. As if we didn't know. I have every one of your albums," the taller of the two brunettes told me, following with a wide grin as she batted a ridiculous pair of eyelash extensions over her fangirl eyes. The shorter woman with her was prettier—striking actually—but she didn't speak until nudged by the one who'd just spoken.

"Sorry," she pleaded, shaking her head. "Excuse me, but this feels... weird, being here in your home when I've seen you in concert so many times." She shrugged her shoulders. I immediately decided I liked her honesty far better than the over-exuberance of her friend's greeting.

"Ah, well, here," I gestured at my property. "I'm an ordinary Joe. The real me," I offered, placing my hand over my heart and giving her a genuine smile. "Please enjoy the food and relax. My daughter is so excited to have your kids over to play. Hopefully as we get to know each other, you'll find there isn't much of a mystery to me, and I'm a dad like any of the others here."

"Kinda hard to imagine that if he was slipping into my bed every night," Cressida mumbled to Harper who shot me a wide-eyed look because it was obviously far louder than Cressida had intended. Harper's cheeks blushed, clearly embarrassed I'd heard, and I bit back a grin at her innocent reaction.

Making my apologies to the ladies, I made my way over to their husbands and found them a far more comfortable proposition than hanging out with their partners, who I gauged—like Matty had already surmised—would have been delighted to get in my pants.

Once the ice was broken and everyone relaxed, the day turned out to be one of the best I'd had in years. I was myself, not Cole the rock star, and the entertainment revolved around playing baseball and water polo with the kids. Later in the day we watched them as they put on a show led by Lucinda.

When the last of the children's energy was spent, a more sedate mood settled on the evening, where the kids sat on the lawn chatting and us adults shared some stories from our pasts.

Night had fallen by the time everyone left, and I heard Cressida praise Jaden for keeping his wiener in his pants. It made me chuckle. Jaden grinned big in return and promptly informed her he'd peed in our pool. Luckily, Paul was dedicated to his chlorine routines, so I figured we were all safe.

Harper came into the kitchen as I stored some food in the fridge. "How are you feeling?" she asked, after everyone had gone. "Layla had a ball today," she added.

"Good. At first, I missed Grace like hell. She was always the more sociable of the two of us. She had this... great ability to make everyone feel at ease. Whereas, I've always been moody, broody... reserved. It wasn't as bad as I thought... mainly because you were there," I added after a hesitation. Credit where it was due. "It was as if you just knew when I needed that extra bit of support."

Harper's lips curved up in a smile as she tore off a large strip of plastic wrap. Placing it over a tray of pastries, she shrugged. "Isn't that why I'm here? To support you as a family?"

I was about to put a lid on a salad bowl when I stopped and gave her my full attention. For a second her comment took my breath away, and I felt a little disappointed. It wasn't until she mentioned this that I reflected on how I'd sought her out at various points in the day when I felt a conversation drying up.

With each situation she was right there alongside me, making my job as their host easy. I was a little shocked to realize it had felt completely natural for me to rely on her. But it never occurred to me once she was only doing her job.

"What?" she asked, staring inquisitively like she'd said something wrong.

I sighed, "Nothing. I mean... thanks. You did support me, and you managed to make it look effortless." It felt strange that I was upset her vigilance was premeditated.

Shrugging her shoulders, Harper gave me a sideward glanced. Smiling slowly, she rolled her eyes a little. "Someone had to protect you from Cressida and Francesca," she replied, winked, and stopped tidying for a second.

"God, this heat," she complained, groaning at the back of her throat. My dick twitched unexpectedly at the sound. "Sometimes I wish it were fashionable to wax this off like I do everything else. This humidity makes my hair go wild."

As soon as her words were out, she looked horrified at her reference to waxing and she stared bashfully at me with her huge blue eyes, like she was trying to decide if she could cover up what she'd implied. Her referencing to waxing everywhere, along with her reaction to her own mistake, made my dick harder.

"I think I know what you meant," I interjected, chuckling.

Our eyes locked in a stare neither of us had seen coming. Her blush grew darker then she averted her eyes and quickly turned away, as she tried to recover.

Setting the bowl in my hand on the counter, I stepped closer and placed my hand on her shoulder.

"Hey, it's okay. You think I've never heard a comment like that before or the double implication? Don't be embarrassed. I know you never meant anything by it. You're a beautiful young woman who takes care of herself." Although I tried to appease my mind, it went to the gutter as I wondered exactly how often she waxed and where.

Harper was a very attractive woman and I considered for the first time why she didn't have a boyfriend already. "You should be out having fun, not cooped up in this ivory tower taking care of someone else's kid." As much as I never wanted Layla to lose her, the words I spoke were the truth.

As I let my hand drop, Harper shook her head, clearly embarrassed by our conversation and began scooping her waist-length dark hair back until she held it in one of her fists. The way she drew it tight behind her head triggered an erotic image of me wrapping it around my hand and tugging it. I shook my head in disbelief at the thought.

Next, she began threading her slender fingers through her long dark brown tresses—another sensual move—and worked it into a high ponytail before she expertly slid a pony holder from around her wrist and pulled it up into place. None of what she did was for my benefit, only her comfort, but when my eyes fell to her slender neck and stayed there, I became captivated by the slender curve from her ear to her collarbone. *Fuck.*

Furthermore, eyeing her delicate golden skin triggered memories of how Grace moaned when my mouth hit a sweet spot she had there. I swallowed roughly as my dick strained tighter in my pants. How Harper affected me was an unexpected response to a perfectly innocent situation, a raw physical reaction I'd rarely experienced from the mere sight of a woman since Grace.

"It *is* effortless," Harper admitted, skipping seamlessly over my previous comment and choosing not to answer. She was oblivious to my enthralled distracted state as she picked up on the comment I'd made before the awkward moment about her shaving her hair. *Was she bare everywhere else?* "I love being around you guys. Nothing feels forced."

That's where she was dead wrong, because the lecherous thoughts in my head and the solid bulge forced painfully against my fly told another sordid story. Her reply barely registered for a moment as I stood a fraction too close to her, still in shock that I'd found Harper's innocent move so alluringly sexy.

Normally, a situation like this could have been excused by an inappropriate response to a large amount of alcohol. Before Grace died, alcohol had usually made me feel super horny, but since I'd been home I had stayed true to my vow to live healthier, and I'd steered clear of the hard stuff.

I could hardly blame my dick's interest on four stubby bottles of beer in a whole day. Forcing a small smile, I lowered my head and turned away, feeling perturbed at the effect she was having on me.

"All right, let's leave the rest and get to bed. The little whirlwind upstairs will be full of beans again in a few hours. Grab some sleep. Matty will sort the rest of this out in the morning."

Without looking at Harper again, I hastily made my way up to my room, cussing myself under my breath. The last thing I needed was to project my fucked-up feelings elsewhere, and add further complications to my life, especially with someone as important as my little girl's nanny.

Rage threatened to roar from my belly as I almost ripped myself out of my clothing, "What the fuck is wrong with me?" I ground out angrily as I climbed into my comfortable bed. It was the only comfortable thing in the room, because I certainly wasn't.

Tossing and turning, I lay riddled with guilt. *Am I overfamiliar toward Harper?* I wondered if I had reacted the way I had because I lacked meaningful female company? This wasn't to say I was a monk on the road. My physical sexual needs had been met by a long series of 'one and done' hook ups during the previous couple of years. My wife may have died, but I had no urge to replace her.

A sudden new wave of grief washed over me, and I needed to see her face. Reaching into my nightstand drawer, I lifted out my favorite picture of her. The small gilt-edged frame had been a gift from Grace to me because I had been carrying the picture of her everywhere in a small padded envelope.

Stroking my fingers down the smooth cold glass, my fractured heart ached as I stared sadly at the beautiful happy face of the woman I still loved with all of my heart. Then I remembered how bright vibrant eyes had dulled with pain until they had looked haunted and sunken, until finally they bulged in her head on that final day.

Sometimes I found it hard to cry—inappropriate to cry—when my anger and frustration wouldn't allow it. But as I lay clutching her picture, the overwhelming sadness, the nondescript feeling of despair beyond words that flooded my mind and steeled my body, brought on tears that were the hardest I'd ever shed.

A sharp pain in my chest stabbed sorely at my heart, squeezing every last flicker of movement within it until it appeared to temporarily stop. Gasping sharply, I realized I'd held my breath for too long. Not deliberately, but like the earth had stopped revolving for a moment and I was suspended in time, absorbing my hurt. Then as soon as I remembered to draw breath everything began to move again.

During the day I'd watched Layla laughing aloud, and I'd found myself swallowing back the simmering swell of grief. The most natural thing to do in that situation would have been to turn to Grace and share the same pride in Layla during those glorious moments. Instead I'd looked to Harper, and she'd taken Grace's place... filled in the gaps in my suffering.

My thoughts turned back to Harper and how I'd felt as I tried to find a reason why I'd reacted to her in the way that I had. Why I'd made stupid comments to her as well. I had no answers.

If we'd known at the beginning the tragic journey Grace would face—that we all would face—maybe I could have done something.

Suddenly the vivid memory of the last time I'd made love to Grace came to mind. The all-consuming, intimately addictive way she'd caught my eyes and held them with hers, the way my hands travelled sensually across her taut warm body, the way her fingers had explored mine. Sliding into her body, her warm tight heat enclosed my cock until there wasn't even a hair's breadth between her skin and mine.

Standing abruptly from the bed, I strode into my bathroom, disrupting the sacred visual and wrapped my fist around my cock. Slapping my hand around the cool tiled wall I tugged slowly at first, my mind trying to focus on something... anything to help me chase a fast release, but the only images my mind would let me choose were all and any that included Harper.

Strands of cum spurted from my cock as my body released the pent-up feelings of want I'd fought so gallantly downstairs. My twisted mind held a mixture of pleasure at the fantasy, and guilt for even having degrading sinful thoughts about how hard I'd fuck Harper, and all the dirty ways I would have had her, had our circumstances been different.

Anger and frustration squeezed tightly at my throat because Harper was the last person in the world I'd choose to fuck with... in any sense of the word. Yet as hard as I thought this, there was no shame in yanking off to the fantasy of a beautiful woman.

There had been many a time where my band members and I had joked about forbidden fruit in one way or another. Truth was, when faced with it under my own roof, it was no laughing matter.

With a pounding in my head, I fished in my bathroom cabinet and took out the sleeping pills William had previously prescribed, and I'd largely ignored. Taking one, I made my way back to bed and stared blankly at the ceiling until I eventually fell asleep.

CHAPTER ELEVEN

In the weeks leading up to Layla starting school, my daughter kept me busy. I'd been thinking long and hard since my near miss with Harper, and the reality of taking responsibility for Layla needed a better balance. I knew how losing Grace had felt, and I began to imagine how Layla would feel when the time came for Harper to go. It didn't bear thinking about.

In truth, Harper was Layla's mother figure and if Layla had a tenth of the feelings in her bones I had, I knew any parting of the ways would devastate her. Because of this, I felt there was no better time for Harper to have regular breaks and share the daily care of Layla.

Looking somewhat dejected, Harper was sent home to rest, giving me two full weeks to spend much-needed and long overdue time alone with my daughter.

Doing all the usual things, like fun inflatables, water parks, the zoo, and a couple of days spent over at Max and Sarah-Jayne's, I got to bond with Layla in the most incredible ways. Building trust and becoming closer made me feel guilty and sad for all the precious moments in her life I had missed. I vowed then to try to go easier on myself and to be the best father I could from here on out.

Harper came home a few days early and although Layla was

delighted to see her, she appeared somewhat reserved. By bedtime that evening, her behavior toward Harper had become ugly and defiant.

Through tears and tantrums, Layla's constant refusal to comply with her routine tested Harper's patience to its limits. A couple of times I went up to her playroom, but before I could interfere, Harper would frown and signal for me to leave with her eyes. I'd never seen anything like it from my daughter, and despite all we'd been through as a dysfunctional family, Layla had been blossoming into an adorable, sweet-natured girl.

Having no real idea what had come over my usually even-tempered, sunny child, I called Sarah-Jayne in desperation to ask for her advice because I had respected her parenting. Frankly, I was stunned when she told me what Layla was doing was a perfectly natural reaction to Harper's absence.

Apparently, according to Sarah-Jayne, Layla's challenging behavior was her way of checking whether Harper still loved her and contended children often try to sabotage relationships, when they are feeling insecure, to see if the person who's supposed to love them really does.

There were two things I took out of the conversation. One, Harper was so important to Layla that leaving her for any length of time had made her feel insecure. And two, Layla had had no such reaction during the times I had gone away... or had she, and no one had told me?

Obviously, after learning all of this, I knew Harper and I had to work closely, and in tandem, to reassure Layla she was everything to us, and we knew this would be made more difficult with Layla starting school. It also sparked a conversation which gave us a stay of execution with Harper, who immediately agreed to extend her contract for at least another year.

Seeing my baby so insecure I was torn about letting her go. However, Harper reassured me all would be fine. And when the time came it was. Once again, Harper had known exactly what to do to make my baby feel settled and safe.

With Layla packed safely off to school, Harper stayed true to her word and took me in hand, devising a pretty stringent fitness program, which initially balanced, suppleness, core strength, and agility. "The cardio and endurance will come later," she told me. "First, we need to relax your mind and body."

For a nanny, she had the stamina of a workhorse and the strength of a grizzly bear... and the patience of a saint. No one—apart from those who had seen me train in the past—really knew how much effort it took to have the stamina and lung capacity to maintain a ninety-minute performance. The searing lights caused exhaustion and dehydration, and the vibrations from the equipment were pretty wearing on the body after half an hour or so.

Saying that, Harper had lived with us for years and I thought she knew me pretty well. She knew I was lazy and stubborn, and all exercise had lapsed, but she also knew from my fame I'd been extremely fit in the past, otherwise it wouldn't have taken as long as it had, for the cracks in my health to show.

That first morning, as we headed back from dropping Layla at school, Harper chatted easily in my car, and all I could think of was making an ass of myself while she tried to teach me how to relax and learn to do her version of yoga. I knew she was good. A few times, not long after Grace had died, and I couldn't sleep, I'd seen Harper by the pool at the break of dawn practicing yoga and meditating by the pool.

Arriving home, Harper got out of the car already dressed in tight yoga pants and a tiny white tank top. She began setting out mats by the pool as I went into the pool house to change. Matty was talking to Harper by the door and smirked when I came out wearing a pair of gray sweats and a T-shirt.

"I'm telling you now, Cole, you're gonna sweat in those. I wouldn't be surprised to see you down to your briefs by the time that girl is finished with you."

Smirking, I raised an eyebrow. "You wish, Matty. I know seeing me in those is your secret fantasy. But I have news for you, real rock stars don't wear underwear." I winked. "Besides, I'm not that unfit, I'll have you know."

"We'll see," she called after me as she made her way back to the house. As I walked over to where Harper was already warming up I was stunned when she suddenly stuck her tight little ass in the air. Placing her head down between her arms, she proceeded to stretch one leg up through her hands, pulling her already tight yoga pants even more taut. A rough swallow stuck in my throat as my cock stirred. *Fuck.* My hand flew to the back of my neck at the sight of her perfect ass cheeks and my mouth went dry.

"There you are!" she exclaimed, turning to look at me. "I found this extra yoga mat, so you won't get knee burn from the patio." The mention of knee burn triggered a sexual connotation.

"Oh, I don't know, I don't mind a bit of knee burn if the activity's been worth it," I replied, and almost choked on my own words.

Harper flushed pink and tucked some stray strands of hair behind her ear. "Trust you," she scoffed, a little embarrassed and rolled her eyes. Shaking her head, she shrugged off my comment and spread her feet in line with her hips to steady her gait.

My gaze fell to her bare feet and slim ankles as she moved, and I slowly dragged my prying eyes up to her face, but not before I noticed she'd discarded the tiny tank, baring her curvy tan midriff. Her ample voluptuous breasts were held together in a black Lycra sports bra, displaying her perfect cleavage. *Fuck. Fuck. Fuck.*

The last thing I had meant to do was check her out, but I had, and my dick had responded in a salute of lustful delight before I had time to compute what I'd done. Harper was a beautiful woman, but I hadn't realized how truly smoking hot she was before.

It was crazy but true. I'd seen her hundreds of times in her swimsuit, in shorts and tops, and dressed up to the nines, but I'd never felt lust like I had when I took her in. It felt all kinds of wrong, and guilt washed over me for finding her so appealing.

"Are you ready?" she asked innocently, with a frown on her face. I guessed it was clear to her my mind wasn't focused on yoga.

"Sure," I replied, shaking my arms out and moving my head from side to side in my effort to shake the new pent up feelings I had. At the same time I was wondering how quickly I could pretend to pull a muscle to get the fuck away from her.

"Okay, we start like this," she instructed, placing her palms together and holding them right in front of the perfect cleavage I'd already noticed and was fighting hard to ignore. I trained my eyes on her hands for a second, but they digressed to the perfectly squashed breasts behind them, then I noticed her nipples were hard. *Fuck me.*

If anyone in my past had ever told me I would feel as awkward as fuck about staring at a pair of pert tits, I'd have had a smart-assed answer. However, that was in a whole other life; because I was so hard up I felt like a ready schoolboy after finding a secret stash of porn.

I felt relieved when she took her hands away and talked me through various positions she wanted me to try, before she proceeded to show me a series of stealthy moves, designed to loosen my shoulder joints and increase their flexibility.

What I actually saw was a range of ways to showcase Harper's tits and ass to the best of their ability as she cut through all the pose changes.

At one point I almost called a halt, as my groin was fucking with my mind, but I somehow struggled through, mainly by staring over her shoulder and thinking about how Peter should redesign the shrubbery bushes over by the south wall. When I looked back at her I swallowed roughly, wondering how I was going to make it to the end of the session without her noting the sizable bulge in my sweats.

If Harper did notice, she never said, but once she'd gone through another impressive set of positions, involving stretching her arms, that included pairing her hands around her back like she had at the front, she smoothly moved onto working our hips. Watching her contort her tight little body became torturous when I hadn't been laid in a while.

Getting down on her hands and knees, Harper darted a sideward glance in my direction. "This is called the table top position." Personally, I'd participated in this familiar position a fair few times in my life, but I knew it as 'the doggy.'

I crouched down to copy her, like she told me, but my hungry eager eyes were stuck firmly on her fabulous toned ass. "This is the cat pose," she informed me, as she curled her hips inward then thrust her ass out, dipping her back, "and this is the cow," she added, and my mind went straight to the gutter.

Then, just when I wondered why the fuck I'd ever agreed to doing this with her, she stuck her ass right up in the air. The sudden upward thrust was totally unexpected and had my jaw hanging slack while my tongue almost fell out of my mouth.

"Come on, you're not trying," she admonished, and I wondered how the hell to try what she was doing without showing the massive, raging boner tenting my sweats.

Slowly I crawled into position and went through the same moves she had shown me. "Great, you're getting the hang of it." I was most definitely hanging, if you catch my drift, but I flashed a grateful smile for her encouragement as I fought desperately to get my head back in the game.

If I had thought Harper's previous demonstrations were enticing, I was ill prepared for some of the more advanced poses she pulled from her body when I'd informed her I'd had enough. Accepting I was new, she continued with her routine while I watched like some sick fuck voyeur. I swear by the time she was done, I had wished I were somewhere else entirely... like balls deep in a tight wet pussy.

From the positions she got herself into, I was convinced Harper had enough bendy talent to kiss her own ass, and I marveled at how unbelievably flexible she was, which did nothing for the state of my sex-starved mind. I pulled off my t-shirt to distract myself from staring at her.

By the time she had finished, there were several damp patches; one of which ran down the seam of her black yoga pants, and her midriff glistened with perspiration from the effort she'd put into her workout. Casting a glance over her body, I imagined her totally naked while she bent to drop the small hand towel she'd used to wipe herself down.

"Cooling down time," she advised me, jolting my dirty mind in a new direction when she told me to lie flat on my back. Sneakily readjusting myself in my sweats, I did as she asked and cussed up a storm in my head when she crawled over and knelt beside me. *Sweet Jesus, give me strength.*

Having her so close beside me almost felt too much as her clean, musky feminine smell surrounded me. Warmth radiated from her tight sexy body as the sun caught her hair, and I swear her face was flushed to perfection, like she'd recently been fucked.

Leaning over me, her beautiful smiling face made me want to wrap my hand around the back of her head and pull it toward mine. Everything she was, suggested, and did, all served to add to the confused and lust-filled feelings I had running through me.

"All right, I know you've probably cooled down by now," she guessed when cool was the last emotion I felt. "I'm going to make sure you know how to breathe properly to help get the most from our sessions."

My self-awareness was at its peak. I had never in my life been self-conscious, but I was learning new capabilities being around Harper.

"I'm going to place my hand here," she advised me, laying her warm sticky palm gently across the center of my abdomen. Her touch only made me want her more. Her ponytail briefly fell forward and grazed seductively across my chest. She smiled and flicked it back over her shoulder.

"And when you breathe out, I want you to pull your abdominal muscles in here." She swept her finger lightly across my midsection and sent a small ripple of electricity across my body, making my insides clench in response. "Make them as tight as you can, like you're tucking them up under your sternum. Each of the exercises I'm giving you will increase your core strength. Now, try to tense on an exhale to maximize the toning effect on your abs."

Staring along her lovely toned arm and up to her face, I nodded and tried to do as she asked. "Shit," I cussed when the effort of holding it for the ten seconds and realized she wanted showed me how out of shape I was.

"Don't worry, looking at these abs," she praised, patting her hand on my stomach before tracing her hands over the ridges of each one, "you'll be tweaked and toned again in no time. These tight lines along here tell me you've probably got a lot of muscle memory."

Harper's hand continued to rest on my belly and for a second her eyes connected with mine. A flush reddened her face and she licked her dry lips before her hand trailed away and left my body. *If I'm not mistaken, her thoughts aren't exactly pure either.*

"Okay, let's do a little relaxation technique." When she lay down beside me, her arm brushed against mine, and another small charge of electricity coursed through my sex-starved body. "Sorry," she murmured before she tilted her hips and shoulders as she edged herself away.

Once there was a little more space between us, I swallowed awkwardly and gave a little cough as another wave of horny thoughts ran through my mind.

Sitting up quickly, I knew I couldn't continue to pretend what was going on inside me wasn't there. "Sorry, Honey, I just remembered something I need to take care of. I've gotta make a quick call to Derek. Thanks for the workout; I really enjoyed it," I lied, standing quickly and taking off toward the house.

"Derek called, he wants you to call him back," Matty called after me, as if divine intervention had occurred. I hurried through the kitchen and took the stairs up to my room.

"Thanks, I'll grab a shower then get to it," I replied over my shoulder, not trusting my flustered mood or the dick bobbing in my sweats not to show.

Stripping by my unmade bed, I made my way into my bathroom and stepped into my hot steaming shower.

As the force of the water jets pummeled my shoulders, I stood staring at the shower door until it went misty and as the bathroom vanity became obscured from sight, my mind fell into an array of thoughts I sincerely wished I didn't have to deal with.

Chaos reigned in my head, invading my mind with a war I didn't want to fight, but defeat was not an option, Harper was a no-go area.

My feelings swung between the never-ending grief about Grace, to the sudden heated desires I had for the deliciously enticing forbidden fruit who lived under my roof.

Then there were guilty feelings, because the woman who still held my fragile broken heart wasn't here anymore, and this time it wasn't only my groin that was nudging me in continual prompts to move on.

In the weeks since I'd been home, I realized I'd thought less about Grace during the day, but I hated that my mind was swapping her out in favor of inappropriate feelings toward Harper.

By the time I left the shower I was squeaky clean and emotionally wrung out, having come twice in my raw need to curb my desires.

It was only 11:00 a.m., and with Layla at school, I didn't trust myself around Harper with all the thoughts running around in my head, so I picked up my cell and called my friend, Max, without another thought.

"Hey, Max, what would you say if I told you I needed a distraction?" I asked, a hint of amusement in my voice I certainly wasn't feeling.

"I'd say, he's right here. What did you have in mind?"

"Escapism," I replied, because God knew how hard I was finding my reality.

"You're in luck, Finley and Grant are here. My driver was just bringing the car around. Can you be ready in ten?"

"What's the plan?"

"Day at the beach. Some surf, a few women, my ball and chain included," he added in reference to Sarah-Jayne. "As a matter-of-fact, she suggested inviting you along, but after I saw you at your cookout, I figured you were nowhere near ready for climbing back in the saddle."

Frowning at his comment, I knew exactly what he'd implied, but I had to get out of the house. "I'm not, but being at home... I could do with a change of scene for a few hours."

"Grab what you need and maybe a change of clothing in case we make a night of it too," he suggested, and then we concluded the call.

Pulling on some board shorts and a basketball tank, I stuffed some clothes in a garment bag and headed downstairs. When I entered the kitchen to grab some water from the fridge I saw Harper sitting at the table reading.

"Hey, I didn't see you there. I'm going out for the day and I probably won't be back before Layla goes to bed. Can you make sure she calls me after school?"

Glancing up from the e-reader poised in her hand, Harper gave me a look of surprise. "Sure, going anywhere nice?" I thought for a moment I heard a note of disappointment in her voice.

"Max and Sarah-Jayne invited me to the beach," I informed her. Why I let her think it was only the two of them and me I had no idea, but I left the kitchen without correcting myself.

CHAPTER TWELVE

An hour at the beach was my limit and although Max, his wife and the boys from his band did their best to keep the day low key and keep me entertained at the same time. I found I couldn't relax.

Max's wife had been Grace's closest friend since they'd moved in to their place a month after us, and even though Grace wasn't around anymore I couldn't bring myself to let go all the while Sarah-Jayne was around.

Thankfully, Max was very laid back and said he understood. Derek only lived forty five minutes away from where we were and he came without question to pick me up. He gave me a meal and a bed for the night, then arranged a ride home for me early the following morning.

As I entered the house I went into the kitchen when I heard Layla talking. She was chatting excitedly in a one-person conversation, asking questions and answering herself about our plans for the day. Harper had been quietly listening but looked up at me when she heard me open the door. Her eyes narrowed suspiciously, checking me out as Layla jumped out of her seat and ran over toward me.

Hugging my leg, she grinned up at me with her cutest persuasive expression. "We're still going to get my puppy today, right, Daddy?" The doubt in her voice melted my heart.

"Of course, Baby, I'd never let you down," I responded, remember the way she'd conned an agreement from me a few days before.

Conscious of Harper watching me, I turned and locked gazes with her and immediately noted she didn't look like her usual sunny self.

"Maybe Daddy needs a nap before we go out, Layla. You need to be patient," she replied to my daughter in a clipped tone. I thought I heard tension in her tone and when she continued to regard me with suspicion, I wondered if she thought my stop out was due to a hook up. Not that it was any of her business, but it felt important to me to put her straight on that.

"Sorry I wasn't home when you got up, Baby. I got stuck at Uncle Max's place and ended up staying at Uncle Derek's."

"Oh I see," she mumbled then flashed me another persuasive smile. "But we're still going to get my puppy, yes?" I nodded. "Absolutely, but I need a short time to clean and smarten myself up to meet it." Tousling her hair, I bent and kissed her forehead. I glanced at Harper who sat quietly studying me.

Excusing myself I went upstairs, stripped, showered and got dressed again before making my way back to the kitchen. Matty was preparing food and had a pile of vegetables waiting to be chopped. Harper was resting her head on one elbow on the countertop and the conversation between the two women stopped when I entered their view.

Matty looked up and there was something in her look that made me think she had been speaking out of turn.

"Something wrong, Matty?" My housekeeper's eyes ticked toward Harper as she slipped off her stool and nodded toward the kitchen door.

"I'm going to get Layla's coat, if you're ready?" she advised me and made her way out of the room.

Matty looked pleased for the diversion, but I wasn't fazed. If they had been talking about me, then I wanted to know why. *If I was to hazard a guess, my money was on them gossiping that I'd hooked up with some woman.*

"If you were gossiping about me being with someone last night, you can forget it. And you don't do that around my daughter."

"None of my business, Cole, and even if you spent the night naked with a harem of nymphs it would still be nothing to do with me. It's beyond my pay grade to worry about your social life. Anyway, I may be an old woman, but if I may be so bold, a few nights away from your grief may be exactly what is needed."

If anyone else had uttered those words I'd have taken offense, but I knew Matty worried about me, and what the future would do to me if I continued to close off the rest of the world. The glare I gave her in response said everything words couldn't. I knew her response was voiced out of love, but in this case, there was nothing to defend.

∽

It was love at first sight for Layla with a scrappy chocolate colored, eight-week-old Labrador. Immediately she stamped her mark on him by naming him Spot after a favorite canine character book series she was obsessed with. I snickered at the irony of the poor dog's name, and my heart swelled to bursting point at the wide beaming smile she had when I told her we'd take him home.

Harper was almost as enamored with the puppy as my daughter, and I didn't miss the pleasure she drew when I gave in to Layla's over-the-top pleas for me to give in to her choice. It also made my heart clench when I heard Layla's serious tone as she instructed Harper how to care for the little dog.

Layla was no stranger to pets. She'd had a Shetland pony since the age of two and had progressed to a bigger pony a few months before. Stuart had taught her right from the start, if she wanted to ride, she had to learn to muck out and take care of her animals. I glanced in the rearview mirror and smiled when I noted her hand resting protectively over the small pet carrier and I was in no doubt she would.

Seeing the proud look on her face in the rearview mirror, my eyes switched to Harper's—who caught sight of mine—and she flashed me a smile before nodding at how firmly Layla had anchored the seat belt around the pet transporter cage on the way back from the breeder's.

Organizing Spot's bed and bowls, food and water, Layla then carried her tiny dog carefully in her arms and gave him a tour of the house. She barely put him down to have dinner; then she tired the poor puppy out by playing little games.

If she picked Spot up off the floor once, she did it a hundred times, and by the time Harper had bathed and put Layla down for the night, I was almost certain I'd heard the poor puppy groan in relief that she'd gone to bed.

The house was sedate and calm by the time Harper and I sat down to dinner together, but the vibe was different from the easygoing one we usually had. I had always enjoyed our friendship, but now I had to remind myself not to overstep.

I wondered if I'd imagined the chemistry I'd felt since I'd been home. The old single and carefree Cole wouldn't have hesitated if he'd thought it was there, but this was Harper, my daughter's caregiver, and no matter what my dick thought, this ass knew not to shit where it ate.

Between us we drank a couple of bottles of wine. It was more than I intended and, if I'm honest, I drank way more than her and became fixated on her smile. It gave me knots in my stomach and sparks of electricity twitched in my dick. Seeing Harper so comfortable around me gave me a warm glow I didn't want to have.

"Aren't you freezing?" Standing up, she wrapped her arms around her body before dropping to her hands and knees and stalked her way over to the fire on all fours. Her ass looked fabulous in her tight black jeans and my gaze focused solely on it.

Padding around, she settled in front of the fire and lay on her side, her elbow on the floor and her head in her hand.

"Not really," I replied.

"So…" she asked, as she lay drawing my attention to the shape of her body accentuated by the glowing light behind her. The dip from her ribs drew my attention to her tiny waist and the raised curve of her hip.

"So?" I mirrored in a gruffer tone. My throat was dry as I basked in her beauty. I'd watched Harper turn from a barely-twenties gorgeous girl to a stunning mid-twenties woman. Everything about her screamed effortlessly sexy and, as I sat there, I wondered why she chose to keep doing what she did. *Men would go nuts for her if she put herself out there. Hell, if I…* I cut the thought dead.

"Did... you have fun last night?" There was both inquisitiveness and hesitancy in her tone.

"Fun?" I narrowed my eyes looking more intensely at her, wondering what she considered 'fun'.

She blushed at my challenge. "Yeah, did you have a good time?"

I sniggered. "I think your idea of having fun and mine would be very different," I replied, before the implication of my statement was thought through.

My response hit home, and I saw her chew on her bottom lip like she was confused by my statement.

"Cole, I know I take care of Layla, but that doesn't mean I haven't lived."

My brow bunched, and I don't know what made me ask but I did. "All right, are you asking if I got laid, Harper?" *So much for not biting, Cole.*

"I wasn't, but the speed of your question gave me the answer to that if I had."

Her eyes darting over my shoulder and around to various points in the room, before retraining them on me, told me she was nervous but testing her boundaries.

"What's that supposed to mean?"

She chuckled, "I figure the fact you thought I'd ask that kind of a question tells me it was obviously on your mind. The speed you answered tells me you're frustrated, so no."

"Correct. The answer *is* no. I never got laid, and I had no intention of doing so when I went out of this house. Could I have? Definitely, with any of the women at the beach I went to, but I bailed."

Silence fell between us and it verged on awkward until I challenged her.

"What about you, Harper? You're a young beautiful woman." She dipped her eyes to the floor and her modest reaction to my compliment only made her more appealing. "You're here with Layla all the time, and you've had what? One day off per week in all the time you've been here. When I offer time off, you always decline. Apart from school days and when Matty does some baking and other shit with

Layla, you're here twenty-four seven. When do you have time for fun... time for relationships? To get laid?" It was a fair question.

"Usually I go to the Sugar Trap bar on the other side of town and hook up. They have pretty interesting bikers over there, and those guys..." she replied fanning herself.

The Sugar Trap was known for being full of rough, hairy-assed bikers and their hos. Those guys made my previous rock star lifestyle look like Bible class.

"You're fucking kidding me, right?" I asked with my eyebrows up in my hairline.

"Absolutely." She chuckled and rolled onto her back on the floor; laughing so hard she was holding her sides. I have no idea why I reacted, but the next thing I knew I was down beside her, tickling her for getting a rise out of me.

Suddenly we both stopped, like my actions had only just caught up with my brain. I was astride her, staring down at my hands currently anchoring her wrists to the floor.

A look of utter shock passed between us. Her jaw gaped, but we held our gazes. I saw two things in her eyes. One, I'd turned her on, and two; she wanted... something.

Licking her lips, she writhed her body underneath me, and wriggled her wrists in my hands. I immediately let them go, stunned at what I'd done. "Fuck, sorry. It's been a while since I had good conversation and the easy company of a beautiful woman. I forgot myself for a moment."

Rising onto my knees, I lifted one leg over her body to join the other and sat down to the side of her.

"Fuck. I'm really sorry," I stated again, my tone laced with frustration.

"I'm not sure why. It's not like you did anything," she offered in an even tone.

"Still, it was inappropriate," I admitted.

"For a rock star? You're kidding me, right?" she goaded, suddenly reaching up and grabbing the back of my head. Rising to meet me, she pulled me close to her face and planted a soft closed-mouthed kiss on my lips. "No, it wasn't inappropriate, but that was."

With the soft imprint of her lips still fresh on my mind, I shook my head, but my eyes fell to her luscious mouth and I took a deep breath.

In that moment of hesitancy my body begged to have her, to give in to my feelings for her and my heart splintered in all directions, because it wasn't only lust I felt. There were other emotions involved. I missed Grace, but she was fading. I loved Layla, and no matter what I felt I couldn't act on my urge for more.

As we faced each other, sharing pounding heartbeats, it felt as if we'd become suspended in time. The whole tentative equilibrium of my family life hung in the balance like a coin spinning in the air, and I wasn't sure where it would fall... or which side it would fall on.

"We can't, Harper..." I blurted in disappointment as I began to breathe again. I swallowed past an emotional lump in my throat when I saw the hurt, dejected look in her eyes.

"Really? Why not? I'm not stupid, Cole. Do you think I haven't noticed how you look at me? How sometimes you adjust yourself during those moments when sparks of electricity arc between us?" *Fuck.*

Stunned for a moment by her honest observations, I realized how naïve I'd been to think she wouldn't have noticed. "No crime in looking, Sweetheart." I recognized the cocky tone from my band days. It was a cheap shot. A pause hung between us and I inhaled then sighed. "Look, you are far more precious to me than being a fuck buddy, because that's all I can offer anyone these days. When Grace died, she took my heart with her."

"You really think she'd want you to walk through the rest of your life like you're waiting to die? Because you sure as shit aren't living. It *is* possible to love more than one person in your life. Do you know that, Cole? Let me ask you this. If Grace were here now, would she still be attracted to you?"

My spine immediately straightened. "That's a fucking stupid question."

"Is it? You've got a daughter who'll be six years old next birthday. She deserves a vibrant, happy father who's not afraid to live for fear of disturbing the dust that's settled in this house since her mother died."

Fury coursed through my veins at her outspoken judgmental attitude.

"You're way off base," I bellowed. "What are you suggesting, Harper? You slot right in and take my wife's place? That I should ignore what my head and my heart are telling me and give you a shot? You're right, you are overstepping, and this is an abuse of your privileged position in this house, because my hands are tied. We need you. You're fucking Rapunzel in that ivory tower."

"Don't quote children's storybooks to me, I'm an expert, remember? Besides, there's more than a passing resemblance between us." I furrowed my brow, confused as to what she meant. Sweeping her hair to the side over one shoulder, she exposed her neck in the same sexy way some women did, a move that had always hit me right in the balls.

"Obviously, my hair isn't quite as long as hers, but I figure in the right hands I could be just as kinky. I'm not averse to a bit of hair pulling."

I stared wide-eyed in disbelief at her; like she'd just told me she'd fucked a horny college football team, and I almost choked on her comment.

"Jesus, Harper, you can't say shit like that to me," I chuckled. "Please understand how flattered I am. I mean you're a gorgeous girl, stunning and in another life..."

"This *is* another life. This is the one *we* have. You've been so consumed by what's happened you've forgotten to live... and in turn you've forgotten to take note that other people have needs as well as you."

Realizing that Harper was telling me she had feelings for me felt like a clusterfuck in the making, because my daughter was at the center of all of this and I changed to a serious tone.

"I'm sorry, but this isn't happening; will never happen," I confirmed, gesturing between us; then I realized how close we were when she sat up. Angling her body toward me brought her face so close her hot ragged breath fanned over my face.

"Do you think I wanted this to happen? It wasn't in my plans to grow up, catch myself a grieving widower and a ready-made family. We don't always get to choose our paths. You're into me, Cole Harkin, I can see it."

The spark of fire in her eyes held my gaze and a lump of emotion swelled in my throat. I swallowed uneasily because she was right. "I know you are. I would never have acted on my feelings unless I saw how you look at me. You just won't allow yourself to let it go," she whispered. I never moved, and I didn't respond.

"You're right. I have overstepped my position, but this has nothing to do with being your employee." I dropped my gaze and looked down at my hands because I totally disagreed.

"I *feel* the way you look at me." Her emphasis on feel made me eye her cautiously, confused by her comment. "That's right, *feel*, Cole. I feel the weight of every stolen glance, every blatant stare, the lustful perusal from a distance, and the way your hungry eyes scanned my body when I took you through your workout yesterday. Your dangerous carnal thoughts shine through in them more than you know, and the searing way you look at me penetrates my skin, ignites flames of wanton desire through my body, and it burns me up inside."

For a few seconds another silence hung heavily in the air until she broke the tension by placing her soft palm gently on my face. It felt so enticingly warm and feminine over my stubbly chin. I should have pulled away, should have stood and left the room, but in a moment of weakness I relaxed, letting her take the weight of it in her hand, because by then I was desperate for any caring touch.

"I wish I'd known you before," she whispered. The sadness in her voice brought another lump to my throat, the torturous moment almost strangling me. "You're a shell of the man you were; the man who fronted SinaMen before his wife died. This isn't my place, and it's not an abuse of power because of my status with Layla, because I am one of the few people who know who you've really become. Cole, I care enough to take this risk because someone has to be the first to help you pin your feelings down."

"Pin my feelings, or pin me down?"

"You're naturally suspicious. I get that, given how people have used you in the past, from what you told me. Personally, my agenda isn't anything other than to be honest about the feelings I've developed for you, and you can deny it all you want, but I know you've got feelings in there for me," she argued, poking my chest.

"No, Harper. You're wrong. The feelings I have are all purely physical. You were spot on because they're carnal... sinful even. Sexual fantasies. Any affection I have for you is related to your capacity as my daughter's caregiver."

"Ouch." With hurt instantly etching her face, Harper pulled her hand away from me, turned onto her hands and knees, and stood up. I followed suit and stood facing her.

"Guess I was way off the mark," she added looking mortified by my words. "Am I supposed to be flattered Cole Harkin would 'do me?'" blunt irony laced her tone.

"Stop," I commanded, catching her by her wrist as she turned to walk away.

Glancing down at my hand on her wrist, then up into my eyes, she shrugged. "The way you hold me isn't unfamiliar, Cole. Your grip feels possessive." Bringing her hand up to show me, she waved her wrist with mine holding it firmly. "But I'll respect your wishes to keep our relationship professional. I'm not sorry I brought this out in the open because at least it's cleared the air."

I dropped my hand from her wrist and watched as she turned and left the room. Closing my eyes, I drew in a much-needed gulp of clean air and prayed I'd handled her advance toward me delicately enough that she'd still decide to stay.

CHAPTER THIRTEEN

In the weeks after Harper pressed her point about the way I looked at her, it had shaken the mist from my eyes. No matter how well I thought my progress was, when it came down to it, I was still stuck on the precarious path I walked between Layla's care and my monogamous feelings of love for a ghost.

Staying home, in the sedate environment of the fortress I had built for my family should have taken some stress from my life, but all it had done was magnify what I was emotionally lacking. Being a single dad was a minefield of negotiations between my head, my heart, and my day-to-day life. And once this attraction thing between Harper and I had come to a head, I knew I had a new dilemma to deal with.

Trying to do what was right by Harper, instead of taking what I wanted, was slowly killing me. I was horny as fuck and I hadn't been laid in what felt like an age. Despite this, I continued my bi-weekly yoga sessions with her. I could have stopped doing them—I'd even considered it—but I figured if I had, it would have only made her feel even more alienated after the way I'd turned her down.

I was emotionally split with half of me wanting to stay home with my daughter, and the other half urging me to get the fuck away before I nailed Harper to a wall, a floor, or a door. No matter what, I had to learn to curb my desires around her, but after her advance toward me I felt the unspoken wedge it had driven between us.

As I became more attuned to my body's responses, I channeled it into the effort I made during my workouts and even added some sessions of distance running to them. Apart from the time we spent together with Layla, I avoided spending personal time with Harper. It was a pity because I had really enjoyed her company.

With my focus less on Grace and more on day-to-day living, I began to feel stir-crazy being around the house when Layla wasn't around. Sometimes I'd write a song, sometimes I'd spend hours on the phone with Fletch or Scuds, and sometimes I took Layla's scrappy little dog for long walks along some of the boundaries to my property.

The novelty of being away from the manic band schedules became mundane. Most of the time when I'd felt caged in, my brother had come to my rescue. Occasionally he'd haul my ass off for the day to a ball game, or drag racing, and when he was feeling pretty reckless to gamble, playing poker on casino boats.

Being in seclusion, I eventually connected reason to my unsettling emotions and decided it was because all the new thoughts in my head were shoving my memories of Grace into the back of my mind.

Even though my late wife was my first thought in the morning and my last at night when I lay in the dark, the images of us weren't as vivid and raw as they'd previously been, and to think they were fading pissed me the fuck off.

With my returning libido and only Harper for company when Dorian was away, I needed some kind of distraction. Luckily, it came in the form of Harper leaving to visit her family, which I knew from the previous occasion would result in tears and tantrums from Layla, but it gave both of us a much needed time out from one another.

Leaving home to attend her brother's wedding in New York, Harper was expected to be gone for four days, which meant she wasn't due back until Christmas Eve, but fortunately my mom and Grace's parents arrived the day after she left and with her grandparents on hand my daughter hardly missed her.

During Layla's previous five Christmases, everyone had ensured she was thoroughly spoiled, but this one was most important to me because I had wanted to make it as perfect as possible for her. We had been making great strides in our relationship and I wanted to work intensively on this during the festive holiday, because I had decided with the sixth anniversary of Grace's passing looming it was time to take Layla to visit her mother's island in the new year.

For a while I knew the day had to come, but no matter how much I thought about the best way to approach the reality of Grace's death, I felt I'd always feel ill-prepared to face Layla. My heart was still sore after all this time and I prayed she never felt the depth of pain I did, so I had to be careful not to make the situation any more damaging for her than it already was.

∼

Christmas Eve was a double-edged event. With Harper returning home, we were a full house, and all afternoon I found myself watching the clock as the time drew nearer to her arrival.

I didn't miss how my heart rate spiked with excitement when I heard the gate buzzer sound as she unlocked them or the undefined glance that passed between us the second she walked through the door.

Angus and Dinah had spoiled Layla with a mountain of the most current range of popular toys, dolls, and board games, which were stowed under the tree, and a battery-operated, remote-controlled toy puppy for Christmas Eve which drove poor Spot insane with jealousy.

Envy was something I faced myself that evening. After dinner, Harper had gone to settle Layla in bed while my mom, Angus, Dinah, and I discussed an article in the news. Suddenly realizing how much time had gone by I excused myself from the table to kiss my daughter goodnight.

When I entered her room Layla was lying on her side; fast asleep, her arm tightly around Spot. I swear the look her precious dog gave me was, 'Go ahead, try to move me, Buddy.' I swear the damned dog knew he wasn't allowed on there. I had forbidden Layla from having him in her room at bedtime.

Despite her defiance, I couldn't help the smile that spread on my lips because the look of happiness and sheer contentment on hers made my heart melt. Closing the door quietly I made my way back down the stairs, and when I heard Harper's voice in the living room, I wandered in to see her.

My breath caught in my throat when I saw my brother and Harper sitting shoulder to shoulder at ease, in a very cozy position. They were sharing flirty opinions about something they were studying on his phone, which he held on his lap. The sight of them together gave me the most uncomfortable feeling.

"Oh wow, this looks cozy," I muttered in a sarcastic tone, as I wandered farther into the room and stood in front of the mantle. Harper threw me a look of indifference, and where I had expected to see a little hesitancy from my comment, I found none.

Instead, she stretched lazily and looked too fucking appealing for me not to stare. The slow and sexy way she moved mesmerized me.

"It is. Best Christmas Eve I've had in years. The last four were miserable, but I've had a great time today with Layla... and spending some quality time with Harper here has been the icing on the cake," Dorian commented, oblivious as to how annoyed I was. Harper drew her hands down from above her head and placed them in her lap.

"Aww, you're so sweet," she gushed, back at my brother. Jealousy tore through me.

"She's not paid to spend quality time with you," I snapped. The snarky abrupt tone with which I delivered my comment even surprised me. I was useless at hiding my feelings.

"Indeed, and no money has changed hands between us. Has it, Harper?" my smart-assed sibling replied. His comment pissed me the fuck off and I couldn't help myself.

"Ah well, sorry to bust up your little tête-à-tête, but Spot's in bed with Layla. What did I say about that damn dog not being in her room while she slept?"

Harper unfolded her legs from under her ass on the couch and rose to her feet. "Sorry, Dorian, maybe another time; it would appear I still have work to do." Her voice sounded flat, yet still dripped with sarcasm.

"Sure, I'll take you to the exhibition next month, if you want."

Crossing her arms over her chest, Harper glanced at me with a smug smirk and flashed my brother a slow lazy smile.

"Thanks, I'd love that. What time does it start?"

"Oh, not until 8:30 p.m. so Layla will be asleep by then," Dorian informed her with a smile.

Heaving a deep breath in my effort to control my temper, I widened my eyes at Dorian and turned my attention to Harper.

"Great, now that you've organized your social life, maybe you can focus your attention to the matter at hand."

Standing behind Dorian, she slowly shook her head and flipped me the bird. "Of course, Cole. I'll get to it right away." The sweet tone she answered with was in complete contrast to her pursed lips and hand gesture, and to the ignorance of my brother who was facing me.

After she'd gone, Dorian stood up and ran his hand through his hair. "What the fuck was all that about? Care to fill me in?"

"I told her about that—"

"That had nothing to do with a fucking dog." His arm jutted angrily in the direction of the living room door.

"All right," I agreed, throwing my hands up in the air as my mind raked around desperately for something to say. "I'll be honest, Dor, I didn't like what I saw. You don't mess around with my hired help, understand?"

"Mess...hired help? Are you fucking serious right now?"

"As a coronary," I bit back without a trace of humor and nodded vigorously.

"Hmm, and why is that? You got designs of your own on her or something?"

"Don't be facetious. That woman is Layla's world. She isn't here to help you fill your nights."

"Fill my nights? Have you taken a close look at her? She's so fucking hot, it's a wonder she hasn't been lured away from the boring domesticity of her life. You've been so caught up in what happened with Grace that you've forgotten there are two sides to everything. Your side appears to be the only one that matters."

"Really, so what are you saying? I'm a selfish prick? I'm a self-absorbed asshole?"

"Normally... before Grace, I would have said you were one of the good guys of rock. Despite all your fame and fortune, your feet were firmly planted on the ground. Now? I'm not so sure. It's like you're using what happened with Grace to excuse any and all behaviors when it suits."

"That is not fucking fair, Dorian. That's not who I am."

"No? Then have you ever thought about doing something nice for Harper?"

"Harper is treated—"

"Bullshit. I'm not talking about pay and conditions, severance packages, and healthcare. I'm talking about treating her like she matters."

"She does fucking matter. That's the fucking point," I roared. "Apart from Layla, she's what matters the most. If I don't have Harper, we cease to function. She's been the constant for Layla, and she's the reason my daughter is as well balanced as she is."

"While all that you've pointed out is true, she's also a beautiful woman. Why the fuck shouldn't she have a life? You don't own her, Cole. Like you stated, she's a hired hand, and as such, she's free to do what she likes, whenever she likes, with whomever she wants, as long as it doesn't interfere with her doing her job."

For a second I almost protested, but I knew he was right, yet I still threw more at him.

"Dorian, if you go after her I will never forgive you," I threatened, sounding completely irrational.

"If not me then it'll only be someone else."

"That's as may be, but I can't have her here and you making what's already a bad situation worse," I replied. I knew if my brother went after her and she took up with him, it would kill me. Especially when she knew I was attracted to her as well.

However, all that aside, if Dorian and Harper did get together and it didn't last, it would be another reason for her to leave.

"Listen, if you do this and it doesn't work out, it's Layla you'd hurt the most. Think about it." Without saying anything else, I strode toward the living room door.

Opening it, I glanced toward the kitchen where all our parents were gathered around the table, then switched and looked up the stairs. Fury motivated me to take the stairs and as I reached the top, Harper was leaving Layla's room with Spot in her arms.

Walking purposely toward her, I grabbed her by her free wrist and almost tugged her off her feet as I dragged her reluctantly along the corridor and into my bedroom. Swinging her away from me, I closed the door and placed my back against it with my hands behind me.

"Got a thing for my brother as well, huh?"

Harper's mouth gaped and she strode over to my bed, placing the puppy carefully down on it. The fucker immediately scooted up to the top and nestled himself between my pillows like he owned them.

Turning to face me, Harper's eyes were ablaze with piss and vinegar, her face flushed with fury. Gone was the calm, even temper I had admired so much about her whenever Layla tested her patience. But fuck if the fuming fire in her belly that showed on her face didn't make me hard. It was the first time I'd ever seen the raw passion that lay underneath her cool exterior.

"You think? And what if I have? You had your chance, Cole, and you threw it away. Look at me. To you I have more value as a child's nanny than a woman. Do I look like the type of girl that has to beg a man for attention?"

Before I could reply, she headed toward me and I stepped forward to meet her halfway, but she strode right past and reached for the door.

My nostrils flared, and in my impulsive frustration I turned and went after her. My hand covered hers firmly as she reached for the doorknob, and I slammed her front flat against the door, pinning her there with my body. *Fuck. What the hell am I doing?* Feeling my raging boner laying the length of her ass, I pressed myself closer and everything stopped.

My heart hammered in my chest as I felt my hard, neglected dick against the firm sexy curve of her tight little ass and it made me sag even closer. No amount of willpower in the world could have prevented it.

Immediately, she was all around me as my senses filled with the fragrant womanly smell on her soft shiny skin, the sight of her long dark silky hair; the feel of it as it brushed against my cheek, and the sound of her short labored excited breathing.

My eyes feasted on the curve of her shoulder a good six inches below mine. Grabbing a fistful of hair, I tugged on it sharply. "Is this what you're after, Harper?" I muttered in a low gruff tone before moving her hair to the side and murmuring in a lower tone close to her ear.

"I know you can feel what you do to my body, but are you prepared for me to manhandle you like you don't matter? How would you feel later if I dragged your jeans roughly to your knees, pulled your panties aside and fucked you raw, right here, right now—against any of these walls?"

My aggressive behavior was nothing like the bereaved, beaten man she'd witnessed in all the time she had known me, but since Grace's death, women were for sex and as poor as it sounded, I'd treated them as a means to an end. Being inside them was nothing like making love to Grace; it was carnal, raw, and purely functional, and it had been mostly angry sex.

"Are you done?" Her salient tone sounded clipped and authoritative. It sparked my awareness as to what I had done. Despite her controlled question, the tension she held in her body betrayed her. Sexual anticipation rolled off her from the moment I leaned in to talk in her ear.

"You tell me, are we?" I shot back, my fingers still laced in the strands of her dark brown hair as I held it tight in my fisted palm.

Long seconds passed between us, the rawness of the moment vibrating like a plucked finely tuned string, and with every second that ticked by, I felt my envy ebb from my body. Then I realized how chemistry and jealousy almost ruined everything. She swallowed audibly and moved her neck to the side like she was considering my question.

The fact she didn't shove me on my ass and cuss me upside down told me the feelings she had for me were more than superficial. For a split second, I wished I could give in to what I knew we both wanted. Probably what we both needed.

Leaning forward, I swallowed past the sudden swell in my throat and ghosted my lips to the back of her head and wished for one night I could just forget the world and all the pain I felt.

Gently, I kissed her hair, because I had to take that slightest taste, then I pulled my head back because I had too many unwanted feelings. Lust and want flowed through my veins and I knew I had never craved anything more.

When I caught a glimpse of the silky skin between her ear and her collarbone, it was my personal weakness about her, and it proved too hard to resist. It had been so long since I had felt this level of want, and I knew then I was feeling and not thinking. *Don't! This is a very bad idea.*

Leaning forward again I inhaled deeply and drew the tip of my nose from her shoulder to her ear. I felt her chest heave and she sighed. I swallowed roughly as every nerve in my body fought against claiming her. "Don't," she whispered.

Harper's one word jolted me to my senses and the moment she stated no, I stepped back, dropping my hand. I turned away.

Staring in confusion at the bed, I ran my hand through my hair as the reality of what I'd done hit me. Glancing up the bed I saw the puppy wrestling with one of my pillows in his mouth. I headed over to the bed and picked him up. In the seconds it had taken to do this, Harper had gone.

CHAPTER FOURTEEN

For ten long minutes, I sat on my bed contemplating what a monumental fuckup I'd made. Fury and disgust flowed through my veins in equal measure as my jumbled mind tried to make sense of the chaos I'd created because of a moment of weakness and envy.

Shoving myself to stand, I knew I had to do something urgently, and in my haste I fired off a text message to Derek.

Me: Set up a small tour from Feb 12.
Derek: You got it!

I reluctantly made my way downstairs, knowing I had to pretend everything was normal. Despite what had happened, I still had people who expected me to entertain them.

"Right, who's up for a game? Let's get some life into us. It's Christmas for fuck's sake."

Patient smiles from my mom and Grace's mom told me they knew it was a deliberate change of subject for me as they rose from their chairs.

"Charades? Haven't played that in years," Angus suggested.

"Oh, what a great idea, though Cole's no good at charades," Harper drawled. The sarcasm dripped from her tongue like melted butter and Dorian raised a brow.

"Do tell," he mused to Harper, and I could have kicked him in the nuts for picking up on her comment like she had a story to tell.

"Let's just say he's not a great actor. He should stick to performing. Isn't that right, Cole?" The challenge in her bright intense stare made me instantly hard.

"It's been a while since I performed," I admitted, flirting back against my better judgment. I saw a wicked smirk tweak Harper's lips.

I was treading water and had been for some time with her. Going back to work wasn't something I really wanted to do, but it was something I had to do to gain some distance and a better sense of perspective where Harper was concerned.

"Which reminds me, early February I'm going back to work. We have a tour set from the twelfth."

The effect my unexpected news had on Harper was immediate. Gone was all sense of having the upper hand, and her expression was a mixture of shock, hurt, and disappointment. My stomach sank because I knew there were unresolved feelings between us. From my perspective they had to remain this way.

"That's fantastic news." My brother gushed immediately. Shoving his chair back, he strode over to hug me.

"I agree. It's time you got your life back, Cole. The guys in the band must be pleased?" my mom added.

Nodding, I looked to my mother and Grace's, and the expressions on both of their faces told me they were happy about my decision; however, when I stole another glance at Harper, she was on her feet, head down, clearing the table.

Moving to the living room, for the rest of the evening we played games: the usual festive ones like charades and Name that Tune. I even sang, but Harper remained reserved and less bubbly than she had been before my news.

Eventually, due to full bellies, heads full of wine, and a tiringly long day, the parents went off to bed. Migrating to the kitchen again with Dorian, he grabbed his jacket and turned to look at me.

"About earlier..." he started.

"No. I was out of order. You're right. She's an amazing girl, and she deserves the world. It's—"

"I was way out of line. I get your focus, but you're my brother. I know you. Don't you think I know how scared you are about the future and Layla?" For a second, my heart stalled as if he was about to tell me he knew how I felt about Harper.

I shrugged. "I know she's going to go eventually, I'm just..." I huffed a heavy sigh, "I'm not ready for that to happen yet, you know? It's depressing because it's constantly on my mind."

"Of course, but one day it's bound to happen, Bro, and when it does I'll be here. If you're this bent out of shape about it, maybe you need to think about a plan B."

Narrowing my eyes, I hated the conversation, but Dorian was right. But there was no plan B.

"There *is* no plan B."

"Then maybe you need to start thinking ahead instead of the past." Stepping forward, he wrapped me tight in a bear hug before stepping back.

"And I promise not to fuck your daughter's nanny," his tone was serious, but I made a joke out of the situation.

"Good to know, but I think a girl like Harper would laugh in your face if you tried." Dorian chuckled and shook his head.

"Thanks for busting my balls and reminding me who the stud of the family is," he replied with a smirk.

"Aw, don't be depressed, someone's gotta be the runt of the bunch," I shot back and winked. Shaking his head again, he scoffed and stepped past me.

"Smug bastard," he muttered humorously, and headed back to the living room where Harper was. She stood and wandered over to my brother.

"I've loved spending time with you today, Dor, we need to do it more," she told him, wrapping her arms around him in a hug. My chest tightened, and a knot formed in my stomach with her obvious show of affection for him.

Dorian looked at me over her shoulder, stuck his tongue out, and winked.

"Anytime, beautiful, just say the word." My heart squeezed with love for the brother who had always been there for me, but I gritted my teeth and mouthed, "In your dreams."

Raising an eyebrow, he pulled out of her embrace and I walked with him to the door. I hugged him again. "Thanks for everything, Bro, you have no idea how much I appreciate you."

"Yeah, I do. It's a lot, but not enough to let me inside Layla's nanny's panties," he muttered, only loud enough for me to hear.

Shoving him out of the door, he chuckled and held out his hands palms up as if to say, 'I rest my case.' I chuckled back and shook my head. "Get some rest, next year's gonna be a doozie when I'm on the road. You're going to have to step up and play Daddy to Layla for the times when I'm gone."

"I'm there, and excited for that. I love her so much… and you, little brother," he said with conviction as he shoved his hands in his pockets. "See you tomorrow."

As he turned away, I stepped back inside and closed the door. Turning around, I faced the living room door and I briefly checked out the stairs, before choosing to go back into the room to face Harper again. When I pushed the door open she was curled up on the couch, in the dark, in front of the fire.

Instead of going in I went to the kitchen and poured us both a fresh glass of red wine. I wasn't sure what I was going to say, but I knew I couldn't leave things how they were. Making my way back to her, I placed her wine on the small end table beside her and took a seat farther away from her on the circular couch.

For a couple of minutes, we sat in a stony silence, both of us staring at the flames licking up the chimney of the fire place and wondering who'd be the first to talk. In my mind I went through several scenarios, all including an apology for my despicable behavior before, but it was Harper who broke the silence.

"You're leaving again." It wasn't a question and when I shot her a glance, she was still staring at the fire.

I took a deep breath and closed my eyes, because the way she learned about me going back to work had been a deliberate piss poor effort to hurt her. I knew it was a malicious attempt to drive her away, but I needed that wedge between us because, the longer I stayed the more likely my resistance would crumble.

"Yeah… are you?" I wouldn't have blamed her if she'd wanted to leave after the way I had treated her.

Staring at me, her eyes widened, and she bit her lip. "Is that what you want?"

"Hell, no. You know that's not what I want." My heart beat wildly in my chest and the sense of relief I felt from her counter question made me more disgusted by what I had done. "Jesus, Harper. I need to get out of here for a while. Don't you see why I'm so averse to messing around with your feelings?"

"Haven't you done that already?" Her eyes glanced up at the ceiling. "I mean, what the fuck was that upstairs?"

"That was me losing control and almost taking what I wanted instead of doing what I need to… what we need me to do. I'm sorry, it should never have happened."

"Why? Because the only emotion you're allowed to feel is how much you miss your wife?"

"Bad form, Harper. That remark is way below the belt."

"From where I'm sitting there was way more going on below the belt up there, than my honesty."

"Don't fuck with me, Harper. All you know of me is the grief-stricken single dad. You said it yourself, you don't know who I really was before and what my capabilities were. Believe me, these days you wouldn't want to find out."

"Wouldn't I? I'm not a child, and to be perfectly straight with you, you have no idea about me. All you know is the efficient surrogate mother your daughter has."

"Is that what you think you are? Surrogate?" I thought for a second and nodded. "Not a surrogate, a substitute, and one day you'll give my daughter's care over to someone else," I replied with a bitter taste in my mouth.

"If you're trying to hurt me, Cole, believe me, it's working; but if it makes you feel better have at it. I'm perfectly willing for you to take all that fucking bitterness and anger out on me if that's what it takes to bring you back to life."

"And you're volunteering for what? To let me use your body? What exactly are you willing to give me, Harper?"

"Whatever it takes to make you stop being the pissy self-absorbed asshole you've turned into these past few weeks."

"Really, and your attitude hasn't been off? You think I haven't noticed the scorned wife act you've been displaying, moping around here like I'm cheating on you or something?"

Watching Harper's neck jut back at the same time as a slight flush crept over her face told me I'd hit the mark. "Ah no, I got it, this is about me finding someone else?"

"That's none of my business—"

"Damn straight it's not. But what do you want to know? Have I fucked anyone lately? What do you think? I see how you look at me," I countered, without thinking.

"Yeah, and I'm glad that you do, because you feel the same way."

"It isn't like that."

"Stop repeating yourself and get your head out of your ass."

Eyeing her with suspicion, I stared closely, "Are you fucking with me?"

"You know the answer to that, but that's your call."

"That was a lapse of judgement upstairs."

"No that was your true colors shining through, Cole. I'm glad they did because it showed me all the eye-fucking you've done whenever we've been in the same room isn't my imagination."

Years ago, if an attractive woman had spoken to me with the amount of confidence Harper had, I'd have slammed her to a wall and fucked her into submission, but I'd been to Hell and was still clawing my way back from there.

"And this brings us right back to the beginning of the conversation, Harper. I'm sorry. It shouldn't have happened."

"But it did, Cole. You can't put the foam back in the can now it's out."

It was clear Harper still wasn't satisfied with my determination not to let things go further between us. Scooping her hair to one side with her hand, Harper let the long dark brown silky strands sift closely through her relaxed fist. Turning her body to face me, she sighed heavily again.

"What you're saying is I'm good enough to care for your daughter, but not good enough for you."

I frowned in frustration. "Absolutely not. What I'm saying is this isn't a matter of whether you're good enough for me, and incidentally you're way *too* good; too... wholesome and pure."

"And Grace wasn't?"

I scowled angrily.

Challenging me with a piercing stare, fury flashed in her eyes. "Say you're not interested, or let *me* decide who I'm good enough for. And while we're at it, newsflash, Cole, you can't control everything around Layla. That girl is going to grow up to be a brat if you let her manage the household. She's almost six years old, and she's going to experience change throughout her life, no matter what. Do her a favor and teach her resilience now or you'll have a neurotic teen who is stuck in her ways."

Her comment stunned me.

"Look, this is about not rocking the boat for Layla, she's more adaptable than you give her credit for. You have to build on that."

I shook my head, because this conversation wasn't going anywhere. I knew she was trying to goad me with the Layla comments and drew her back to the matter at hand.

"Back off, Harper, like I said, you have no idea who I am."

"So you keep saying. Fuck, Cole. Get. A. Life."

"I had a life and look how that turned out," I ground out.

Harper's eyes softened, and she edged her way forward in her seat. Clasping her hands in front of her brought my attention to her pert cleavage, which heaved as she inhaled and sighed. "I get you're scared. Fuck, if it were me I'd be petrified, walking in your shoes."

"Yet you're willing to bust my balls for a fuck? Because that's all it would be between us, Harper."

"Are you telling me you've been celibate since your wife died?"

My heart faltered, and my chest felt tight at being called out. There had been a lot of women, but I didn't talk about them, especially not at home. When I didn't respond, she huffed out an indignant reply. "Huh." Her flat huff confirmed she knew there had been others.

"None of them meant anything."

"None of *them?*"

Frustration got the better of me, "Yeah, if we're airing my dirty laundry then sure, them, as in multiples. See, I'm not a fucking saint. I lost my wife… the love of my life. I don't want to feel those feelings again." My words were sculpted to have a negative effect.

"Fuck you," she whispered and rose slowly from the couch. "Have it your way, but this isn't a tour for the sake of it. You're running away from your feelings. Well, newsflash, Cole, you're too late, because they've already caught up with you, and you'll be taking them with you."

Before I could protest, she stood swiftly and left the room. I didn't go after her. There was no point. I sat staring at the fire, and when the flames died and all that was left was the dim glowing embers, I wondered when I had gotten so adamant about trying to do the right thing.

∼

My relationship with Harper was strained after our Christmas night blowout and I avoided being around her whenever possible. None of the family noticed, as they focused their attention on Layla. As soon as my daughter went to bed and everyone settled down to watch a movie together, I made the excuse of a headache and went to bed early because I was concerned I'd lose my temper or worse if I had to face another confrontation with Harper.

Thankfully, I caught a break and Harper and Layla were busy with play dates and parties. And it was easier with all the time my mom and Grace's parents were around because Harper made some space by driving home during the day to spend time with her own family. In the evenings when she came home, she went straight to her room.

Layla was her usual self, totally unaware of the rift between Harper and me, but since Grace's parents had been around, she had more and more questions about her mom. After talking to everyone about my intentions, they agreed with my plan to teach Layla what death meant and show her Grace's final resting place.

Angus and Dinah stuck around for Layla's sixth birthday and Harper threw her a huge party, which I only attended briefly due to the number of parents and kids. I didn't want to take the glory off Layla's day. Besides, Layla's birth had left me with bittersweet feelings about the gift Grace gave me, and the life we'd both lost.

CHAPTER FIFTEEN

When we reached the landmark six-year anniversary, Layla and I were swept up in a wave of love I could never have expected.

The dreary January morning had started out just as I had planned. The house was still and deserted save for Layla and me. Instead of a family pilgrimage, I'd arranged that Dorian have everyone over for breakfast leaving Layla and I alone to talk.

Packing a small picnic basket, I strapped her into the booster seat of the small Jeep to drive her down to the long meadow and toward our manmade lake. I thought I'd done a great job of preparing her for the graveside until a comment she made almost choked me.

"Are we going to see Mommy now?" My heart squeezed painfully tight by the innocence of my daughter's tender years.

Fighting desperately against a swelling emotion constricting my throat, I struggled under the weighty strain of my fury at God for putting me in this position. It was clear from my daughter's incontainable excitement she had expected to see Grace. Eyeing her warily, I bit back the words I knew would slaughter her as soon as I uttered them. For a second my heart faltered right there in my chest. The crushing sensation leaving me even more breathless.

Gasping, I suppressed the suffocating feeling and barely managed a stolen shallow breath. I had painstakingly poured my all into making Layla ready, but it appeared I had overestimated her level of understanding.

"We're going to visit Mommy's grave, Sweetheart. Remember Mommy's in Heaven now... so you can't see her." Inadequacy weighed like a heavy stone on my soul as a feeling of utter helplessness took over.

"So, she's invisible? Like she has a superpower? That's what Gregor in my class says. He told me if I can't see Mommy, but I know she's definitely there, she must have a superpower."

Narrowing my eyes, I cussed the meddling know-it-all kid I'd never even met. "Baby, we talked about this, remember?" I prompted, "You can't see Mommy because her soul's gone to Heaven and that means she's a beautiful angel now, but we're going to a place where we can remember her."

Pursing her lips, Layla eyed me with suspicion. "Then why does Harper always tell me no matter where I am my mommy's watching over me?" My breath hitched, remaining inside my lungs when it was stolen by the things we say to others to help them come to terms with the loss of a loved one.

Pulling over to the side of the road, I killed the engine and leaned over to unbuckle her seat. "Come here, Baby," I told her in a gentle tone. Layla slid out of her seat and stood on the floor, then climbed nimbly between the seats before squeezing herself between the steering wheel and my chest to sit on my lap.

Staring up at me with bright inquisitive eyes, my daughter waited patiently for me to come up with an analogy that would somehow sooth her in the fucked-up situation that Grace had left behind for us.

"Okay. How do you know when Matty has made your favorite cinnamon cakes?"

"Because she leaves them on the counter in the kitchen to cool?" I sighed and tried again.

"Well, say you had gone out and came back to the house and Matty had already stored the cakes in the tin box in the pantry. How would you know she'd made them?"

Tapping her finger on her little lips, Layla's eyes furrowed in thought. "I'd know because I'd smell them. You can't hide the smell of cinnamon," she replied, giving me a big smile that said, 'I'm smart.'

"Right," I enthused. "So what smell reminds you of Mommy?"

"Betty." Betty was Layla's teddy bear, Grace bought it the week before her birth. She sprayed perfume on it and told me Layla would be comforted by the soft toy because it smelled of her. "From the pink bottle of perfume you showed me, the one you keep in the drawer in the dresser?"

"Oh, you're so clever," I praised because I still sprayed it on her teddy bear.

Looking at me like I had sprouted an ivory horn, she lifted her hand and placed it on my cheek.

"Daddy, Mommy's not in a cookie jar in the pantry," she informed me, like she was breaking news that was sure to disappoint me.

Despite the sadness in my heart, I couldn't help but smile warmly, seeing the humor in her comment. "No, that's true, she's not, Layla. But, Mommy is all around us, like the smell of cinnamon. We only have to spray her perfume and our head reminds us about her."

Layla frowned and placed her other hand on my cheek, squeezing them both together slightly and relaxing her hands.

"I see what you mean. Even though we can't see Mommy, we know she's there." I nodded, choking up again.

"Now when we go to the cemetery, we won't be able to smell that Mommy's there because," I paused trying to think.

"It's outside so the smell of Mommy's perfume will be blown away."

At a loss for anything better to offer, I agreed. "Kind of... I mean Mommy's soul got carried in the wind when she went to Heaven, but things here on earth keep our memories of her alive, but inside our heads."

"But I don't really have her in my head. I don't remember. Daddy, I don't want her inside my head. I want her here, like you are. I want her to read me stories and chase me in the garden, and swim..."

Cradling her head to my chest, I stroked her hair as we sat right there at the side of the small private road. "I hear you, Baby, but no matter how hard we want something, sometimes it just isn't possible."

Falling silent, Layla huffed out a huge sigh in defeat and sagged sloppily in disappointment, all tension in her tiny body instantly giving out. Wrapping my arms around her, the only thing I could do was wait it out until her discontentment at my reply passed. I'd have given anything to give her what she wanted—what we both wanted—but it was beyond my control.

I concluded my daughter was far braver than I was, when minutes later, she pushed herself away and stared up at me with compassion in her eyes.

"It's okay, Daddy. I know you can't make her be here, and you can do *everything*, so I guess bringing Mommy back is the hardest thing in the world."

Her words were like a sharp stab in the neck and winning an Emmy simultaneously, because she had expressed in one sentence my limitations, and at the same time, she had no expectations of me taking away her excruciating hurt.

We continued in silence, Layla huddled over against the wind with her hands stuffed deep in her pockets. A few minutes later we had finally made it to the boat, and the exposed position out there made the air feel even colder.

Placing my brave little daughter into the pontoon boat with its small outboard motor, a blustery wind played into the earlier conversation and Layla seemed to cling to this, observing it as the reason why she could still tell her mommy was close by.

Without disagreeing, I pulled the cord and started the engine. Steering the rudder, I took us to the island in less than two minutes flat.

Although my heart lay heavy inside my chest, its beat was slow and deliberate as I lifted Layla out of the boat and placed her feet on the soft earth. I didn't visit the island often, but the few times I had ventured there before had brought about a calm feeling.

After I had spent a short time explaining about her mother's grave, Layla and I stood and said a short prayer, our heads bowed. I then asked her to think about the things she wanted to say.

Watching her little eyes lift in thought, I waited patiently for her to come up with something.

"Um, hello, Mom. It's pretty here," she said, glancing around at her lush green surroundings. "I want to tell you something. You going away made my daddy very sad. Harper, that's my nanny, she said that's what made Daddy grumpy."

Her honesty stunned me, and I stood wondering if that's how she saw me. When I asked if she had anything else to say, she thought for a moment then shrugged when nothing was forthcoming.

"Nope, I'm good. I just thought she should know about you being sad."

Pain shot through my body as her words tugged at my heartstrings, and I guided her away from her mom's final place and lead her back to the boat in silence. Starting the engine, we slowly made distance from the island, and with every foot closer toward the meadow, my heart hurt a little less.

Deciding to take Layla to visit Grace's grave so young had been a bit of a gamble, but my precious little daughter had taken the painful short journey in her stride. My intention had been to give our daughter partial closure by taking her over to Grace's resting place, and to my surprise, she weathered the experience well. It wasn't as traumatic for either of us as I had expected it would be.

CHAPTER SIXTEEN

Three days later, everyone had gone, Layla was back at school full time, and everywhere I went Harper was always in my face. This wasn't her intention, but with the house being quiet she appeared to be all around me.

With the tour looming in less than a month, I camped out at Dorian's more often than not to help me keep my distance from Harper, but I also hoped it would help Layla to get used to the idea of not seeing me every day.

Obviously, the yoga had stopped because I didn't trust myself around Harper anymore; after pushing the boundaries between us, and with a little time to reflect I wondered whether our attraction was down to lonely infatuation.

We were vastly different people: me the once laid-back rock star now broken with a head full of dark thoughts; whereas Harper was beautiful, bright, bubbly, and kindhearted. The enigma was she could also be boldly forthright and sassy and wasn't afraid to go after what she wanted in life. That part I did relate to because I once had all those attributes myself.

By the end of January—on a superficial level anyway—it appeared as if the challenges between Harper and I, although still present, were manageable. A civil, professional relationship was reestablished between us, and we kept our distance when no one else was around.

January rolled into February and as rehearsals for the band took up a lot of my time, I wasn't home that often in the daytime. For all my push to get back on the road, I had insisted the band rehearsals take place during the day, so that I could catch Layla on the flip side before she went to bed, a couple of nights a week, because I wanted her to know I was still there, but not to feel insecure when I didn't come home.

Packing up to leave was the most difficult part of the whole experience because Layla wanted to help. Every T-shirt she stowed in the suitcase had a question attached: about the tour, about me, about Harper and her.

Keeping the conversation light was a struggle because I knew at some point the tears were going to flow, and when they did, I hugged her tight, told her I loved her, but reasoned firmly I needed to go to work. The way she held me broke my heart and for a long couple of minutes I struggled to let her go.

It would have been different if I hadn't been the front man; the main man, as the band had been built around me. My bandmates had been monumentally patient with me and it had been the second time they'd had their careers put on hold.

The reality was a mixture of privilege and ugly, but I reminded myself there were many others in life that worked away from home... and for a lot less reward than I'd been given for doing my job. At least I could rest easy, knowing I had a fantastic support network of people around Layla, and my brother on my doorstep.

Angus surprised me when he called the night before I left for the tour, and although the conversation started normally enough, I sensed there was something he wanted to say. When the words between us dried up and he hadn't, he suddenly cleared his throat and in the gruffest tone he boldly told me he thought I'd grieved long enough and to go and live my life.

"Six years is a long time to be lonely, Cole. Before now, I've watched from a distance. Dorian's kept me abreast of your progress, and let me tell you, it's been a painful journey for us, made all the worse for knowing how Grace's death has affected you."

I sighed, "I'm on it. Taking Layla to visit the island was a turning point for me."

"I know this. It was the sign I had waited for, but you need to start really living again. I know it's hard but it's time to let Grace go. Something as profound as this will always stay with you, but you need to come to terms with it or it will destroy you. Don't let it do that, otherwise you may as well all have died that day. Layla deserves a dad who is happy. You owe it to her as well as yourself. Most of all you owe it to Grace's memory."

"Angus…"

"Dorian has a letter for you. Grace gave it to me, and I have always carried it with me when we visited, but she made me promise only to give it to you when I thought you were ready to read it. I never felt the time was right until you told me you were taking Layla to the island and going back to work. Before I left I gave it to Dorian and told him to give it to you tonight because I felt if I gave it to you myself before you left it would have given you time to find something in it that stopped you from going again.

My heart raced knowing Grace had sent me a message from beyond the grave. Initially I was angry he had been judging me all this time and held back, and he was right my resolve suddenly wavered about me leaving Layla behind when the insecurity of what I was about to do washed over me.

"Gotta go, I'll call you," I mumbled, not trusting myself to say anything else, because I knew what would leave my mouth would be full of hate and angry words. I closed out the call and slumped slowly onto my bed. A tight knot formed in my stomach, my chest felt tight and the all too familiar feeling of loss of Grace threatened to overwhelm me again.

Fighting back the suffocating feeling, I stood and then ran down the stairs and tore out of the house. Seconds later I banged repeatedly on Dorian's door. He opened it with a shocked look on his face, then his expression changed as he realized why I was there.

"Angus has spoken to you?"

"Give me the letter."

"Come inside," he urged, and I shook my head.

"Give me the fucking letter," I repeated in a more forceful voice, tears brimming in my eyes.

A look of resignation passed over his face and he turned, walking away from me.

Following him into his living room, he went to a small box over by the chair he always sat in and pulled out a long white envelope. I stuck out my hand to take it and he hesitated, pulling it slightly away.

"This is to help you, Cole, not to set you back, you hear?"

I gestured a 'gimme' wave with my hand and nodded.

Placing the letter in my hand, Dorian grabbed me and hugged me tight to his chest before I had the chance to move. "Angus told me he was with Grace when she wrote this, she told him she loved you but she was ready to go."

Stepping back, I separated from him and shook my head. "No mother is ready to die when they have just brought a new life into the world."

I turned away from him, needing to get out of his house, and ran outside into the cold February air. Feeling the wind on my face, I glanced in the direction of the house then over toward the meadow. If I was reading words from Grace, I wanted to be close to her.

My chest had never felt tighter, and no letter had ever burned my fingers the way hers had as I sprinted down the hill from my house and all the way to the boat dock. Ten minutes later, I was pulling the frost-covered canopy off our pontoon boat and climbing in. Five more minutes and I was on the island, standing in front of Grace's gray marble headstone.

Scanning the hollow letters that spelled out her name *Grace Harkin*, I traced them slowly and stared through tears at the dates. The birth and death digits were far too close together. My beautiful wife had gone too soon.

"Baby, you wrote me a letter," I hesitated, choking on the emotion in my throat before roughly swallowing it down. "I... it's been six years since you passed, and you had no idea how hard it would be for me walking this life alone without you." More tears blurred my vision for a moment and I blinked them back before I slid my finger into the seal and tore the envelope open.

Heaving for breath in the suffocating situation, I sniffed, my chest catching the sharp, cold air I took into my lungs. With a racing heart, I pulled out the envelope. *To Cole, my husband, my lover, my life.*

One page, two sides of Grace's distinctive scrawled handwriting.

Hello, my beautiful husband. If you're reading this, then my wonderful dad thinks the time is right. No, don't shake your head; don't cry. See? I know you well (smile). In life you gave me everything a woman could have wished for. A love that was pure, a life that was so full it often overwhelmed me, adventures beyond my comprehension, and action... plenty of action; both in and out of the bedroom (wink).

Was it too short? Absolutely. Are we angry about this? Yes, like raging bulls to a matador... I know this... me too. But I could never have wished for a better person to spend the whole of the rest of my life with, since I met you... and I did. You may not have realized this, but I was the lucky one. The one who got to live the perfect life with the only man who held my heart. The man who gave me so much love my heart was fit to burst every time he looked at me with so much love in his. You did this, Cole, and I felt it every day.

The ache in my heart made my eyes close, blinding me from her words, like I was shutting out the wave of excruciating emotions washing over me, coursing through me. My fist tightened, crushing her words in my fist momentarily, as dealing with them cast a heavy shadow over my soul.

Standing, silently I allowed my turbulent emotions to run their course until my strength returned and the tears subsided, before I smoothed out the creases from the paper and returned my focus to her letter again.

I want you to know I'm sorry. Sorry you didn't get the happily ever after I had with you. Sorry you were the one left behind. Sorry you faced the future with Layla alone. But you see, Cole, had it been you who went first, I know my heart would never have survived the pain. God knew this, and it's why he took me first.

Time is short, too short for all the things we needed to say to each other, but really the only things that are important to say are these. I'm leaving this earth with a settled, happy soul, but in so much pain I am resigned to my fate. I have no fear for Layla because I know if anyone can protect our daughter, and do what's right for her, it's you.

Go with your gut, Cole, it's never done you wrong. I'd always suspected you were in touch with your feminine side with that intuition of yours (smile).

Now for the part you won't want to hear (nods). Yes, I know you so well, as to know how hard my passing would have been for you, but, my darling Cole, it's time. Time you let me go. Time you began to move forward. Time you put the wonderful memories of us to one side and learned to live again. No. More. Tears.

My dying wish is that you live for the both of us, experience that full to bursting joy in your heart we once shared together. Laugh breathlessly, get fall-down- drunk, find a beautiful girl and fall in love; fall for her so hard and deep it washes away our tragedy and the searing pain you carry in your heart. I want you to write her love songs, sing them to her in the rain. Hell, strip naked and dance in it if that's what floats your boat... but I want you to feel the passion of living again.

Do this not only for yourself, do it for Layla. The rest of your life is a gift, Cole. You walked one path and now you need to walk another. Don't walk it in pain and anguish; instead do what I know you can. Fly in the face of your sorrow, and love with all of your heart. The person you choose doesn't deserve to live with a ghost.

Thank you for the tremendous joy you brought me, the incredible life that we lived, and the precious beautiful child we made that lives on, with you. You were my world and I was yours, but hear me when I speak from beyond, and say now is the time to discover another life that's waiting out there for you.

My blessing is yours. Whatever you do, whomever you choose, I give you gladly to her, if she is deserving. My only wish is she loves our amazing daughter as much as we do.

Grace x.

For long painful minutes I stood silently weeping. No longer angry about the love I'd lost, my only feeling being immense sadness. Eventually the biting cold wind cut into my senses and stirred me from my trancelike state. I turned my focus to the letter again. Folding it carefully in the fading light, I slipped it into my jacket pocket and turned to walk back to the boat. Suddenly a sharp gust of wind unsteadied me, and I glanced back toward Grace's grave.

"Damn, was that you?" I joked then smiled at my spontaneous reaction. Then I thought, just like in life, Grace had knocked me off of my feet. Giving a rueful smile, I turned slowly and headed back to my life.

Stepping onto the boat that day, I felt a shift inside of me, like the burden of grieving for Grace had been lifted. It terrified and relieved me in equal measure, but I didn't know what the emotional weight of those feelings meant for my future.

CHAPTER SEVENTEEN

When the house came into view as I walked back from the meadow, Layla was waving excitedly at the front door. Next thing I knew, she started running toward me. Seeing her welcome lifted my heart and I bent down, holding my arms wide, waiting patiently to receive her into them.

When she reached me, I enveloped her in a loving embrace and spun her in fast circles on the lawn. I'm almost sure her high-pitched screams and infectious giggles were heard for miles.

"Stop, Daddy. Put me down," she shouted in protest, but I knew it was all for effect because the look of glee on her face assured me she never wanted me to stop.

"Oh, I don't know. I could do this all day," I teased, but obviously I couldn't. She was growing fast, and the weight and orientation meant I almost lost my footing. Placing her on the ground, I watched her stagger dizzily until she fell on her ass. I chuckled.

"What's gotten into you today?" she asked, mimicking something Harper would have said to her.

I grinned then tried to bite it back and looked at her more seriously. "You. You've gotten into me. Can't I spend time with my favorite girl without you busting…" I stopped because I had been about to say 'busting my balls' then remembered who I was talking to.

"What? Busting what? Your balls?" I stared wide-eyed and almost swallowed my tongue.

"Where did you learn that?" I asked, running my hand through my hair, guilt-ridden.

"You. You say it to… Matty, Harper, and Uncle Dorian," she replied with her hands—one on her hip and one counting each person on her fingers. "What does it mean anyway? What balls? I've never seen them, where do you keep them?"

If ever there was a moment when my words had come back and bitten me in the ass, it was at this precise second.

"It's only a saying, Baby," I offered, trying to dismiss it.

"Well you say it *a lot*." She paused, blinking for effect as she thought more about it. "You say it so much, if there really were balls, there would be none left to bust."

I couldn't help the chuckle that escaped my lips. "You're so right. I really need to say something else when people are getting my goat."

"Who's getting your goat? You've got a goat?" she asked excitedly, her eyes big as saucers and her face full of expectation.

"What? No. No goat… another saying… never mind." I sighed and looked down at her innocent little face, knowing in my heart Grace was right. I owed it to Layla to do better. "Let's go to the house. Do you know what's for dinner?" I asked swiftly changing the subject.

"Meatballs and sketti," she immediately replied. "I wanted mac and cheese, but Harper said I'd turn into macaroni, but sketti is the same thing just designed differently." Her rationale was spot on; pasta was pasta no matter how it was shaped.

When I pushed open the front door, the heat from inside engulfed me. I stepped aside, letting Layla walk in first. "Boots off, young lady," Matty called from the kitchen.

"All right, stop busting my balls, I'm doing it," Layla shot back.

Coughing back a laugh, I gave her 'the look' that warned her she'd gone too far, and she bowed her head to look down at the floor. The last thing I wanted was me admonishing her right before I went away, so I scooped her up and whispered in her ear. "You can only say that to me, Baby Girl."

"I'm doing it," she called over my shoulder to Matty again, and I smiled in awe at how quickly she caught on.

Wandering into the kitchen with Layla in my arms, the wickedly mouthwatering smell of basil, garlic, and red wine permeated the air and my stomach groaned as pangs of hunger shot through me.

"Smells delicious," I told Matty as I stood Layla down on her feet. Matty gave me a second look and frowned, and I guessed she had noticed I'd been crying again.

"Can you help set the table?" Harper asked Layla as I slid onto the stool next to the fridge, leaned over, and pulled a beer out from the already open door.

Twisting the bottle cap with my teeth, I took a long drag from the cool, bitter tasting liquid.

"One of these days, you're gonna give yourself a cavity doing that," Matty scolded.

"Yeah, I suppose," I mused, checking out the cap on the counter and chugging down the rest of the beer.

"Dinner is set," Matty informed us and dished it up into large serving bowls.

"Go wash up, Layla," Harper told my daughter.

"You too," Matty prompted in my direction.

Nodding, I slid off the chair and wandered around to the sink.

"Not here," she scolded stepping in front of it. "I prepare food here," she reminded me.

Shaking my head, I turned and wandered out of the kitchen and down the hall to the first available bathroom, washed my hands, checked out my red-rimmed eyes, and returned to the kitchen.

Harper placed a huge platter of cheesy garlic bread—Layla's favorite—at the center of the table and sat down. Matty followed suit with deep dishes full of her amazing meatballs and lightly buttered spaghetti. Turning back, she placed a large bowl of grated Parmesan cheese near my setting and stood back wiping her hands.

"There, I'm done for the day. Cole, I'll see you in the morning. I hope everyone has a great night." We all called out our goodbyes as Matty left and turned our attention to our food.

"Delicious," Harper groaned, slumping back and sliding down her chair; her hand over her stomach, she looked totally sated from the taste of her food.

"Yum," Layla agreed, her clothes splattered in Bolognese sauce with a face to match, "I'm stuffed."

When Harper was finished she stood up from the table, pulled Layla's chair out, and helped her to her feet. Lifting her sweater over her head, I noted the tiny sparks of electricity as her hair made static electricity from the wool.

"Yikes," Layla commented and laughed as her hair crackled for a few seconds before she quickly smoothed it down.

"Bath time," Harper informed her, "I'll go start it, Honey. Don't forget to come up before the water gets cold," she added. Without looking at me, she left the room and Layla came around the table and climbed up on my knee.

Placing her hands on my face like she always did when she had something serious to say, I waited patiently for her to let me know what was on her mind.

"You won't forget me when you go to work tomorrow will you, Daddy?"

Her words crushed me. "Baby, look at you. I could never forget you, not even if I wanted to. You're so precious, you know that?"

"Mm-hm," she muttered, not totally convinced.

"Baby, it's three weeks. Twenty-one sleeps. Now I know you can count to twenty-five, because we did that leading up to Santa's visit, right?" She nodded. "So, you can count the sleeps down until I get back, and meanwhile I'll Skype every day." I watched her consider my reply in the intelligent little way she had, and she nodded again.

"Okay, I won't be sad because I'll still see you every day and you came back last time, so I know you'll come back." My heart squeezed again at how grown-up she was attempting to be about me leaving.

"Baby," I said, taking her tiny hand and placing it over my heart, "You feel my heart beating?" She nodded. "Every single beat in here has your name on it. Every single pause in between is your smile. I'll be back before you know it, and we'll do something fun together, okay?"

Nodding again, she squeezed my cheeks together, pursing my lips, and she rapidly peppered a bunch of small kisses over them. She kept on doing it and I had no idea what was going on in her head. Eventually she stopped. "I lost count, but I think there's enough there to last until you come home," she informed me, and I realized the significance of what she had done.

Feeling my throat close, I knew I had to move before I broke down and cried again, so I set her down on her feet and began running toward the stairs with her. "Thank you. Now we need to move before we both get into trouble with Harper for letting the bath get cold."

∽

With Layla in bed, I packed the last few things I intended on taking with me and stowed them neatly in Stuart's car. He had left it open outside the house, ready for me to load, and was driving me to the airport to meet the guys at the private airplane. I closed the trunk, went straight back inside, and up to my bedroom.

Stripping off my clothes, I took a hot shower, dried myself off and lay naked on my bed. Even though it was a bitterly cold February night outside, my bedroom felt stiflingly hot. I flipped through the TV channels on my remote and lay back to watch a biographical documentary on David Bowie to distract myself from darker thoughts. It must have worked because I don't remember falling asleep.

My TV timing out woke me up. The room was in darkness, but somehow, I knew I wasn't alone. My bedroom door was ajar and there was a distant light somewhere down the hall. "Layla, is that you, Baby?" I asked shifting onto my side and pulling the comforter over the lower half of my body.

"It's me," Harper mumbled in a low tone.

"Harper? What are you doing in here? What's wrong?" Shifting up onto my elbows, I tried to focus in the dark.

"Nothing," she sighed, "No, that's a lie, everything. I'm sorry. I heard the TV from outside and I knocked, but when I opened the door, it switched off. I thought you did it when you saw me come in."

"No, I was asleep, it timed out. What can I do for you?"

Harper chuckled in the dark, "You can't say stuff like that, Cole." I got the double entendre as soon as she said this and my dick bounced with interest against my leg. The flirty sound of her voice tugged at an invisible cord inside of me, sending sparks of possibility I was tired of fighting.

"Why are you here?" I asked, trying carefully to keep any encouragement from my voice.

"To make things right between us."

I sighed because the attraction that had built between us during the previous months, and the subsequent rift it had caused, was torturing us both.

"What do you want me to say, Harper? You're a beautiful girl. But you're the light to my dark. We would never work, and I'm leaving tomorrow."

"Which is why I decided this couldn't wait another day. You may meet someone…"

"You deserve way more than I can offer. More than I'm ready to give… may ever be ready to give."

"Noted. I get you."

Walking past the window, her slender silhouette cast a darker shadow as she moved across the room; then I felt the mattress dip near my knees.

Drawing in a deep breath, I sighed. "Harper, this is not a good idea. If you stay in here, I guarantee you this won't end well," I warned, feeling my restraint slipping.

"If I stay here, it could be the start of something," she argued.

"Is that what you think? The start of what? More heartache for me? For you, when I make you feel you're second best for my affections? Do you really want to compete with a ghost? If not, then it's exactly why you shouldn't be here. Have you not been listening to me?"

"I've listened, Cole, and I've made my own observations, years of them. Don't you think I've tried to be objective about this, wondering if this isn't some stupid crush I've developed for the unobtainable? After six years, very long years I might add, I'm sure it's not."

"I'm your employer for Christ's sake, my daughter relies on you." I knew it sounded conceited and aloof because we both knew she was more than this.

"Despite what you say, your actions speak louder than words. Verbally, you've been extremely clear in what you don't want to happen, but how you've behaved, the way you almost lost it on Christmas night, how you've avoided being in the same room as me..." She left the rest of the explanation for me to decipher. "We both know this attraction isn't superficial, even if you tell yourself it is."

I closed my eyes to shut out my feelings, even though she couldn't see my face in the dark. Deep down I always knew Layla wasn't the only reason for not being with Harper, that reason alone would never have stopped me in the past. It was because when I was with her I had started to feel things, other things; she stirred my emotions in ways I felt uncomfortable with.

I felt frustrated by the way my body reacted around Harper and hated the thoughts I had no business having. They weren't welcome. When I looked at her she triggered butterflies, excitement, dark moods, and feelings of guilt and disloyalty to my late wife.

Harper's advances had also prompted me to face the fact that I was conflicted between feeling excited and the need to cling to a memory because I was petrified I was falling from Grace. Falling away from a part of my life so significant it had paralyzed my soul and rendered me terrified of opening my wounded heart to someone else.

My raw attraction for Harper left me with an ache of want in my stomach and a heart torn in half between grief and something else— possibility.

I had tried everything to resist this beautiful, trusting woman who was willing to take a chance with someone as damaged as me. Why was I resistant? Grace was gone. There was a wall around my mind and I'd hid behind it for so long, I had no idea how to behave. I knew if I stepped out in front of it the world would have changed.

I was torn between being with a gorgeous girl made of real flesh and blood and remaining loyal to a ghost. Yet, the letter from my wife had spelled it all out. I had her blessing. Facing my denial meant admitting my thoughts and fantasies no longer included Grace. They were unequivocally full of Harper.

Lastly, the passionate memories of my time with Grace were fading and no longer wounded me in the same way that they had; replaced by my curiosity and wonder of how it would feel to face my vulnerabilities about falling for Harper. *Is this what's happening?*

When the mattress decompressed as Harper stood, I figured my words had done the trick and she had risen to leave. I heard her move away, but when I saw a glimpse of her frame fleetingly move past the door and the crack closed, and the sound of the lock engaging told me this wasn't the case.

When I felt the mattress dip again, this time the impression deeper on Grace's side of the bed, something inside me snapped. The last thing I would have done was take any woman in the bed that had held so many memories of my wife. The bed where Layla was conceived... the bed where we drew plans for a family and had lived, laughed, and loved.

CHAPTER EIGHTEEN

*P*rior to Grace, my life as a rock star had been full of debauchery, with one-night stands, lewd, often public sex acts and propositions, but the man I'd become was so far removed from the carefree risk-taker I had been back then.

Subsequently, I was drowning in responsibility; a broken man, perhaps beyond repair. With Harper testing my position, I found myself less forceful and more reluctant to make a decision about how to respond to her advances.

Reaching over, I tapped the light on the nightstand and stood up naked off the bed. Harper's eyes flew to mine then down my body. Her eyes widened. "Up. Get the fuck off the bed, now."

Sitting curled up in my bed in a tiny pale pink tank, her hard nipples visible; and some short pajama bottoms, she looked paralyzed by my reaction. When she didn't move, I strode around the bed and dragged her to her feet by her wrist and made for the door. "What the fuck..." No matter how appealing she looked, I wasn't fucking her in my bed.

Fueled by anger and conflicting feelings, I pulled Harper down the hall. Her long hair whipped from side to side in her silent struggle as we passed by Layla's room. Opening Harper's bedroom door, I swung her roughly inside, closed the door softly behind me, and shoved her crudely down on her bed. Determined to keep the upper hand, I caged her to her mattress with all of my limbs. Her breath hitched, and her eyes filled with fire.

"You're determined not to take no for an answer?" My question was laced with a mixture of frustration and anger as I shook the mattress beneath her, bouncing her on the bed.

"You want this as much as I do," she spat back, her eyes ablaze with the same sass I'd witnessed before when she'd almost pushed me too far. Placing her hands on my sides, she forcefully pulled me closer. I landed heavily on top of her and she let out a grunt.

My taut, ready body lay against her soft heaving chest, down her whole front actually, and I felt myself weaken when my cheek brushed softly against hers. Leaning up on my forearms, my felt my cock grow thicker as I watched her staring back in defiance. My restraint... disintegrated.

For a few long drawn out seconds, our powerful gaze turned to unbridled desire as the weight of her stare tipped the balance. My ragged labored breaths masked her more rapid breathy ones as our next move depended on her.

My gaze warned her, 'Don't,' my primed and wanton body asked, 'Why not?' If I had to trust anyone to open my heart to, Harper would be the one... then I reminded myself I'd already had 'the one' and look how that had turned out.

Lighting doesn't strike twice in the same place—mostly anyway, I told myself. Then again, the chances of it striking at all were slim at best. Yet it had struck... and we'd crashed and burned. Pushing those thoughts from my mind, I intensified my gaze, and the longer I searched into her soul, the more I feared this was a mistake.

Despite all my reservations, my indecision turned to dust as my need for female attention and my blistering lust for Harper took over.

Suddenly the waiting was done, and I couldn't wait to touch her any longer. I surprised myself by how tenderly I smoothed down her hair and carefully cupped her head in the palms of my hands before my lips took hers in a punishing kiss. She kissed me back with as much passion as I gave—harder in fact— biting my lip and sucking greedily at my mouth,

Feeling her sense of urgency as she took what she needed from her frantic first real taste of me stoked my desire all the more. Surprisingly, Harper wasn't afraid of the chance we were taking and felt every bit as confident in her actions as she was with her words. There was no holding back.

"Oh," she let out on a moan and the soft seductive sound vibrated into my mouth as her hands threaded through my hair and gripped it possessively. It undid me, and my hands swept into her hair, pulling several low growls of satisfaction from her throat.

"Mm," I murmured, my reluctant response to the pleasurable pain she spurred within me. She set me on fire as she touched me gently in all the right places that left me weak to resist and determined to satisfy the rising passion within her.

I became aware of my weight pressed heavily against her and rolled her onto my chest. My hands found her shorts waistband, and I slid one inside.

Groping a large handful of her smooth silky flesh made my pulse kick up a notch, and my eager cock pulsed in reaction. It was a simple move, but I'd fantasized about grabbing her ass since the first day I'd seen her doing those sexy yoga moves that had taunted me.

Pulling her hair back, I stared up at her in the dark, silent room and slid my middle finger farther round and into her warm wet folds. She was barely visible in the dark, and apart from our excited exchange of breaths, we stalled, in limbo.

Harper placed her forehead on mine. "Don't think, feel," she whispered, her hot breath fanning my face as she leaned forward and kissed the corner of my mouth. Aroused beyond measure, I yanked her hair back up again and gazed intently into her eyes, as love and hate warred inside me. Every cell I possessed screamed at me to forget the past and act.

I'd already passed the point of no return when I had made the conscious decision to remove her from my bed, because my subconscious mind knew how this would end, but not in my marital bed.

Until then I had never expected to feel this level of intimacy for anyone other than Grace. My thick hard cock strained in desperation. The undeniable want in me dripped from my slit as precum prepared my body to betray my tormented mind.

Taking my hand out of her shorts, I moved both to the bottom of her tank top, grasped the hem and slid it up and off her body. At the same time, I rolled her over onto her back again and covered a dark-pink pebbled nipple with my mouth. Harper gasped with the greedy suck I took. "Oh God," she said through a breath at the long awaited contact followed by, "Jesus," in reaction to the small sharp bite I couldn't resist.

Seconds later, I stripped her down, tearing the pajama shorts roughly down her legs, and tossing them over my shoulder.

As soon as my mental barriers fell, my hands trailed from her thighs back up over her breasts and I stilled when the sight of her totally naked took my breath away. *God she's beautiful.* I took more than a few rapid heartbeats to appreciate her as she wrapped her hand around my thick girth, gazed up at me with eyes full of lust, and gave it a firm squeeze.

"Fuck."

The relief I felt at her touch was immeasurable and the sudden pang of desire which shot through me made my cock strain harder in her hand. I leaned over her body on all fours, she stroked steadily at my dick as I swept her long dark hair over her shoulder revealing the pale creamy skin on her neck.

For a split second I hated how my weak, wanton body deceived my hurt and damaged mind, until Harper's soft breathy moans demanded my undivided focus on pleasuring her.

"Mm," she murmured as my hand slid down her ribs, across her hip, and between her legs. She shivered in reaction before they spread wide and willingly, and my fingers found her hard swollen clit and her soaking wet seam. "Oh, Cole," she murmured in a breathy tone.

Squeezing my hand between her ass and the mattress, I pressed her closer as anticipation and want riddled my whole body with a vibratory hum of coiled restraint. "Fuck, look at you," I cussed, taking her in, desperate for more. Spreading her long, toned legs wider, Harper wrapped them around my back and pulled my body down on hers.

My hard, throbbing cock nestled along her soaking seam, her desire coating it with her wet, warm nectar, and nothing in this world could have prevented me from grinding urgently against it. It felt like Heaven and Hell, just like she was light to my dark, then the dam within me broke.

Elbowing my way down the bed until my knees hit the floor, I moved my straining arms around her thighs and dragged her swiftly down the bed. She yelped in surprise, "Ah," before I positioned her so that her gorgeous little ass hung free of the mattress.

Palming her globes in each hand, I glanced up at her face. "Look at me," I commanded as I tilted her warm wet pussy up to my mouth and held it poised there for a second. Harper's pulse beat wildly in her belly as her body hummed with need, and it drew a smile from my lips to see how much I affected her.

Ducking my head between her legs, I closed my eyes, and breathing slowly through my nose, inhaled deeply, savoring the moment. Opening them again, I fingered gingerly at her beautiful pink folds, noting how bare and smooth she was, and then at how perfectly her outer lips parted and displayed her intimate wet warm flesh inside.

Sliding my cheeks up her silky thighs, I held her gaze and blew on her white-hot heat. A tremor of anticipation thrummed in her tight fleshy thighs, and I swiped her clit once with my tongue, catching a first taste as I eyed her reaction and basked in her response.

Harper's lust-filled eyes rolled back in her head as she dropped off her elbows and fell backward into the mattress. I hadn't performed oral sex on any woman since Grace, and I felt strangely emotional when a soft "Oh," fell from her mouth.

For many men, oral sex was par for the course, something they did frequently, but for me it was reserved for the handful of women who mattered. I'd always known Harper mattered to me, but when I performed the intimate act on her I ignored the frightening realization she could easily matter even more.

Harper looked beautifully vulnerable as she came around my fingers, and on my tongue; my head clamped between her legs as they shook uncontrollably. Pinning her lower limbs almost too tightly, I held her in place and continued to pleasure her. She began to scream when it all became too much and I clamped my hand over her mouth in my effort to muffle the sounds.

From my perspective I hadn't even started with what I could have done to her, but as she caught her breath and climbed back up onto her bed I lay on my back beside her.

"Damn," she muttered in a tired gruff voice, and I chuckled.

"I know, right?" I agreed, stretching my jaw left and right to ease the cramp.

Scooting down the bed, she grabbed my dick in her fist and covered the tip with her mouth. I felt too desperate for relief to resist her.

Tightening her grip on my cock, she took me deeper; her teeth grazing the underside of my dick and I immediately fisted her hair. "Oh, God," I muttered as shivers of delight passed through my body and I began setting the pace by tugging on her hair as her head bobbed up and down. In mere minutes I began fucking her mouth, chasing my release.

Rolling her over onto her back, I stood off the bed and fucked her mouth faster, "Grr, fuck," I grunted loudly until her throat relaxed, and I bottomed out. With my cock squeezed tight, I stilled. I almost came right in that moment, but I breathed deeply and held it there for a few seconds. "Fuuuuuuuck."

Feeling my cock deep in her throat, on the edge of orgasm was almost overwhelming. Choking, she tapped my leg, and I looked down at her watery eyes and I let her go. Harper gave a small cough then gasped loudly as she came up for air.

With her still on her back, I took her hands and placed them on her tits, pushed them together and slid my long, swollen cock between them. As the pressure of my release built rapidly inside, I fucked her enveloping flesh, gritted my teeth, and I chased my release. When the sudden lightheaded wave of ecstasy rushed through me, my heart immediately slowed to a strong and healthy beat and I spilled my seed on her neck and hair.

Afterward, she rose on one elbow, smiled in her post orgasmic haze and stared at me pointedly; like she expected me to comment. Nothing came to the forefront from the sudden chaotic thoughts in my mind.

When I had nothing to say, Harper rolled away from me and rose off the bed before quietly going into her bathroom. Seconds later I heard the shower water running and her sudden change of pace gave me time to think.

Fooling around was one thing, fucking her when I was leaving wasn't how I rolled, no matter how much either of us would have wanted to do it. I'd been weak, jumping off the fence for one night, but the last thing I had been willing to do was fuck her and run.

Lying in her room suddenly felt all kinds of wrong, and when I heard the shower start, I remembered I'd come on her hair. I quickly got off her bed, left her room and went back to mine before I changed my mind.

After cleaning myself off, I slid between my sheets and fortunately in the aftermath of my orgasm, I quickly passed out.

CHAPTER NINETEEN

Waking to a pair of freezing cold feet frightened the crap out of me. "Fuck," I cussed, grabbing a small ankle and realizing Layla had snuggled in.

"You said fuck," Layla scolded, wagging her little finger at me as she stared out from under my comforter.

"Geez, Baby, you can't do that stuff; you gave me a fright."

"Matty told me to come and get you up if you're taking me to school, like you promised. Squinting bleary-eyed at the clock on my nightstand, I saw it was less than an hour before it was time to go.

"All right, Sweetheart, please tell Matty to give me ten. I want three pancakes, two strips of bacon, and two sausage patties. Can you remember all of that?"

"Yep," she replied, climbing backward off the bed with purpose.

"Gotta grab a quick shower, so no coming back and..."

"Get cleaned up and don't be all day about it."

I sniggered at her sassy order because I'd heard both Matty and Harper use it on Layla regularly.

My daughter left the room, and I hurried through my morning routine of showering and shaving before I made my way out to Stuart's car with the last of my toiletries.

I was thankful I didn't have long to be around Harper after what had happened between us. I figured the best thing I could do all round was to act normally and accept it happened. *At least I didn't fuck her.* Feelings aside, we had both scratched an itch in a moment of weakness, but I felt confused by the feelings I had.

With everything packed away, I had no excuse to stay away from the kitchen, and I wanted to spend my last twenty minutes at home with Layla.

Entering the kitchen, I noticed Harper was pouring coffee on the other side of the counter, so I focused my attention on Layla. "Hey, Baby," I cooed, bending to kiss her head and stealing a strawberry from her pancakes.

"Stop, Daddy, I only have four left," she protested, and I grinned.

"Clever girl, you can count," I teased, and she smacked my hand away when I reached out pretending to go for another.

"You're taking me to school, right?" she queried.

"Yep, Stuart is driving us, and Harper will pick you up," I informed her, glancing at Harper properly for the first time since I'd been in there.

My heart stuttered in my chest when I saw the tired, drawn look on her face and noted her eyelids were puffy. *Shit, she's been crying.*

Matty had been busy with her back to us, putting my breakfast together on the plate, but turned to look pointedly at me. "You almost didn't get any breakfast. Imagine sleeping in this morning of all mornings," she admonished, as she put the plate in front of me.

"Sorry," I mumbled. *I never got to sleep until around 3:00 a.m.*

"You feeling okay?" I glanced at Matty and saw her eyeing me with concern.

"Sure, I'm just tired. It must be the cold weather." Cocking her head, she considered my answer and nodded before walking back to the sink.

Harper took her coffee and wandered over to the couch in the den at the end of the kitchen. Sitting down, she placed her coffee on the table and picked up her phone, then appeared to be texting with someone. I ignored her presence and focused on Layla again as I ate my breakfast.

As Layla and I chatted, I could feel Harper's eyes on me. I wanted to look over at her, but I knew if I saw a hurt look on her face I'd have needed to say something; something that wouldn't take five minutes or be resolved before I had to leave. *What was I thinking?* Truth was I had let my cock do the thinking for me because I was too busy feeling.

As I was finishing my food, Harper stood up, pulled her figure-hugging sweater into place and called out to Layla. "Go get your backpack and your coat, then put your pink sneakers on."

Layla scooted down from the table and made for the kitchen door. Matty tied a plastic bag full of trash and left the kitchen to dispose of it as Harper approached me.

"That was a shitty move you made last night," she muttered, as she walked past me and out of the door. I never went after her like I should have, and I didn't reply.

I wasn't proud of the way I left, but I wasn't the one who had made the move this time, and nothing that happened changed the fact I had to leave.

By the time I went to the hallway to pick up my jacket, Layla was swaddled up in her coat, scarf, and gloves and was ready to go. Harper reminded her she'd pick her up, and instead of addressing me, she turned and headed upstairs. As Layla made for the door, I glanced over my shoulder and watched her go. When she was out of sight I turned my focus back on Layla.

"Weren't you even going to say goodbye?" Matty asked as she came running from the kitchen. Turning to face her, I gave a sheepish grin, and she stepped forward and hugged me. "Sorry, this one distracted me," I lied.

"Have fun, Cole. You deserve to be happy. And don't worry about this little one; she'll be fine with us. She's loved and adored, so you have nothing to think about." I smiled warmly and nodded.

"I'll miss her and home every day, but I know she's in the best hands," I admitted ruefully and my throat constricted.

Hearing Matty talk about her, Layla hugged my leg and my heart squeezed tight because the reality of what I was doing brought a swell of emotion to my chest. Clearing my throat, I rubbed Layla's back.

"All right, Baby, let's get this show on the road."

Road work had meant the usual route into the airport had been blocked, and I had been left with no choice but to run the gauntlet of this public display leveled at Cole Harkin, lead singer of the band, SinaMen.

As I entered the concourse I had my first reminder of my life as a celebrity. I was a little unnerved by the groups of guys who obviously recognized me, but they stood in a huddle glancing enviously while their girlfriends fawned over me. Some looked awkward and shy, but still gravitated toward me; and there were those that suddenly ran away from their partners and came running toward me.

I'd temporarily forgotten the manhandling aspect of my job where women grabbed my face in their hands and planted rough stolen kisses on my cheeks. Having my ass felt by strangers in public wasn't my idea of fun either, but I had experienced all of those things by the time I'd passed through the airport concourse on my way to the VIP lounge.

Once I was safely on the plane, I had time to reflect on the steamy session between Harper and me. It was stupid letting it get to me because she had been the one to force things when I was in a highly emotional state after being given Grace's letter.

Still, I figured a few weeks away from home would hopefully give us both the space to realize we were driven by lust. Living in close quarters the way we did, it was natural there would be some magnetism in the absence of anyone else.

The flight to LA gave the guys and I time to catch up, and it was the first time since Grace had died my heart wasn't swamped in sorrow.

I'd all but forgotten what it was like to belly laugh, until Scuds told us a story involving a fan and we roared so hard I was breathless. Grace's letter came to mind, it was one of the things she had mentioned, and I felt free to do it for the first time in years.

As a band we owned several houses, preferring not to stay in hotels on the West Coast whenever possible. Over the years we had acquired four properties with one in Seattle, San Francisco, Los Angeles and a place in a mountain celebrity community in the Mojave Desert.

As our label also had a studio out west, we had spent a lot of time there in the past and it gave us a break from hotel and tour bus life, if the stint away from home was a bit longer.

The transition from the airport to our place in LA was much smoother than the one I'd experienced at the start of the journey. Thankfully, the landing went smoothly and we were on the road to our home away from home in LA just after 1:00 p.m. Flying against time from east to west had bought us three extra hours on our day on the Pacific coast.

During the transfer, "Highway to Hell" blared from Fletch's phone and he reached into his pocket and pulled it out.

"Yo," he answered, and we all smirked, because he was a pretty nerdy looking gay guy and it sounded stupid every time he did it.

"Sure, yep, just landed," he confirmed, nodding even though the person on the phone couldn't see him.

"Sounds awesome. I'll tell them, yep." He glanced at me. "I dunno about that, we'll do our best." He listened for a moment and nodded again. "All right, text the address and we'll see you later." Without saying goodbye, he closed the call out and shoved his cell phone back in his pocket.

"Donny Chambers has invited us to an after-party gig later. It's local, so I said we'd go."

Scuds shrugged. "We don't have the first interview until 2:30 p.m. tomorrow, so I'm game."

Moz glanced at me. "You going?" I already knew this was part of the conversation Fletch hadn't mentioned; the look of uncertainty he'd given me told me I'd been discussed.

"Sure," I replied and felt all eyes on me. I went on to tell them about the letter Grace had left for me but left out what had happened afterward with Harper.

"Good job, Cole. I'm excited you're coming with us. The whole band together," Moz mumbled with a wide grin.

"No one is ever gonna judge you if you find someone else. I'm sad for you that it's taken so long," Scuds informed me in an encouraging tone.

"I'm not looking," I said, quickly. "For a long time, I was so fucking angry, I couldn't even contemplate living without Grace, yet here I am six years later, still trying to recover. Reading her thoughts before she died really shifted my views and what she'd said was correct. I can be a shadow of myself and exist, or I can learn to live without her. Unless someone walks the path I've been walking, it's impossible to know how much it affects those of us left behind. But my family is right; it's high time I got my shit together. Grace isn't coming back, and no amount of sitting and waiting for a miracle is going to make that happen."

Watching them all nodding, I reminded myself how fortunate I was to have these guys behind me. Never once had they complained about the disruption I'd caused to all of their lives, nor had any of them become frustrated with me as I worked through my grief. Maybe because they had seen the mess I was.

Setting my overnight bag down on the luggage rack in my bedroom, I checked the three suitcases of clothes already left there for me and wandered in to my adjoining bathroom to take a shower. Once refreshed, I pulled on some shorts and a T-shirt and headed downstairs to relax with the others.

The housekeeping staff had set out a buffet of food and I helped myself to a plateful of pesto pasta and an ice-cold beer.

It had been a long time since it was just the guys and me, and because of my mindset, it had felt more like the old times for a change. Grace wasn't mentioned once, and listening to them talking about normal life made me realize how much I had missed.

Checking my wristwatch, I noted it was 3:30 p.m.—6:30 p.m. at home. Excusing myself from the group, I took off back to my bedroom to call Layla before she went to bed. We'd negotiated her bedtime to 7:00 p.m. while I was on the road.

Setting up my laptop, I climbed onto my bed, leaned back against the headboard, and hit the icon connecting me to Harper's Skype with a mixture of feelings from excitement to dread and guilt after what had happened and how I had subsequently left.

Instead of Harper answering like usual, it was Layla's face that came into view on the screen. From what I could see behind her, I knew she was sitting in my office in front of my desktop Mac.

"Daddy!" she exclaimed excitedly. "Are you with all the band?"

"Yes, I am, Baby."

"Did you eat yet?" she asked.

"A little. Pesto pasta. What did you have?"

"Noodles, beef and vegetables... and Lemon Drizzly cake."

"Aw, sounds like I missed a good one. How was school today?"

"So-so," she replied, and I chuckled at her facial expression like someone had pissed her off.

"How come?"

"Both Jaden and Tom had a fight. They both said I was their girlfriend and Jaden didn't like it, so he punched Tom on the nose."

"Wow, you already have the boys fighting over you."

"Mm-hm," she replied, "anyway, I told them they were both being silly because it was up to me who my boyfriend was, and they both told me it was none of my business and to butt out."

I laughed softly and Layla immediately scolded me. "What are you laughing at? This is serious. What if one wins I don't want?"

"Well, who do you want?" I asked, and she looked at me like I was nuts.

"I would rather have you. I told them I already had a boyfriend and they said I can't have you." My heart ached to hug her.

"Aw, you are too cute, Baby, but it's true. I'm your dad, I can't be your boyfriend as well."

"Then I'm having Stephen Moody because those twins are just ridiculous."

"Sounds like you've got it figured out," I replied, and chuckled again.

After a few more minutes, we ran out of things to say, and usually when that happened, Harper interjected and helped me conclude the call. When there was no sign of her, I eventually had to ask where she was.

"Is Harper there?"

"Yep, she's in the kitchen with Uncle Dorian." My stomach knotted.

"She's not there with you?"

"No, I just told you she's *in the kitchen*. She said when I'm done I'm to let you close the call and not to touch *anything* on your computer. She'll come and shut it off when I go back and tell her."

Fuck.

"All right, Sweetheart, I'm going to get off now and go out with the guys."

"Where are you going?"

"I'm heading to a party at one of Scud's friend's places."

"Yay. How lucky are you? I'm going to bed, but it's night here and it's still a little bit day there, right?"

"Right, Baby. You are so smart. I'll call you tomorrow around the same time, okay?"

Layla nodded and brought her face right up to the screen. "Mwah," she gushed, kissing the lens.

"Love you, my gorgeous girl."

"Love you too, Daddy," she replied and jumped down from the screen. I sat waiting as I heard her feet pitter-patting down the hall, and in the distance I heard her shout, "Harper, we're done. He's gone now."

I sat for another five minutes thinking she'd come and switch the computer off, but when she didn't appear I let the call drop.

A new frustration had taken precedence in my mind and I knew, although I hadn't initiated what had gone down between Harper and me, I knew I'd fucked up.

CHAPTER TWENTY

Stepping into the smoky, noisy atmosphere of the packed out after-party, I felt a little out of place. It had been a long time since I'd bothered to show up at parties, but I knew it was something I had to get reacquainted with. It had been years since I'd partied hard.

The one thing that hadn't changed was the number of women pursuing me, especially one in particular.

Angela Barnett had always had designs on me, and although I'd enjoyed more than a few steamy nights in her company, I wasn't interested this time around.

"Well, aren't you a sight for sore eyes," she asked in a full-on predatory tone. I'd put in a lot of time working on my health and I knew I looked better than I had in the previous few years.

"You think?" I asked, pretending I had no idea what women thought.

"Absolutely. Look at you, all lean and *hard*," she gushed with emphasis on the word hard.

"Yeah, I figured I had to work out to get back in shape for the tour."

"Well, let me tell you, it worked; you look incredible." Glancing around, I saw a girl I'd spoken to a few times who was a backup singer from Donny's band, and before Angela could monopolize my company for the night I quickly excused myself.

"Thanks, Angela. You look great too, by the way. If you'll excuse me, I promised Barna Graham I'd meet her here tonight." I'd promised no such thing, and I prayed Barna didn't have a guy in tow.

Stepping past Angela, I felt the weight of her stare as I left her behind and moved over to where Barna stood.

"Hey, Honey, how are you doing?"

"Oh, wow, Cole. I didn't know you were here. I'm good, you?" She was so casual it was like a breath of fresh air to have a woman make normal conversation with me.

"Doing better," I nodded. "First time out at a party since..."

"Yeah, I was so sorry to hear. How's your daughter doing? Lydia?"

"Layla," I corrected, "she's amazing... my whole world now."

There was no hesitation when Barna stepped forward and hugged me. "Good to see you out and about again. If you need someone to talk to, you can always call me."

"What's new on your end?"

"Same ol', supporting Donny's crew, but I'm getting married next month," she informed me with a beaming smile, as she wagged a big-assed diamond engagement ring at my face.

"Congratulations."

As Barna's fiancé was back in Arkansas, it left her free to hang around with me, and before I knew it, we had joined a group of her friends.

By two in the morning, I was very relaxed from the wine. When one of our band's slow songs came on, JoAnn, a cute, flirty dark haired friend of Barna's grabbed me by the hand and yanked me up to dance.

"This is a trip, dancing with the guy who's singing the song," she said, chuckling. "I love this tune, by the way. It's so fucking sexy." The song was about a guy pleasuring a woman with his tongue and it reminded me again of the mess I'd left behind at home.

"Yeah?" I asked, pushing the thought away and concentrating on the moment. It had been a long while since I'd danced with any woman. Previously it had been one of my favorite simple things to do in life.

"Yeah. You smell amazing. What's that cologne you're wearing?"

"Dunno, some shit in a blue bottle I got for Christmas, I didn't look at the name. I went by the woodsy smell and this one was the subtler of the ones that I got."

"Testosterone," she offered, "Smells masculine, makes you smell hot."

Chuckling, I tightened my grip on her. "How does someone smell hot?"

Placing her head on my chest she muttered, "Alluring then, you smell sexy." I scoffed at her response and we danced in silence for a minute while I mulled over her reply.

JoAnn was almost as tall as me and as I got caught up in the music, my hands wandered from her mid-back to the more natural position over her ass and I pulled her closer. Her hands immediately mirrored mine.

Fighting the instant tension I felt, I closed my eyes, pulled her flush against me and basked in the warmth of her tight warm body next to mine.

"I can feel you're enjoying this as much as I am," she taunted, lifting her head from my shoulder to look into my eyes as she rubbed her groin seductively against mine. There was no mistaking the lust in her eyes.

"Yeah? And you know this how?"

"You're not exactly small in front," she replied.

"In front?" I had a semi hard-on from her rubbing against me, but I wasn't fully erect.

Sliding her hand from my ass to my front between our bodies, she brushed her fingertips along the outline of my cock. Being slightly drunk, I let myself go and gave over to the sensation as my cock grew under her touch.

"Want to get out of here?" she murmured in my ear and our cheeks brushed as she moved away.

I shook my head because I'd already left one clusterfuck at home and I didn't have the stomach to jump from Harper's bed straight into another. "Thanks for the offer, but I'm not looking for a hookup, Sweetheart." I replied as we made our way back to the seating area we'd left for the dance floor. She grabbed a small jacket and threw mine at me. What do you say we get out of here anyway?" she suggested.

Seeing how unfazed she was by my rejection I decided to go with her because she was cool company anyway. I was shrugging my shoulders into my jacket when I eyed the door and caught Fletch watching me.

Instead of making a deal of me leaving with someone like he would have at one time, he tipped his beer in my direction and placed his bottle to his lips. Turning away, he continued talking to the group he was with and I was thankful he didn't draw attention to me.

"Your place or mine?" she asked in a confident tone.

"You live here?" I enquired.

"Ever since my daddy came here to make his first movie," she advised me.

"Your daddy?" I asked in disbelief, because I had no idea who she meant.

"Leo Moranelli, she replied, looking a little embarrassed.

"The guy with the bear and the boxer dog? You're JoAnn Moranelli?"

She sniggered and nodded. "Yep, that's me, and why is it out of all his movies, everyone remembers that one?" she asked, cringing and clearly embarrassed.

"Whoa, don't knock it. I loved it. The TV scheduling wasn't kind when they showed that movie, but it was worth it because man, that dog could sing," I replied jovially, while I chuckled and she texted into her phone.

We wandered out into the driveway and I expected to grab a cab, so I was surprised when a sleek high-end BMW drew up in front of us.

"I take it as you didn't answer my question, you're either in a downtown hotel or you're sharing a place with your bandmates."

Before I could answer, a huge beefy guy in a crisp dark suit climbed out of the driver's seat, came around the hood, and opened the back door for her. "Harold, this is Cole Harkin. Cole, meet my muscle come driver, Harold. Can you take us home," she instructed and slid elegantly into the back seat. *Muscle come driver? Now I know who she was texting.*

For a second, he hesitated, looked at me then back to JoAnn, before he replied, "Very good."

There was a time when no one could pass a billboard without seeing JoAnn's father's face plastered on it. Everyone wanted to know him, and he was still one of the most expensive actors in the business.

JoAnn's father's wealth was apparent from the moment we drew up to her property. Several armed guards with dogs guarded the high double walled property and CCTV traced our every move as we traveled along the tree-lined driveway, which eventually led to at an imposing Tuscany-style villa with terracotta tiles on the roof.

Harold exited the car and locked us in before he headed up some stairs to the double glass doors of the house. Seconds later he went inside and two guys with guard dogs appeared from either side of the front of the house.

"Is this thing bulletproof?" I asked in jest at what I deemed the security paranoia surrounding her home.

"Yeah, and bomb proof," she muttered, watching the door without any hint of humor. "He's just checking the place out before I go inside. Unfortunately, when you have a rich daddy he comes complete with a bull's-eye T-shirt." My attitude changed immediately when I vaguely remembered someone had tried to kidnap her once.

I'd always been a bit security conscious, and I knew our ranch-style home was vast, but it was as secure as I could make it from the accessible areas. Layla having a famous father was something I'd considered, and until now I had been happy with Stuart or Paul, my two burly cowboys, supporting Harper to transport Layla around, but since she was now at school and mingling with kids and adults we didn't know I had already decided security had to be improved.

Harold's return was signaled by the locks disengaging on the car and he purposefully made his way back to us. JoAnn leaned over and opened it before he reached the handle. "All clear, Jo, is there anything else?" After discussing her next day's agenda her guy was dismissed, JoAnn smiled warmly and led me inside.

For all my wealth I'd never seen anything like JoAnn's place. It was huge, long, and open-plan, but with three defined sections. At the far end, facing the pool, were rows of floor-to-ceiling bookshelves packed with novels and journals, ancient and new. A massive square wooden coffee table was situated between two velvet designer couches.

The rest of the space was filled by a state-of-the-art kitchen; a larger, more formal seating area, furnished with expensive bespoke sofas and real wood furniture, and a huge natural gas fireplace.

Strolling over to the kitchen area, I noted how it flowed seamlessly from the main living room. Yanking the tall fridge door, JoAnn grabbed a magnum of French champagne. Swiping two glasses from a low cupboard, she kicked both the cupboard and the fridge doors closed with her heel.

Making short work of the cork, she poured two glasses, held them both between the fingers of one hand and carried the bottle over toward the smaller, more intimate area I'd noted first.

Sitting down, I glanced up in time to see her place the bottle on the center table and turn to face me. Something in her smile as she handed me a glass held my gaze. Taking the drink from her, I leaned back against the couch and was surprised when she straddled my lap and sat down with her face inches from mine.

"Now, where were we?" she asked in a teasingly seductive tone.

"I turned you down, but I'm here, anyway."

"Is this is where you tell me I'm not your type?"

"No. You're gorgeous. Shit, I'm sorry, but it's nothing to do with the way you look or that I wouldn't… you know?" my voice tailed off as I ran my fingers through my hair. JoAnn deserved an explanation for me ruining her night.

Shrugging, JoAnn stood up, reached over and grabbed her glass. "More champagne?" she asked, waving the bottle before she poured herself another drink.

"If there's some on offer." I glanced at my wristwatch and saw it was 4:15 a.m.

"Do you have to be somewhere else?"

"Yeah, but not until this afternoon though," I admitted.

"Good, then we can get to know more about each other, okay?" she asked, signaling I was clearly forgiven for leading her on.

Relief washed through me and I shrugged. "Sounds good to me."

During the following two hours, JoAnn gave me invaluable insight about how to parent Layla in the future.

I had no idea why I trusted her, but like with Harper before her, I poured out my heart about missing my wife, but also shared how confused I was about what I'd done with Harper... and most importantly, my admission of doubt about my ability to be everything my daughter, Layla needed.

Listening quietly, she nodded, gave me paralanguage cues such as uh-huh, mm, and kept her eyes trained on me, even during times when I disclosed some of my more uncomfortable thoughts.

I already knew some of JoAnn's background, such as how her mom had been a beautiful Hollywood starlet, contracted to the same studio as Leo and much younger than him, and that she'd died of a drug overdose when JoAnn was almost five.

After this happened, JoAnn explained she had been brought up by a series of nannies and was homeschooled by governesses as a way of her father managing her upbringing without much involvement from himself. I decided on the spot that if Harper ever left, my music career would be done. There was no way I'd pass my daughter from person-to-person to keep making music.

"People wanted Dad's money or access to me as a way of getting some of it," JoAnn disclosed, deadpan. "It took me a long time to realize they didn't like me for who I was. They liked the thought I had access to my dad's deep pockets. His fame and fortune made me a target for social climbers, speculators, and would be kidnappers. God knows how many death threat letters my dad received about me."

"Hell, that must have been a tough upbringing."

"It was, Leo Moranelli wasn't only famous as a movie star. It didn't help he topped the Forbes Rich List for years. His shrewd investments also raised my profile as his daughter because of the trust funds he'd set up in my name. That's when the kidnap attempts led my dad to buy this place for me."

From the various documentaries that I'd seen over the years, the iconic Leo Moranelli had a ruthless reputation as a ladies' man to rival Hugh Hefner's, and growing up even I'd been aware of the vast number of women her father had been linked to.

"Well, Sweetheart, you appear pretty together to me," I remarked.

"Why are you telling me all of this?"

"I'm making you aware of how my life has been growing up motherless with a father who is famous. Layla may be small right now, but she won't always be. From all that you've told me about Harper she's a genuine girl."

"Oh, she is. I've no doubt I've seen her true colors. It hasn't stopped me from being wary about getting involved with her, though. When I think about the attraction between us, I can't help asking myself if Layla is our only real connection, and we've just been thrown together in this emotional situation."

"Why should that make any difference if you're both attracted to each other?"

Pressing my lips together in thought, I came up with a possibility. "When I'm at home we live a pretty secluded existence, much like you've talked about here," I replied gesturing with my finger at her room. "I can't help thinking had Harper and I met in different circumstances, we may not have looked at each other twice."

"And maybe you'd have fucked one another's brains out? Who knows? It is what it is, Cole. And for the record, I think Harper may be onto something. This could be the start, not the end. If, like you say, there's a genuine attraction, why wouldn't you go for it? I know you said it was because of Layla, but don't you see, Harper will leave at some point whether you test the water or not. Who knows, she may stay? I can only speak with a degree of expertise from Layla's position; it's fucking hard growing up without a mom."

"I'd never been adverse to take a risk with my music, women, or Grace. Everything was steeped in possibilities. Then one day my world as I knew it was gone. Since the day Grace died, I haven't allowed myself to think about anything other than the love I had for my wife, my loss and distress at missing her and my daughter's day-to-day needs."

The empathy in JoAnn's eyes for Layla's situation crushed me because I was staring at a woman who had walked in Layla's shoes. I loved the very bones of my daughter but hadn't shown her as much love as a father should have.

I sighed, "I've not been the best father to Layla. Going on tour when she was so small, I figured she wouldn't even notice if me being away became part of her routine. Now I feel…"

"You can stop that pity party, Cole. You're not my father, and from the conversation we've had tonight, you care very deeply for your daughter. In fact, you're sacrificing your happiness because her stability matters so much."

"God knows, I'm scared to do anything that will bring a change for her. Maybe because I don't feel totally confident I can give her all that she needs on my own. Like you already said, a young girl needs a woman, you know?"

"That's a natural reaction given what happened to Grace and how suddenly life changed for the worst. In times of tragedy, money helps but it isn't everything. Look around you, Cole. It provides a luxurious but lonely prison. Harper has been there since shortly after Layla's birth, and you've always known you could buy the services she's needed, but what about her emotional wealth and security? Yours or Harper's?"

I nodded, taking in her comments and shrugged. "Well, JoAnn, I hate the thought of you being lonely, Sweetheart, and I definitely don't want anything from you, but I'd be more than happy to call you a friend."

Smiling, she raised her champagne glass in salute. "I really get you, Cole. To friends." She clinked her glass and threw back her drink in one hit.

When I glanced at my watch and told her I had to go, we exchanged numbers, and JoAnn reminded me again to think about Harper and what it could mean for Layla and me.

"You've been so busy living in fear you've let it define you, Cole. Time to reclaim your life and remind yourself of who you are. Whatever's going to happen is going to happen. You can't will it not to. So, stop worrying about the things you can't control and enjoy the things you can. I'll give you a call in a few days and we'll talk again."

Calling a car service, JoAnn pecked me on the lips and I headed back to the band house. Everything she'd told me made sense. For someone with such a disjointed background, she had shared her sound insight and I most certainly had learned from it.

CHAPTER TWENTY-ONE

Sneaking into the house at 8:00 a.m., I felt relieved everyone else was asleep and when I climbed the stairs to my room, I finally admitted to myself I'd made a mistake in trying to ignore what was going on with Harper.

JoAnn had given me a lot to think about, but with twenty more days away from home, I figured it would give me time to work through some of the feelings I had. Then, if I still felt the same about Harper, I'd face my feelings head on.

Being out on the road kept me busy and my mind focused on my job, and the way Derek had planned the schedules for promotion with a good mix of TV, live performances, podcast and radio interviews stopped me from procrastinating. As long as he had cut time into my schedules to contact Layla before bedtime I was happy.

I surprised myself by how outgoing I'd become, and with each event, interview, and gig we played, I felt parts of my old self coming back. Banter with my bandmates helped keep my sense of humor on the road, and between us we had it in spades, but it was only when Moz pointed out how funny some of my stories were that I realized I was contributing to this more often than I had in a long time.

Probing questions regarding my love life were the focus for a couple of the interviews we had, but Derek and the PR team had ensured no one asked about Grace or Layla. I was there to spread the love of the band, not my personal shit, and I had threatened to walk away from any TV or radio show host that invaded my personal life in this way.

I was touched by how protective the guys were of me, but I could feel I was healing because my smart-mouth had returned with a vengeance, and from the challenges I'd faced from hecklers and would-be reporters looking for exclusives, I was ready to fend for myself.

With each day that passed I found myself living more in the 'now' instead of the past. Like my mindset had somehow undergone a mental reset since Grace's letter, and I was surviving instead of merely existing after the death of my wife.

My first thought in the morning, when I lay in that quiet time between consciousness and being fully alert, was still always about Grace, but the catastrophic hurt in my heart about my loss of her had become a dull ache, and my thoughts would quickly digress to the living and the near future, but mostly about the now.

During the tour, my days were so wrapped up in the promotional side of my work, there was little time to think and plenty of doing, but the evenings were mainly social or gigs, and my music brought a lot of light to my soul once again.

The real turning point for me was when I sang in the shower. It had been years since I'd done it. It may have been inconsequential to anyone listening, after all, I was the lead singer in a band, but to me it gave me the understanding I was finally moving on.

Talking to Layla on Skype was the only part of my day that brought me down because I would rather have been there to tuck her in. She missed me almost as much as I missed her. The separation made me want to be a better dad to my daughter.

Harper had gone from being absent to indifferent when I called, passing the cell phone to Layla and making herself scarce during our conversations, but I would always ask Layla to pass the phone back, and ask pertinent questions about my daughter's welfare and discuss any issues that had arisen during her day. I had fucked up with Harper, but she still had a job to do, and I was still Layla's father.

Being on tour sometimes excited me, but I missed Layla, and my heart squeezed at the thought of not being with her. I realized I missed the closeness I had with Harper too. I told Scuds everything and what JoAnn's opinions were.

"Tell Harper how you feel," Scuds advised me with only two nights left before I flew home. We were chilling out late into the night after playing a small gig at a TV host's live show.

"I intend to. When I first planned to come out on the road again, I was in denial. Harper's the reason I'm here. The tension between us put a huge strain on our relationship. I'm scared how this will affect Layla."

"Layla's a kid. She's adaptable. They take more in their stride than you give them credit for... and they're fucking observant. My nephew has the eyes of a hawk and the ears of an elephant. The stuff that kid has told me about my brother would make your hair curl," he said, chuckling.

"God, I hope so, because if I fuck this up, it's Layla that'll suffer."

"Look, like this JoAnn woman pointed out, Harper will leave anyway, at some point. If I were you, I'd tell her you want to talk. Don't just show up and switch it up. You left her hanging, man, you can't expect to waltz straight back in there and pick her up now that you've decided what you want."

"Guess you're right. I'll talk to her when I speak to Layla tomorrow and smooth the path a little for when I get home." *How the hell do I do that?*

"You should never have been a rock star, Cole. You're the least likely rock star legend in the whole history of the genre. Hell, Dorian's more rock star than you," he informed me with a roar of laughter.

"Nah, that's not true. I used to be a party animal until real life burned the fuck out of me."

"Yeah," Scuds agreed, his smile fading, clapping his hand on my knee in support.

"You've had the roughest deal a man could ever face. We were all devastated for you, and for a long time we felt you'd never recover, *but* here you are, and I for one am so fucking pleased to have my buddy back." It wasn't often Scuds offered personal feelings, so his admission tugged at my heart.

The following morning I took Scuds' advice and decided to warn Harper I was ready to talk. All day long, after I'd made up my mind, I'd watched the clock. Time appeared to drag, and even though the day's schedule was short, everything we did felt like it took an age.

When the time finally came to make my Skype call with Layla, my heart pounded in my chest and my nerves kicked in as I set up my laptop. It had been a long time since I actively pursued a woman, and given how I'd left things with Harper, I wasn't so naïve as to think she'd make it easy for me. Nevertheless, I had butterflies inside as I sat down and made the connection, and I liked the feeling.

For a few moments I was disappointed to see Layla sat in my office on my desktop Mac again. After the previous night when I'd spoken to Harper, I thought I had shifted us forward. Pushing my feelings to the side about her, I focused on Layla who talked about her day, and I chuckled at some of the comments she made.

"Miss Wild wrote a note to Jaden's mom about what she called his toilet habits, and I heard Cressida tell Harper she thought Jaden's only hope for a job when he's an adult was as a human sprinkler system." The way her nose wrinkled in disgust was too cute.

"Hm, he hasn't gotten over that one yet?" I asked sounding serious.

"Nuh-huh, and Miss Wild got pretty red in the face and gave him the same look Harper gives me when I know not to mess with her," she added.

Our conversation turned to me being home and the look of delight on her face made my heart twinge because it wasn't sooner.

"Tell you what, how's about when I come home, we saddle up your pony and we can hit the trail? What do you say to a night of camping under the stars with me?"

"Like a daddy-daughter date?" she asked, clutching her hands over her heart. Her eyes widened with excitement.

"Yeah, a daddy-daughter date," I mused, realizing apart from taking her to see Grace's grave; I'd never done anything *with* her before. She'd had parties, and I'd taken her places, but I'd facilitated her play and she'd done the activities alone. This was something we'd be doing together.

"You'd ride out with me?" she asked, and I nodded.

"Yeah," I replied. I hadn't ridden since Grace had passed. I was rusty, but I'd been riding since I was a child and no matter how long passed in between, it was pretty much like riding a bike—so long as I knew the horse's temperament.

Bouncing up and down with excitement, she squealed with delight, and the next thing I knew Dorian's face was staring down the lens at me, his hands braced on my office desk.

"Don't go exciting Layla when I'm babysitting, she won't go to bed for me," he joked, smiling warmly.

Babysitting? "Babysitting? Has Harper gone home for the evening?"

"No, Daddy, she's out on a date too. Not a daddy-daughter date or a playdate. She's going out with Ruth's daddy."

"Ruth's daddy? Layla, go get your pajamas on while I speak to Uncle Dorian for a few minutes, then you can come back," I told her, my heart rate erratic with the shocking revelation Harper was out with some other guy.

Pouting, she thought for a moment then complied with my request, and Dorian sat down in her chair. "How's the tour going?"

"Great, almost done. Can't wait to come home." The last thing I had wanted to do was to talk about my work. "Harper's on a date?"

Dorian gave me a wry smirk, "Yeah, she looked happy about it. Luke, a single dad who has a child in the same class as Layla. From what she says he's a great guy. Divorced, one kid, and he works from home."

"I don't want Layla around strange men," I snapped. It was true, but I also mentioned it as a condition to keep Harper away from him as much as possible.

"Layla has only met him when he was with his kid. They're in the same playgroup."

"So, what? This guy just rocked up and hit on my kid's nanny when she was waiting for my daughter to come out of school?" I knew I sounded ridiculous, but the question sounded reasonable enough when I thought it up in my head.

"Whoa, where is this coming from?" Dorian's eyes were huge as he stared at my anally retentive response to the situation.

"I'm serious, Dor, I don't want guys I don't know around Layla. He could be a fucking kidnapper for all we know. Have you read the newspapers?"

"Jesus, you are the last person who should be throwing that sentence around. Look at the way they've tried to crucify you over the years."

Hearing his comment made me stop ranting and absorb what I'd said. He was right, of course. I couldn't believe everything I read, because in my case it was one-percent truth, nine-percent bending the truth, and ninety-percent bullshit.

Dorian tried again. "Look, according to Harper, they got talking. He was having some issues with his kid, Ruth, since his wife abandoned them, and he asked Harper for some behavioral advice."

"Well, he gets six out of ten for originality," I replied, fighting to keep the bitterness from my tone.

"Cole, can't you just be happy for the girl? She's gorgeous, and she's given Layla a good six years. Think of it this way, if she gets with this guy, nothing much will change. She'd still be living locally, his kid is at the same class as Layla, and she'd probably still be available to work for you."

Not once during the conversation had I thought about it from Layla's future, because I felt stronger to face the daunting task of bringing my daughter up and taking full responsibility for her. I was acting out of envy for the single father who was able to see what a catch Harper was.

"How often has she met him?"

"Christ, I don't know. Not when she has Layla, I know that much. Maybe a few times for coffee when the kids were in school, but tonight is their first real date."

I felt crushed at the words 'real date.' Jealousy reared its head for the second time in as many months about another man courting Harper. First Dorian, now Mister No Name.

"Ask her to call me when she gets in, will you? It doesn't matter how late. I'll be up," I requested, not knowing what the hell I'd say if she did.

"Can't it wait?"

"No. I want to take Layla out the day after tomorrow when I get back, so there's a lot to arrange," I answered with a grain of truth in my response.

Layla came back and climbed on Dorian's knee. "All set for bed, Daddy. Two more sleeps until you can read and tuck me in, right?"

I nodded, my jaw slackening from the tension I felt from my conversation with her uncle. "That's right, Baby. I can't wait."

Concluding the call, I closed the Skype out with my stomach churning and a head full of doubts. Leaving my laptop running, I sat at the side of the bed, grabbed the remote and switched on the TV.

CHAPTER TWENTY-TWO

The boredom of watching five grown gold miners digging for pay dirt for an hour lulled me into a fitful sleep, until I woke with a start at the familiar and distinctive Skype call tone. Stretching my way out of my sleep I sat upright, my heart rate spiking at the sudden disturbance. I grabbed my laptop, resting it on my knees, and leaned back against the headboard as I connected.

Harper's face appeared on the screen. She looked gorgeous. My heart clenched at how happy she looked and a knot formed in my stomach because this was the effect of being with another man.

Glancing at the clock a quick calculation told me it was 1:30 a.m. back home and my heart sank because she was late home from her date.

"Dorian told me I had to call you no matter what time, what's up?" The casual way she addressed me was less hostile than before.

"I'm taking Layla camping this weekend. I need you to make sure she has everything she needs for a night under the stars. We're saddling up and I'm taking her for a father daughter camp out."

"Gotcha. I'll make sure Stuart has the farrier check out her pony's shoes. Anything else?"

Sighing, I ran my hand through my hair and prepared to eat crow. "Yeah, there is," I muttered, clearing my throat.

Glancing seriously at the screen, I took a deep breath. "I'm sorry for running out on you like that," I mumbled, then held my breath when she didn't immediately reply.

Twisting her lips, like the topic was distasteful she shrugged. "Okay."

"No, I really am," I protested.

"It's fine. You're right, it was a bad idea," she offered and shrugged.

"Was it?" I asked, pushing for a different response.

For a few seconds she averted her eyes and slowly nodded.

"It was wrong of me to attempt to force something you tell me isn't there," she muttered.

"Or was I the one in the wrong?"

"Meaning?"

"Meaning I've had time to think about everything… time out to view things objectively."

When she nodded in agreement, I thought she was going to accept that I'd sorted through my feelings, but her unexpected reply floored me.

"Me too, and I was wrong to push myself on you like that. I took advantage of your vulnerabilities."

"I may have been distressed and depressed about my life, Harper, but despite those facts I have always been conscious of any decision I've made. If I was as vulnerable as you think I was, I'd have taken what I needed from you without considering the consequences."

Shrugging again, she scooped up her hair and tied it up in a ponytail. My eyes cut to her neck, and for a moment I remembered the way I had kissed, licked, and nibbled it in the dark. My cock pulsed at the memory.

Realizing a long pause had stretched between us, I waited for her to reply. Eventually, she sat back in my office chair and rocked for a moment, then tilted her head to the side.

"I'm glad you stopped short, and we never fucked. At the time I felt hurt and rejected… like I was only the nanny and not good enough for your bed."

"That wasn't it at all," I protested again.

"Wasn't it? Isn't it still? While I believe everything happens for a reason, I was way out of line. You're right, I'm your employee and what I did put Layla's stability at risk."

Fuck.

The call was supposed to be about apologizing and letting her know I'd changed my mind about what happened; to hint at the possibility we could be more, but when I heard how resigned she was as to my previous point of view. I had no choice but to open up and tell her how I felt about her.

"Whether or not you are my employee has nothing to do with how I feel. Since I've had time to think I've realized how focused I was in the past. Even though Grace isn't here anymore I thought having some of those feelings for another woman meant I was being disloyal."

"So, in three weeks you've found some capacity in your heart to fit me in there?"

"That's a crass analogy," I argued.

"Is it? Can you hear yourself, Cole? *Some* of those feelings? Do I look like someone who'd be happy to be squeezed in like some consolation prize? From all accounts Grace was a wonderful woman, a beautiful woman. I'm sorry I never met her, but you're right, I can't replace her, *nor* would I want to."

"Can we talk about this when I get home? That's what this call was about."

"Was it? Or was it that Dorian told you I had a date?"

Fuck.

"It was my intention to talk to you when I called Layla this evening."

"Are you sure about that, or did it become a priority when you knew I was with someone else? I mean given your reaction when Dorian and I were alone, sharing a joke?"

"This isn't the same thing at all," I urged.

"If you say so, Cole, but if it makes you feel less anxious, Luke and I… it's very early days. One date doesn't mean I'm going to desert Layla. It'll take something special to lure me away from supporting her."

"This isn't about Layla," I argued again.

"No, Cole it's about you deciding what you want, when you want it, and how you want it. Unfortunately for you, I have a life too. You and Layla have been my priority in every decision I've made for the past six years, but I'm almost twenty-seven years old. I need to start making decisions for me." Her eyes searched my face for a few seconds. "I've got to go to bed, Layla will be up in a few hours."

By disconnecting the call, Harper gave me no opportunity to defend myself, but was right to be angry with me. I had been so absorbed in my own situation I had completely ignored hers.

∼

Moz was the first to comment about my snarky mood the following morning, not that I cared. During our radio interview I barely spoke, letting Scuds and Fletch do most of the talking. When we were finally done, I pulled out my phone and called JoAnn.

"Hey, Cole, to what do I owe the pleasure?"

"I could do with some advice," I admitted, because I wanted her opinion since she knew my story and relayed the Skype call from the night before; including my plans with Layla.

"Sounds to me like Harper's got a diversion."

"But what if he's not? What if this guy is everything she wants? I mean he's not fucked up like me. He's got a kid at the same school as Layla and he works from home."

"Or is she passing time with him? Does she really believe it's never going to happen with you?"

"I don't know what to say. How can I say I'd give her everything? Sure, I've got feelings, but I'm not ready for any kind of commitment. Lady, I lost the person I expected to spend my life with, how do I risk that kind of heartbreak again? Fuck, I sound like a broken record. One minute I think I'm moving on and the next I'm being backed into a corner."

"No one is boxing you in, Cole. This is about Harper. She has every right to make her own life. Look, all is not lost; she's had one date that you know of. You have a choice now. This girl can't be just enough for you, she needs to be *everything*. Why shouldn't she expect this? You gave that to Grace. If you can't do this, then she's a poor second, just like she feels she is."

"I know," I replied and sighed heavily. "It's too soon to know if..."

"If what? If you love her? Do you love her?"

"No... that's a lie," I amended quickly, "Yes, I do, but it's different. Different from Grace."

"Could that be because you feel disloyal by sharing yourself with someone else?"

"Of course. I never wanted anyone else. No one appears to understand this."

"I do. I get it. Someone doesn't have to die in order to break your heart, Cole. Some people experience a love that's shallow, perhaps one full of passion, and when the passion dies, they move on. Problem is not everyone loves in the same way. Some people love so deep, their mind absorbs so much pain, they never love again. Then from what I've seen in the little time I've known you, there are people like you who because you loved Grace deeply you feel it would be a betrayal to love someone else."

"Where the fuck did you get all this wisdom?"

"From experience. Like I said, you're not the only one whose heart has ever been broken."

"Tell me," I urged, because I needed to know she had connected with someone in the same way I had with Grace.

"I was seventeen."

"A crush?"

"You'd think, but no. It was the real deal. Problem was he was ten years older and married, but it was real enough."

"What happened?"

"I was mad about him, he paid me so much attention in the beginning. After a while I became his booty call. He played me for a year and I tried to be patient when he promised me the world. I guess I was vulnerable, lonely... and stupid, because I believed every one of his lines. Eventually he told me his wife was pregnant. It was a real eye opener as to who he was as a person and I dumped his ass."

"Fucker. Glad you got rid of him. He didn't deserve you."

JoAnn flashed me a forced smile, and I grinned, then her eyes grew serious. "Okay, so you have the weekend at home with your daughter."

"I'm taking her on an overnight pony trek," I reminded her.

"Sounds great. Go home and spend time with Layla. Forget Harper for a few days. Let her miss you."

"I'm not into playing games or mind fucks," I stated, frowning.

"Well, sometimes they're necessary to make someone see what's in front of them." I wasn't so sure about this, but my judgement was off, and I had to admit JoAnn appeared more clued in to how relationships worked than I was.

CHAPTER TWENTY-THREE

Layla was at school when I first arrived home, and Harper was nowhere to be seen. Dorian was busy doing a crossword puzzle in the kitchen with Matty, their heads bowed over like they were formulating a war strategy plan. Matty glanced up when she heard me enter the room.

"Cole," she said, dropping her pen on the table as she stood and rushed over toward me. "Layla is so excited you're taking her on a trail with her pony later. She's been packing and her poor pony is going to look like a mountain Sherpa's mule."

I sniggered and glanced at Dorian. "Hey, Bro, did you miss me?"

"Like a bad bout of dermatitis," he shot back.

"Yeah, you're only saying that in front of her. Once Matty leaves the room, you'll be all over me," I teased back.

"What were you two like as kids? It's a wonder your mother still has hair," she scoffed, chastising us both.

"What do you mean? We're the reason she still does. Those real hair wigs are fucking expensive I'll have you know," I joked.

Dorian was about to take a swig of coffee and sprayed out his nostrils, sending the coffee out of the cup and over the table.

"And he's back," he announced standing up and wiping the wet patches down the front of his T-shirt.

"Jesus, you see why I have to go to work? I gotta keep this deadbeat, who can't even drink a cup of coffee without help." As we all laughed, the gate buzzer sounded, interrupting us and signaling the return of Layla and Harper.

Turning, I stepped over the weekend bag I'd dumped when Matty came at me and headed for the front door. As Stuart drove up the driveway, I could see Layla's hand waving frantically from the rear passenger window.

Harper sat in the front, her large shades giving her the advantage over me because I couldn't tell what she was looking at, even if I felt it was me.

When the car came to a halt, I jogged down the few steps and opened the back door.

"Daddy!" Layla exclaimed, excitedly.

"Layla!" I mimicked back, and she giggled. Her sound was so infectious it even pulled a smile from Harper's lips.

"What time are we hitting the trail?" she asked, sounding like she'd heard the line from an old cowboy movie, and I bit back a grin. Layla could neither tell the time or knew what 'the trail' was.

"I figured we'd have a snack and a drink then we'd saddle up. How does that sound?"

"Like a plan," she replied, and I grinned again.

Bending toward her, I lifted her up into my arms. Wrapping her little ones around me she squeezed me tight. "I missed you so much, Daddy," she mumbled into my neck.

"I missed you too, Baby." Inhaling her sweet little scent was my smell of home. Pulling away from me, she cupped her hands to my face, her usual way of grabbing my attention and holding my focus.

"It's you and me... nobody else?" she asked.

I glanced toward Harper, who quickly averted her eyes by turning her head, and I nodded. "Yep, Layla, just me and my girl." I knew it was a low blow, but Harper had made it clear the day before she wanted nothing from me. If I drew a reaction, it was on her.

Sliding Layla to her feet, I took her hand and led her inside the house. Entering the kitchen again I saw Matty had pre-empted the snack and drink and had laid a pitcher of milk, freshly baked bread and some sandwich meats on the table.

Inhaling deeply, I sat quietly making up a small sandwich while Layla filled me in on her day at school. Harper had gone straight up to her room and I decided to let her stew for a day, because as much as I wanted my thing with her resolved, Layla came first.

∽

Watching the excitement almost burst from Layla's chest as I sat her on her pony was an uplifting feeling. Holding onto her reins, I led her sedate little pony, Glitter, out of the paddock as I sat on my own mare, Elbe.

Stuart had been giving Layla riding lessons on a little Shetland pony since she was old enough to hold the reins, but these days it kept her newer pony, Glitter, company in the stables. This ride was the first time Layla had been outside of the paddock with me on Glitter. I had a lot of trust in the fifteen-year-old and I'd bought her because her temperament was placid and she didn't spook easily.

"I love your cowboy hat, Daddy," Layla said, chatting easily.

"Me too, Sweetheart; it's very cool, right? Makes me look like the Lone Ranger."

"Who's that?"

I smirked, "Never mind, it was a character in a movie before your time."

Leading her down to the meadow, we followed the river east along the south side of the property. We weren't going far, but I took it slow. An hour in the saddle felt like a day at Layla's age, so we stopped at a place where I knew it was safe and we set up camp.

Naturally I cheated with a new pop-up tent Harper had ordered online and there was a box in my saddlebag crammed full of fresh morning rolls, beans, sausages, relish, and tomatoes, but we gathered dry wood and I taught her how to safely make an open fire. The look on her face was sheer delight when it began to smoke and the small kindling, tumbleweed, and twigs caught fire.

Taking a small cast iron frying pan, we cooked some sausages and beans over the fire and Layla behaved as if it were the best meal she'd ever tasted. When night fell, I took our sleeping bags outside of the tent and spread them on the ground, then lay my baby down on her back.

As we were a little way into March, it was still chilly once the sun had gone down, so I covered her up with a thermal blanket and I lay down beside her. All around us was silent, except for the crackling logs on the fire, as we both gazed up at the clear night sky.

It didn't matter that I hadn't paid attention during the astronomy lessons in science, and because Layla knew no better, I made up stories about the ones I could make out, like the Big Dipper, the Three Sisters, and Orion's Belt.

Lying beside me, her little head turned left and right and her huge doe eyes were totally enthralled by everything I told her. She even added some narrative when she tapped into her own imagination.

I was so impressed by my daughter's ability to adapt to her new situation, because it was far removed from the comfort and safety of her bed, yet she showed no fear from being out there with me.

"Which one is Mommy?" she asked, and I suddenly stopped mid-sentence from an explanation I was attempting to make about the Milky Way.

I'd never made mention of Grace being a star and I guessed it was something Harper had told her in an effort to comfort my daughter.

"Which one do you think?" I asked, feeling concerned I'd say something wrong.

"That one," she said pointing to the North Star.

"There are millions of stars up there. You sound pretty certain in your choice," I replied.

"I am because Harper said Mommy was the brightest star in the sky, and if I needed to find her, she'd be easy to spot." My heart clenched because the significance of the sentence told me Harper had anticipated times when my daughter would feel lonely and need something to identify her mom with.

"Ah, that's why you knew." I stated, agreeing with her choice.

Turning on her side to face me, she scooted over and nestled in my arms. "Yeah, you're not going to be a star soon, are you, Daddy?"

Hearing those words choked me. "No, Baby, I've no plans for that. I've got a gorgeous little girl to take care of. I aim to be around for a long, long time."

Glancing up at me, she flashed me a beaming smile and I swear she lit up the dark. "Good, because I was worried about that."

"Sweetheart, sometimes I have to go to work, and that's unavoidable, but take it from me, as soon as I can come back, I'll always be here. You're my heart and I need you as much as you need me."

Satisfied with my response she sat up and looked down at me.

"Okay, my butt feels icy, and the dirt is hard, can we get into the tent now?" she asked, moving swiftly on from her deep conversation and back to the practicalities of our night under the stars.

Sleeping with her clothes on, Layla snuggled into her sleeping bag and wedged herself up close. "Night Daddy, I love you," she confessed, sounding groggy in minutes from the cold and the late hour of nearly 9:00 p.m.

"Night, Baby, I love you too," I replied, yawning myself. It had been a very long day.

～

A freezing cold nose trailed down my neck as little iced fingers snuck under my layers of clothes. I woke with a start as my daughter struggled her way inside my sleeping bag.

"Damn, where are your socks?" I mumbled, scooping her little body into my side.

"Lost them inside the sleeping bag," she mumbled, shivering with the cold. Her cold nose skimmed my neck again, and I hissed with fright.

"Okay, Baby. It's still dark, let's go back to sleep." Snuggling her closer, I wrapped my fingers around her feet, and I sighed as we resettled comfortably. Feeling the warmth we generated between us made me tighten my grip, and my heart swelled with love for my sweet little girl.

"Glitter's hungry." Cracking open one eye, I smiled affectionately at my gorgeous hot mess of a daughter, who was standing, looking disheveled, by the zipper opening of the tent. One jean leg was tucked into a tiny scruffy cowboy boot, the other half in half out. With her hands on her hips and her crazy tousled mass of bed hair, I'd never seen her look more adorable.

"Is that right? And what about Layla? Is she hungry as well?" I asked, talking about her in third person.

"Welllll," she began, dragging the word out. "The fire's out. How will you cook something?" she asked, as she held her arms out in a helpless gesture and twisted her body to look back at the burned-out fire again.

Sitting upright, I pushed my way out of the sleeping bag and clumsily climbed out of the tent. "It just so happens I brought a little stove with us. How does fried egg sandwiches with ketchup sound?"

"Like a plan," she nodded. "What did you bring for Glitter and Elbe?"

"Look around you, Sweetheart. The land is their food, and by the looks of them they're food drunk after eating all this lush green pasture overnight. Matty did put some carrots and apples in as treats for them though."

Turning away from me, she hot tailed it over to the saddlebags and rummaged inside. "Careful, remember the eggs are fragile," I warned.

Between us we managed to make breakfast, feed the animals, and take down the tent all before 8:30 a.m. "Are we going home now?" she asked.

"Do you want to? Have you had enough?"

"Well, we could go slow, but it's mac and cheese night," she informed me.

"Good to know a trip with your dad comes second to a plate of mac and cheese."

"Don't be silly, Daddy, I can't eat you," she replied, using her innocence to answer.

Still smiling I felt a small amount of disappointment our trip in the wild was coming to an end, and strapped the rolled-up tent onto my saddle. Lifting Layla up, I sat her back on her pony and we headed back toward the house. I guessed sixteen hours with a guy six times her age got wearing after a while.

During the slow ride back toward the house we spoke about her classmates' antics. She even spoke about liking Ruth, but she didn't mention the guy Harper was seeing, and I never asked. The last thing I'd have stooped to was pumping my daughter for information, no matter how curious I was.

We arrived home just before lunch, reeking of bonfire and horse sweat, but I'd never had a better time with my daughter since the day she'd been born.

Layla had barely cast off her mucky boots before she rushed upstairs to find Harper to tell her about her adventure. Following suit, I walked past Harper's suite and into my bedroom, listening to Layla's animated storytelling about our adventure.

Stripping out of my clothes, I turned on the dial in the wall of the shower. Stepping under the hot steamy spray, I closed my eyes at the luxurious feeling of the warmth invading my bones. My back, ass, and neck ached from my night on the hard ground, but I wouldn't have swapped it for the world.

For a second I wished Harper would be as easy to please as Layla had been, but somehow I knew if I was ever going to stand a chance with her, I'd have to work hard to convince her.

Showered and dressed, I was tying my sneakers when Layla burst through my bedroom door, hair still wet and squeaky clean from the shower. "Turkey or ham?" she asked.

"Both... and tomato," I called after her as she had already turned away and was heading back to the kitchen as soon as my first word was out. Staring after her, I marveled at the energy she still had after a night of broken sleep and a few hours in the saddle.

The first person I noticed as I entered the kitchen was Harper, head down engrossed in her phone. "Anything interesting?" I asked because I was done being ignored in my own home, and I wanted her to look me in the eye. I felt buzzed from being in the same room as her again, which was a different feeling for me. I studied how beautiful she looked as she replied.

"Yeah, I have date number two tomorrow. Luke's mom is keeping his daughter this weekend and he's taking me to see Ed Sheeran." From her body language I knew she was going for a casual disclosure, like she was only dropping it into conversation, but the challenge in her eyes when they met mine told a completely different story. The arrangement was supposed to have an impact on me.

It reminded me of JoAnn's comment about sometimes games being necessary, and I nodded. "Good, I hope you have a great time," I replied, managing to sound authentic, knowing full well she'd be pissed at my nonchalant reply after the conversation we'd had via Skype.

My father used to say sometimes you need to keep women guessing, and he used to tell Dorian and me it was this tactic that had helped him snare my mom's interest and keep it. There was an almost overwhelming attraction between me and Harper, but I wasn't going to beg her to rethink her date.

CHAPTER TWENTY-FOUR

Watching Harper stroll around the house getting ready for her date almost killed me, and when she came downstairs rocking a casual but chic outfit of my favorite tight black jeans and her off-the-shoulder figure-hugging sweater, I almost growled in frustration.

Dorian had buddies down from Maine and I'd invited them over to my place for a game of poker to keep my mind from dwelling on Harper being out. As I set up the card table, I tried hard to hide my irritation at the way both Dorian and his friends checked Harper out, but I could hardly blame them. Knowing she had chosen what she wore for another man annoyed the fuck out of me.

God alone knew how I managed to play it cool, but I reasoned with myself I wasn't emotionally ready for a knockdown, drag out fight with Harper about dating someone else. Who was I to object, when I had only recently convinced myself there could be more between us?

From how Harper behaved cordially toward me when others were present and ignored me in private, I knew there were fences to mend between us, but the way she soaked up the attention from the others I could see she wanted to make me jealous.

This had given me hope. If she hadn't cared, she wouldn't have gone to all the effort of trying to get a rise out of me. She was good, but not good enough to fool a guy who'd been around thousands of women who had tried every trick in the book to make me interested.

Knowing all this wasn't enough to push past the worry of what Harper already had going with her new guy. *How can I have expectations of her when I don't know if I could give her everything she needs from me?*

Lust and raw physical attraction, friendship and trust, we already had, but did all of that equate to love? If anyone had ever told me in the past, I'd have been so indecisive about being with a woman I'd have laughed, but the future wasn't only about me, it was Layla's future too.

Despite Harper igniting feelings in me I thought died with Grace, I still couldn't help wondering if staying friends would be better than any potential broken romance for the sake of Layla.

"All set, Harp?" Stuart asked from the doorway as Harper fixed a clasp on her earring and picked up the purse she'd left on the chair.

"Yeah, thanks, Stuart." Turning to address Dorian and his friends, she flashed a beaming smile. "Nice to meet you, boys, see you tomorrow, Dor." Glancing toward me, she bit her lip and flashed me a smaller smile. "Nice to have you home again, Cole. I'll try not to make noise when I get back. Can you please make sure Paul doesn't turn on the alarm? I'll set it when I get in."

"You can relay that message to Stuart to text Paul yourself, I won't see him this evening, we're going to be busy here," I shot back curtly, picking up the deck of cards and shuffling them. For a second Harper looked unsure of herself and then turned around and left. *Fuck, I hate games.*

During the poker game I spent half of my time trying to keep my shirt on my back due to a lack of concentration and the other half checking the clock. Dorian pissed me off when he shared that Harper had sent him two short video clips of Ed Sheeran singing "Perfect." I took those videos she sent him personally, even though I knew she'd sent them, knowing he'd share them with me. *If I'd wanted to impress her, I could have flown her to the UK to meet Ed.*

Eventually, at almost 2:00 a.m., I was three grand down because my mind had been on the wrong game all night. Dorian was all in as well and we called it a night.

Seeing the guys out of the house, I glanced down the drive in an absentminded gesture then wondered why Harper wasn't home. With a wry smirk, I scoffed, closed the door and headed up to bed.

I had barely stripped out of my clothes when I heard the gate buzzer signal Harper's return. For a second my body tensed, and it was only when my jaw relaxed, I realized how keyed up I'd been because she'd stayed out so late.

When I heard her coming upstairs, I almost opened my bedroom door, but decided that would be a bad idea. Changing my mind, I pulled on some sweats and sat heavily on my bed and turned on my TV. I expected her to go into her room and was surprised when she gently knocked on my door.

Eager to see what she had to say, I wandered over and opened it. Harper stood in my doorway looking very drunk and more than slightly gorgeous. "I just want you to know I had a brilliant time, and Ed Sheeran is a much better singer than you," she said, her words slightly slurry.

"Yeah, and a good deal less drunk than you, I bet. What kind of guy have you got in tow that lets you get into this drunken state?"

"Fuck you, Cole," she barked, swiping her hand half-heartedly in my direction. "It's called fun." When her hand missed me, she lost her balance and fell forward into my room. Catching her by her waist, I dragged her inebriated body up and onto my bed.

With her flopping like a rag doll, I repositioned her, sitting her on the end of the bed at my side, and I held her up by putting my arm around her back, my hand on her upper arm. I'd never seen Harper get wasted before and I even wondered for a second if her date had spiked her drink.

Brushing her long silky hair away from her face, I caught her chin in my free hand and tipped it up to get a better look at her face. Squinting with one eye open to focus, she raised her hand and traced my jawline affectionately with one finger.

"Anyone ever tell you what a beautiful man you are?"

"Baby, I don't think you're in any kind of position to throw pickup lines at me."

"But it did get you to call me Baby," she responded with slurry speech, and she smiled like she'd won a small battle.

Ignoring her, I focused on her condition. "This Luke is one classy guy who lets his date get so fucking drunk she can't stand up at the end of the night."

"Really?" she questioned, staring vacantly at me for a few moments before she drew breath and blinked in slow motion. "Luke didn't *let* me do anything. How much I drank was *my* choice. Unlike you, Luke doesn't tell me what I can and can't do. I don't work for him."

"All right, so you let this guy think you're a lush?"

"You're jealous because he's hot and available and you're not."

"And now you're talking nonsense," I chided.

"Not nonsense," she slurred, as she hiccupped and blinked again.

"You don't even know what you're saying."

"Sure I do. Luke likes to fuck me, and you wish you were him, only you can't allow yourself to act on what we both know you feel in here," she told me, taking her hand off my face and poking a finger at the center of my chest. I growled that she'd let him inside her already.

Confirming she'd had sex with the guy made me want to vomit, but who was I to judge? My only hope was he hadn't taken advantage of her while she was drunk.

"Now I know you're way past smashed with comments like this," I remarked in frustration, noting the tension in my jaw once I'd stopped talking.

"Oh, I know what I'm saying. And do you want to know why I'm so drunk? It's *your* fault. After I slept with Luke I hated myself, because he's a really, *really* nice guy. We could go somewhere if I wanted it to, but it won't because he isn't you," she admitted, stroking my face again slowly.

"This isn't fair, Cole, none of this is fair." Tears welled in her eyes and from my perspective there was only one thing worse than a drunken female, and that was a crying drunken female.

"Look, let's get you along to your bed," I offered, trying to avert her becoming a sobbing mess.

"Yeah, and we know what happened the last time you did that. Anyway, don't. I'm not finished. The injustice of the sadness in this house is heartbreaking. I'm sad for you, Grace, Layla... what happened to you guys, but this..." she shrugged, her eyes rolling to the top of her head in thought, "this chemistry..." she paused again and inhaled deeply then stared pleadingly into my eyes. "Don't look at me like that, like you're being fucking tortured; you know what I mean? Don't deny what you feel about me."

She wasn't in any position for us to have the kind of conversation I wanted to have with her. "Go to bed, Harper. We'll talk tomorrow—"

"No! I want to talk now," she demanded and attempted to hold herself up. Flopping again, her head landed on my shoulder and she passed out. It was as if she'd used the last of her energy to assert herself. I sighed, wondering how to get her back to her room.

Glancing at her limp body, I knew she'd be a dead weight. Although I could carry her easily enough, I was concerned about leaving her. *What if she gets sick and chokes in the night?*

Moving her onto her back I gently removed her shoes and her jacket, being careful to leave her clothes on, then I picked her up and lay her on my side of my bed. Turning her onto her side, I stuffed two pillows behind her back to prevent her from rolling and pulled the comforter up to her neck.

Walking around the bed, I climbed onto Grace's side and lay staring in the dark at Harper's silhouette lying beside me.

Grief was exhausting and the climb to recovery steep, but the previous few weeks had taught me life was for the living. With that mindset I slid slowly into a restless sleep, deciding if I wanted Harper, I'd have to take a leap of faith and hope the rest would figure itself out in time.

∼

Startled awake by the bed covers sliding over my body, I rose up on one arm and realized Harper had pulled them all off of me and was lightly snoring. I snickered because I'd never seen her this way... ever. I wondered how she'd react when she woke up and found herself in my bed. My bet was she would be mortified.

Turning to see the time and noting it was almost 6:00 a.m., I slid out of bed, quietly pulled on some jeans and a T-shirt and went down the hall to wait for Layla to wake up. The last thing I wanted to happen was for Layla to find Harper in bed with me.

Like clockwork, a few minutes later she came shuffling out of her bedroom and into her playroom.

"Hey, Baby." Greeting her in a soft tone earned the same response from her as she mimicked my tone.

"Hey, Daddy, why are we being quiet?" I smiled. She was way too astute for a little kid, but I guessed this was how life was for a child in a world full of adult influences.

"We're gonna let Harper sleep in this morning," I informed her in the same quiet voice.

"Good, then I can have as much bacon and maple syrup on my pancakes as I like," she replied, conspiratorially. I chuckled softly and lifted her up in my arms.

"Sounds like a plan," I offered, and she grinned in the way kids do when they're in cahoots with an adult who's doing something they shouldn't.

Taking her downstairs and into the kitchen, I saw that Matty had already set up the coffee machine, and the mixture of the smells of that and fresh pancakes made my stomach grumble.

"My goodness, you're up early," Matty stated, narrowing her eyes at me.

"What?" I asked pretending to be shocked by her statement. "I want to spend every minute I can with my baby. Is that okay with you, Nosey Parker?" Layla giggled, and I smoothed down her hair as we took our seats at the table.

True to her word, Layla smothered her pancakes until they were swimming in syrup and had four strips of bacon. I didn't stop her indulgence, figuring everyone should live a little sometimes. Even children.

Strange thing was, I didn't find Layla's conversations trivial. I wanted to know as much as I could of her thoughts, encourage her opinions, and figure out what made her tick; but the one thing I noticed above all else was how like her mom she was.

There were these little facial expressions and mannerisms, which had nothing to do with me, but were undeniable traits of Grace, and instead of being hurt when I saw them I felt comforted.

I was thinking about this when Stuart turned up just after 8:00 a.m. and his appearance was timely as Layla was asking about Harper. Needing her to be distracted, I asked Stuart to take Layla for a morning ride, and as he told me he was going into town afterward with Peter and Diane, Layla kind of invited herself to go with them.

This couldn't have worked out better for me, because with everyone safely off the premises I was free to have the potentially explosive conversation with Harper I knew had been long overdue.

When I opened my bedroom door, I noticed the bedding was neatly in place and Harper had vacated my room. Closing it again, I made my way down to her room and knocked on her bedroom door.

Getting no reply, I opened it slowly and stepped inside and heard water running in the bathroom. I was about to call her when she shuffled through the door. She was startled to see me, and her legs buckled in fright.

"Jesus Christ!" she exclaimed, clearly shocked. "What are you doing skulking about in my room?" Her face flushed immediately, and I knew she was embarrassed about her behavior.

"I'm skulking? I knocked, you were the one who didn't answer. How's your head, by the way?"

Instantly, her shoulders sagged, and her blush crept all the way up her neck, before her questioning eyes narrowed in defiance.

"You've never seen a drunk woman before?" she asked with a raised brow.

"Oh, yeah, I've met plenty of those, but I think when you told me the guy who's fucking you was a replacement for me, I felt disappointed because I expected more from you."

Insulted by my comment, Harper flew at me in a rage and I caught her raised hand.

"Never had you down as the violent type, Sweetheart. First you want me, then you don't, and then you turn up at my door, rat-assed drunk. Are you unstable?"

"If ever there was a man who brought out the worst in me, it's you," she admitted.

"Seriously? Why, because I couldn't be what you wanted me to be when you accosted me in the dark? You think I rejected you because you weren't good enough? I was a mess, Harper. Parts of me still are, and I felt you deserved better than a man who's struggling with the collateral damage of cancer."

"Isn't that for me to decide? Don't I get the right to choose?"

"Yeah, of course you do, but I'm so fucking scared of hurting you... of being hurt like that again. Every word you said last night was the truth. None of this has been fair to you. You were dumped in the middle of a clusterfuck with a man so entirely broken it's taken years of mental reasoning for me to function properly again. You're young and beautiful and what happened in my life shouldn't be allowed to taint yours."

Harper's eyes softened. "No, it doesn't, nor was what happened my problem, but I've been here since it happened. I've seen how your wife's death almost destroyed you, and if I may speak frankly, there were times when you were a fucked-up, stubborn pain in the ass."

"Tell me about it, Baby," I agreed and ran my hand through my hair.

"Sometimes you wallowed in self-pity so often I wanted to scream when I saw what you were doing to yourself. But I've been happy to support you and your daughter through all of that because I could never imagine the pain of losing someone like either of you had."

My eyes softened. "Sweetheart, at first I saw you as a temptation; like you were somehow sent to test my commitment to Grace, even though she was gone. Then I wondered if you were a distraction, and at other times I considered whether this thing between us was because of what you meant to Layla. At those times I wasn't ready to face the future with her alone."

"Stop. Please just stop. I don't want to do this." Stepping to the side, Harper tried to get out of my way, but I blocked her.

"No, I want you to hear me out. At that time, I wasn't in control of my own world, so I knew I couldn't help Layla to manage hers. If I could take back everything that's happened between us and start again I would, but we both know that isn't possible."

Harper fell quiet and I could see her thinking. Her eyes searched the room without focus on any one thing in particular; then she glanced up at me, blushing again. "What did I say?"

"Wow, you really *were* drunk. You don't remember?"

"Bits and pieces... mostly pieces," she replied sheepishly. She winced and shrugged at the same time before she lowered her eyes like she was ashamed.

Taking her hand, I led her over to her bed and I sat us both down.

"Well, I know that you've slept with this guy," I disclosed, my jaw tightening immediately as the words left my mouth. Her guilty eyes darted to mine; yet she had no reason to feel that way. We weren't together.

"Like you were a saint while you were away," she shot back. I swallowed as I considered her statement because her assumption was wrong.

"That isn't true," I replied honestly, and I hate that you let that guy inside you."

"If we'd..." She wagged her finger between us. "I would never... but the way you left me..." She shrugged, helpless and lost for words until she added, "You were a dick leaving me like that without a word."

"I know," I admitted, feeling like a real asshole, "but I did it because the last thing in the world I had wanted to do was to use you. I've voiced it before, Harper; you matter to me. Maybe if it hadn't been my last night here, and I hadn't only just been given the letter from Grace... or if I'd made the first move..." I left the end of the sentence hanging because there were too many variables to have made the right decision. Gazing into her gorgeous trusting blue eyes I saw immediate forgiveness.

"Where does this leave us? I mean do I still have a job?" I knew she was joking, and I chuckled, then I tenderly smoothed down her hair. Holding her head in my hands, I looked into her questioning eyes as they searched mine.

"Can I take you out on a date?"

Harper's eyes widened, and she smiled. "Seriously? I should kick you in the nuts, Cole Harkin."

"Yeah, I'm serious, but only if you promise not to be knockout drunk at the end of the night," I teased.

Looking embarrassed again she laughed softly, "Depends on the company. If you become whiny and boring..." She trailed off, making a smile tug at my lips. My curious eyes ticked over her gorgeous even features for a moment and I leaned in closer.

Tracing one hand over her brow, around her cheek and down her nose, I savored the moment of being able to touch her properly for the first time without feeling riddled with guilt. My mouth watered, and I swallowed audibly at the significance of the moment. I was touching Harper intimately because I felt compelled to.

A soft sigh of relief escaped her lips, and she closed her eyes as she basked in the moment. Tipping her chin higher, I brought our lips closer and our shallow breaths quickened in anticipation of the kiss we both wanted to share. In the end it was me who took the initiative.

Pressing my lips to hers, a soft breathy moan of relief immediately passed them. "Cole," she murmured as I pulled back and pressed another to the corner of her mouth. Pulling back to take another look at her, I smiled small, then bigger when I saw her smile in return, and then I kissed her again, really kissed her.

Unlike the raw, desperate, lust-filled, frenzied kisses we'd shared in the dark many weeks before, this one was slow and unhurried—a sensual kiss that was different from any other I'd had since Grace.

Palming the soft skin of her jawline, her cheek, I trailed my fingertips up her neck, before I buried them in her hair. Harper's warm hands explored me in return, sliding under my T-shirt to trace the lines of my ab muscles, smoothing her palms over my pecs, and skating them around to my back. Both of us shivered; reacting to the firey chemistry igniting between us.

It wasn't long before a burst of adrenaline bumped up my heart rate, and I tore my lips away because one small kiss between us was all I could trust myself with, deciding if we were going ahead and exploring our feelings, then there was a condition attached.

"I'd rather Layla didn't know about this for now, and I want you to know it's not because I don't think we'll go anywhere—"

"No, I get it," Harper quickly agreed. "We shouldn't risk disrupting her. You don't have to worry, no matter what happens, I'll be in Layla's life for as long as she wants me to be."

Relief washed through me, because although it wasn't a very romantic start, the decision to keep our feelings a secret at least until we knew what they truly were, felt like the right thing to do.

CHAPTER TWENTY-FIVE

"We need to take this downstairs." Leading Harper out of her bedroom, we headed to the kitchen as I cleared the husky lust from my voice. I poured us some coffee and placed the mug on the table because I felt a physical barrier was needed to keep us in control. I wasn't willing to jump her at the first opportunity and our experience of being alone in a room together had a poor track record.

If we were going forward, I knew when I finally did take Harper, I wanted it to mean more than a frantic lust filled twenty-minute ride.

"First things first. Text that guy and tell him you're done."

Harper pulled her phone out of her pocket but placed it on the table. I knew she'd probably talk to him later about it, but I wanted to voice my request to ensure the significance of what I was saying.

"Before we go ahead with this, I want you to understand what you're getting yourself into. I want you to understand how numb I sometimes feel, like my heart has stopped beating, yet somehow I'm still living and the never-ending hurt continues to live on. It's like I wish my existence on Earth would hurry up and be over in this life. A thousand nights full of breathless tears, that's what I'm clawing my way back from."

Glancing up, my eyes met Harper's across the table and she winced at my description of my loss.

"That's how I felt about losing Grace. Coming back from something like this takes a huge amount of bravery, and if I've learned anything from this whole horrifically raw experience, it's that I wasn't an innately brave man; it's been an extremely tough skill to learn."

Leaning over the table, Harper placed a hand over mine. "You're right, I don't know the feeling, but I know how it feels to watch someone walk that walk, Cole, because I've been here every step of the way." For a long moment I stopped thinking and stared at her before I considered her answer. I'd never viewed it this way before, but she was right. I nodded, accepting her point and my heart squeezed at the dedication she'd shown my daughter and I.

"Everyone suffers love and loss at some time. Some feel it harder than others. The length of time it has taken for you to pick up the threads of your life tells me you love deeply. I'm not a replacement for Grace... I'd never want to be. If we do this, you need to be prepared for risk, but it's not one-sided. There's a bigger risk here for me than for you."

Nodding slowly, I accepted her comment because what she said was true. How does a girl go from filling one role to one person to being two people's everything? Then I considered maybe Harper had been everything to Layla and I a long time ago and I'd been too selfish to see it.

"Indeed, and you have to believe me when I say the reasons for holding back with you were mainly for your benefit... and Layla's of course."

"I got that. I've always accepted Layla's needs are your priority, but one day she will be grown. Before then, it's up to you to teach her how to live. The life you lead means she will undoubtedly be of interest to the public because of who you are. I can teach her manners, humility, caring, kindness, assertiveness, and etiquette, but I can't teach her about wealth and fame." I sighed.

"You are a fabulous person, you know that?"

"Ah, now he gets it," she teased and flashed me a soft smile.

"I don't deserve someone like you in my life," I stated with the self-loathing view I had of myself since I'd lost Grace.

"Yeah, you do, and you deserve to have fun." Harper's eyes darted around my features, taking me in, then in a softer tone she squeezed my hand. "You deserve all that life brings. So far you've only seen its extremes, the fame, adoration, fortune, and all the ugly, painful and heart-wrenching misery it has to offer. Maybe it's time to learn about all the simple pleasures in between."

"You're a philosopher, you know that?"

"Not really; just someone who cares."

"Then I'm a lucky man you landed on my doorstep."

"Indeed. I was wondering when you'd notice," she replied and winked.

My lips curved in a smile and I was thankful for the frank exchange, because nothing I'd confessed had made any difference to the way she looked at me.

"I'm excited to get to know you, Harper," I told her, finally accepting it was okay to take a chance. "I may fuck up from time to time, but if you are willing to tolerate my demons then I'm looking forward to seeing what happens between us." Lifting her hand in mine I turned it over and placed her palm to my lips. "You're a lifesaver, you know that?"

"Mm, what flavor?" she joked, referring to the LifeSavers brand of hard candy.

"Obviously not cherry," I replied, referring to her non virgin state, chuckling and ducked a swat again. "No, you're a combination of lemon and lime, because this feels kind of bittersweet."

"Damn, you're corny for a rock star," she teased, laughing softly.

"And you're way too much of a distraction to be my child's nanny," I retorted back. We both grinned, and I pressed my lips into her palm again. "Thanks for putting up with me," I muttered.

"Does this mean I get a raise?" she asked in a serious tone.

"No, I'm the one that gets the raise, Baby, but if you're good I'll let you play with it sometime." My double entendre made us both laugh aloud. Letting go of her hand, I sat back in my chair, my hands clasped behind my head and I knew I sounded cocky. As I did this move, Matty bustled her way back into the kitchen.

"Jeez, guys, never get old. I'd forget my head if it wasn't attached these days," she muttered. Opening the pantry door, she pulled out her purse, looped the straps over her arm and headed back over toward the door.

"Matty, don't bother with dinner tonight. I'm driving up to the mountains later. I'm taking Harper and Layla with me."

Turning to look at me she smiled. "That's a great idea and the fresh air will do Harper good after all that alcohol she had last night."

My eyes went wide, and I glanced back at Harper with a smile, wondering where Matty had been and how much she'd heard of Harper's drunken disclosures when she came to my room the night before.

As soon as she knew Matty had gone, Harper exhaled heavily. "Ah fuck," she muttered, and I chuckled at how mortified she looked.

"You think anything gets past her? Matty's nose is far superior than any bloodhound's. There's not an event that goes by in this house she isn't aware of."

Harper's face grew scarlet, and I figured she was remembering the noises she made the night before I left. Leaning her elbows on the table she rested her chin in her hands and groaned.

"Tell me something personal about you," I asked, because I felt ashamed she had lived alongside me, and apart from knowing her parents lived nearby in Draper, she hadn't disclosed much and I'd never asked.

Everything I had needed to know about her was on her resume and background check, but I knew very little about Harper's life before she came to live with us.

Gazing up to the ceiling she gave me a soft smile. "Well, I'm the middle child of three children."

"Three?"

"Yeah, there's my brother, Baxter; I went to his wedding remember? And I have a younger sister, she's twenty-one in a few weeks."

"Oh, yeah," I agreed, a little embarrassed when I remembered the information which was in the background check we ran on her.

"Ariana is at college— MIT. She's a computer wiz and wants a career in cyber intelligence."

"Damn, bright girl."

"Yeah she is. She's pretty similar to Dorian actually. For your information, her other passion is graphic design, and it was some of her stuff I was showing Dorian the night you got jealous."

I smirked, sheepishly. "Yeah, seeing you both like that crushed me, and I had no right because I wanted you, but was still in a bad place in here," I told her, pointing at my head.

"I love Dorian, but like a brother," she stated firmly. "Anyway, what else do you need to know about me?"

"Parents?"

"Robin and Tracy. My dad's a construction worker; my mom has a small soft furnishings company, you know drapes and—"

"Jesus, I know what soft furnishings are. They sound like hard working people."

"They are," she said, smiling affectionately at the mention of them.

"What else?"

"Not much. I was a good kid, good scholar, good girl until I met Millar Sorenson. He promised me the world and broke my heart. Made me jaded about men. I decided after him I never wanted to get married."

"Never? Hm, tell me about him."

"Well, unfortunately for me, Millar was too good of a teacher. He took my virginity and taught me everything I know about sex. He was a good lover and according to him he'd taught me well... which would imply I was better than average as well."

I waggled my eyebrows and smiled then my expression fell serious again. "So, what happened?"

"Anal sex was my hard limit, so he slept with my parents' next-door neighbor. When I challenged him, he told me it was my fault for not being experimental enough," she replied flatly, and shrugged.

"Wow, what a douche."

"Anyway, once a cheater, always a cheater. She's welcome to him. When he moved in with her, I put it all behind me when I came here to work."

"Don't tell me they still live in the house next to your parents?" I quipped, half-joking.

"Yep and he's still there; hence the reason why I don't make it home too often now. However, the last time he saw me he begged for my forgiveness and told me he wanted me back."

"Fuck. I hope you told him where to go, but no one should make you feel you can't go home."

"It's fine. I'm long over him now. I don't know what I ever saw in him, to be honest. Besides, he's starting to go bald. Not that I have anything against bald men, they can be very sexy, but if you knew Millar, damn he was vain," she mumbled through a soft laugh.

As we were talking, the gate buzzer sounded and minutes later Layla came running into the house. "Daddy, can we go buy some new boots? These are getting pretty snug," she asked, dropping to the floor and wrestling one off her foot.

"Of course, Baby, but wouldn't you rather go to the mountains with me this afternoon?"

A huge smile spread on her face, and she glanced at Harper. "Can we take Harper?"

I glanced at Harper like it was Layla's idea, "Wow, that's a great idea, Baby. Harper would you like to come for a ride with Layla and me to the mountains?"

"I'd like nothing better," she replied, trying to sound surprised. "Go get a warm coat and some sneakers, Layla. Let's see how fast you are, I'll race you." Both Harper and Layla took off up the stairs and Stuart glanced over at me with a knowing smirk on his face.

"She was as drunk as a skunk last night, huh?" he mused.

"Yep," I replied, not giving anything away and waving my fingers in a 'give me' sign with my hand for him to pass me the car keys.

"Poured her heart out on the way home," he stated dryly, as he held them up and dropped them into my hand with a knowing grin.

"Fuck off, Stuart," I warned and tried to bite back my own grin. I failed.

"Yep, I'll just go right ahead and fuck off in this direction," he replied, chuckling as he turned and wandered away toward his apartment. "Oh, and Cole…" he added without turning around.

"Yeah?"

"Don't forget to wrap it up and good luck. It's nice to see you getting back on your feet... or whatever you're getting on," he laughed. "But fuck with Harper and you'll have to find yourself a new estate manager," he warned.

As he made off down the hall, I heard the girls' voices getting closer as they made their way back. I shook my head and glanced toward the stairs. Seeing them come into view I wondered if my attraction for Harper hadn't been as covert as I'd thought.

CHAPTER TWENTY-SIX

Living in the valley with Draper Mountain in our sights, meant the short drive only took fifteen minutes to the car lot at the top. Stepping out of the car, I inhaled the fresh air deep into my lungs and slipped Layla's hand into mine.

Although the sun shone, a brisk wind created some fast-moving clouds. They cast shadows, which crept over the land below as they moved past the sun. As each one passed, bursts of brilliant sunshine made the color of the lush green meadows more vibrant each time it appeared. When the wind died down, and the clouds moved slowly, we had the spectacular view of crepuscular rays breaking through.

Our clearly defined plot of land was visible from the main vantage point. However our large Colonial-style house was obscured from view behind a dense woodland. Layla was very interested in the geography of her home below and pointed out some of the landmarks she recognized. After she pointed out Grace's man-made island she fell quiet.

"Are we in the sky, Daddy?" she eventually asked.

"The sky? No, Baby, the sky is always above us," I told her, as I tried to figure out how to explain it better.

"Oh," she remarked sounding disappointed.

"We are on a planet... it's like a huge ball. We live on the outside, but it spins all the time and there's this thing called gravity, which you can't see, but it keeps us from falling off. The sky is all around the ball, so it's always above us."

Layla looked at me like I was insane, and I could see she'd dismissed my descriptive attempt to get into the mind of a small child.

"And Heaven is in the sky, right?" she asked.

"Heaven is a place you can't see, and it's really far away. You don't go there until it's your time," I blurted out because the thought of anything happening to her was unthinkable.

"My time?"

"What your dad means is no one knows exactly where Heaven is, Honey. That's why it's so special, but we think it's an incredible place where no one feels pain or suffering, and it's much higher than a rocket can reach."

Layla nodded and appeared to accept this, and I glanced at Harper who shrugged and gave me a sad smile.

My daughter then began to play a game where only she knew the rules, skipping and jumping, running back and doing it again. Ten minutes after this she became attention seeking and bored.

Proceeding to use me as a form of entertainment in the absence of anything else, she demanded a piggyback ride then this advanced to sitting astride my shoulders. As we walked along like this, Harper sneakily slipped her hand into mine, and for some reason, the simple contact of them both together made me feel whole in those moments for the first time in a long time.

"Excuse me, would you mind taking a picture of us?" A short stocky couple wearing matching waterproof coats stood looking expectantly at us. The woman glanced at me as if she knew me, but I stared through her and I saw her dismiss me. *Thank you, God.* The last thing I wanted was anyone disrupting my beautiful private moment by talking about my band.

"Sure," Harper agreed, taking the camera as I moved Layla and I out of the way. The couple struck a holiday snap pose, the man hugging the woman's waist as Harper lined up the shot of them against the view of Pulaski County down in the background.

After three quick snaps, Harper checked the pictures with the couple and handed the camera back. The small woman turned and glanced up at me. "You look like someone famous... I can't remember his name. Has anyone ever told you this?"

Squeezing Layla's leg, I shook my head, "No, I can't say they have," I replied with an innocent smile.

"Well, anyway, you're a very handsome man and you have a beautiful family."

"Thank you," Harper responded before anyone corrected her. "Hope you like the pictures; we need to be on our way," she added, concluding the interaction. We turned and walked away before the woman said anything else.

"Did that woman think you were my mom, Harper?"

"I think so."

"Everyone does. I guess it's because we're together all the time, huh?" Layla mused.

"Guess so," Harper replied, not making a big deal of it.

"I wish you were," Layla said, totally unfiltered.

Harper's eyes flicked to mine, but she didn't respond... and neither did I.

The conversation turned less heavy when Layla claimed she was starving. I lifted her off of my shoulders and stood her back down on the ground. Layla immediately attempted several cartwheels against a backdrop of Draper, entertaining us both, until she gave a theatrical bow and we clapped.

When Layla told us her tummy was grumbling again for the fourth time, we all piled in the car, and at her request, went to her favorite restaurant, 'Tha Dawg House II'. It had been years since I'd visited a restaurant like it, but the food was plain, good, and wholesome. The surroundings were simple and spartan, but the atmosphere was perfect because it was empty apart from us.

"Excuse me, Mr. Harkin, my boys just love your music," a woman gushed in a soft Southern tone. "May I ask you to sign these napkins for them? They'd be thrilled to know their momma met y'all," the middle-aged hostess probed interrupting us at our booth. She blinked slowly as she held the napkins out.

I smiled courteously and took them from her. "Sure, what are their names?"

"Wyatt, Jordon, and Nate," she replied, with a smile of affection at the mention of them.

"How old are they?" I asked, making conversation without looking at her as I got to work autographing the paper napkins. "Fifteen, thirteen, and twelve," she replied.

"Oh, my. Weren't you a busy lady?" I teased, and she glanced coyly, covered her mouth with her hand and laughed.

"Yeah, seems so," she replied as she took back the napkins I held out and examined each of them in turn. "Thank you so much for taking the time. They'll be thrilled when I give these to them."

"My pleasure," I replied, and turned my attention back to my girls. Layla looked puzzled.

"Why did you put your name on her napkins?" Layla asked.

"Because some people are strange," I replied with a small laugh.

"Harper said you shouldn't speak to strangers."

"That's right, Baby, as a child you don't. You'll learn all about this as you grow up. You see, because of my work, a lot of people listen to my music, and they know my name because they've seen me on TV. Lots more because of my concerts, right?" Layla nodded. "So, although I don't know them, they all know who I am, and because they like my music, they want to own something I've touched or put my name to."

"What? Why?" she asked incredulously with her little hands up in the air.

"I guess so they can prove they really did meet me at some time."

Layla thought for a moment then sighed and shook her head. "You're right, Daddy, some people *are* strange."

Glancing over to Harper I saw her slowly smile, and figured on this occasion, I'd hit my pitch right in explaining away my fame as our food arrived at the table.

When Layla had filled her belly full of hot dogs and milkshakes, she yawned repeatedly.

"Are you tired, Baby?" I asked glancing in the rearview mirror five minutes after we'd gotten in the car.

"If I say no, can I stay up later?"

"No," both Harper and I agreed in unison. Harper chuckled and hid her reaction behind her hair.

"Well, can I have a TV in my room?"

"No," we both agreed again, and Layla twisted her lips, her eyes narrowing in suspicion.

"Are you both having a 'No' day? Because if so, I can ask again tomorrow."

Grinning, Harper and I made eye contact, but it was Harper who spoke.

"Layla, did I teach you no means no?"

"Yes," she admitted slowly then her eyes flicked over to look at me. Glancing in the rearview mirror again she twirled her ponytail looking innocently at Harper, before looking more sheepishly at me.

"Sometimes if I ask Daddy, he says no, and if I ask him again as many times as I can, he says yes," Layla disclosed to Harper.

"Oh, does he, now?" she replied, glancing toward me and narrowing her eyes.

"Only sometimes," she added quickly, and it was so cute the way she realized she had ratted me out and tried to defend me again.

When Harper didn't say anything else, Layla fell quiet and stared out of the window. I knew from her lack of questions she was done for the day. She'd been up since 6:00 a.m. and it was almost 8:15 p.m. by the time we arrived home. Killing the engine, I turned around to look at her and my sweet little girl was hanging from her booster seat like a discarded rag doll.

"Aw," Harper and I said together in whispered voices. "Isn't she the sweetest little girl?" I asked, sounding like the doting dad I was.

"She is. There is no malice in Layla whatsoever," Harper agreed. Turning, she opened her car door before I could even think about helping her out of her seat.

"Harper," I called after her. Turning, she looked with a questioning expression.

"You're doing an incredible job with her," I praised.

"It isn't only me, everyone has a hand around here... and her dad's upped his game considerably lately." She winked.

Watching Harper as she walked around the hood gave me butterflies, because the more time I spent with her, the better I liked her. I felt as if I were seeing her through fresh eyes, or perhaps it was because the guilt that usually had accompanied my attraction to her wasn't there anymore.

Catching my eye, she became a little self-conscious and ran her hand through her hair, licked her lips, and dipped her head so I couldn't see her face in the low light. It was a rare lack of confidence from her, but my dick grew semi-hard in response.

"Leave her, I've got her," I told Harper as I exited the car. Stepping back, she made way for me to gain access and I opened the door. Unbuckling Layla from the seat belt, I gently lifted her out and put her over my shoulder. Immediately, she clutched a clump of my hair.

My heart swelled, comforted by her touch and the feel of her little body draped against mine. "If you carry her up, I'll change her and put her to bed," Harper offered. I nodded and did as she asked.

Stretching lazily, I helped Layla out of her clothes, leaving her in an undershirt and panties, then I moved out of the way and allowed Harper to finish dressing Layla for bed. Tucking her bear between the sheets, I smoothed down her hair and placed her threadbare stuffed bunny under her chin.

Signaling to Harper to make for the door, we had almost reached it when we heard a small voice. "Night, Daddy, I love you. You too, Harper," she mumbled.

Closing the door, we began to make our way downstairs.

"Thirsty?" Harper asked.

"Yeah."

"Wine?"

"Yeah, grab a bottle and a couple of glasses; I'll go check on the fire.

A few minutes later, Harper was curled up on the sofa next to the open fire with a large glass of red in her hand. "Thanks for today," she said sounding grateful, "it was nice to spend time with you and Layla like that," she added.

"Yeah, I'm trying harder to be spontaneous," I agreed.

Harper chuckled, "The point about being spontaneous is you don't have to try to do something, it just happens."

Laughing, I nodded. "Yeah, I suppose."

"That was my world before... Grace," I offered.

"Before you met her or after she passed?"

"Everything I did before I met Grace was spontaneous. I'm not the most organized person. Meeting Grace was spontaneous. She wasn't in my plans for living life as an eternal bachelor," I mused and shook my head. My voice sounded melancholic and Harper obviously noted this.

"How did you meet? I mean..."

"In a Walgreens," I blurted out and chuckled. "Hardly the most romantic place, and I'd love to tell you some amazing anecdote about how I swept her off her feet, but it was the other way around."

Biting her lip, I could see her absorbing my affectionate recollection about my late wife and I relaxed, relieved because she didn't view Grace as competition.

"How so?"

"We'd been on the road for sixteen hours straight and my mouth felt as furry as a bear's ass. I'd left my electric toothbrush at the hotel we stayed in the night before, and I guess I was being obnoxious, because I insisted the driver stop the bus so I could grab a new one."

Glancing at me like it was the most boring story on earth, I saw Harper stifle a yawn and I chuckled. "Anyway, turned out Grace was buying a toothbrush as well, and we both went for the only one either of us would use.

"Flashing her one of my best Cole Harkin rock star smiles, I gave Grace a sob story about being on the road and it being the only brand of toothbrush I used, and Grace handed me my ass on a plate about gentlemen and manners, then suggested she arm wrestle me for it."

We both cracked up laughing about Grace's sass and it dawned on me it was the first time since Grace had died I had given anyone who never knew her alive an insight into the funny side of her personality.

"So, who won?"

"I did, but I offered to swap the toothbrush for a date and she accepted. Three weeks later she gave up her job and came on the road with us, and I married her a month after that."

"Wow, so in like two months you were married?"

"Yep, and it was seven weeks too long to wait for me. I asked her to marry me every morning until she gave in." My smile froze on my face because I'd totally forgotten who I was talking to. I gave her a small smile and shook my head. "I can't apologize for how I loved her, Harper, she was my world," I stated, unashamed.

"I asked the question, Cole. I'm glad you loved her so deeply. It's good for Layla to know all of this. Who knows, maybe one day you'll love someone else in the same way. I'm not a fool and I'm not going into this blind, but if I do this with you, I expect you to respect me."

"You deserve the world, Sweetheart, and I know you make my heart lighter," I said, putting my wine glass down and moving beside her on the couch. "I'm broken, we both know that, but I'd never compare you to what I had with Grace. You're two different people and you're the two most special women I've ever known in my life... after my mom, of course," I added, and winked again.

"Wow, how did I get included in there?"

"Grace gave my baby life, and you've given me the child we shared today. She's an amazing little handful so far, and both Layla and I owe that to your dedication and support. The last few years in this household couldn't have been fun to live in."

"That's not the way I saw it. Maybe in the beginning... yeah. You were in such a dark place for a while, I wondered if you'd ever bond with Layla. Watching someone so heartbroken with the responsibility for a helpless newborn baby was overwhelming at times."

Staring into her eyes, I expected to see an element of anger or some other judgment for my lack of interest in Layla as I tried to come to terms with something that shook me to my core, but all I saw was understanding.

"Thank you for all you have done for us. I've never really voiced it before because I don't have the right words. For someone who used to write song lyrics all day long, I have nothing in me which would adequately describe how I feel about the person you are or what you have done for my daughter."

For a moment Harper's eyes ticked over my face and she shook her head. "No words are needed. When I saw you with Layla today, it reminded me of how far you've both come. You're developing a beautiful friendship with Layla, and to see this, is all the reward I need. You don't need to say the words."

As if our gaze became too much for her, she glanced down at her lap, her hair falling over her face.

"So, this guy of yours?" I asked taking the conversation back to her.

"He's not my guy," she replied giving me eye contact again.

"But he's still a sore point," I stated.

"Perhaps, but I don't love him anymore."

"No?"

"No. For the first two years here I never went home. I mean who does that? Cheats on their girlfriend with her next-door neighbor?"

"Yeah, which was the main reason I figured we were a bad idea," I disclosed. Seeing her eyes narrow, I expanded. "Not the cheating part, but you know, being attracted to you, but the thought of me fucking up the status quo here in the house made me determined not to act on it. You have *no* idea how difficult it's been, and it's the main reason now why I want to take this slowly."

"Thank you, and I get it now why you didn't sleep with me. You were acting maturely while I was acting on impulse."

Cupping her chin, I leaned in and pressed my lips to hers then pulled back without allowing it to turn into more. "Exactly, but now that we've spoken and cleared the air, I think we both know where this is heading."

If I could have captured Harper's secret smile as soon as I'd shared this, I would have locked it in a box for when I got old. Delight flooded my veins, and a happy feeling settled inside my heart, as I looked forward to getting to know her better. After what happened with Grace, it was something I never thought I'd attempt again.

CHAPTER TWENTY-SEVEN

*L*ying in bed the following morning, I tried to think of the best way to take Harper on dates without it impacting Layla. It had been obvious from Matty and Stuart's comments they knew something had gone down between us. I figured the best way to keep Layla out of the loop was to enlist the support of those in the house.

It felt weird calling a house meeting of the staff while Layla and Harper had left to go to kindergarten, and once Stuart came back, I had a word with him in private about it.

"There you go, I told you," Matty lectured at Diane and Peter and gave them a smug smile. "I've been telling these two since Christmas I thought there was something going on. The tension between you two has been so tight, I almost banged your heads together. I saw the way you looked at her, Cole, and I think Harper is perfect for you."

Matty and Diane offered to be on call to take care of Layla in the evenings after she'd gone to bed, and this would give Harper and me some time alone together.

I'd never had to enlist the help from anyone to spend time with a woman that wasn't a driver, bodyguard, or a PA, but the fact was that no one was in the least bit surprised. Dorian, the least astonished of all.

"About fucking time," he stated, shaking his head. "It's been torturous watching you two, the angst has been so intense, there were times I felt you'd combust."

I chuckled at his animated opinion. "You weren't goading me on Christmas Eve by any chance, were you?"

Smirking, he shrugged. "May have been. You only have to see the way Harper looks at you to know she's nuts about you."

"I want to do this right, you know? I'd hate for her to get hurt."

"She's tougher than you know and you're in deeper than you realize. Whether you understand it or not, she's incredible and you'll never find anyone better."

"I wasn't looking for anyone else."

"You weren't looking for Grace either, remember?"

Before I could respond, Harper strolled into the kitchen. She smelled fucking edible and looked divinely elegant in a black silk button-down blouse, black slim-fitting pants, and a white sweater tied around her neck. Her long shiny blonde hair was flat-ironed straight and hung loose. I finished taking her in and my hungry eyes settled on her pert little cleavage. She looked effortlessly beautiful.

When she suggested a movie, I knew it would take a bit of ingenuity to make this happen with any degree of privacy. Of course, I could have made some overtly romantic statement by hiring a private viewing, but I knew Harper, she was a normal girl who liked doing normal things, and while I would have been happy to do this for her, it would have made her uncomfortable.

Deciding the time for grand gestures was somewhere down the line, I enlisted the help of my brother who booked the tickets, buying just enough seats around us to give us privacy without being obvious, and spoke to the manager about having drinks and snacks already in place for us when we arrived.

Wearing a baseball cap, we entered the auditorium after the lights had dimmed and the beginning credits for the movie had started. Seating Harper first, I slid in the aisle seat and took her by the hand.

Clasping my fingers with hers, I glanced apologetically at her for having to sneak around, but the smile on her face when she looked back at me made me feel the fact we were there was all that she needed, how I made it happen was of no consequence.

During the movie, I found it hard to concentrate, with Harper smelling so alluring and sitting so close to me. Turning to look at her, I found myself engrossed in her reactions to what was happening on the screen rather than with the movie itself. I scared myself by admitting I could fall hard for her.

Eventually she caught me, her eyes going wide and her expression rather self-conscious as she mouthed, "What?"

I slid my hand around her head as if I was pulling her closer to talk, but instead I took her by surprise and I kissed her. It was slow and sensual, and I was in no hurry to ramp things up, nor were either of us ready to break the kiss either. Pressing her hands gently, she held both of my cheeks and it felt as if she was making sure I couldn't get away.

Eventually the movie ended, and out of the corner of my eye I saw the end credits for the minor roles pan up the screen. I had a minor awareness of people rising to their feet around us. I had a semi-awareness of them shuffling past us, but neither Harper nor I made to move as I experienced the longest, most sensual, yet innocent kiss of my life.

As the lights came on we broke the kiss. Harper stared passionately into my eyes, her cherry red lips, swollen and wet, and her cheeks flushed with desire.

"Wow," she whispered quietly, and continued to stare.

"Yeah," I muttered, my voice husky and my boner straining, desperately wanting to know what would happen next. Glancing around me, I saw we were the only people left in the auditorium.

"Home?" she asked, a small smile curving her lips.

"That would be dangerous," I replied with a small chuckle.

"Hence the suggestion," she stated in a serious tone.

Clearing my throat, I smiled widely, "Home it is then," I agreed, with excitement coursing through my veins.

My initial wish to move things slowly conflicted with what I'd learned from the past. Time was precious. None of us knew when ours was up. It had been a long hard fight for me to finally accept that it was possible to love someone again without diminishing the love I had for Grace.

As we left the cinema though an emergency exit Stuart was waiting in the alleyway in front of us, and as he closed the car, I had a sense of smugness about having an evening in plain sight of a hundred other people and no one had known I was there.

"Enjoy the movie?" I teased, knowing she'd only seen about half of it.

"Yeah, it was... intense," she answered, as her eyes flicked to the back of Stuart's head then looked back to focus on mine. Glancing down at our hands resting side by side, she laced her fingers in mine.

"What part did you like best?" I enquired, my eyes darting briefly to the rearview mirror to gauge how much attention Stuart was paying us.

"Call me a romantic, but the kissing scene took my breath away," she remarked, and a secret smile tugged at her lips.

"Yeah?" I asked.

"What did you think of it?" she probed.

"I reckon her panties were soaked by the end of that scene," I replied and chuckled. Stuart glanced in the rearview mirror and bit back a grin as he tried to pretend he wasn't listening. Harper squeezed my hand so tight she almost broke my fingers in her attempt to shut me up, and I decided it was fun pushing her buttons.

Leaning in toward her ear so as only she could hear, I whispered, "Your pussy just pulsed there, right?"

Watching her jaw drop and her eyes widen told me she was shocked. She had yet to learn how filthy my mind could be.

In the past when I'd wanted a girl, I took what I wanted; but Harper was different because her home was also her workplace, her work colleagues were also her friends, but more than that my daughter worshipped the ground she walked on. I'd wanted to tread with caution, but all things considered I had to be true to what was happening between us.

The rest of the journey was flirty, and Stuart largely ignored us until he dropped us off and we went inside. Suddenly for the first time, Harper looked unsure of herself. Seeing this, I grabbed her hand, smiled reassuringly and led her toward the stairs. She had gone from this self assured woman to someone who looked at a loss on how to behave now that she had what she wanted.

For a moment, I didn't know where to take her because the odds of Layla finding us in Harper's room were too high-risk a bet. I glanced at my bedroom door and dismissed it. I wasn't in a place where I felt mentally ready to take her to my bed.

"Follow me", I urged, tugging her past every bedroom door to a spare bedroom at the end of the hall no one ever used. Pulling her inside, I closed the door and led her over to the bed. "You're sure you want to do this?" I asked, giving her one last chance to back out.

"I've never been as sure of anything in my life," she replied quietly, as she stood staring into my eyes. "What about you? I'm not going to go to the bathroom in the middle of the night and find you gone again, am I?"

Guilt panged in my chest in reaction to her comment. "Definitely not. The moment I give myself to you, is the minute the uncertainty stops."

My reply brought a broad smile to her luscious lips and her eyes dropped to my mouth. Wetting my lips with my tongue, I leaned in and pressed them firmly on hers. Sliding my hands around her waist, they wandered down to her ass and pulled her closer.

"So, where were we before the lights went up again?" I asked, referring to the long hot make out session we'd had in the theater.

"I believe you were making me wet," she declared, as if she were reading the news on TV and I chuckled.

"Baby, you have no idea what I could make you do," I replied, playfully.

"No, I don't, but it's been fun guessing," she replied. I shoved her back on the bed, spread her knees wide, and settled my hips down in between them. "Oh," she gasped.

My hungry eyes fell to her cleavage as her chest heaved when she caught her breath. Instantly turned on, I felt her body vibrate with anticipation and she looked back at me, her eyes heavy with lust. As I stared at her trusting gaze I realized I desperately wanted her—no—I *needed* her.

Physically, I was a starving man; emotionally, a man deprived of the soft love of a woman, but none of that was Harper's fault. For months I'd not only been blocking my physical attractions to her, I'd been denying there were feelings I couldn't compute for someone other than Grace.

Rolling slightly to the side, I slid my hands across her blouse and tore it open in one swift desperate move. Buttons scattered around the bed and everything briefly froze as I took the time to admire her voluptuous tits and the sheen of her smooth silky skin. Her cleavage was held perfectly in place by her soft lacy bra.

Licking my lips, I held her gaze as my thumbs grazed over the center of each breast where her hard, pebbled nipples lay beneath her bra. Pushing it up I freed them, and I immediately sucked greedily at one while palming the other.

Working my way up to her neck with small kisses, I slid a hand down her belly and into her jeans. Harper gasped again, "Oh," and her head rolled back as she moaned. "Oh God," she cried repeatedly as my hands explored and my mouth tasted her body.

Sliding my finger into her soaking wet seam, my cock ached when I found her hard nub. Harper instantly tilted her pelvis toward it for better contact and ground herself with more than a hint of desperation against my hand. "Fuck," I muttered as my dick grew painfully thick and strained urgently at my jeans.

"Please," she begged, her head rolling to the side in submission as her hands fisted in frantic grasps through my hair.

Slipping my hand back out of her jeans, I unsnagged the button and slid down the zipper, grabbing both sides in my hands. Rising up on my knees, I tugged roughly at the sides as she tilted her hips to aid their release as I pulled them down. She barely got one leg free before the scent of her nectar lured me in and I hurriedly sank my head between her thighs.

"Watch me," I commanded, as I bent my head and laved my tongue hungrily along her slit. "Oh, fu…" she muttered, then let out a long breathy moan before rising up onto her elbows to do as I'd asked.

I moved my head roughly between her legs as I licked and sucked, and she bucked and moaned in response. "Oh my God. Yes, Cole." The raspy, husky tone in her voice sounded desperate.

"Fuck," I muttered, spurred on by her reaction. Climbing up off the bed, I quickly stripped out of my clothes. Grabbing my cock, I pulled on it to ease the ache; then quickly resumed my position between her legs again.

With my mouth on her pussy and my tongue buried in her entrance, Harper's legs quickly started to shake. She yanked on my hair. "No. Not like this, you. I want you." Glancing up her body, my eyes locked into hers and she silently willed me to give in to her demands.

"What do you want?" I mumbled against her pussy, because I wanted her to say it out loud. I sucked hard on her clit and her head lurched forward, her chin on her chest, her eyes widening in surprise at the sensations I evoked in her.

"Jesus," she heaved breathlessly. "Fuck me, I want... Oh," she gasped again. "Fuck me, Cole. Please." Her needy pleas dragged me up from between her thighs, and I turned to grab a condom from the back pocket of my jeans.

Making short work of putting it on, I turned back, climbed onto my knees and spread her legs wider, holding her calves in my hands. "Is this what you want?" I teased, my tip barely touching her entrance.

"Yes," she murmured.

"You don't sound very sure," I teased.

I smiled when she glared in frustration, lifted her ass off the mattress, and attempted to wiggle closer.

"Oh, my, you're so impatient," I said playfully, and she grunted and growled her displeasure. My balls were killing me, but she looked so fucking sexy when she was riled. "Hm, tell me again what you want me to do," I demanded.

"Give it to me... inside me," she demanded disjointedly in a more forceful tone, as she tried to free her legs to wrap them around my back. I gripped her legs tighter.

"I'm calling the shots, remember?" I emphasized firmly, keeping her pinned where she was by my strength.

"You're a pig," she replied, and I chuckled at how frustrated she was. Reaching between her legs, she grabbed my balls then slid her hand to my cock. Watching me intently, she grasped it and slid her fist up and down with just the right amount of pressure. I groaned, deep and she smiled.

"Fuck. You're making me feel so good, Baby," I goaded, but I made no attempt to progress things. Seeing how wound up she was, and how much she wanted me, only made me more determined to control the situation.

"Fuck me," she ordered more forcefully, gritting her teeth in frustration. When I continued to hold back, she took her other free hand and placed two fingers on her clit, rubbing in small circles and trying to get herself off.

"Fuck, that's hot," I muttered huskily, as I tilted my hips forward giving a little more pressure to her entrance.

"Please," she whispered, then mouthed the word again.

Edging my way forward on my knees, I crouched over her body and placed my forehead on hers. The gaze between us grew intense, and I cradled her head between my arms. Gazing into her eyes, I watched her tongue dart out and wet her lips.

"Take me; don't make me wait anymore," she whispered. Her lips barely moved but something in the way she whispered shifted within me. I finally acknowledged it wasn't only lust I felt. I'd held back, because I knew once I had her, my late wife's ghost would disappear. She was right; it was the start of something more; something bigger than I ever imagined I could feel for someone after Grace.

"Keep looking at me, I want to see your eyes," I ordered as I pressed myself toward her. Harper's beautiful, trusting face morphed in ecstasy as my cock slid deep inside her. Her gorgeous blue eyes first widened, then closed in a blissfully contented reaction to my thick cock filling her up inside. Her luscious lips made a silent 'O' in response to the overwhelming sensation of her tight walls stretching as I bottomed out inside her.

"Oh, damn," she husked. "So full," she gasped, and I waited a few seconds, because I wasn't a small man. When I figured she was comfortable, I began to move, speaking softly to her as I rocked gently in and out. "Is this what you were after, Sweetheart?" I asked, giving her a knowing smile.

"Feels so good," she mumbled in a breathy tone.

"How good?" I probed.

"Feels so full," she tried again and closed her eyes as she basked in the sensation.

"Open your eyes," I demanded as I rose up on my hands. I lifted my body clear and quickened my pace. Harper spread her legs wider and wrapped them around my back. Digging in her heels, she tilted her ass and took me in deeper. "Fuck," I hissed because she felt so good, then growled involuntarily at my rising desire to unleash the pent-up animal inside me.

"Don't hold back, just be yourself," Harper murmured against the corner of my mouth as if she'd read my mind. If I'd had any doubts about how to gauge how she liked it, they disintegrated the moment she uttered those words. I gave her what she wanted and fucked her totally unrestrained.

Suddenly her warm giving pussy walls resisted as her body became a tightly coiled ball of tension, her muscles squeezed my cock as her legs quivered, then shook uncontrollably as she screamed so unexpectedly loud, I had to cover her mouth with mine to swallow her sounds.

With her pussy clamped like a vise around my cock, I watched in wonder as she orgasmed and shuddered, waves of unadulterated ecstasy coursing through her body.

Letting her recover briefly, I flipped her over on her hands and knees, stopping for a moment to bask in the sight of her table top yoga position. Immediately, my carnal thoughts met my raw lust for her when I took in the naked sight of the perfect uncovered ass I had fantasized over many months before.

Naked, Harper had an ass built for sin and I couldn't resist smacking it hard and watching her sweet fleshy globe ripple seductively before I entered her again.

Of course, as soon as I slid inside, it was no longer a yoga position, but the very immodest doggy one. Gripping both hips, I glanced at the red welted mark I had branded her with, and in another burst of carnal desire, I pounded into her harder.

"Ouch," she said loudly, right before I rammed into her again, taking all memory of the pain from her as she quickly got lost in feelings of ecstasy and another unexpected orgasm. "Damn, oh," she muttered again and again, her hands gripping the sheets beneath her. Watching her twisting them tight in her fists until her fingers blanched as she moaned was incredible.

The voyeuristic view of her virgin asshole from behind made any resistance to explore it futile. Despite Harper's admission to her hard limit, I couldn't stand not to touch it.

Feeling how wet she was, I pulled out my dick, sunk two fingers deep inside her and rubbed her G-spot hard. I growled at how responsive she was to my touch and immediately I felt her walls clamp down around them as she came again.

Pulling my fingers out, I sunk deep inside her again and watched her shoulders slump down to the pillow, making the visual I had even sexier than before. Sliding my coated finger across her asshole, Harper instantly froze.

"Relax, Baby. I promise I won't penetrate unless you beg me for it," I coaxed, in a calm even tone. "Do you trust me?" she hesitated then relaxed and murmured her reply.

"Mm-hm," she agreed at last.

"Then give me your body. Nothing I've done so far has freaked you out, has it?"

"No."

"Then you have nothing to worry about," I stated and continued to move my finger gently again.

After a couple of minutes, I spoke again. "Are you still worried?"

"No," she stated, clearly.

"Do you like it?"

"I'm not as afraid of it as I was," she admitted. It was a start.

"Good, remember this, because at some point you're gonna want to tell me there are no hard limits when you're with me. My body is yours to do what you want. If you are serious about giving me your body, I want it all. When two people truly connect, there should be no limits with total trust."

As soon as I had left her feeling positive about the boundary I'd tested, I turned her over and sat her astride me.

"All right, I've done most of the work tonight, let's see what you've got," I teased cockily, and I grinned as I positioned my dick under her entrance again. Sinking down onto me, she bent her head and pressed a kiss to my lips, my tongue slid inside her mouth.

"Mm," she moaned, as her hips gently began rocking back and forth until we both came up for air and Harper sat up straight. Placing her hands on my chest, she began moving her ass and within seconds she was in total control.

When she rode me, the pressure on my cock was perfect and a few minutes later I felt my own orgasm build in my balls. As they tightened, I glanced up at the intense expression on Harper's face and my heartbeat raced. "Fuck, I'm going to come."

No sooner were the words out then I saw Harper's face relax as she let go. My balls tightened as her walls gripped me tighter and we both gave way to the pleasure that coursed simultaneously through our bodies.

"Oh, fuc...jeez," I cussed none too quietly as Harper lunged forward, worn smooth out by her effort. Her hair was soaked, her lungs breathless, as she lay on my chest. We both chuckled without any hint of shame after our marathon session.

"Goddammit," she muttered in a tired mumbled voice.

"Yeah," I agreed, my mind blown as my heart pounded steadily in the afterglow of it all. Easing her to the side of me, I rolled over and immediately dealt with the used condom still wrapped around my dick.

"We're definitely doing that again," she blurted out, unabashed, and I chuckled at the enthusiasm in her tone. "But maybe tomorrow... or definitely tomorrow," she decided, and I laughed.

As I tied the condom off and chucked it at a trash can by the nightstand, I turned, giving her a wicked smile. "Or maybe in a few hours," I agreed, with a tired smile on my face then I grinned wider.

CHAPTER TWENTY-EIGHT

"Cole," Harper whispered, as she gently slid her hand under the sheet and wrapped it around my morning wood.

"Hm," I murmured stretching lazily, as I turned my head and squinted up at her, sitting upright in the bed.

"I've got to go back to my own room, it's almost 5:30 a.m.," she informed me in a reluctant tone.

Grabbing her by the wrist, I pulled her down beside me. Turning to face her, I slid my arm under her neck. Pulling her close, I slipped my free hand over her hip and hauled her warm delicious body flush with mine.

The look between us immediately became intense, and I was torn about letting her go.

"Thank you. I had an awesome time last night," I whispered, stealing a small kiss.

Biting back a grin she nodded. "Yeah, it was a great movie, huh?" she joked.

"As first dates go, you were a bit of a slut. I mean who puts out like this on the first date? I never even bought you dinner," I goaded, and chuckled.

Moving her face closer, she went to kiss me but caught my bottom lip between her teeth. Pinching it to the point of pain, she let it go, slipped her hand lower and grabbed a firm hold of my dick.

"I wonder if it's possible to snap this?" she asked with a straight face, as she gave my cock a gentle squeeze.

"You know, I've often wondered that myself," I joked, rolling her onto her back and settling myself between her legs. My tip brushed her wet heat and I stilled. It would have been the easiest move in the world to slide inside.

Tempting though it was, my life was on the cusp of being better and I wasn't about to change it by pulling a dick move. *With my luck it would probably backfire.*

Glancing up at Harper's face, my breath caught in my throat at how gorgeous she looked in her sleepy morning state.

"Pity the condoms are all the way down at the bottom of the bed in my jeans pocket and my daughter may discover us at any second."

Genuine concern flitted through Harper's eyes at the thought and her body tensed. I loved her for thinking of Layla before herself.

"Move, she'll be awake at any time now," she ordered, trying to free herself from my hold.

Reluctantly, I shifted to her side but grabbed her and kissed her quickly again. Struggling free, she stood off the bed and grabbed her blouse off the floor. "You owe me $119.99 plus tax for this," she barked, sternly shaking it out at me before pulling it on.

"Worth every penny," I agreed, chuckling.

I especially enjoyed watching her pull on her pants and jump as she tugged them up over her ass, and I lay mesmerized by the way her tits jiggled freely in the ripped open blouse while she quickly got dressed.

Yanking the two sides of her shirt closed, she leaned over and opened the door. I called after her and she turned to face me again.

"I really did have an amazing time last night, and I can't wait until we do it again."

A wide smile spread on her lips, her blue eyes brightening in pleasure at my words. "Yeah?"

"Hell, yeah," I replied. Hesitating for a moment she stared pointedly and narrowed her eyes.

"Then you'd best get dressed, grab a hearty breakfast, and get out there and train, because you're gonna need all your strength for later."

When she closed the door softly, I flopped back down against the mattress and stared at the ceiling. The smile on my face was like nothing I'd felt in a long time and my internal feelings were somewhere between scared shitless and fearless about my budding romance with Harper.

"Daddy, are you getting up today? What are you doing in here?" Layla asked, pushing the door open and looking around the room.

"I wanted to try something different," I replied, the amusement in my own voice almost making me laugh.

"Why was Harper in bed with you?" *Fuck.* I blinked.

"What makes you think she was in bed with me?"

"I didn't think it, I found you both here. It was noisy in the night and I thought Spot was hurt, so I got out of bed and went in to wake Harper. She wasn't there." *Fuck. What did she see?*

"She wasn't in her room?" I questioned, and a small pang of guilt hit my chest at asking a question I already knew the answer to.

"Nope. Then I came to get you because the noise happened again." *Fuck.*

"And you weren't in your bed either."

"You came here?" I asked and heard the alarm in my own voice.

"Uh, huh."

"Did you open the door, Baby?" My heart beat fast at the thought she'd witnessed some of what had gone down between her nanny and me.

"Yep." I stopped breathing for a few seconds. "You and Harper were lying down. Were you having a sleepover?"

"We *were*, how clever are you?" I asked going with her theory.

"Is this a sleepover room?" I nodded.

"Did you have a good time, Daddy?"

"Oh yeah, Baby it was a lot of fun," I admitted.

"Can I have a sleepover with you and Harper next time?"

I chuckled, nervously. "We'll see," I replied, like I think most adults caught in this situation would have offered.

"Yay. So, are you coming to breakfast?" she asked, either satisfied by my reply or having her little mind's priorities right.

"Sure, Baby. Go tell Matty to start my bacon and I'll be down in a few minutes."

Layla took off along the landing and I slid out of bed, shaking my head and grinning as I thought we hadn't been half as careful as we'd thought we were.

∼

When I walked into the kitchen, Harper shot a secret glance in my direction, a smile quirking her lips.

"Morning," I offered in a cheery tone.

"Wow, you're bright this morning," Matty quipped then I saw her cringe.

"Am I?" I asked, drawing a grin from Harper.

"Daddy's happy because he had a playdate with Harper last night and they had a sleepover," Layla informed Matty. Our housekeeper almost choked, and I burst out laughing, while Harper hid behind her hair by pulling it in front of her face.

"Sleepover?" Matty's tone sounded amused.

"Yeah, I found them in the sleepover room," Layla informed us all.

Matty immediately clicked it was the spare room on the landing. "It's good that your daddy and Harper have become such good friends," she offered, trying not to look at either one of us.

"Are we baking cinnamon rolls today?" Layla asked Matty, letting the conversation drop as I approached the table and sat down next to Harper.

Sliding my hand under the table, I squeezed Harper's leg and left my palm resting on her knee. Turning to face me she gave me a small smile, but her focus was on Layla who was busy getting ingredients out of the pantry with Matty.

Sweeping her hair over her shoulder, I leaned in quickly and pressed a kiss to her neck. She shuddered, her eyes flicking from mine back to my daughter, then she boldly slipped her hand under the table too and ran the heel of her hand firmly over my semi-errect dick.

"It's a beautiful morning out there, who wants to go for a swim?" I asked, trying to ignore what she was doing.

"I have my yoga regime," Harper said.

"Me. I want to swim, Daddy."

A little disappointed Harper wasn't coming in; I coaxed a little more.

"You can come in afterward," I replied, persuasively.

"Maybe, I'll see how hot I get," she answered.

"You're already hot," I countered, no longer caring who heard it, and my open confession about what I thought earned me a seductive smile. It felt liberating to say what I felt.

Not wishing to disrupt what Layla was already doing, I went down to my office to check my snail mail from the previous few days, but seconds after I entered, Harper came rushing in after me and quietly closed the door.

"Tell me she never saw anything," she pleaded, her eyes wide.

"No, it's fine. She said we were lying down, but she asked if she could have a sleepover next time with us, so I think we're in the clear," I whispered in a low tone and we both laughed.

Stepping closer to her, I placed my hands on her hips and walked her back against the closed door. "Is it too soon to say what I'm feeling terrifies me?"

"Only if the feeling is horrible," she warned.

"It's a great feeling, but that's what's scaring me."

"What is your gut telling you?"

"It's telling me, 'Hell yeah, there's no guarantees in life.'"

"What's the worst thing that can happen? What do you fear the most?"

"You know what that is."

"No, I don't. I need you to spell it out for me."

"These feelings I have for you. After last night, I could easily go all in. I mean we've known each other for many years now and we've lived in the same house. I know you as a person. I know your personality: likes and dislikes about bands, music, movies; the way you parent my daughter... all the things it would take years to learn if we were a couple starting from scratch."

"Yeah, I get that..." Harper looked as if she was mulling over my explanation.

"What you're saying is, even though the sex part is new, we're already living as a family together?"

"Yeah. I fought what I've been feeling for the right reasons, but now I've had this mental shift in my mind. I don't want to live alone, but I'm scared to give everything in case I lose it.

"Cole, I know you've heard this all before... multiple times, but what happened with Grace was a freak event. Statistically it's extremely rare. You need to remind yourself of this and challenge it, not let it disable you from finding happiness."

"I know. I'm trying," I replied, as I gazed seriously into her eyes and smoothed down her hair.

"Try harder," she prompted, her smile softening the words. "You deserve to be happy, but you have to allow yourself to be. Believe it and you'll make it happen."

Pulling her close, I kissed her gently and pulled back. "Thank you for putting up with me all this time, I know it hasn't been easy."

"No, there are times when it hasn't, but to see you recover from then until now has been a privilege."

"All right, go and get those sexy-as-fuck yoga pants, I've got some voyeuristic tendencies," I joked. Giving her an affectionate pat on the ass, I opened the door and gently shoved her through it into the hallway. "Because if I keep you here, you'll be over my desk any second."

Walking backward, Harper grinned. "Promises, promises," she goaded, then turned and sashayed away. I smiled at her playful tone, and the seductive way she swayed her hips was designed to get a rise out of me. Adjusting my dick in my pants, I realized she already had.

During the following weeks life didn't change that much between us, apart from the fact I was more open with my feelings for Harper. Also, now that we were together, there were many more opportunities to get to know my daughter better, and Layla loved all three of us doing things together.

For a while Harper and I continued to meet in the 'sleepover' room, but the rest of the time we kept to our separate spaces, and from my point of view, this began to irritate me. With every day that passed, I found myself waiting for the times when we could spend some quality time alone. Nine weeks after Layla had found us in bed together, I'd had enough of this.

When Harper and Layla had left for school, I asked Matty to call the interior designer Grace had used. Explaining the situation, I asked her to redesign my bedroom, and after a few emails, I'd swapped out all the dark wood furniture that Grace had loved and replaced it with white high-gloss stuff instead. The bed went as well and was replaced with an awesome new custom made one. The designer informed me the changes could be completed in less than a week.

After Layla had gone to sleep that night, I told Harper what I was thinking. "What would you say, if I said it was time, we told Layla about us?"

Smiling widely, she nodded. "You're sure?"

"I am. What do you think?"

"I think it's my turn to be scared," she replied quietly, and grabbed my hand. Placing it over her heart, she prompted, "Feel." Her heart raced.

"Ah, so that's what it takes to scare you?" I asked, because she was normally so laid back.

Harper dropped my hand and hugged me tight; then she pulled her head back just enough to look at me. Her eyes softened.

"This is a massive step you're taking, Cole. I want you to be sure you're doing this for yourself and not just for me or Layla."

"Believe me, Baby, this is a move for all of us. I don't know about you, but I'm tired of sneaking around. I miss you from the moment you leave my bed until you're back there with me."

"What will Layla think?"

"Layla will think we're together."

For a moment Harper was quiet, then her eyes searched my face. "Given that I know how wary you were about shaking Layla's emotional stability and routines, do you think you're ready for this kind of commitment with me?"

"Baby, it's being sure of what was right for her that's kept me out of your pants before."

"So..." she trailed off.

"So, I'm asking you if you'll move in with me."

"We have to be sure."

"Agreed, and I am. Are you?"

"Yes," Harper interjected before I repeated the argument I had used so often before. Seeing her beaming smile made my heart squeeze at how happy I'd made her.

~

"Hey, Layla, Baby. Can you come and sit down for a few minutes please?" Harper asked as she wiped her hands nervously on her jeans and gave me a forced smile.

"Is this going to take long? I'm coloring in a unicorn in my pad."

"No, only a minute or two. Your dad and I want to talk to you."

Huffing noisily, she jumped down from her chair at the table and wandered over to the couch at the far end of the kitchen that turned into a den.

"Make it quick." Her sassy made me smirk, because she was as impatient as I was and thoroughly focused when she was doing something she enjoyed.

I glanced at Harper and bit my lip, but I wasn't worried about telling my daughter because I knew she'd be happy about the new arrangement. "What would you say if I said I love Harper?"

Harper's eyes shot to mine. I did, I just hadn't voiced my feelings to her. I hadn't intended to say it to Layla first either, the words just came out.

"Daddy, we all love Harper," she replied, impatiently.

"Yes, but because I love Harper, and Harper loves me, we're going to have sleepovers every night. If I said Harper's my girlfriend now, how would you feel about this?"

"Does this mean if Steven Moody from school is my boyfriend he has to sleep in my room?"

"God, no," I chuckled. "Harper and I are going to live like Max and Sarah-Jayne."

"Okay, so now Harper's my mom? Do I call her mommy?"

"No, your Daddy and I aren't married, but we live like I am."

"But if you get married, I can?"

"Yeah, but that's way in the future, maybe," Harper said, stumbling over the question.

"Good, now can I go back to my coloring book?"

"Sure," I told Layla, and both Harper and I shrugged at each other because she was my kid and was unfazed by our revelation. Harper and I began talking about the remodeling of my room and Layla dropped her crayon and came back to sit beside us. Suddenly she was far more excited about new furniture and cutting in on the deal, even managing to snag herself a Disney Princess mural.

When the remodel started, Harper was quiet, and I knew something was wrong. When I challenged her, she told me she didn't want to sleep in the room where I had so many memories of Grace.

"Changing furniture won't erase how you feel in that room. Please can we move into another one?"

"Fine, we'll take yours," I replied sounding indifferent, but I was pleased she'd spoken up, because she was right, and in the nine weeks we'd been together I'd never taken her in there.

Asking the designer to work with Harper on the remodel gave Harper the opportunity to choose how she wanted things to be, and it gave me the chance to spend time with Layla while the changes took place.

I was fine with everything we'd planned until it came to changing the nursery walls. My heart had felt bruised watching some of the most poignant memories from my time with Grace being harshly erased with the sweep of a rolling brush. However, although the design had held significant memories for me, Layla had no such attachment to them, and as they were in her room, it was only right I let my daughter choose.

Moving on took strength, and going forward with a new relationship, I wanted to consider Harper's feelings, and ten weeks after our first date the décor had all been done, and we finally made the shift to living openly together in Harper's newly decorated room.

"Does this mean you're my new mommy now?" Layla asked again when she saw both our clothes hanging in the closet together.

"What do you think, Baby? Hasn't Harper always been like a mom to you?"

"I suppose," she scowled with a knitted brow, "but she's *really* my mom now because you *live* in the same bed."

Her comment about living in the same bed made me chuckle because my desire for Harper was almost insatiable and life in bed with her sounded idyllic. The more time I spent with her, the deeper my feelings became. I missed her when I was without her, and like it is with any new relationship, the time we were alone together never felt long enough.

Another shift with all the changes that had happened was how I felt when I looked out toward Grace's final resting place. I no longer had the same dark angry feelings about it. Instead my emotions were more melancholic and affectionate. This comparison was something I'd have considered inconceivable before I fell for Harper.

CHAPTER TWENTY-NINE

For four months we managed to keep our relationship out of the press, until one day Layla drew a picture of her family in school. The picture was of a man, a woman, a child, and a dog. Labeling the picture Mommy Harper, Daddy, Spot, and me, naturally her class teacher, Ms. Bell, gently challenged this, but when Layla remained persistent her teacher called us in for a meeting, concerned about my daughter's perception of her family.

When we put her right on the subject and told her that Harper and I were in a long-term relationship, and Harper was indeed a mother to Layla, we never thought for one minute she'd blab her mouth to someone else who immediately sold our story to the press.

For the following week, my daughter couldn't go to school due to her class teacher's loose mouth, and we were under siege at home, as helicopters invaded our privacy overhead and media vans blocked the driveway down to the house.

Poor Harper was painted as a gold-digging money grabber who had put herself before my child, which pissed me off because it couldn't have been farther from the truth. Derek, my manager, and the Public Relations team felt the best way to head them off was to be up front with the media. Following this it was decided we should do a short TV talk show interview as a family. Harper readily agreed and I felt dreadful she had to face this to defend her position.

This was a huge step for me, because publicly airing my relationship with Harper was a declaration of my commitment to her and Layla, and most poignant evidence I had moved on from Grace's death.

∼

"Cole Harkin, you are one dark horse," the talk show host gushed in a patronizing tone, like she knew me. "How long has this been going on?" she enquired, directing the question to Harper and me.

"How long has it been, Baby?" I asked, smiling and prompting Harper on the studio couch like she was born to do this. I directed the question to her, as I wanted people to know Harper as I knew her. She wasn't a puppet who only spoke when she was directed, my girl was strong and opinionated, and I wanted them to hear what she had to say.

"Obviously Cole and I have always had a good professional relationship since Layla was a baby. We've always done a lot of activities together, and sharing the same home, we're very comfortable with each other. Over time we've become great friends, but I guess romance began to blossom about a year ago.

"Who made the first move?" the interviewer asked, sitting forward on her chair, looking keenly from one to the other of us.

"I did, of course," I said, because to my mind it was me. I'd kissed her in the kitchen once and looking back there had been several near misses to something more. "I overstepped the Christmas Eve before." Harper absentmindedly placed her hand on my thigh and I looked down at it and back up to her. I smiled.

"I think in fairness, when we both realized how attracted we were to each other, it was a very awkward time. Neither of us were willing to make the first move because of concerns about the impact on Layla."

"Okay, but Cole has told us he eventually did. What did you think, Harper? I mean, Cole is your employer—"

"Was. I was her employer. Harper is in a different role now, we're a family," I corrected.

"Actually, Cole, I don't mind answering this because it was part of the reason why it's taken us so long to get together. The attraction between us started a while before this... maybe about two and a half years after Grace had passed, but Cole was still grieving and I wasn't about to act on my feelings."

"So you waited it out?"

"I guess we ignored it for a long time. I was naturally resistant and wondered if the feelings we had were due to us living so closely together, but once we realized this wasn't an infatuation, or a case of familiarity being the key, we stopped fighting our feelings." I concluded.

"Are you happy?" The interviewer asked, directing her question to me.

Turning to look at Harper, I smiled adoringly at her and my heart clenched for having such an amazing second chance. "Look at her. Of course I am. She makes my heart race, but this woman is beautiful inside and out." I reached up and brushed her hair over her shoulder, so I had a better view of her slender neck. "She makes me very happy... *we're* very happy. It's crazy because Grace's death shattered me, and I was so devastated I never expected anyone could make me feel the way I do now about Harper. I suppose I never expected to find a love like this again."

"What about you, Harper? It must be difficult to know you weren't Cole's first choice?"

My fists immediately balled in my lap and Harper instinctively knew the interviewer's remark would rile me. Her hand slid over mine, tamping my rising temper.

"What kind of a question is that? No one has walked in our shoes. In my opinion, you don't choose to love someone; you are stricken. Harper has seen me at my worst, and I don't think she's experienced me at my best yet, but I know for sure this girl loves me no matter what. It wasn't a conscious decision to love either of the two women I've loved. I believe it was fate that we found each other."

"Fate?" the interviewer scoffed and glanced at the studio audience.

"Yeah. In my experience, both times I've fallen in love have happened when I least expected it to. With Grace I was riding high at the pinnacle of my career. Who knew that something as simple as forgetting my toothbrush, could have led to me meeting and falling so deeply for Grace, leading to our wedding in a matter of weeks? During my time with my late wife, I thought there would never be anyone else who lived up to her... that she was the love of my life."

I saw the interviewer's eyes dart to Harper for a reaction, and I did the same. Harper sat passive in her seat, but when our eyes met, hers immediately softened and she gave me a small smile of reassurance. I knew my explanation didn't hurt her because she got me. Taking her hand, I lifted it to my lips and kissed it.

"What this experience has taught me is not to compare. For a long time, I felt as if I couldn't go on. Being honest, I didn't want to live, but I couldn't be that selfish because I had a tiny helpless baby who needed me. For the first year I didn't really pay much attention to Harper. She was someone who'd taken the weight off me and provided awesome care for my daughter."

"Are you saying you're with Harper because it's good for Layla?"

"Not at all. What I'm saying is grieving was a very long process for me, but I knew I had to keep going, and having Harper there for Layla meant I could take the time to find some normalcy in my otherwise sorrowful existence. Going back out on the road quite early on was a mistake. I had thought if Layla grew up with this arrangement, it would feel normal to her. Obviously, I was naïve and my daughter eventually demanded my attention."

"Is that when you cancelled some of your tour?"

"Yeah, I was emotionally shut down, and it wasn't until I burned out a couple of years ago, I realized I wasn't compensating for losing Grace, I was allowing her death to consume me. I was also anxious about what was ahead for my daughter growing up without her mom."

Clutching Harper's hand tight, I brought it to my lips again. "Since then Harper and I have lived alongside each other with the single focus of making Layla as emotionally secure and protected as we could, given her loss. I wouldn't have gotten through it if it wasn't for this amazing woman."

Harper responded to my comment by cupping my face in a tender gesture, completely forgetting where we were, and we had this split-second moment. Smiling warmly, I eventually broke eye contact with her and refocused my attention on the interviewer.

"People can say what they want about me. I really don't care what they think," Harper stated in a defiant but nonconfrontational tone. "Neither Cole nor I expected any of this to happen, but Layla thinks it's fabulous, because according to her, the two people she loves the most, love each other."

My heart swelled at her honest admission, and I was impressed by her ballsy attitude during her moment in the limelight. Some of the reports had been less than favorable about our relationship, but they had no understanding of how much Harper had helped me during those early days and how incredibly loyal she'd been toward me and Layla.

"Can you give our audience an exclusive... is marriage on the cards?"

"No plans for marriage," Harper informed everyone quickly. "I don't believe Cole needs that kind of pressure with what happened to Grace, and I'm not in any hurry to replace her as his wife. Our relationship doesn't need labels because something has changed in our living arrangements. We've been together before in a different way, but apart from sharing a bed, nothing much else in our household has changed. We both still parent Layla, we all love each other, and we love spending time together."

As Harper continued to talk, my heart pulsed affectionately in agreement because it was clear how much she understood us. The audience's ripples of applause were an indication of their growing admiration for her.

I also realized the time Harper had been with us had given her the confidence to speak with some authority when managing people.

"Let's bring out the little girl who brought you guys together," the hostess said, and the show theme suddenly played as Layla was labeled the matchmaker.

Walking calmly toward us like she'd been taught to do, I saw her smile widen the closer she got to Harper and I. Both of us naturally parted on the sofa to make room for Layla to sit, and after hugging us both, she turned, sat politely, and faced the camera.

"Aren't you a pretty girl?" the talk show host asked her.

"I guess," Layla replied, looking bashful, and was rewarded by a ripple of laughter and an 'aw' chorus from the audience.

The host then asked some general questions, to which Layla gave a few more cute answers and then she asked Layla if she was looking forward to Christmas coming.

"Yep." She nodded, enthusiastically with a beaming smile and this was followed by the question of what she wanted from Santa.

"Well, I'd like a baby, but Harper says I have to wait until I'm older," my daughter replied in all seriousness.

The audience laughed again, and the hostess immediately jumped on her comment, while my reaction to this almost put my brain into meltdown. The thought of Harper becoming pregnant terrified me.

"Is there anything you'd like to tell us?" the talk show host asked Harper, amused by Layla's comment.

"No... but if we do have children, it will be to our timelines and not at the pressure of the media," Harper responded.

Sensing the question had knocked the wind out of me, because having another child was the last thing on my mind, Harper answered in the same vein as the previous question, and I somehow got through the remainder of the segment before the interview ended. I pushed the subject out of my mind and was beginning to feel settled again by the time we left to go home. It had been a big day for Layla, but once in the car on the way home, she brought up the subject again.

"How long does it take to make a baby?"

I felt my hands grip the sides of the seat. Fortunately, I was in the front beside Stuart, with Layla and Harper in the back.

"A long time," Harper replied, curtly in an attempt to shut the conversation down. She knew it made me nervous.

"Is it long until Christmas?" her enquiring mind asked.

"Not long enough for a baby," Harper answered, anticipating where Layla was going with her question.

"Now that you and Daddy have sleepovers all the time, do you think we can get one?"

Harper fell quiet and didn't answer the question, but her lack of answer spoke volumes, and the thought of her ever becoming pregnant terrified me. When Layla got no reply I asked her if she enjoyed being on TV and my daughter quickly picked up on this topic of conversation.

CHAPTER THIRTY

"Shit the condom's split," I gasped, cupping my hand underneath. It was only two days after the television interview and Layla's question about a baby was fresh in my mind.

"Stop. Stop freaking out," Harper ordered.

"I can't feel anything. It must have happened after you took it out," she commented, swiping her hand between her legs.

"You have to go to the pharmacy and get the morning after pill," I demanded.

"No. Stop panicking about it. I'm not going to some drug store to get a pill. I disagree with abortion, but it won't come to that. I'm sure I'm not pregnant." This was the first time we'd had any real disagreement since we had been together.

For almost two weeks after this I counted down the days until Harper's period came, worried she was pregnant. Relief washed through me when she wasn't and I felt as if I could breathe deeply for the first time in weeks, but I didn't miss the glimmer of disappointment in Harper's eyes. It crushed my heart because I knew I was being selfish, I had a child already.

Layla was already as much Harper's child as she was mine. I may have fathered Layla, but Harper was most definitely the mother figure to her. I even thought of suggesting adopting because Harper was such a natural mom, but I couldn't bear the thought of her being pregnant, because the risk of losing her felt too great.

Gradually, we moved on from the scare and our relationship grew stronger than ever, but with Christmas coming, we faced the new challenge of Grace's parents coming over. It was Matty's question about who to expect for Christmas when I broached the subject of Harper not being particularly close to her own family.

From the conversations we'd had, I knew she was the middle child, and as such, didn't feel she had much individual attention from her parents. She excused this as being circumstantial as her mom and dad had three children in quick succession, and then her mom went back to work.

Part of me wondered if Harper living with us, and the time demands of caring for Layla, had actually stilted her from developing her relationship with them, but she disagreed, stating when she was at college she had only seen them twice a year.

When I suggested Harper invite them for Christmas, she told me they already had arrangements with her younger sister to spend Christmas with her brother's wife's parents. She told me she had been invited to this as well, but she had declined.

~

"Will you take me to meet your parents?" Harper had never suggested we go. We had been collecting a gift for Layla's pony for Christmas and I'd noticed it was only a couple of miles from her home address. I sensed reluctance to take me there, but I'd already decided this was as good a time as any.

"Not sure they'll be home from work yet," she replied, frowned and glanced at her wristwatch.

"Do you mind?" I asked, checking for an honest answer.

"Yeah, my mom will flip, she's a bit of a fan," she smirked, and I realized this was the issue.

"Yeah?"

"Mm-Hm," she nodded.

"Dad, not so much. He thinks you must be wild as you're a rock star, and he hates our living arrangements, because he thinks you're using me."

"Is this why you haven't taken me to meet them before?" I sounded concerned, she'd kept this to herself.

"Perhaps."

"All right then, let's do it. If your dad's got issues, let's air them and put them the fuck to bed, because you and I know what's going on is real. Next time we'll bring Layla with us. I don't know if you want to text or call them to warn that we're swinging by."

Harper dug out her phone and fired off some texts, one to each parent, I presumed, and we drove the ten-minute car journey from where we were at, to their place. We pulled into a single driveway off the main road that forked, with a couple of houses on separate parcels of land.

Pulling up in front of the garage, I slid out my side of the car and wandered around the hood to help her out. As I held the door open for her, I saw a tall balding guy come out from the house next door. I didn't need Harper to tell me who it was; she'd described him to a tee.

Closing the door, I grabbed Harper by the wrist as she was about to walk past me and leaned her seductively against the car door.

Reducing the distance between us, I flattened her chest with mine. Sliding my hands into her hair at both sides of her head, I whispered, "I love you, Baby," in a rare public display of affection.

Guiding my nose along her jawline and up her cheek, I playfully brushed our noses together and was rewarded when a gentle smile spread on her lips. Bringing her head closer toward me, I kissed her in my favorite way—at a slow, leisurely pace.

Separating, breathless, Harper's lust-filled eyes darted to her left and her body steeled when she saw her dickhead ex-boyfriend staring at the scene I'd staged. Slipping my hand into hers, I squeezed it tight in a silent I-got-you gesture, and I whispered in her ear. "Breathe, Baby." I smiled when I heard her exhale.

"Hey, Harper, looking good, Honey," he called out, totally unashamed of his previous behavior toward her and smiled at me like we were buddies.

"You need an eye doctor. My girl doesn't look good; she looks incredible. Who the fuck are you, anyway?" I asked curtly, like I had no idea who he was.

"Oh, Harper and I go way back. Don't tell me you didn't tell him about us?" he asked, sounding like he had this big fucking secret and was manipulating the situation.

"Told me?" I asked him in a curious tone. My hand tightened around Harper's when she tried to pull away from me.

Glancing toward her parents' place, I ensured there was no one around and they weren't aware we'd arrived before I replied.

"What exactly was she supposed to tell me?"

"We were an item for almost two years," he informed me looking proud, even though the fucker hadn't treated her right. I stared pointedly at him for a few seconds, wondering if he'd forgotten this small detail.

"Is this the guy you refused to have anal play with?" I asked, addressing Harper bluntly with a raised eyebrow.

Harper's eyes went wide in horror. "*Cole,*" she admonished, mortified I'd blurted out the one thing she felt she'd told me in confidence.

"No, Babe, it's fine. All I want to do is tell... what's your name?" I asked, my fingers waving in a hand it over gesture.

"Millar," he informed me in a far less confident tone already.

"Yeah, Malcolm, Harper did mention you, now that I think about it. You apparently dumped her ass when she would let you near it." I knew I was making Harper feel uncomfortable, but I wanted her to walk away from this with her dignity totally intact.

"What you obviously don't realize is there are two types of women who have no boundaries with their bodies. There are those who don't respect themselves and are happy for any guy to stick it to them in any hole they want. Then there are women like Harper. Winning the trust of a woman like *my* girl takes a real man. A man who takes his time to truly connect with her. Someone she trusts. Believe me, when a woman trusts in the right way, there's no part of her body that's out of bounds."

I could almost hear the cogs whirring inside the asshole's head as he stared at Harper.

"So, I guess what you got is a keeper like the first type I've just described. Good luck with that, by the way, because you obviously don't have what it takes to keep a girl like Harper, and the first type don't take much to stray. Hell, I should shake your hand for being such a dumbfuck in choosing the one you've got, because I'd never have had such a beautiful second chance."

Even as I spoke, I watched Millar's eyes rake over Harper's body, and where normally I'd have throat punched any guy who eye-fucked my woman, in his case I was thrilled to have him look. My words had hit him where it hurt, and I saw the realization as to what he'd lost because Harper was now a woman far beyond the reach of a stupid guy like him.

"Nice to meet you," I lied, in a voice laced with a small degree of sarcasm and amusement, as I brought Harper's hand to my lips. Looking up at him one last time, I flashed him the smuggest smile I could manage and winked. "Trust me... no part of a woman's body is out of bounds in the hands of the right man." Placing my hand on her back, I steered her in the direction of her parents' front door.

Feeling how tense her body language was, from what I had done, she leaned in and groaned. "Thanks, Cole, that didn't help because now he thinks I do anal sex."

"Ah, no, did I say anal sex? I don't believe I used those words, Harper. I'm not a liar... because one day you will, I have no doubt about that, but what I said was *anal play*."

Harper's eyes connected with mine and I saw relief flicker there. "Just don't try to win my father over with that example you just gave Millar," she told me, and although her voice sounded stern, I didn't miss the small smile that curved her lips as she shoved open the door with her shoulder and led me chuckling inside.

Everything Harper had ever told me about her parents, Robin and Tracy, was exactly as she'd said. Her mom was a tall, slim, and warm-natured woman, and I could immediately see where Harper got her gorgeous looks. The genes on her mom's side were great. My girl also had her mom's sense of humor and we gelled right off the bat.

Winning her father Robin's blessing about our living arrangements was a far harder feat. It was clear from the moment he and I shook hands there were bridges to mend. We had barely been introduced when he confronted me by asking if I saw Harper as a new mother for my daughter.

"Actually, I do, Robin," I replied, honestly, "but not in the way you probably see our family situation. Harper and I were great friends before we got together. She has been part of my daughter's life and mine since the week my late wife died. It's been an extremely tough journey back from the sudden and devastating loss my daughter and I suffered, but I'd go as far as to say what I feel for Harper is probably a deeper love than what I felt for Grace."

Both Harper and her father looked shocked by my statement and Harper's breath hitched in her throat. It sounded like I was diminishing what I had with Grace, but from my reasoning, this wasn't the case. I forced myself to go on and voice some of the thoughts I'd had in the previous few weeks.

"What my wife and I had was a very fast, romantic, and passionate relationship, full of impulse, exploration, and making life up as it happened. It was less than three years from the day I met Grace until the terrible day she died. Harper and I have known each other for several years longer than that. More than twice the time I knew Grace, and I'd go as far as to say this beautiful, sweet-natured woman saved my life."

"Gratitude isn't the same as love," Robin ground out, his eyes flicking from me to his daughter.

"And I'd be the last person to disagree with what you say. While it's true, I will always be eternally grateful to Harper because she was a godsend to me in the beginning, I can guarantee I know the difference between gratitude and love."

"Is that so? Then you won't mind explaining that difference to me," he stated, not convinced and sat back in his armchair with one leg across his knee.

"Sure," I replied unperturbed by his challenge. "Gratitude is a reaction to an act of kindness. In most cases the person receiving this act is thankful and sometimes may even want to offer something in return for the favor being received. They may even feel warmth, affection, or a loyalty toward the person who performs the kindness."

Robin stared me down for a few moments then nodded. "Sounds about right."

"Love on the other hand is an entirely different feeling, and as we know, the kind of love we feel may differ from person to person. For example, loving someone is different from being in love with someone."

"How can you be sure that what you have with Harper, and indeed what my daughter feels for you, is real love? Like you said, you've lived in close contact for years."

Taking Harper's hand in mine, I rubbed my thumb over her knuckles and stared intently into her eyes. "It's no secret I've been in love before. Harper knows this more than anyone else because she saw how losing that love devastated me. Having these feelings again for Harper may even mean my love for her runs deeper than it does for Grace. Otherwise, how could I have survived losing Grace and then have fallen for Harper if this wasn't the case?"

Looking away from Harper, I questioned Robin with a stare. "Harper makes me forget. When I'm with your daughter it's her I want to be with. Not my dead wife. When we're apart, I miss her more than I ever missed Grace, and believe me I missed her too. But I miss Harper more because I know her better than I did Grace. Do you understand?"

"I believe you," Robin conceded, then he turned to Harper. "I'll admit I was worried about you, Honey, but no man could explain it in the way Cole has, if he didn't feel strongly for you. What he's confessed takes a lot of thought."

The transformation in Harper's father's demeanor following our conversation was nothing less than remarkable. I was glad to see it, because it meant he cared about Harper's future. I also made a mental note about my future expectations of any man Layla brought home when the time came.

CHAPTER THIRTY-ONE

"Can we talk?" Harper knocked softly on my office door and I swiveled round in my office chair to look at her. I'd been staring out at the incredible winter scene through the window where a white-tailed deer and her two fawns were trudging slowly through the snow, less than thirty feet from our house.

"Yeah, I wasn't concentrating anyway. Check this out." Standing up, I led her over toward the window.

"Aw, they're gorgeous. We should call Stuart and get him to put some food out for them. It can't be easy finding much to eat and drink in these conditions," Harper mused, her eyes full of wonder.

"Is there anything you don't want to take care of?" I asked, sliding my arms through hers and clasping my hands at her lower back.

"Hm, now you mention it, this is what I came to talk with you about."

"If it's the extra puppy Max and Sarah-Jayne have, the answer is no. Layla grumbles about walking Spot, unless it's to go down to the stables to see Glitter."

"It's not about the puppy," Harper stated firmly.

"Good. Then I'm listening, what is it?"

"I'm pregnant."

My heart stopped for a beat, then electricity jolted through my body, my veins cramping from the sudden lactic acid as I struggled for breath.

The beaming smile and the sparkle in her eyes when she gave me the news disintegrated in front of me, and all I could think about was what had happened after last woman I loved said those words.

"Breathe, Cole," Harper ordered, sternly. The devastation I had caused Harper by my reaction crushed me. I couldn't speak. I didn't want to talk, because I knew if I did, my thoughts would hurt her even more.

Conflict reigned in a raging battle within me. Although the last thing in the world I wanted to happen was to leave a scar, which would remain in her mind forever, the words stuck in my throat held no joy or encouragement, but were rather more sinister and foreboding in nature.

As I tried to block out my nightmare memories of the past, I fought through the internal anguish and pulled her hurriedly into my chest. Hugging her tight, for what had felt like an age, didn't come off congratulatory like it should have been. Even I recognized it was a hug of desperation.

Pulling back from me, Harper gazed up into my worried eyes, hers full to the brim with unshed tears and my heart slowed from the panic I'd felt inside. Pushing her hair away from her face, I held her head in my hands in the same affectionate way I always did. "I know what you need from me, Harper, but I can't bring myself to say it."

Tears slid down her face unchecked as she stood silent for a moment, then she took a step back and shook her head. The wounded look in her eyes shattered me. I'd hurt her badly with my lack of response.

"I didn't plan this, Cole, and I'm not even going to dissect how it happened, but we're having this baby," she said in a flat even tone. "I'm not Grace. What happened with her never should have, but it won't happen to me."

Nodding, I still couldn't speak, because I knew whatever words came out would be wrong.

Turning away from me, she wandered slowly back through my

office door and closed it behind her. As soon as she was gone, I dropped to the floor and prayed to God this wasn't history repeating itself.

Leaving the song I was halfway through writing, I fought the meltdown brewing inside, because the last thing I wanted to do was lose my shit with Harper. Swiping my cell from my desk I called down the hall to Stuart.

"Can you saddle up Elbe for me?"

"Now? It's freezing outside; some of the pastures are two feet deep in snow."

"If I'd wanted a fucking weather forecast, I'd have called a meteorologist, just do what I asked," I snapped, cutting off the call before he'd had the chance to argue back. Opening my office door, I headed down to the utility room at the back of the house. Pulling on some chaps, my boots, an extra sweater, and a long waterproof coat, I stepped out the back door and immediately felt the biting wind sting my face.

Entering the stable, I saw Stuart had saddled and tacked up my mare, and was in the process of placing the saddle on his large temperamental stallion, Electron.

"Where are you going?" I asked, tightening the girth one more notch and taking a hold of the reins to my horse.

"Depends where you're going," he muttered, and continued to secure the saddle rigging.

"Sorry, I don't feel like company," I replied, shaking my head as I turned Elbe around and headed for the door. Stuart ignored my comment and followed suit.

"Did you hear what I said?" I asked, my anger barely contained in my voice.

"Yeah, I did, and I don't know what's wrong, but I got the vibe that it's big when you need to ride out in this weather. Forget going alone, Cole, it's not happening. You're a good rider, but the safety etiquette of any good rider is no one leaves home on a place this size alone in weather like this."

I glared at him, frustration building inside, but I was too pissed to argue; because every moment I stayed close to the house made me think about what Harper had disclosed.

"Fuck, then don't talk to me." Turning away from him, I led Elbe out into the stable yard and mounted her, not waiting for Stuart to catch up. My horse led me down toward the meadow, like she knew what was on my mind even before I did. Following the curve in the river, she trudged through the two-foot snow and came to a halt by the empty boat mooring by the jetty.

"Boat's in dry dock for the winter," Stuart pointed out, riding alongside me as I stared over to where Grace was buried. Parts of the lake had ice forming.

"I know. I didn't intend on being here. I suppose I've brought Elbe this way so often over the years she's on autopilot," I replied.

"Want to tell me what's on your mind?" Stuart gently probed.

"Want to mind your own fucking business?" I muttered back.

"I figured the fact I'm freezing my balls off in sub-zero temperatures kind of hints at the fact I think you are my business," he scolded.

Glaring with narrowed eyes, I sized him up for a few seconds then figured he was right. Although he was an estate manager, he was also the most loyal of friends. Most of all, he deserved to know why I was in such an angry place after I'd dragged him out in the cold.

"Harper's pregnant," I mumbled, and I felt my heart clench in desperation as I struggled internally with my fears.

"Congratulations," Stuart mumbled cautiously, as both horses whinnied when a swift gust of wind spooked them both.

"From where I'm standing, it doesn't feel like a celebration," I snapped back.

For a few minutes Stuart sat quiet, then as I started to turn away, he shouted after me, "She's not Grace, Cole."

Glancing over my shoulder, I narrowed my eyes and thought that was easy for him to say, he had never been where I was. I tugged on the reins and changed direction. "You're not helping, leave me alone."

I rode through the silent winter scene until my hands were numb through the thick leather gloves, and when the late afternoon light began to fade, I headed back to the stables.

"Leave it, I'll do the tack," Stuart told me as I lifted the saddle from Elbe and placed it over the wooden rack where it was kept.

"Don't shut her out. We all know what happened; we lived it too, remember? Harper's a good woman. She's raised Layla for the past six years, and no matter how much you want to keep her safe, you need to understand it from her point of view. Don't begrudge her a child of her own. She loves Layla with all that she is, but you have what she has never had, a child that's part of you.

"Do you think I don't know this? To tell you the truth, I don't want her to have this kid. I hate that she's pregnant, and I'm scared shitless she'll die a horrible death like Grace did. Now I know these are all irrational thoughts, and my mind feels heavy from the weight of them," I explained, pointing to my head.

Slamming my palm hard against my chest, I eyed him angrily and shook my head. "But in here, I'm consumed by dread. Since the minute Harper told me today, my heart has stuttered uneasily, fighting for rhythm. No matter how many times I chant *it's not going to happen*, there's an echo from my past, which immediately counters with the nagging doubt, *but what if it does?*"

Stuart left the girth strap he had started to unbuckle and grabbed me into a hug. "You got to fight those thoughts every step of the way. We all know there's no guarantees, but believe me, Cole, for the sake of your relationship with Harper and Layla, you have got to fight against the devil on this one."

"Anyone who understands what I've been through would accept I want to protect what's mine. I know I'm hypersensitive when it comes to childbirth because of what happened before, but the thought of anything going wrong again is so uncomfortable I don't want to upset the status quo as we are right now."

Taking a step back, he patted my back and dropped his hands. "No matter what you're feeling in there," he scolded, pointing sharply at my breastbone, "you've got to get back in that house and appear interested in the news you have learned for Harper's sake. She's been living with the ghost of Grace from the moment she walked through your door. Don't make her sorry she can't compete with what happened to her." His tone was firm and almost admonishing, and I'd never heard this side to him before. Turning away without a backward glance, he began seeing to the horses like I was dismissed.

Pulling off my gloves, I smacked the ice off them against my thigh as I thought how protective he sounded, then turned and walked back to the house without replying. Stuart was right; it was sad that Harper didn't get the response she should have, because as a newly expectant mother, it should have been one of the happiest days of her life.

When I entered the house, the heat stifled my breathing immediately and my face stung from the thaw of being out in the cold. Stuart's words had resonated with me. I knew no matter how fearful I felt, I had to find a way to protect my feelings from overwhelming me and support Harper and Layla at the same time.

"Where's Harper?" I asked Matty when I entered the kitchen. Layla was covered in flour from the dough they were kneading.

"She's lying down, she has a headache," Layla told me, as she picked up Matty's huge rolling pin and clanked it down on the countertop.

"Careful," Matty warned as she stretched over and moved it to a safer position. Leaving them, I headed up to my bedroom and pushed open the door.

"Are you okay?" I asked in a low voice as I crept toward the bed in the darkness. The hallway light shone from the doorway and was bright enough for me to see Harper was lying on her side, but she hadn't heard me because she was sound asleep.

Still being cold from the ride, I left her to rest and went into our bathroom. I relieved myself, washed my hands in the hot water to thaw them out, and dried them. As I turned to go back into the bedroom, I caught sight of the pregnancy test Harper had used lying in the trash can by the sink. My stomach rippled with nerves.

An instant flashback of Grace bouncing on her toes with delight when she shared hers with me came to mind. I pushed back the thought and went back into the bedroom.

"Hey, are you okay?" I asked again when her red-rimmed eyes opened and stared at me.

"I'm fine," she answered quickly, but her clipped tone barely held back her true feelings.

"I'm sorry," I murmured, as I sat on the edge of the bed and brushed her hair clear of her face. It was damp, and my heart squeezed tight at the thought I'd made her cry.

"Your news was so sudden, you know?" I argued, gently trying to explain my reaction.

"Our news, Cole. It's *our* baby," she muttered.

"I know. Please don't be mad at me."

Glancing up at me, her eyes shone with tears. "I'm not mad. I'm hurt and disappointed."

"As you should be. I don't expect you to understand—"

"No, Cole, you missed the point, I do. Everyone knows what you went through. If I had one wish, it would be for you never to have experienced that, but I need you to look at this from my perspective, because I'm on this journey with you now too."

"I know," I agreed, feeling like the worst man in the world for how I took the news.

"Understanding is a two-way street. I'm walking in a dead woman's shoes unless you accept this is about us. My pregnancy, the child we've made together, has nothing to do with her or what happened before."

I straightened my spine, instantly pulled up by her comment and I nodded in agreement. How I behaved affected everyone around me. Harper's condition no longer allowed me the familiar indulgence of dwelling on the past.

Since I had gone all in with my girl, I had felt more emotionally stable. My heart and moods were infinitely lighter, and my sense of humor had returned. I was a different man to the one before Grace, but for knowing Harper I'd grown to be a more considerate version of my old self.

Reaching out, I grazed my thumb over her lips and bent to press mine to hers. "Baby, I agree. I was off, and I'm sorry it's taken me so long to come back, but I didn't want to say anything to you that would diminish the significance of what is happening."

Changing position, Harper shifted until she was sitting up, resting against the headboard of the bed. I took her hand in mine and slowly stroked my thumb over the back of it. I found it comforting to know she let me.

"Baby, when you told me, I was stunned. You being pregnant was the last thing I had expected you to say today. If I had gone with my gut and responded, I would have commented from a totally selfish perspective. That would have been wrong, and that's why I went for a ride."

"I'm listening," she confirmed flatly.

"Where I've been, my situation doesn't allow for spontaneity and being able to indulge in the beauty of something most people would see as a happy miracle. Though it is, so I don't want you to think I don't know this. But I had to sort through the shit going on in my head and to come back and address this without all the negative feelings associated with my experience from before."

"All I wanted to hear was you welcome this baby."

"And I will. What is going on inside has nothing to do with not wanting a child with you, Baby. What I went through has everything to do with the shock of what should have been a very normal experience, for most couples, becoming a membership to some very exclusive horror club. Grief isn't something I can switch off, and the trauma associated with it will always live inside me."

Cupping my face with her hands, Harper leaned forward and placed her forehead on mine. "I really want this baby, Cole. Layla will be ecstatic when she knows, but I understand you need time to come to terms with the change. Nothing is going to happen to me. We're going to have a beautiful baby, a brother or sister for Layla, and the happy ever after we deserve. Nothing is going to get in the way of this," Harper stated with conviction.

CHAPTER THIRTY-TWO

Finding out Harper was five weeks pregnant bought me some time before I had to deal with the obvious signs of our growing baby. I figured it would let me get used to the idea, and as Harper kept Layla's routines tight, it was easy to forget she was expecting at busy times.

This worked for most of the time, but even with my best attempts, there were times when dark thoughts would creep in, and I felt panic rise from my gut. It helped that Harper knew me so well, because she recognized the times when I wasn't receptive to what she wanted to tell me.

During these times, she would either moderate how and what she said or drop the subject until she felt I was more receptive to the information. No matter how long it took her, she always eventually got her point across.

My girl had the patience of a saint, never showing any obvious anger or frustration with me if I shut her down, especially when she spoke about tests or examinations. From my point of view, I knew I sometimes sounded absurd or unyielding, and I was always quick to apologize to her on the occasions where this happened. Fortunately, they weren't too often, and Harper had great empathy whenever she thought I was scared.

Despite these internal battles, I tried to remain positive during the early days, and I was determined to act on the sound advice Stuart had given me when he had ridden out with me that day.

I made a conscious effort to be more attentive toward Harper in regard to her pregnancy; asking how she felt, both physically and emotionally, and I'd tie up her responses with what I saw from my quiet observations of the subtle changes in her moods and body.

Although Harper was occasionally nauseous, thankfully she didn't suffer at all from morning sickness, which was completely the opposite of how Layla had affected Grace.

When Harper went for her initial OBGYN appointment without telling me until afterward, I felt oddly disappointed; guilty for not being with her, half pissed at not being given the choice, yet relieved not to have been there.

There were times I felt my head was about to explode under the pressure of facing the unknown, like when life had been so dark after Layla's birth. Restraining myself, I didn't know how to react for fear of getting my hopes up, in case something went wrong. It was possibly my indecision that made Harper appear to do what her instincts told her was best.

We had discussed at length about how she wanted me to support her, and although I was nervous, I was happy for Harper to set the pace. It made sense when she'd like to keep me informed, but without going into too much detail, because she figured the less stressed I was, the more she'd enjoy the experience.

I loved her logic, but there were times when I pushed for more information and at others she actively encouraged me to opt out, especially her visits to her obstetrician.

Between hospital appointments, Harper kept Layla's routine much the same with school, playdates, and outings, so unless something was looming with her physician or specialist, life ticked along in the same vein.

It was Harper who always initiated sex in the first few weeks after she told me about the baby. Until she pointed this out, it hadn't been anything conscious on my part, but I guess the news must have affected me to the point where it suppressed all thoughts about anything else. It wasn't like I didn't still find her attractive; it was due to the potential risks to my girl consuming me.

By the second trimester, my libido had returned, and as I had found with Grace, Harper's changing body sent my desire for her through the roof.

Watching Harper blossom from her first to the second trimester made me realize how fast time had passed. We'd both agreed not to tell Layla until Harper was safely past the first twelve weeks, and everyone in the household found this a hard-kept secret. All the staff knew our news and Harper had confided in our friends and neighbors, Sarah-Jayne and Max.

At almost fifteen weeks, both Harper and I felt it was time to spell things out for Layla, and Harper and Diane came up with an ingenious plan to help us to do this.

Friday nights were traditionally Layla's late night for bed. We had all been watching a family movie in the living room. When the movie finished, I turned the TV off and Harper nudged Layla.

"Hey, how would you like to have a sleepover with your dad and me tonight?"

My daughter's eyes grew huge from the drowsy ones ready for bed, to bright, wide, and alert.

"Really? Can I really, Daddy?" she asked turning to me, not entirely believing her luck.

"Sure. I think it's a great idea. Obviously, it's a very special occasion, because usually the sleepovers are adult only, but I think we can do it just this once."

Unbeknownst to me, Harper, Matty, and Diane had been in the bedroom earlier and worked their magic while I'd kept Layla busy, and when Layla opened the bedroom door, she squealed in delight. Glancing past her, I saw the room was bathed in white string lights. The headboard of the bed had softer blue, pink, and yellow ones running the length of it.

Running full blast at the bed, Layla quickly climbed up on it and stood at the center, then jumped up and down with excitement.

"Come on, let's get into bed," she shouted. Spot came scuttling into the room, slipped on the wooden floor and went skidding into the side of the bed. From the puppy he was he'd grown into a huge clumsy lump.

"No. No dog. I'm drawing the line, Baby. Spot sleeps downstairs or the party is off."

Immediately Layla placed her hands on her hips without missing a beat and scolded the dog, when normally she'd have moved Heaven and Earth to have Spot included.

"Sorry, Spot. You know my daddy doesn't allow you in the bedroom," she scolded, like she was full of wisdom and jumped down off the bed. Grabbing his collar, she dragged her reluctant dog over to the door and led him out of the room.

Harper passed her on the landing, her hair neatly braided and wearing short pant pajamas, and we both chuckled when we heard Layla admonishing her dog all the way down the stairs.

Stripping out of my clothes, I quickly pulled on some boxer briefs and went to the bathroom to brush my teeth. By the time I returned, Layla was back in the room and she and Harper were already in bed. She'd snuck into bed with me hundreds of times, but this was a first lying between Harper and me.

Harper clapped her hands and all the lights in the room went off apart from those over the headboard. "How does this feel?" Harper asked Layla as she wriggled excitedly in between us.

"Magical," she immediately offered, and the sound of wonderment in her tone touched me. I smiled, and my heart filled with love that something so simple could have had such a huge effect on her little mind.

"I agree it is magical, Layla," Harper started, "in fact I can only think of one other thing that would make this sleepover even more magical," she added.

"A unicorn? They're magic, aren't they?" Layla asked, her eyes darting around the room as if looking for one to appear.

"Yeah, they are, but I was thinking of something that's real, not a mythical creature," Harper replied.

"Hmm, then I have no idea. Do you, Daddy?"

Letting Harper lead the way, I shrugged as her little bright eyes stared quizzically at me from my side.

"What would you say if I said you were going to be a big sister?" Harper asked gently.

Layla's feet immediately cycled their way from under the comforter and she climbed out on top. Kneeling to face us, she sat back on her heels and her huge bright eyes sparkled with excitement.

"Me? Where's the baby?" she asked with her hands wide and her eyes twice as big and round as they were with her reaction to the sleepover.

"It's in my tummy," Harper told her.

Layla frowned and glanced at me then back at Harper. "But you're not my mommy," she replied. "How can I be your baby's big sister?"

"Because I'm your daddy and I'm this baby's daddy as well," I explained.

Layla squealed with excitement and jumped up and down, bouncing on her knees completely unable to contain her pleasure and asked Harper if she could see her stomach. Harper gladly obliged by pulling up her tank top, but with her belly still largely flat, there was nothing much to see.

Patiently, Harper stroked her hair and smiled.

"Right now, my baby is only the size of a lemon, but it's getting bigger every week, and by the time it's ready to be born, it will look like a real baby."

Eventually Layla calmed down enough to slide back into bed between us, but her questions continued, and although at this stage we had very few answers for her, she was clearly accepting and enthused by the news. Harper had been a little worried about how Layla would take it but the look of pure joy was evident.

It was almost two hours later that my daughter finally fell asleep and Harper's hand slid across to rest on my hip. A sigh of contentment left her lips and I turned to look at her face.

"Thank you. I know all of this isn't easy for you," she whispered.

"Baby, it's me who should be thanking you for putting up with my whiny ass."

"I've never thought you were whiny, Cole. You love deeply and knowing that, and that you found it in your heart to love again, makes me so happy it's me you love now. This event is bound to stir up horrible memories you thought you'd dealt with."

Turning on my side, I rose up enough to perch my head on my elbow and looked past Layla at her. "I keep telling myself this is different. This right here is different," I admitted nodding at Layla lying between us. "This was a great idea and, Baby, right now my heart has never felt so big."

My comment earned me a beaming smile and brought tears to Harper's gorgeous blue eyes, and I thought she'd never looked so beautiful. "You're so good to me," I told her.

"I know," she replied, a grin widening on her lips as a tear trickled down her cheek.

Leaning across Layla, I cradled her face with my hand, brushed her tear away then stroked her lips with the pad of my thumb. "Thank you for loving me."

"Aw, I guess someone has to," she teased, taking the seriousness out of the moment, and instantly making my heart feel light.

"I want to come to the ultrasound scan," I stated impulsively, making Harper shift onto her elbow too.

"Yeah?" she asked in a tentative tone, as her curious eyes searched my face for the truth.

"Yeah, I want to support you. It has never been that I don't want this. I want this baby as much as you do, I'm just... scared, you know?"

Harper didn't reply, but stared long and intently as her thoughts took over.

"Get some sleep, Baby. God knows when this one will be awake, and I'd place a bet it'll be even earlier than normal."

Grabbing my hand from her face, Harper kissed my palm, let it go then settled down on her side, still facing Layla and me. I lay down doing the same, and for the first time since Harper had told me about the pregnancy, I fell asleep without the deep dark thoughts in my mind about what could go wrong.

"Are you my brother or my sister? What's your name?" I heard the sweet muffled voice of Layla coming from under the sheets and felt her wriggle around, shoving my thigh out of the way for a better position.

"Daddy, move," she ordered, huffing in frustration. "Why are your legs so hairy and yours aren't?" she asked me then Harper, who stretched her arms above her head and cracked open her sleepy eyes.

Working her way out of the covers, Layla's head popped up alongside me, her hair wild and full of static electricity. Her little hands cupped my cheeks in the special way she had of keeping me where she wanted me. Pushing them together to make a pouty mouth with my lips, she bent over and kissed me. "Good morning, Daddy. Does this baby have ears yet?" she enquired, staring expectantly into my eyes.

"No, Baby, it can't hear you yet, that doesn't happen for a couple of more months." I suddenly had a vague recollection of having read something to this effect.

"Well, that was a waste of time. I thought it was ignoring me."

Harper turned on her side and scooped her into a hug. "I love that you want to talk to this little bean, but it won't have all its little bits until it grows some more."

"Is it a boy or a girl baby?" she asked with a frown.

"We haven't asked because we want it to be a surprise," I offered, knowing Harper wanted to wait until the birth like she reckoned everyone should. I loved that about her, she had no preference; then again neither did I. As long as they were both okay I didn't care about anything else.

"When will it get here? Will I be in school when it comes?"

Sitting up, Harper pulled her onto her lap. "Well, this is what I was thinking," she began, her eyes darting to me, and then back to Layla. "If everything goes well, I figured I should have it right here in the house, maybe in the huge square bath on the ground floor."

We hadn't discussed this, and I almost choked at the thought of her taking a risk like this when I knew exactly what could go wrong. "Oh, now wait—"

"Yay, and I can see it come home?" she asked a little confused at what Harper meant.

"Actually, Layla, if everything is going well with me and the baby, then yes, there's no reason why you couldn't see your new baby arriving here in the house."

"Baby, can you go tell Matty we'll be down in ten minutes for breakfast, let Spot out the back too. I want to talk to Harper for a few minutes alone; then we'll be right down." Immediately, she scooted down the bed and out the door, her feet thundering down the hallway like a baby elephant. For someone so little, she sure made her presence felt.

Throwing the comforter off, I slid off the edge of the bed and I could feel my blood running hot from the bomb she'd just dropped.

"You're not having this baby at home," I stated categorically.

"We'll see," she replied calmly, and rose to her feet from the other side of the bed.

"No, Harper, you can't take chances with something like this."

"Something like what? Natural childbirth? Women have been having babies for centuries, Cole. I'm healthy and we live in a first world country, why wouldn't I take responsibility for where it's born?"

"You're terrifying me," I told her.

"You're affected by the past," she countered, "I'm not Grace and there's no reason to think there will be any problems."

"But if there are, you'll be miles from help," I argued, as my chest tightened when the idea of what she had stated gripped me. Feeling distressed, I shook my head and grabbed my jeans, shoving one leg in then the other. "This conversation is far from over," I ground out and stepped out the room, banging the door behind me.

CHAPTER THIRTY-THREE

Reaching the bottom of the stairs, I saw Stuart come out of his quarters at the end of the hall, and I could tell by his face, he'd heard my raised voice. Striding toward me, he stood between me and the kitchen door, preventing me from going inside.

"Breathe, Cole. What the fuck's going on?" he asked, concern etched on his face.

"I'm getting some coffee. Saddle me up, I'll be over in twenty minutes," I barked, not entertaining his question at all.

"Calm down," he warned. "Remember Layla's in there, and you throwing a hissy fit won't be good for the baby either, you need to modify your volume."

If anyone else had spoken to me the way he had, I'd have decked the fucker and stepped over his body, but Stuart had earned an opinion after his years of dedication where his even temper and loyalty told me he'd never do me wrong.

"Just do what I've asked." My tone was low; my temper sounding more contained than it was from the first time I'd spoken to him. Satisfied I was now in control, he grabbed his jacket and headed down the hallway, past my office and out into the yard.

Entering the kitchen, Matty eyed me with concern and glanced toward Layla. "Did you shout at Harper?" Layla asked, completely unfiltered, and with tears brimming in her eyes.

I sighed, heavily. "Oh, Baby, adults often shout at each other. It doesn't mean we don't love each other. It's only that living in the same house and having different ideas can get frustrating sometimes."

"But if you shouted at Harper, you shouted at our baby as well. I'm really glad it doesn't have ears yet," she informed me in a voice that was far more scolding than anything Stuart had said to me.

"I'm sorry, Baby, I didn't mean to shout. Sometimes when we are afraid or passionate about something, we don't always deal with situations in the right way."

"That was bad," she told me in a stern voice, and my heart squeezed tight that my baby could differentiate to the extent that she had. I knew then my reaction had affected her in a negative way.

"You're right. I'm going to apologize right now," I agreed, placing the coffee cup down Matty had put in my hand.

As I walked toward the hallway, I heard the front door close, and through the window I saw Harper get into Diane's car. "Fuck," I muttered, knowing immediately she'd left the house to make space between us.

I felt ashamed that I hadn't found the confidence to deal with what Harper had told me in a far more rational way.

The caveman in me would have jumped on my motorcycle and gone after her, but I knew if I had, it would have only taken the tension between us outside the home. I could understand Harper's need to get away from me because she'd seen how dogmatic I could be when I really disagreed with something.

I figured right then, no matter what words I chose to argue my choice for the place of the birth, any suggestion I put forward for going to the hospital would inevitably be mute, and all because I hadn't been able to keep a civil tongue in my head.

～

With asking Stuart to saddle Elbe up and Harper disappearing, I decided to use the morning to take Layla for a pony trek. I think if I hadn't suggested this, she wouldn't have spoken to me at all. Stuart offered to tag along, but I thought it would be better to take Layla on my own because I had some fences to mend with her.

The atmosphere was frosty, and I had to accept responsibility for how Layla had viewed me. Riding mellowed Layla after a while and eventually she addressed the topic, which had caused the rift between us.

"Why did you shout at Harper?"

"That was naughty of me, Layla, and I'm sorry. Harper didn't tell me what she had in mind for where our new baby is to be born."

"Where else would it be born?" she asked, her eyes wide and round and staring at me like I was crazy for not agreeing to this.

"I'd prefer our baby to be born in the hospital where it's safe," I reasoned.

"I don't want my Harper to go to the hospital," she suddenly stated. "It wasn't safe for my mommy when she had me."

Grace's situation wasn't the same, but in the simplest terms, I couldn't argue with that, and the way she'd referred to Harper as 'my Harper' spoke volumes on where Layla's loyalties lay.

"I'll speak to her and make it right, I promise."

"And you won't do it again?" she asked, the questioning tone held another hint for a promise.

"No. I can't guarantee I won't raise my voice, because that's what normal couples do."

"But Harper isn't a couple."

"Harper and I are a couple."

"Then you should do what makes her happy. That's what The Beast does for Beauty." I couldn't help smiling when she used the analogy for Harper and me, but I promised to try harder to make Harper feel happy about having our new baby.

After a three-hour ride, we made it back to the stables and the first thing that caught my eye was Diane's car parked again in front of the drive. My heart rate raced knowing Harper was home and I couldn't wait to talk to her to make things right again.

Ten minutes later, after settling our rides in the stables, Layla opened the back door and I immediately heard Harper's voice in the kitchen. Reminding Layla to wash her hands, I was annoyed when she began to do this, but ran off in search of Harper before we were finished.

By the time I reached the kitchen, I saw Layla was on Harper's knee with her arms around her neck. I caught Matty's attention from the doorway and asked her to distract Layla so that I could speak with Harper.

Matty asked Layla for some help in filling the small flour canister from the larger one in the pantry, and once they had gone, I wandered into the kitchen and sat down beside Harper at the table.

Taking Harper's hand, I lifted it gently and brought it to my lips. "I'm really sorry, Baby. I've been known to have a temper when I'm stressed, but I've rarely raised my voice in this house. I hope you know I'm better than I behaved today." Harper's sad tear-filled eyes stared intently into mine.

"You have to know I'm trying… and I know you're doing everything you can to keep the stress levels down for both of us; but making a decision like that without any consultation with me wasn't right. Of course, it's your body, Harper, but you're so fucking important to us, the thought of anything risky is out of the question."

"No, it's not. There is probably more risk of intervention and something disrupting the natural process of giving birth in the hospital than there is here at home with a good midwife and a doctor standing by."

Gazing intently, I knew not to push any more at that time and shook my head. "We're going to discuss this again. I appreciate you've tried to protect me, but this should have been a discussion before you calmly announced to Layla what the plan for the birth was, without even attempting to check out what my thoughts were."

Before I could smooth things out further, the gate buzzer sounded and Layla came running out of the pantry to see who had arrived. "Uncle Scuds is here," she shouted excitedly, jumping up and down beside the close circuit monitor. I hadn't been expecting him, and I glanced at Harper with a look that told her we'd be picking this up later.

"What brings you to town?" I asked, opening the front door to let my bandmate inside.

"Meeting with Max and Finley. I promised Finley the next time he was down visiting Max I'd have dinner with him. Obviously, I couldn't come to town and not call in on my favorite dude," Scuds offered, then turned to Layla and fist-bumped her.

"You're going to dinner this evening?"

"Yeah, boys' night with the three of us."

"Why don't you go with them?" Harper prompted.

"I wasn't invited." My tone was laced with sarcasm. I knew she probably wanted me out of the way because she knew our conversation was far from done.

"Yeah, you are. It goes without saying," Scuds replied in an even tone.

"Thanks, but I'll pass if you don't mind," I answered again, determined not to go to bed without us hashing out the earlier debate.

Leaving Harper after a rare row wasn't an option for me. I'd never been someone to start something and walk away, and I would never have left her without trying to find a compromise that suited us both.

Scuds stayed for a couple of hours and left when Matty made dinner because he knew Layla would be following her bedtime routine afterward. When Layla went to bed and Harper and I were settled in the living room, I attempted to talk to her again.

The disagreement we'd had didn't have any easy fix, I knew that going into it, but I was determined to have my say.

"Look, Harper, I don't want an argument, but I don't feel comfortable with you putting yourself and our baby at risk."

"What you don't understand is midwives are very skilled to bring babies into this world. I don't want to go to the hospital. I want my care to be given via the River City Birthing Center. All this stuff around normal childbirth has been made out to be far more complex than it is. Having a baby isn't an illness, so why should I go to the hospital to give birth?"

"The hospital is the safest place for you to have our baby."

"Is it? I mean statistically? Here." She dropped a book and a few leaflets on the table in front of me. "I'm trying to make this easier on all of us. I hate having to keep saying this, but what happened with

Grace was a horrible fluke of nature, Cole. I know you know this deep down, and you're fighting against a program of trauma inside your head, but I wasn't a part of that."

I toyed with the colored leaflets and picked up the book, thumbing through the pages.

"Read these brochures, then tell me if you would rather me and our baby be assisted by someone who brings babies safely into the world every day, or a doctor who sees me maybe four or five times and catches it after meeting me at the hospital? These women are experts who are trained in all aspects of prenatal, labor, and postnatal care. Whoever we choose will know us as a family, discuss all your issues, and help me devise a plan of care that is the best for me and our baby."

"You make it all sound so simple."

"Because it *is*. Providing everything is going well, these people are the best for me. If not, then they'd refer me to my obstetrician for him to take over."

The last comment made me feel slightly easier about her choice. "Do we get to meet these people?"

"Of course. I was going to talk to you about it; it was unfortunate that I slipped up with Layla. I guess I got caught up in the moment. Which doesn't happen often enough around here."

Staring quietly, I conceded that point because there were times when I needed to know the ins and outs of a bee's ass for anyone to gain my permission for something to change.

"Fine, set us up with an appointment, but I want to talk to the OB doc about this as well."

"Good, we can do this at the 3D ultrasound scan," she replied in a clipped tone.

"Come here," I ordered, opening my arms, because I needed to feel close to her.

"No, you come here, I'm pregnant," she replied playfully.

"No, because if being pregnant is no excuse for anything, then you can get off your ass and come please your man," I stated firmly, with more than a hint of amusement in my tone. I wasn't totally satisfied, but I did feel slightly better informed about what Harper wanted to happen, so for now at least I was willing to let the subject slide.

CHAPTER THIRTY-FOUR

True to her word, two weeks later Harper had set up a meeting with two midwives from a place called the Riverside Birthing Center.

I still had reservations, but kept my thoughts to myself, because I figured if I was going to counter her decision, I should at least hear her out.

The midwives visited when Layla was at kindergarten, and it was obvious from the start, Harper had filled them in about my thoughts and feelings. As the story had been extensively covered in the news and media, none of it was confidential anyway.

Karen, the older and more senior of the two midwives, initially did most of the talking. She was friendly, and from the conversation she sounded caring and kind.

My immediate thoughts were Harper doesn't need caring and kind or friendly, she needed a medical activist with serious skills, capable of springing into action. Glancing at the plump middle-aged woman again, I didn't get the vibe she did anything much in a hurry.

The other midwife, Natasha, was younger, more agile looking, and she began talking about ultrasound scanning, and monitoring Harper through a series of appointments. When she charted the growth of the baby and ensured Harper's blood work was normal, I relaxed a little. From then on, their service had begun to sound more like the regular examinations Grace had been given at the doctor's office.

"By giving Harper continuity of care by the same person, we can often detect if anything falls out of what we regard as normal. In those cases, we'd refer her to her obstetrician for care.

"How often does this happen?"

"In a woman of Harper's health maybe one in a hundred."

"What kind of conditions would they be referred for?"

"It may be if blood work changes, or the baby's growth slows down, or if blood pressure problems occur, to name a few examples. We deal with women who are healthy, and because of this, we can identify most issues before they become emergencies. We don't take chances, Cole. We're a professional, highly-trained service for women."

Natasha nodded. "We would ensure Harper has her baby in a comfortable place where she feels safe and supported by people she has built a relationship with and she trusts. Research has shown when women feel psychologically supported, they are more in control of their pain and their birth is a more positive experience."

"How long have you been doing this?" I asked them both.

"Twenty-seven years certified," Karen replied with a smile.

"Eleven," Natasha offered.

Dr. Ken had been an obstetrician for six years, and the two women in front of me had two degrees and thirty years on him at least, yet I continued to question their abilities.

"How many babies have you lost?"

"Cole!" Harper admonished.

"What? I think that's a fair question since the hospital is about five miles from here."

"One," Karen replied honestly.

"See that's one too many," I replied, pointing at her before running my hand through my hair.

"I think if you directed the same question to any obstetrician this figure would be much higher. They deal with more medical cases.

What I'm saying is if any doctor gets involved with our women, it's because they already have a complication.

"The mom in question, who lost her child, refused our advice to deliver in the hospital in the first place. She was determined to give birth at home when we had already advised her a home delivery wasn't in the best interests of her or her baby."

"And if Harper does this, you'd be referring her to someone?"

"Harper already has an obstetrician. We simply inform him this is the route Harper wishes to take."

"What if I want the doctor tagging along in the background?"

"Absolutely, but that would depend on whether he was willing to be here for her labor. It's really not necessary, but if it will give you more confidence, of course you can ask. We wouldn't ask for their assistance unless there was an issue."

"Fine. If you've got your heart set on having this baby at home, then I'm going to make sure if something goes wrong we can get you help as quickly as humanly possible."

Frustration passed through Harper's eyes, but she shrugged and remained silent. She'd won her battle, but the emotional war going on in my head was far from over.

After the challenging questions were posed, the midwives explained how it all worked, and an hour after they'd arrived, they left with a rudimentary birthing plan in place to support Harper.

"Thank you, Cole. This really does mean a lot to me."

"You, Layla, and this baby mean the *world* to me, so this is a tough negotiation," I countered.

"You'll get used to the idea," she started to say, then she clutched at her baby bump. My heart sank to my stomach like a heavy lead weight.

"What? What's wrong?" I asked urgently, suddenly petrified at seventeen weeks something had gone wrong. My heart raced so fast it triggered tiny electrical charges pinging around inside my body, making me feel lightheaded. The metallic taste in my mouth made me feel sick as I fought off the urge to panic.

"I think I felt the baby move," she murmured quietly, her eyes were big and round, and her mouth circular and wide to match them in surprise. For a second my heart skipped a beat, and it should have been a moment to cherish, but the enormity of my anguish took yet another step toward the day I couldn't wish was over safely fast enough.

∼

With Harper's swollen belly, I could no longer pretend in my head nothing was changing, but as she was carrying our child differently to Grace's front bump, and with Harper's preference for loose clothing, she was less noticeably expecting until it was almost time for her scan.

When my hands skated over her stomach, or I held her by the hips, her figure felt fuller, but these changes were most notable for the first time when I was brushing my teeth and Harper came into the bathroom.

I glanced at her over my shoulder as she leaned on the bathroom door, then turned back to rinse out my mouth. As I was straightening up from the sink, I caught the sight of the obvious neat bulge in her belly and I stopped moving. A wave of anxiety gripped me as the reality of seeing my baby growing inside my girl overwhelmed me again.

No matter how ridiculous I tried to tell myself my fears were; they remained imbedded in my mind. The chances of Grace dying like that were millions to one, yet she had. This point kept me from discarding it from ever happening again.

As part of my psyche involved a great deal of self-preservation, I found I couldn't let myself go all in and be excited like Layla and Harper were... like everyone else around me was.

It wasn't until Harper was twenty weeks along that our situation turned a corner. Our ever-vigilant little princess, Layla, knew that by then there was a good chance the baby could now hear some sounds inside Harper's belly.

Observing how Layla interacted by constantly chatting and trying to share her earbuds with our unborn baby by tucking one into Harper's belly button, my heart squeezed at how she loved this baby already, and it finally sank in I was missing out.

At the time, we were all sitting on the sofa with our feet stretched out on the coffee table and I suddenly reached across and gently smoothed my huge palm protectively over our growing baby bump. Feeling the solid little bundle growing inside Harper made my chest and throat tighten with emotion.

"You have to hear this, it's my favorite song," Layla coaxed as she glanced up at me and smirked wickedly. "If you're going to live with me, we can sing it together and drive Daddy nuts because he *hates* it," she gloated sadistically, with her mouth almost touching Harper's stomach as she mumbled conspiratorially.

The whole *Frozen* movie soundtrack drove me crazy, so I wasn't sure which one she was referring to, but I chuckled that she was recruiting her unborn sibling to wind me up.

Harper immediately turned her head in my direction, her eyes narrowed, as she gauged my response. "Scan tomorrow," she murmured encouragingly. Like I'd forgotten.

"I know, it's been on my mind," I confessed, and she smiled, placing her warm soft hand over mine on her belly to keep it in place. I spread my fingers wider—more protectively—and it was the first time I had shown any obvious affection to physically acknowledge our baby to her.

∼

I was fine so long as we were living in the 'now' talking to Harper about the pregnancy, but there were still things neither of us were saying, like what if something went wrong? When I had to speak with anyone else about her condition, it gave me the jitters.

Being physically involved took effort, as my mind was still blocking events around my nightmare scenario first time around. To some I'm sure I sounded ridiculous, but trauma is trauma.

Harper's opinion was the only one that counted, and I was making small steps each day to push over the invisible line between my past and my present.

After I let myself go and showed real interest, it was like a dam had broken and I couldn't have been more focused on every aspect of our baby's development.

Layla's innocent excitement toward the pending arrival humbled me, and although I'd been carefully observing how Harper was coping, I knew my somewhat standoffish behavior had failed to make her feel attractive. This wasn't because I hadn't thought she was; it was more of a case of burying my head in the sand.

The morning of the scan, my nerves were frayed, and I had found myself having quite regular conversations with God about what this would mean to me if he let us catch a break with our results.

My mom said prayers always came in handy—something I didn't believe in when faced with Grace's sudden and rapid illness—but I figured anything I could do to create a positive vibe was worth a try.

As the sonogram technician set Harper up on the table, the lights were dimmed, and I wiped my sweaty palms before clutching Harper's hand. Watching with a racing heart as blue translucent gel was applied to her belly, I took a deep breath and tried to look relaxed for Harper's sake.

The blank screen transformed immediately when the transducer spread the gel across Harper's bump, and we saw our baby's little gray, grainy form appear on the screen. My heartbeat stalled for a second at the sound our baby's strong, steady heartbeat and my breath caught in my throat.

Harper squeezed my hand tight, drawing my gaze from the screen to her eyes, and her wondrous smile made me swallow hard. My eyes filled to the brim with tears and I blinked, letting them fall one after another. It was a totally unexpected reaction, but one I couldn't control.

"Is everything okay?" I asked nervously, wiping tears from my eyes with my sleeve, both eager and reluctant in equal measure to be reassured, and Harper squeezed my hand again.

"Isn't this beautiful?" she asked, and I almost missed her question because the rapid volume of blood rushing through my ears distracted me.

"Baby's doing perfectly. Length, abdominal circumference, head circumference, heart and heart rate are all within normal range." My shoulders instantly slumped in relief and I realized how tense I had been. Harper squeezed my hand again.

"You okay?" I nodded, too choked to speak.

Switching to the 3D scan, I marveled at technology and concentrated on taking in the features of our baby's face on the screen. My heart squeezed again, and I looked at Harper who was staring at the screen, tears streaming down her face and grinning widely. "Wow," she whispered, turning to look at me.

The love in her curious eyes threatened to overwhelm me again, and I swallowed past another lump in my throat. Bending down, I kissed my girl softly on her lips as her hand automatically cupped my cheek. The affection in her gaze made my heart swell with love, and I thought what a truly remarkable woman she was to have put up with all the different sides of me she'd witnessed during the time she'd known me.

"Would you like to know the sex of the baby?" My eyes snapped to the technician then back to Harper.

"No. We'll love it no matter what it is," Harper quickly replied.

The attendant replaced the transducer back in a cradle at the side of the machine and cleaned Harper's belly, then I helped her pull her clothing back in place and eased her up to stand.

As we left the scanning room, she tugged on my hand and we ground to a halt. "You did great in there, Cole. I'm so proud of you. We're halfway there and everything's going to be okay." I smiled, grateful for her encouraging words and a little embarrassed that I'd felt so weak before.

Pulling her close, I rubbed my hand gently over her belly through her dress and Harper instantly smiled. "I love you so much, Baby. Thank you for being so brave for the both of us. Your strength is incredible, and I know it's been hard for you at times, but I promise I'm trying to be a better man."

"You're doing just fine as you are, Cole. You're the man I fell in love with, and I'd rather have you with all your honest flaws, than a man with no feelings. Your past is bound to have shaped you. If anything, I'd probably be more worried if we were sailing through this and you were blocking it all out."

Waving the small envelope with the 3D and other scan pictures in it, Harper's eyes brightened and a grin spread over her face. "Come on, I can't wait to share these with Layla. What's the bet that as soon as she sees them, the first thing she'll say is 'Oh look, our baby has ears'?"

We both laughed heartily, and I pulled her into my side, gave her an affectionate peck on her forehead, and we made our way back to the car. Hope rose inside me for the first time since I learned she was expecting our new baby.

CHAPTER THIRTY-FIVE

As each month went by, I got more used to Karen, the older of the two midwives, visiting us at home. Greeting her like she was an old friend, Harper appeared relaxed and felt confident she'd made the right choice about where she wanted our baby to be born.

As the due date drew nearer, the midwife service visits became more frequent and Harper arranged some of them to coincide with when Layla was at home. Personally, the thought of Layla being present at the birth freaked me the fuck out. I had no idea what to expect myself. I'd never attended a natural birth... or a birth of any kind for that matter, and at the back of my mind I figured Layla may herself back out when she saw Harper in pain.

Karen encouraged me to express all my concerns and reassured me I wasn't unique in being worried about the birth, reassuring me my feelings were the same as most fathers. While Harper was dealing with Layla at one point, Karen asked me how I thought Harper was coping, and when I called Harper an Earth Mother, the midwife's eyebrows rose in surprise.

"You know this term?" she probed.

"Yeah, Harper's an angel and a natural mother. She cares for everyone and sees everything in the simplest terms. She takes everything in her stride. Apart from the biological aspect, Harper's been a true mother in every other sense of the word to Layla. Even before we got together, she always challenged me if I went against the grain to what she believed was in Layla's best interests."

Since we'd been to visit Harper's parents, and I'd broken the ice with them, her mom and sister had made more of an effort to visit, but it was apparent to me none of her family were close. I guessed some just weren't. Part of me wondered if Harper's closeness with Layla filled a void she'd missed out on herself.

No matter the reason, I was deeply grateful she'd come into our lives. When I thought back to my conversation with JoAnn, it challenged me to look objectively at how I now treated Layla. It had made me realize how special Harper was, because if it hadn't been for Harper's care and encouragement of me, my daughter may well have felt how JoAnn did about her father.

"Your belly looks like a huge pumpkin. It's going to burst," Layla advised Harper as she lay back on the couch with her T-shirt pulled up and her belly sticking out.

"Our baby is growing fast now," Harper informed Layla, as my daughter stroked her bump over and over.

"Wow, did you see that, Daddy?" Layla asked in an excited tone, as the baby's movement rippled beneath Harper's taut skin.

"Yeah, watch this," I told Layla as I crawled over the floor on my hands and knees and placed my lips to Harper's belly, I began to sing "Baby I Love You," by The Ramones. What neither Layla nor Harper knew was it was the tune I used to sing to Layla before she was born. There was something about this song that touched my heart and it had made every playlist I'd ever put together.

Halfway through the song, I glanced up at Layla and noticed she was sitting back on her knees beside Harper, swaying gently to the song, and Harper's bump began to roll back and forth from left to right, in the same way Layla had when she was inside Grace.

"Oh, look, our baby is dancing to Daddy's song," she marveled, her eyes glittering with excitement.

Gently, Harper caressed my head and my throat immediately constricted. Suddenly, my voice cracked, the emotion of the moment preventing me from continuing and I sat up. Tears spilled from Harper's eyes and Layla immediately cuddled her.

"What's wrong, my Harper?" she asked, her little voice full of concern.

"Nothing at all, Baby, I'm really happy," she replied, pulling Layla and me forward to cuddle us both at the same time.

I glanced, concerned for Layla, and noted again it was the second time she'd used the word my before Harper. "Why do you say my Harper?" I probed.

"Because you say my girl. She's not my girl, she's my Harper," Layla explained with a shrug. Harper and I shot each other a look that said we'd come back to this later and let it slide.

Later that night in bed, I thought about what Layla said again. In fact, Harper and the new baby's status had been on my mind since the day she'd told me she was pregnant. Although I regarded all of them as mine, it began to bug me that Harper and the baby would have different names to Layla and me.

As Harper Tennison, Harper had stated the baby's surname would be Tennison-Harkin, and that immediately set Layla and her sibling aside. I wanted both my babies to have the same name, but more than that, I wanted Harper to have mine.

"Harper?" I murmured, turning to spoon behind her, as best I could, with the pillows anchored between her legs and another stuffed under her bump.

"Mm?" she mumbled, sleepily.

"Do you want to marry me?"

Harper's body stiffened.

"Can you ask me again tomorrow," she muttered in a sleepy state.

"I'd rather know now," I insisted.

"Why?"

"Because I don't want to lie awake all night wondering," I replied.

"No, not that, I mean why ask?"

"Because I think I'm ready... no, I'm sure I'm ready to take this step with you, and I couldn't have gotten here without your love."

"Good answer, but I'm quite content, Cole. We don't need anyone to officiate what we've got."

"Are you reluctant because you think I'm replacing Grace? That's not what I'm doing. This is a second chance at a new beginning I never thought possible, and it ties up who we all are to each other perfectly."

Turning slowly, she molded herself to me as much as she could and wrapped her arms around me.

"Explain."

"My girl doesn't begin to describe who you are to me. I want you to be mine. That means you taking my name, our children having my name, our family having a family name. Layla having a mother for the first time in her memory, both kids having a mom as well as a dad."

"Having your name has never mattered to me. Having the man is much more important. If it makes you happy we'll get married… make it neat for the kids, but it won't change how I feel about you and it won't—"

"I know, but I think it will make our children feel we all belong together. You'll be Layla's mom, that will go a long way when this little one comes. She's had you to herself until now, Harper. When the novelty wears off and your time is split between them, she may feel pushed out, no matter how hard you try to reassure her."

"Yeah, I've been thinking about that too," she admitted, "maybe we *should* make what we've got official, but I want a prenuptial agreement," she added, firmly.

My body steeled, and my heart rate spiked in shock as I moved my head back enough to see her face in the darkness.

"What? Where the fuck has this come from?" I asked, suddenly hurt that she'd think I'd want that.

"I'd hate people to think I snared you for your money by having your kid."

I remembered the newspaper articles and sat up quickly, putting the nightstand light on. "Who the fuck put this in your head?"

"Look, it doesn't matter. If we're getting married, I want one. If anything happens to you, I want any assets you have to go to the children."

"Jesus, Harper, you really *have* thought about this," I ground out; furious she'd even have to think of such a thing.

"It's not fucking happening. No prenup, we both know this is the real deal; I won't have it. Now I'm gonna ask you again, who put this notion in your head?"

Rolling over she sat up, got out of the bed, and sighed. For a few seconds I watched the internal struggle and knew she was breaking a confidence.

"Sarah-Jayne has one with Max. She told me Max's management and law firm wrote one for Max and she was asked to sign it a few days before their wedding."

"All right, first let me say, I'm not Max, and I'm surprised he put that on Sarah-Jayne, but that's between them. We have no idea what goes on behind closed doors, so I can't comment on his situation. But this right here," I wagged my finger between us, "this is real love, and let me tell you, even with what I felt for Grace, it's not the same... what we've got is far more."

"Don't get upset about it. I can understand your managers and lawyers wanting to protect what you have," she pleaded.

"Baby, look at where I've come from... what I've been through... what I survived. If this is all that's holding you back from being my wife, forget it. No fucking prenup. What's mine is already yours. The moment you became pregnant my will was rewritten, ask Derek and Dorian, they were witnesses. You've never asked for anything, never wanted anything."

Blood and heat rushed through my veins in frustration that thoughts like this had been put in Harper's head. To think those thoughts were put there by someone who knew us, but had no idea how deep our feelings ran, pissed me off.

There wasn't even a discussion about a prenuptial agreement when I married Grace, and I certainly would never have entertained such a suggestion from someone who put money and business before my wife.

"Why haven't we had these discussions before?" Harper asked.

"I don't know, but I want you to be my wife, and not for the kids, for all of us, you included."

"Well, when you say it so romantically," Harper replied, lightening my mood.

"Will you marry me?"

"What an amazing romantic proposal, you sitting half-naked in bed with a face like thunder, and me standing here in my huge maternity shorts and tank," she chuckled.

"Sorry, I didn't mean for it to be like this. I acted on impulse. I should have thought it through before I asked."

I know I should never have compared them, but my proposal to Grace was also spontaneous and without thought. It was as sudden and passionate, yet I realized Harper saying yes meant more than when Grace had.

"Tell me what you want, Harper? I'm yours with or without the romantic gestures. It isn't that you don't deserve the hearts and flowers and the serenades, but I think I know you, and doing any of those things would be seen by you as empty gestures."

A smile spread on her face and she knelt on the bed, leaning toward me. "Kind of having an issue with being called Harper Harkin right now," she giggled. "It's kind of freaking me out."

I chuckled. "Well, as I'm the famous one, it's going to have to be you that concedes on that one, but I think you can keep your name and use it as normal. How often would anyone refer to it anyway? You'd be Harper, Cole Harkin's gorgeous wife," I told her tongue in cheek.

"If we get married—"

"When," I countered.

"I haven't said yes yet," she scolded.

"You will," I teased, pulling back the covers to reveal my junk. "Where else would you find a package like this at your disposal with a kid in tow?"

Giggling, she shook her head. "You're ridiculous." Her smile told me I was winning her over.

"I know, right? That's what men say when they check me out at the urinals in public restrooms. I give them inferiority complexes I'm told." I winked and grinned wickedly at her gaping mouth when her jaw dropped.

"Wow, you made that up on the spot?"

"You'd be amazed at what I can do on the spot." I winked again.

"You need to get that eyelid pinned back, it keeps falling over your eyeball."

"Now you're ridiculous," I countered.

She waved her hands over her huge bump. "Yeah, that's what all the women say..." she chuckled, "at the birthing center prenatal classes." She giggled and tried to continue, "they have inferiority..." giggle, "complexes as well when they check this lump out."

Opening my arms, she climbed back into bed then quickly turned around and climbed back out. "Hold on, I need to pee," she advised me as she waddled into the bathroom.

"I'll hold yours, if you hold mine," I called out after her.

"Pfft," she replied, "You're an opportunist, you know that?" My heart stopped for a second, and I felt as if I had been punched in my chest. Grace used to say this to me all the time. A lump formed in my throat and I felt weird for a moment, like it was a sign of some kind.

A minute later I heard the flush and the faucet being turned on and I pulled the comforter back to clear Harper's space for her to get back into bed. She bumped around getting comfortable with the pillows and shit, then her breathing slowed as she settled.

"I'll marry you, but here, at the house. No cameras, just the band guys, our families, and the household. If the press gets wind of it, I'm not doing it. I'll take your surname and be the ridiculous Harper Harkin because I love you."

An emotional swell rolled through me and my throat constricted. "Don't you ever knock my unromantic proposal; that acceptance was ten times worse," I choked out, then I pulled her as close as I could get her to me and kissed her softly on her neck.

"Can we go to sleep now? I'm almost due and this may be one of the last few good night's sleep I'll get for a while," she drawled.

Kissing her neck again, I squeezed her hip gently and whispered, "Sure... love you, Baby."

Not long after Harper's breathing evened out and became deeper, I fell asleep listening to the breaths of the woman who breathed new life into me.

CHAPTER THIRTY-SIX

"Jesus, you're cutting it short for a shotgun wedding," Dorian stated, with his hands on his hips, as he stared at Harper's belly when I asked him to be my best man. The method to my madness was that he'd arrange everything while I concentrated on my girls.

Four days later, I got my wish to marry Harper, and she got hers to marry in privacy on our property. The similarities for privacy between Harper and Grace didn't pass me by.

Harper knew exactly what she wanted, and even though I offered her a far more befitting event, she was determined to have the last say and had Matty, my mom, Dinah, and Diane do the catering. The food was simple: beef Wellington or chicken Parmesan, and an assortment of delicious salads and noodle dishes, joking a carb heavy diet was every expectant mom's right.

Angus and Dinah, Grace's parents, were delighted when Harper called them to tell them our news. They had already given Harper their blessing. Dinah cried, but she knew about the letter, and although it must have been hard for her, she told Harper she couldn't have wished for anyone better for me. Dinah told Harper it was bittersweet, but she was happy that my girl was going to be Layla's new mom.

ANOTHER LIFE

The wedding itself was a very low-key affair, but perfect according to Harper. As our close families and friends gathered around in the meadow, our altar was an arch made of fall colors and a carpet of fallen leaves in vivid oranges, reds, greens, and browns lay beneath our feet.

Harper insisted on no new dress. Instead staying casual in a white smock top and matching stretchy pants and flip-flops, because her feet were so swollen, joking was her final defense in the event the guys from *People*, *Cosmopolitan* or *Rolling Stone* magazines came snooping.

The only concession she made to her appearance was a Grecian braid with a few pieces of baby's breath threaded through it. She looked radiant and stunning. Naturally Layla had the same hairstyle, but had a new pink frilly dress and wore this with some new tan leather cowboy boots underneath.

The pastor was one my mom had talked into coming with her from Delaware because Harper was paranoid about asking someone local, in the event it sparked interest from the press. Derek and Dorian sorted out the license; all we had to do was sign it.

It may not have appeared special, but we thought it was perfect, given our circumstances. However, Harper insisted she'd made no compromise, because pregnant or not, famous or not, our wedding was exactly how she had wanted it to be— minus the bump.

We wanted a fresh start from the moment our new baby was born, and for us that meant making sure Layla was happy and knew the plan before the baby's arrival.

The most notable thing about the quick no fuss exchange of commitment was our vows. Harper humbled everyone with her sensitivity and unreserved thought for Grace's parents and all who knew her.

My Vows to Harper

Take my hand; let me guide you from the darkness of grief.
You never spoke those words, Harper, but you silently showed me the way.
You taught me grief can't be rushed; to each person it's an undefinable question of time.
My time was long; in my mind, my soul was lost forever—but I was wrong.

Finding it was a troubled path but a path that led to a new destination.

You, Harper, are my new destination.
Love isn't only experienced, defined as passion, or the feeling of excitable butterflies and skipped heartbeats.
Sometimes love is born from nurturing, from having empathy, from wiping tears, and facing fears.
Through you, I've learned there are a hundred ways to love.
Each one an eternal blessing, each one a valuable lesson, each one a special gift.
I give myself to you and thank God for the new joy I have found in being with you.
Thank you for being the light in my darkness, Baby. I'm forever yours.

Harper's Vows

Cole, I stand before you today, not to take a place or replace,
but to fill the space in your heart you truly believe is mine .
Through your darkest days I'll be by your side. Through your brightest, I'll help you shine.
I give you my heart, my body, my mind, my trust,
Cole, I'm not your past, I'm your present and future, another life to add to your journey.
thank you for trusting your instincts about what we could be, for being brave, for facing fears and for loving me.

One week later

"Matty, can you call Karen? The number is on the address book over there, on the fridge," I heard Harper ask calmly, from my office down the hall. Harper was three days after her due date and she hadn't had so much as a twinge the previous night.

"What's happening?" I asked, jumping out of my office chair and striding hurriedly down the hall to where Harper was standing holding a bath sheet between her legs, in the kitchen.

"My water broke," she informed me laughing. "I've been having some weak contractions since about five this morning, but they began to heat up right after Layla left for school." I immediately stood by her side but panic rose in my chest.

"Please, would you ask Diane and Stuart to pick Layla up for us? When Karen gets here, she'll tell us if we can wait for her to come home at the normal time," she asked, matter of fact, as Matty pulled the number from the fridge door and began calling the midwives.

"Shouldn't you be lying down or something?" I asked, holding her arm in support.

"I'm not tired," Harper replied, chuckling, and her smart-ass answer told me she was going to deal with her labor the same as she dealt with everything else—practically.

"I mean get off your feet," I prompted, trying again.

"No. It's better if I'm mobile. Gravity will help the labor and it's more comfortable if I move around."

Stuart wandered into the kitchen. "So this is it?" he said, almost as excited as Layla had been in recent days when the due date came and went with no movement.

"Either that or my bladder exploded," Harper said, chuckling, then she winced when a contraction gripped her. The way it took her breath away also took mine, and for a moment I was back in the car with Grace on the way to the hospital in my mind. Pushing the thought aside, I eyed Harper with concern.

"Anything I can do?" I asked, hoping there was, because the sudden feeling of helplessness was crippling.

"Yeah, can you go fill the tub?" Harper asked.

"I'll start it, but I'm not staying in the bathroom with you in here."

"Just do it, Cole," she barked sternly and shook her head. Pulling her to me, I softly kissed the stress from her temple and went to do as she asked.

The tub was big enough for eight people, and I used to think the people who had the house before must have had orgies in it, because I couldn't imagine what else something this big was used for.

I waited until there was a couple of inches in the bottom and had set the faucet to balance the temperature between hot and cold, then I left it running and went back to the kitchen. To be honest, I felt I could have left it running for the day and it would never have overflowed.

"Tub's filling? What's next? I asked; looking for direction to keep me busy and my mind off wigging out and letting my nerves get the better of me.

"Music? The sleepover room playlist," she suggested.

Pulling my phone out, I scrolled through my lists until I found it. "Where?"

"Here, put it on now. I want to listen," she said, then wandered over to the kitchen counter and leaned over it to deal with another contraction. Without thinking, I went over to join her and began rubbing her lower back.

Setting my phone up with the Bluetooth speaker, I put it on shuffle and let the music fill the room. "September" by Daughtry was the first song up, and both Harper and I shot each other a look, because the lyrics were so poignant to everything that had passed and our current situation. It was also the last day of September.

"You're doing brilliantly, Baby," I encouraged, suddenly brave and fiercely protective. "Check the tub will you, Matty?" I asked, and then I concentrated my attention on Harper.

Matty nodded and left the room while Stuart had begun to pace. "What do you need from upstairs, Baby'?" I asked.

"There's a bag by the side of the dresser, everything else I need is already in the bathroom down the hall." Stuart looked relieved at the delegation and left the kitchen.

Ten contractions later, we'd established they were coming every three minutes, each lasting a minute or so when the gate buzzer sounded. Checking out the CCTV monitor, we saw it was Karen's car, closely followed by Natasha's. Relief flooded through me and a couple of minutes later they wandered into the kitchen in an unhurried fashion.

Karen smiled. "Hello, Harper, Cole," addressing my girl, then nodding to me.

"Who's having a birthday, today?" she gloated. "Tell me what's been going on, Harper, then we'll go in the living room and check you out. Meanwhile, Cole, we could use a coffee if there's one going," she instructed me, and I knew she was making me feel useful.

I wandered over to the coffee pot, nerves making my hands shake slightly, and I poured them a couple of mugs of coffee. "Milk's in the fridge behind you," I said, knowing I couldn't get anywhere near it for the bags they'd dropped by their feet.

Between contractions, Harper sat on one of the breakfast barstools and conversed with everyone as if nothing was going on. The respect I had for her was immense, and I felt guilty when she caught my eye and mouthed, "Are you okay?"

"I'm fine, it's you I'm worried about," I snapped, aloud.

By the time Stuart took Diane to pick up Layla, Harper had been examined and she was well over halfway to fully dilated.

"Whoa! That was intense. I think it's time for the tub," she said when a contraction took her breath.

Shit. I'd forgotten about the tub and prayed Matty had taken care of it.

Assisting Harper down the hall, I was relieved to see it was halfway and the faucet had been turned off. I'd been too focused on what was happening with Harper to care about it.

"Can you give me a hand here, Honey?" Harper asked, taking her sweater off as she went into the throes of a new contraction. We waited for it to ebb as she breathed through the pain, and when she was done, I helped her get naked and she climbed into the tub.

For a few minutes she appeared to cope better for being in there, but soon after she was wriggling around restless and couldn't get comfortable, even on her hands and knees.

Natasha narrowed her eyes like she was sizing me up. "Do you think you could get in behind Harper and support her in the water?" she enquired.

They'd spoken about this during their visits, and each time, I kind of backed off figuring I'd be more of a hindrance than a help. I knew the deep-rooted fears I had from Grace's labor still plagued me, but when faced with the real-life scenario, I nodded immediately.

"Sure. What do I do?" I asked, and Harper glanced up at me in surprise, obviously gauging whether I really was okay with Natasha's suggestion.

"Strip down and get in behind Harper. Let me adjust the water temperature first," Natasha replied.

"Oh, sounds like an offer I can't refuse," I replied, reading the comment both ways.

"Ignore him; he's such an opportunist," Harper told them, laughing before another contraction interrupted her scathing comment.

Thankfully, she was too distracted to see how her comment had floored me. It wasn't something she'd ever said to me before, yet she had mentioned it twice lately, once when I asked her to marry me and at this, another significant turning point in my life. Either I was turning into a pussy or there were signs everywhere.

Natasha emptied a little water out of the tub and added more hot water.

"Are you getting in then?" Harper asked, eyeing me curiously, when her contraction had ebbed and Natasha had turned the faucet back off.

"For you, Sweetheart', anything," I confirmed, tugging on the buckle of my belt.

"No, you have to put a swimsuit on," Harper cried out, her voice high pitched.

"What? Why? You're naked?" I nodded at her body. "What's the difference? Best you look away now, ladies, rock stars don't wear underwear," I stated as I undid the fly on my jeans and shoved them down my legs to the floor. Gingerly, I stepped out of them and into the bath, with Harper trying to catch my dick and balls in her hands to hide them.

I chuckled. "Jesus, woman, you're in the middle of giving birth and you can't keep your hands to yourself," I teased, as a new contraction came on and the atmosphere tensed again. Nudity had never been a problem for me, and I wasn't leaving her to go upstairs and find some board shorts.

Positioning myself behind her with my legs open, I slid down against the bath, pulling Harper's shoulders back to take her weight.

Heat radiated from her to me and her hair was stuck to the back of her neck, so I set to work cooling her down with a washcloth and scooping her hair together again, retying it in her pony holder. I kissed her neck and talked her through breathing for the next half hour.

Suddenly the door burst open and the patter of feet running down the hall was quickly followed by heavier ones.

"No, Layla, you have to wait here until someone comes and gets you," Diane called out after her.

"It's okay, she can come in." Harper called out, sounding relaxed, but my body stiffened. I wasn't sure how Layla would take to what was happening, and the last thing I wanted was for her to be scared.

Discarding her coat and shoes, she came and hung over the side of the bath with her head resting on her forearms.

"Wow, you're naked," she observed. "It's really coming?" she asked Harper excitedly.

"Yeah, Baby, it is." Harper sounded tired this time, and I noted she had become more restless since Layla had come home. At first, I wondered if it was because she was naked, and Layla was checking her out, but something inside me sensed Harper's situation was changing.

"Can I get in?" Layla asked, after Karen had used a handheld monitor wrapped in a waterproof glove to listen to the baby's heartbeat. She'd been doing this regularly throughout Harper's labor. "Sounds good," she reported and jotted it in Harper's notes.

"Yeah–No," both Harper and I said simultaneously.

"Yes, you can get in for a few minutes, but you have to promise to get out as soon as Karen or Natasha tell you to because the baby will be coming." I was stunned by Harper's cool head; she was unbelievable.

Layla peeled down to her panties and climbed in the water. "It's nice and warm," she commented, as she settled at the side of my leg and leaned over carefully to kiss first Harper's cheek then mine. Her sense of occasion was spot on when she slipped one of her hands into Harper's and covered the one of mine nearest to her that I was using to support Harper.

A few contractions later I'd noticed Harper was shifting about more and had begun to make some grunting noises at the height of her contractions. I'd forgotten all about calling the doctor. It all felt how it was meant to be.

"Harper, you're doing incredibly well. Remember the longer you can resist pushing; the less work there will be to deliver. Babies know their way out, and as long as it isn't distressed, we allow things to happen naturally," Karen instructed her calmly.

Turning to address Layla, she smiled. "Layla, Honey, I think it may be time for you to get out for a bit. I don't think the baby is going to be long before it arrives now." I expected a protest because of how protective Layla had been since she'd found out Harper was pregnant, but she stood up and allowed Karen to help her out.

"Should I get dressed?" she asked.

"If you want to," Natasha replied, and Layla went and grabbed a bath sheet, wrapping it round herself, then came to settle by my head. Ignoring the fact, she was wet.

"I may miss something," Layla mused, and I smiled at her. She was so astute.

The two midwives began to open packets and prepare an area for the baby. As soon as I saw suction tubes, I almost allowed my fears to return, but Karen had obviously been keeping an eye on me.

"It's fine, Cole. This tube is just if there is any mucus in the baby's airway, so we can clear it out. It's a perfectly normal precaution," she informed me, right as Harper could no longer resist pushing and moved her arms under her legs, grabbing her thighs.

"Ah," Harper called out and hissed. "It burns," she gasped in pain. Karen snapped on some rubber gloves and dipped her hand in the water between Harper's legs.

"Good girl," she told Harper, "your baby's head is right there. That burn you feel is your perineum stretching. If you can, when you get the next breath, try to give me some short pants instead of pushing. The baby's head will crown in the next couple of contractions. You've got this far, and it's nearly over. Keep listening and this will be a beautiful calm birth."

Another contraction came, and I automatically began to coach. "Short breaths, Sweetheart', you're doing fantastic. I love you so much," I babbled, almost beside myself, because I was on the verge of panicking. Layla stayed silent, resting her chin on her forearms, watching.

The contraction ebbed, and Karen checked the baby's heartbeat and felt in the water for the baby's head again. "Wow, it's crowned, the baby's head won't slide back now, Harper, good job. The head will be born in the next contraction, keep panting if you can," she added.

Once again, Harper did as she was asked, and the baby's head was out in less than a minute. Peering over her shoulder, I could see a mound of black hair in the water, but I couldn't make out much else. I glanced at Layla who was now standing on tiptoe, craning her neck for a better view, and taking it all in her stride.

I became distracted again by Harper when she began shaking violently.

"What's happening?" I asked, unable to keep the panic from my voice.

"Stay calm, Cole. It's nothing to worry about. This is the effect of the physical effort to stay in control. Next contraction your baby will be born, Harper."

No sooner were the words out than Karen dragged our limp baby, soaking wet, from between Harper's legs and laid it on her chest. Harper's hands immediately cradled its back and I stared, concerned when it lay still for more than a few heartbeats, then it caught a breath and opened its eyes.

I groaned loudly with relief. "Oh, it almost gave me heart failure there," I admitted.

"You're so dramatic," Harper chuckled.

Karen leaned over and lifted one of the baby's legs, "What do we have, Mom?" she probed.

I looked when she was directing Harper, but heard Harper say, "It's a boy," before my eyes confirmed that it was.

Layla squealed with delight, then her face fell serious. "We can't let him play with Jaden, Harper, he'll teach him to pee on the plants," she replied, like it was the most important advice Harper would ever receive.

Turning to look up at Harper's flushed face, her bright eyes stole my breath. Flashing me a beautiful smile she said, "I'm so proud of you." Her comment sounded as if I was the one who had pushed a watermelon through a tight little hole.

"Sweetheart', I don't even have words for what I've witnessed in you today," I replied, and bent over to kiss her softly.

"Yuk!" Layla shouted, and I pulled my face away. Tracing her gaze, I saw Natasha doing something funky with the placenta. "We don't have to keep the jelly fish as well, do we?" Layla asked in all seriousness.

"Cole, maybe you can take her through to the kitchen now for cookies and milk and let me get out of here," Harper prompted. Moving forward, I stood up in the bath and Layla shook her head.

"Daddy, where are your pants?" she asked, running over to the towel shelves and dragging a hand towel over for me. I chuckled as I took it.

"Something wrong with this picture, Sweet Pea. How come you got the big towel?" I asked.

"I was covering my whole body; you only have a little bit to cover." All three women laughed, and I smirked as I climbed out of the bath holding the towel over my dick.

∼

Less than an hour later, Harper had fed the baby in the bath before she'd been cleaned up, and strolled through to the living room with the baby in her arms like what had gone on was no big deal. It was the last thing I'd expected to happen.

"What are you doing? You should be resting in bed," Matty admonished, as she gushed over our son.

"I've been sitting on my backside all day," she countered.

"Here. It's your turn," Harper offered, wandering over to me and placing the baby in my arms. Layla immediately squeezed down the side of the couch next to me. Harper eased down on the soft cushion beside me and winced. I immediately frowned, and she smiled. "I'm fine."

I turned my attention to our son and he lifted his outstretched hand. Touching it gently, I then placed my index finger along his palm and he immediately made a fist around it. He opened his eyes and blinked, and his tiny red lips made a neat little 'O'.

Then he stared unfocused, but my eyes connected with his and it felt as if my heart had burst open in my chest. "Hello, little man," I cooed, instantly recognizing the feeling of pure joy I'd missed out on when Layla was born. There are no words that could accurately describe what went on in my head at that moment. All I knew was I didn't know my son yet, but I knew I loved him so hard and I'd give my life for him, just as much as I would have for Layla.

Blinking up at me like he'd been woken up abruptly, he pulled a face and pursed his lips like he was saying 'oo' and we all smiled.

"Twenty-one inches; seven pounds two ounces," Harper informed me proudly. My seven-pound guess was almost spot on.

"So, what are we calling him, Mom?" I asked Harper. "Nine months and we've still not decided," I mused.

"Can I name him?" Layla eyed first me, then Harper.

Harper smirked but decided to indulge her anyway. "What were you thinking?"

"Simba or Abu," she said deadpan.

Both Harper and I bit back grins and Harper shook her head. "I think you have to be a lion to be called Simba," Harper reasoned with a straight face.

"Abu Harkin... not really a big name is it? We need something special for him," I suggested.

"Special?" Layla asked, tapping her lips with her forefinger. "I know," she squealed, suddenly excited.

"What's Santa's name again?"

"Kris Kringle?" I asked and I couldn't hold back my chuckle.

"No, the holy one?" Harper frowned for a moment; then it was as if a light bulb flashed behind her eyes.

"St. Nicholas?"

"That's him... or Jesus?" she added. I looked toward Harper to rescue this.

"Nicholas? Nick Harkin? Not bad," she mused. I had to agree, and we knew it would mean the world to Layla to be responsible for naming him.

"All right, Nicholas Harkin it is."

Layla jumped up and down and ran to tell everyone else the baby's name, as the midwives packed their equipment in preparation to leave for the night.

Turning to Harper, I cradled our new son in one hand, shifted to face her and cupped her cheek with the other. "Baby, you are nothing short of a walking miracle to me. You emit so much light you blind me. You have made Layla and I so happy."

Tears welled in Harper's eyes and she touched my face in return. "Cole, it's me who should be thanking you, for letting me in when life was so tough, for trusting we could do this when you had experienced so much hurt. Our baby's birth is a new beginning, our new beginning. We've just got to believe this and it'll work out."

"I believe you, Sweetheart. I used to think my life was over; I didn't want to go on. Now I can't wait for each tomorrow, to get to know this tiny bundle of love and hope. To watch our children grow. What I witnessed today was an incredible show of strength; you have an amazing and beautiful soul. Thank you for my precious son, for being everything my beautiful daughter needs, and for loving me."

For years I was stuck, my soul buried in tragedy, along with who I thought was the love of my life. Consumed by my heartache to the point I almost missed the joy I never thought it was possible to feel again. Where a sudden catastrophic event turned my life on its head as I clung to the memories of a love that was lost.

When my heart wanted to heal, I had feelings within me I couldn't bear to have, because my mind wasn't ready to trust that things could be other than the desolate despair of the path I was walking alone.

Truth was: I was never alone. I was just too damaged to notice; too afraid to climb out of the shell of who I once was, to be the man my daughter needed.

I thought Grace was my life, when she was an important part, but not the whole. Loving Harper wasn't a choice, and I finally faced my fears enough to grab onto my second chance for another life, with both hands.

Through faith and trust, Harper not only mended my heart, she made me stronger, and I learned to love her in ways I never knew existed during the time I had with Grace. I also discovered, by finding the courage to sidestep the darkness grief and sorrow brings, it may be possible to find true love more than once within the same lifetime.

The End

OTHER TITLES BY K.L. SHANDWICK

THE EVERYTHING TRILOGY

Enough Isn't Everything

Everything She Needs

Everything I Want

Love With Every Beat

just Jack

Everything Is Yours

LAST SCORE SERIES

Gibson's Legacy

Trusting Gibson

Gibson's Melody

Piper

READY FOR FLYNN SERIES

Ready For Flynn, Part 1

Ready For Flynn, Part 2

Ready For Flynn, Part 3

OTHER NOVELS

Missing Beats
Notes on Love
Free To Breathe

ACKNOWLEDGMENTS

Editors

Andrea Long Editing Services 2nd Edit by Karen Hrdlicka

Proof readers
　Rosa Sharon, I scream ProofReading Services,
　Lisa Perkins and Heather Woodman.
　Cover by Jay Aheer— Simply Defined Art
　Cover Image: Alicia Erwood— Alicia Erwood Photography
　Cover Models: Charlie Garforth and Baby Amara.

～

Beta Readers
　TL Wainright, Ava Manello, Elmarie Pieterse, Emma Louise Moorhead, Nikki Costello, Wendy Hodges, Chele McKenzie, Riah Piling, Anne Dawson, Danielle Brass, Trudie Harley Quinn Moore, Tracey Pearson and Fiona Wilson Sarah Lintott and LJ Knox.

A special thank you to my awesome indie author friends, Ava Manello,

TL Wainright, for their fabulous beta support, to Tracie Podger for prompting me to get the book finished, and to my promotion team members not mentioned already. They rock with their constant dedication and support to helping me share the word about my latest releases.

Promo ladies

Serena Worker, Valerie De George, Colette Goodchild, Tricia Dransfield, Ann Batty, Tammy Ann Dove, Ann Meemken, Theresa Ritchie, Nese Cimener, Clare Beale Cook, Sue Robertson, Wendy Porter, Joanne Bulmer, Donna Tripi Salzano, Janet Boyd, Jeanette Kennedy, Kristi Iogha.

∼

What happens to Grace in this the story is an extremely rare event.

With the story's potential of a worldwide audience, I cannot suggest specific helplines. However, if you have been affected by any of the themes mentioned in this fictional story you may find services online which are available to gain more information or support.

Common searches : Cervical Cancer Support, McMillan Cancer Support, Cancer Research Trust and the American Cancer Society.

There are many bereavement support groups which may be specific to the needs of the individual and can be researched online; two of which are Cruse and Macmillan Cancer Support.

Printed in Great Britain
by Amazon